A HERO IN SCOUNDREL'S CLOTHING

Prudence Thorne wasn't the sort of woman a man touched on a whim.

She was the sort of woman a man could drown in.

But he was already turning her toward him, drawing her closer, his fingers clasped gently around her wrist, her impossibly soft skin gliding under his thumb, and she was so close he could taste her scent, honeysuckle rushing over his tongue with every breath he drew.

She didn't resist when he urged her closer, nor did she protest when he lowered his mouth to hers, but only gazed up at him with darkened hazel eyes, her lips soft and open with wonder.

He couldn't do anything else then but take her mouth in a dizzying rush of desire. She let out a soft gasp when his lips brushed hers, her warm breath a maddening drift over his lips, but she didn't draw away, and he let his hand settle on the back of her neck, a low moan tearing from his throat . . .

Books by Anna Bradley

The Sutherlands
LADY ELEANOR'S SEVENTH SUITOR
LADY CHARLOTTE'S FIRST LOVE
TWELFTH NIGHT WITH THE EARL

The Somerset Sisters
MORE OR LESS A MARCHIONESS
MORE OR LESS A COUNTESS
MORE OR LESS A TEMPTRESS

Besotted Scots
THE WAYWARD BRIDE
TO WED A WILD SCOT
FOR THE SAKE OF A SCOTTISH RAKE

The Swooning Virgins Society
THE VIRGIN WHO RUINED LORD GRAY
THE VIRGIN WHO VINDICATED LORD DARLINGTON
THE VIRGIN WHO HUMBLED LORD HASLEMERE
THE VIRGIN WHO BEWITCHED LORD LYMINGTON
THE VIRGIN WHO CAPTURED A VISCOUNT

Drop Dead Dukes
GIVE THE DEVIL HIS DUKE
DAMNED IF I DUKE

Published by Kensington Publishing Corp.

Damned if I Duke

∾ DROP DEAD DUKES ∾

ANNA BRADLEY

ZEBRA BOOKS
Kensington Publishing Corp.
www.kensingtonbooks.com

ZEBRA BOOKS are published by

Kensington Publishing Corp.
900 Third Avenue
New York, NY 10022

All Kensington titles, imprints, and distributed lines are available at special quantity discounts for bulk purchases for sales promotion, premiums, fund-raising, and educational or institutional use.

Special book excerpts or customized printings can also be created to fit specific needs. For details, write or phone the office of the Kensington Sales Manager: Kensington Publishing Corp., 900 Third Avenue, New York, NY 10022. Attn. Sales Department. Phone: 1-800-221-2647.

Zebra and the Z logo Reg. U.S. Pat. & TM Off.

First Printing: April 2024

ISBN-13: 978-1-4201-5540-2
ISBN-13: 978-1-4201-5543-3 (eBook)

10 9 8 7 6 5 4 3 2 1

Printed in the United States of America

CHAPTER 1

Hamilton Terrace
St. John's Wood, London
August, 1818

Jasper St. Vincent, the Duke of Montford, had a talent for sin.

Some gentlemen excelled at sport, others at art or music, and still others were notable for their wit or fashionable eccentricities, but there wasn't a single gentleman in London who could rival him for creative, inspired wickedness.

It was a curious gift, really, and not one he'd chosen. It had been foisted upon him, bred into his bones, a bequest from either his mother or father. He couldn't be certain which, as both of them had been felled by a fever before he'd reached his sixth year, but one or the other had infected the St. Vincent bloodline with a truly dazzling streak of devilishness that was as much a part of him as the dimple in his left arse cheek.

Some days it was a blessing, others a curse. It depended on what was passing at the time.

"You've the most absurdly bewildered expression on

your face, Your Grace. One would think we were playing chess rather than a simple game of vingt-et-un."

Tonight, it was a curse. A scourge, a plague, a torment visited upon him from the very depths of the fieriest pit of hell, and atop a shockingly bright green silk divan on the other side of a baize table perched Satan's favorite mistress herself, the plump, scarlet lips he'd once found so alluring curled in a malicious smirk.

Pure poison, those lips. It was a pity he'd drunk so deeply from them before he'd regained his wits. It had been a temporary madness only, but getting free of her had been no easy feat. She'd left scars behind. Not figurative scars, either, but actual mutilated flesh. He touched a finger to the thin, jagged line her silver hairbrush had left on his forehead. Half an inch to the right, and he might have lost his eye. As it was, his eyebrow would never be the same.

The scuffle with the hairbrush had put a final, irrevocable end to their affair—he drew the line at maiming, as every proper gentleman should—but in the month since he'd broken with her, Lady Selina Archer, once his delight, had become his greatest torment.

"It's your play, Your Grace. Do try and attend to the game, won't you?" Her smirk widened, her lips pulling back to reveal sharp, gleaming incisors. "Oh, dear. Are you unwell? You're rather pale."

Dear God, that smile was chilling, and how was it he'd never noticed before how unpleasant her voice was? Like the grind of shattered glass under a boot heel. His shredded nerves shrieked in protest with every word that fell from her lips. "I'm aware it's my play, my lady."

"Indeed? Forgive me, Your Grace. It's been so long since you stirred, I thought perhaps you'd fallen asleep. It wouldn't be the first time you'd slipped into a doze in my dressing room when you'd much better have remained awake."

Once. That had happened *once*, and he'd been in his cups at the time.

But she was only trying to distract him, and he wouldn't allow it. *Couldn't* allow it, not when there was so much at stake. Another outrageous scandal was lurking on the horizon, right on the heels of the last outrageous scandal. That one had sent his grandfather to his bed for a week, and the one brewing now was a good deal worse.

If he didn't put an end to it tonight, it might finish the old fellow off for good.

"Let's get on with it, shall we, Your Grace?" Selina rapped her knuckles on the table. "Unless, of course, you wish to forfeit? Luck hasn't been with you tonight, has it?"

Luck be damned. Luck hadn't a thing to do with it. There was only one way to win a wager, and that was to never risk anything you couldn't afford to lose.

He eyed the earrings she'd tossed on top of the pile of discarded cards.

Too bloody late for that now.

A bead of sweat inched its way underneath the white linen of his cravat and joined its brothers at the base of his neck. He longed to tear the damn thing off and toss it on the floor, but he wouldn't give Selina the satisfaction of knowing she'd rattled him.

He was Montford, for God's sake. He didn't *get* rattled. He didn't panic, fret, fuss, agonize, or fall prey to excesses of emotion of any kind. Once he made up his mind to transgress, he did it with a style and aplomb that made him the envy of all of London's scoundrels, and he was never much troubled with regrets afterward.

He was *meant* to regret it—there must be some Bible

passage or other that warned a man's past sins would catch up to him sooner or later—but there didn't seem to be much point in fretting over some hazy, far-distant future punishment when the sins of the present were already crashing down upon him with all the brutal force of a runaway carriage.

"It grows late, Your Grace. I have another engagement this evening, and I'm certain you're eager to return to whatever shiny new bauble has captured your attention. I daresay you've already replaced me. You'd think nothing of humiliating me in such a cruel manner, would you, Montford?"

"Ah, we're back to this now, are we, my lady? Yes, I'm a rake and a scoundrel, a man devoid of all proper feeling, a man of no tenderness, a cold-hearted blackguard who treats his lovers as if they're nothing more than playthings."

And so on, and so forth. It was her usual harangue. In the end, her dramatics and endless recriminations were the reason he'd put an end to what had been a rather agreeable arrangement between them. Well, that and the fact that she'd been encouraging the attentions of other gentlemen. He'd never been particularly good at sharing with others. It was an affliction, alas, common among young children, and dukes.

"You're a beast, Montford." Selina thrust out her lower lip in a tremulous pout. As recently as a month ago, that pout would have so inflamed his passions he'd have tumbled her into the nearest bed, but he was no longer taken in by her performances.

Now, it left him cold. "A beast, indeed. If I recall correctly, you rather liked that about me at one time."

"Is mockery the best you have to offer, Montford, after

we once meant so much to each other? After months of only living when we were in each other's arms?"

"So romantic, Selina, but do permit me to point out that you appeared lively enough when you hurled your hairbrush at my head, and I don't recall you being in my arms *then*."

"Oh! I might have known you'd throw that in my face."

"Mere words, my dear. They land rather more gently than your hairbrush did."

Selina's face darkened, two ominous spots of color rising in her cheeks. "That's it, then, Montford? Reproaches, and accusations? You have nothing else to say for yourself?"

"Not a blessed thing. I believe you've said more than enough for both of us." At this point, the less he said, the sooner he'd be free of her forever.

"Well, I don't know why I'm surprised at it." A sneer turned Selina's lovely face ugly. "My mistake was in thinking you cared about my feelings, but you care only for your own selfish pleasures."

"Then you're well rid of me, aren't you?" And he of her, and not a moment too soon. After an hour with Selina, his head ached as if a swarm of miniature she-devils had insinuated themselves into the veins at his temples and were stabbing at him with tiny pitchforks.

Wasn't having a mistress meant to be pleasurable? Hadn't there been a time when Selina's smile had transported him? There must have been, but it was all a blur now, like a mirage shimmering just out of his reach.

"That, Your Grace, is the one point on which we can agree." She tossed her head, her dark curls tumbling over her shoulders. "As I said, I've another engagement this evening. I can't sit about all night while you puzzle over your cards."

"Far be it for me to delay any pleasure of yours, my lady." He ran his finger under the damp linen clinging to the moist skin of his neck. The gold earrings glinted dully in the firelight, the enormous, teardrop-shaped rubies winking at him like a pair of blood-red eyes, a glittering symbol of his folly.

The earrings were part of a parure he'd given to her as a token of his affection from their earlier, fonder days together. Extravagant little baubles, those rubies, but the expense was nothing. Jewels came and went, much like mistresses did. He didn't give a damn about the other pieces—a magnificent ruby necklace and a set of diamond and ruby combs. She'd kept those, with his blessing.

But the earrings were another matter entirely.

If they'd been ordinary jewels, she might have kept them, too, as a token of his once-ardent affections, but there was nothing ordinary about those rubies. He'd given them to her during the most violent throes of his lust, when nothing less than the most, er . . . intimate expression of his regard would do for his lovely Selina. It had given him a thrill to see them dangling from her ears, knowing what was hidden inside.

Now his reputation, such as it was, hinged on him getting the earrings back. Christ, what a bloody fool he'd been, handing such a weapon over to a viper like Selina, but God knew there was nothing more ridiculous than a man with an aching cock.

It had taken another, far more valuable sapphire parure to persuade her to even *wager* the ruby earrings tonight. She'd refused at first, claiming she couldn't bear to part with a gift he'd given her in the first flower of their love.

Flower of their love, indeed. What bollocks. Selina only understood one kind of love, and that was the love of money. As for true love—the hearts-and-flowers, yearning-sighs-and-breathless-kisses love? She wouldn't know it if it reared up and bit her on her big toe.

But then, neither would he. They were the same sort of creature, he and Selina. It was a humbling thought, indeed, though at least he lacked her viciousness. His heart was impenetrable, yes, but it wasn't the black, shriveled thing that lurked in the deep, cold depths of Selina's chest.

But for all that Selina was the devil's handmaiden, she wasn't a fool.

Those ruby earrings were the perfect cudgel, the sword hanging above his head, the blade at his throat. As long as she had them, she still had power over him, and she knew it well. She wanted to keep them nearly as badly as he wanted to take them from her.

Not because she loved them, but because she despised *him*.

Fortunately for him, there was one thing Selina loved even more than revenge.

Jewels. Sapphires were her particular weakness, because they brought out the deep blue color of her eyes. In the end, the lure of the sapphire parure had proved too tempting for her to resist, and so, here they were, a fortune in jewels tossed carelessly onto the table between them.

"Come, Your Grace." Selina studied her fingernails, all casual negligence. "Show your hand, or forfeit the game."

He glanced down at his cards. A queen, a seven, and a three. Twenty points. It was a promising hand, yes, but like all of Satan's minions, Selina had the devil's own luck. Still, there was nothing for it but to lay down his cards and pray she hadn't drawn an ace.

He spread them out on the baize. "Twenty, my lady."

Selina's face went white, then red, and he held his breath as slowly, slowly, she lowered her cards to the table.

"Dratted, cursed thing!" Prue snatched up her ruined letter, balled it in her fist, and in a fit of pique, threw it on the floor next to the four other crumpled bits of paper.

The fire had burned down to embers in the grate, and the garden beyond the glass doors behind the desk had turned an inky, impenetrable black, yet all she had to show for her efforts were a few scrawled lines and a heap of ink-blotted paper.

No matter how much she scribbled, her brain refused to produce a single line of the cheerful, amusing letter she'd envisioned flowing from the tip of her pen, and now she'd made a mess of the Duke of Basingstoke's study. He'd regret his generosity to her when he sat at his desk tomorrow morning with a dry inkwell and an empty drawer where his paper had been.

Try as she might, she'd been sitting here for hours with her pen poised above a blank page, her head empty of words. The trouble was, she had nothing to *say*. Well, no, that wasn't it, precisely. There were plenty of shadowy thoughts tumbling about in her head that she might have spun into a dark, dramatic tale of the evils that befall penniless young ladies who get too far above themselves and gad about London with the aristocracy when they'd much better have stayed at home.

But she didn't like to trouble her father with her dire predictions. It would only worry him, and he'd had enough worries these past months to last him a lifetime. No, only sunny, optimistic thoughts would do.

Surely, she could think of *something* pleasant to say?

Her journey from Wiltshire had been agreeable, the weather dry, and the roads tolerable. Lovely views, as well, with the English countryside dressed in her best gold and green summer garb. The duke's carriage was as comfortable as any she'd ever traveled in—it was astonishing, really, what a difference superior springs made—and the duke's coachman only permitted the finest carriage horses near the equipage.

Yes, that would do. Her father was always interested in horses.

She drew a fresh sheet of paper from the drawer, carefully blotted her pen, and ignoring the cramp in her neck, bent over her task and let her pen flow over the page.

Her dear friend Franny, now the Duchess of Basingstoke by a truly stunning twist of fate worthy of a fairy tale, was in the pink of health, as was her husband, the duke, and their eight-month-old son, Giles Frederick Charles Alexander Drew, the future Duke of Basingstoke.

It was a mouthful of a name for such a tiny mite of a boy, but then that was the way with dukes. He was called Freddy, and he was a perfect, laughing cherub of a child, a tiny prince blessed with his mother's bright blue eyes, his father's crown of curly golden locks, and a sweet, toothless smile.

Yes, that was very good. It was best if she focused only on pleasant things. Dinner menus, the baby's antics, harmless gossip, and the like.

She dipped her pen into the inkwell again, prepared to launch into a description of the excellence of tonight's curried eggs and the beauty of the roses still in bloom in the gardens, but she'd only gotten as far as "a spectacular array of blushing pink," before the study door flew open and a whirlwind in dark evening dress stormed into the room. "How d'ye do, Basingstoke?"

Her hand froze, but her fingers went so tight around the pen she tore a jagged hole in the paper underneath it, and a pool of dark ink blossomed under the nib.

That *voice*. It made no difference that she hadn't heard him speak in more than eight months, and then no more than a few dozen words.

She'd know that voice anywhere. Since her disastrous first season, that voice had crept its dastardly way into her dreams every time her head touched her pillow.

Jasper St. Vincent, the Duke of Montford.

Scoundrel. Rake. Blackguard. Villain.

She hadn't had a single moment of peace since her father had lost fifteen hundred pounds to His Grace, the Duke of Montford, during a game of piquet at Lord Hasting's ball last year.

Fifteen hundred pounds, lost in a single evening. Poof, and just like that it was gone, vanished into the ether as if a magician had waved his wand over it.

Or not so much the ether, as the Duke of Montford's pockets.

Because of that wager, Lord Hasting's ball had been both the first and the last of her season. She and her father had hardly had a chance to unpack their bags in their rented lodgings before they were back in Wiltshire, in far tighter financial circumstances than they'd been when they'd left.

It had been an ill-conceived wager, and it made no sense that her father should have made it at all. Major Thomas Thorne wasn't a man who wagered money he didn't have.

That is, he *hadn't* been, until he'd stumbled across the Duke of Montford.

She didn't excuse her father's part in it, any more than he excused himself. She'd never seen him more ashamed than he was when he'd confessed the whole of it to her. For the first time she could recall, he'd looked every one of his fifty years.

It had been one of the most dreadful moments of her life.

Her father had realized soon after they arrived in London that the expense of her season would far exceed his means, yet he'd been desperate to see the thing through, for her sake. The worst of it was, she hadn't even *wanted* a season. She was the last lady in the world who should be twirling about a grand ballroom in a tight silk gown.

But there they'd been, in London, and by the ugliest twist of fate, in the same ballroom as the Duke of Montford.

Her father's desperation had led to predictably catastrophic results.

But surely most of the blame for their ruination must rest upon the Duke of Montford's shoulders? He was known to play deep, and often. A man so accustomed to wagering must have seen at a glance that her father wasn't a gaming man, yet he'd sat down with him anyway, and in the space of a few hours, he'd taken every penny they had.

No, *more* than that. Every penny they had, and every penny they could ever *hope* to have.

"Christ, what a bloody disaster of an evening." Montford threw himself into one of the chairs in front of the fire and propped his booted feet on the table in front of him without sparing a glance at the desk. "You won't believe where I was, Basingstoke."

Indeed, the mind boggled. A Covent Garden brothel,

perhaps? A gaming hell in St. James's Street? His mistress's bedchamber? She set the pen aside and rose to her feet with a smothered sigh. She'd best stop him now, before he launched into a lurid description of his debauchery. "I beg your pardon, Your Grace, but I'm *not* the Duke of Basingstoke."

One would think that would be obvious, but here they were.

Montford peered over his shoulder, but when he caught sight of her, he leapt to his feet and whirled around to face her. "You!"

"Me, indeed. Miss Prudence Thorne, Your Grace." She offered him a reluctant curtsy. "We met at the theater at the end of last season," she added, as he certainly wouldn't remember someone as insignificant as *her*.

He let out an impatient huff. "I know who you *are*, Miss Thorne. What I don't know is where the devil you came from, and what you're doing *here*."

"I came from Wiltshire, and I was writing a letter, if you must know."

"In Basingstoke's study? How singular." He threw himself back into his chair, his boots landing atop the table with a thud. "Where's Basingstoke? He might have warned me you were coming to London."

Yes, it would be disconcerting to have one's nemesis spring upon you from cover of darkness, wouldn't it? Goodness only knew what he'd nearly just confessed to.

Then again, Montford likely hadn't any notion she *was* his nemesis. Fifteen hundred pounds was a mere pittance to him, and nothing to bear a grudge over. "The duke and duchess have retired already. I believe they gave up on you when you didn't turn up for dinner this evening."

He blinked. "Was that tonight?"

The sweep of his long, dark lashes against his cheeks

was irrationally irritating, and her reply was sharper than it needed to be. "It was, indeed. If you'd turned up as you'd said you would, you might have avoided being so startled by my presence, and—"

"Is this going to be a long lecture, Miss Thorne?" He flopped his head back against the chair with a yawn. "If so, you won't mind if I have a nap, will you?"

Odious man! "It's nothing to me what you do, Your Grace, though one might ask why, if you're so fatigued, you don't return to your own house."

He peered up at her for a moment, then a slow, infuriating grin curved his lips, and he settled himself more comfortably in the chair, his long legs sprawled out in front of him. "No, I'm quite content as I am. So, Miss Thorne, what brings you to London? I trust you had a comfortable journey from . . . er, from . . ."

"*Wiltshire*, Your Grace, as I said. It's a small county in southwest England, near Trowbridge. Perhaps you've heard of it?"

"It sounds vaguely familiar, yes. I believe I visited some ancient stones there once that used to be some sort of burial ground or other. Dreadfully dull, really. I do hope you didn't come all the way from Trowbridge just for Basingstoke's dinner party."

Why, how absurd. "It's a two-day journey from Trowbridge to London, Your Grace. You can't truly think I'd come all that way for a plate of roasted fowl."

He shrugged. "I don't see why not. Basingstoke's cook does a very nice roasted fowl."

She glanced down at her unfinished letter sitting on top of the desk and stifled an impatient sigh. For pity's sake, did he really intend to make her stand about while he chatted about the merits of roasted fowl? "I've come at Franny's . . . that is, at Her Grace's invitation, though why that should matter to you—"

"Your timing is a bit off, Miss Thorne." He eyed her, one long leg crossed over the other knee. "London's as dull as a tomb, now the season's ended."

"I've no interest in the season, Your Grace." To put it mildly. It was closer to the truth to say she'd rather die than ever set foot in another London ballroom. Franny had offered to sponsor her for a second season, but she'd refused, not only because she wouldn't put her friend to such an expense for her sake, but also because the mere thought of it tied her stomach in knots.

"Perhaps not, but if you're on the hunt for a husband, Miss Thorne, you've quite missed your chance. You should have come weeks ago."

Goodness, that was rather too close to the truth for comfort, wasn't it? "I just told you I've come to London to visit the duchess. How curious that you should take that to mean I've come to London to hunt for a husband. I can't think of any reason why you should make such an assumption."

A lie, of course. She could think of fifteen hundred reasons, and if the duke had any sense at all, he'd wish her luck in her matrimonial endeavors. If she didn't make an advantageous match, he may as well have set fire to the last five hundred of his fifteen hundred pounds, as he'd never see a penny of it again.

Her father was a proud man and would never willingly default on a debt of honor. He'd already sold the property that surrounded their small estate to a neighboring squire, who'd bought it as a favor to them. But the land had only fetched a thousand pounds. They still owed Montford the remaining five hundred, and there was nothing left to sell but their home and their cherished possessions.

Even if they could sell it, it might not bring in enough money to settle the debt. What would become of them, then? One couldn't get blood from a stone, no matter how hard they squeezed. And once Thornewood was gone, then what? Where would they go?

It didn't bear thinking about.

"Come now, Miss Thorne. There's no need to be coy. Every unmarried lady in England is on the hunt for a husband. Preferably a wealthy, titled one."

"On the contrary, Your Grace. I can think of few things more troublesome than a husband." That was true enough, but that she didn't want a husband, wealthy or otherwise, mattered not a whit. She'd be obliged to have one, and it was all the Duke of Montford's fault.

"Unless it's a wife." He tipped his head back against his chair again and scowled at the ceiling. "It's odd, Miss Thorne, but those ladies who claim a disinclination for the married state inevitably change their minds once they've sunk their claws into you."

Dear God. Had there ever been a more arrogant man than he? No doubt he thought every lady in England was angling to become the Duchess of Montford.

Indeed, perhaps they were, but *she* wasn't. "Not to worry, Your Grace. The gentlemen of London are safe from my claws. I've come to visit the duchess. That's all."

It *wasn't* all, not by a good measure, but the Duke of Montford didn't need to know about her matrimonial schemes. Or, more accurately, Franny's matrimonial schemes on her behalf. Oh, he'd find it out soon, along with every other scoundrel and gossip in London.

There were no secrets among the *ton*.

Until then, however, she didn't intend to provide him with any illumination about her reasons for being in London. It was bad enough she'd be plagued with his tiresome presence on this visit, yet there was no helping that, as he was a good friend of the Duke of Basingstoke's.

But he was no friend of *hers*, and thus there was no reason for her to be standing about chatting with him. "If you'll excuse me, Your Grace, I believe I'll retire for the evening."

"You're excused, Miss Thorne." He'd closed his eyes and didn't bother to open them, but merely waved his hand, as if he were dismissing a servant. "Go on then, off to bed with you."

She turned to go, but before she could even reach the door, a low, buzzing drone made her pause, and she turned back around to find the Duke of Montford still sprawled in his chair, his head thrown back and his mouth wide open.

He was *snoring*. She slapped a hand over her mouth to stifle a laugh.

Why, how mortifying for him! So very . . . un-ducal.

The kind thing to do would be to wake him so he might be on his way, but she didn't owe the Duke of Montford any kindness. So, she left him where he was, in front of a dying fire with his boots propped on the table and his head tipped back against the chair at an awkward angle.

It was too perfect.

She skipped out the door and hurried up the stairs to her bedchamber, and if she wished him an aching back and a crick in his neck, well . . .

No one ever needed to know it but her.

CHAPTER 2

The searing pain began below Jasper's left ear. The icy burn of it would have been enough to jolt him from his slumber, but it didn't end there. It streaked from his neck to the hollow between his shoulder blades before it slid down to the center of his back.

And there it stayed, throbbing with enough intensity to wake the dead.

It was the villainess again, the one with the glittering red rubies where her eyes were meant to be. She was creeping about in the darkness, her glassy gaze locked on him, her bow lips curled in a ghastly smile full of sharp, gleaming teeth. She'd buried a blade in the arch of his neck, right where it gave way to his shoulder, and she was twisting, twisting . . .

He let out a pained groan. "Begone, witch, and let me sleep!"

The villainess didn't answer, and when he reached out blindly to slap the knife from her hands, he found only emptiness.

An invisible villainess then, wielding an invisible knife. "Loftus, the villainess has gotten loose in my bedchamber again. Toss her out at once, will you?"

There was no reply from Loftus, which was strange. His valet was always fluttering about in the mornings, brushing coats and sharpening razors and whatnot. Had the villainess stabbed poor Loftus, too?

That wouldn't do. Not only because Loftus was a kind, gentle soul who didn't deserve such a bloody death, but also because Jasper would never find another valet who'd take such exquisite care of his linens. "Loftus? Are you there?"

Still no answer, only the twist of the knife in his neck, his blood gushing from the gaping wound. He could taste it, thick and coppery on his tongue. She'd take his eyes next, then his heart, skewered on the tip of her blade, and his grandfather would be left with his mangled body—

"No!" His own shout woke him, and he struggled upright, the remnants of the dream still clinging to him as he shook the grogginess from his head.

There were no glittering red eyes, just the last few coals still glowing in the grate.

It wasn't a dream at all, but a nightmare. Just another nightmare, bloodier than the last, to be sure, but there was no villainess, no knife, and no . . . pillows?

Where the devil had his pillows gone? And why was it so damned cold in his bedchamber? He fell back against the bed and threw his arm over his eyes. "Someone has taken my pillows, Loftus. Fetch them for me, will you, and stir the fire? There's a good fellow."

No answer, still. What had become of Loftus? He was always in the bedchamber when Jasper woke, hovering and clucking over the state of his clothing.

He rolled over, but the other half of his bed had vanished as well, and he hit the floor with a bone-cracking thud, flinching as pain exploded in his hip. "Damnation!" He peeled his eyes open, blinking to dislodge the grit sealing his eyelids together and peered up at the beamed ceiling above his head.

Beams? No, that wasn't right.

Damn it, someone had made off with his valet, his pillows, and his green silk bed hangings, and now there were beams where beams had never been before.

Either that, or . . . he blinked again.

Where *was* he? Not in his bedchamber, that was certain. Good Lord, had he fallen asleep in Selina's dressing room? That would explain the red-eyed demoness and the stab wound to his neck, but no, he distinctly recalled leaving her townhouse last night and directing Knapp to take him to Park Lane.

Right, that was it. He was in Basingstoke's study.

He must have fallen asleep in the chair. He struggled onto his knees and heaved himself up. His coat, cravat, and waistcoat were tangled in a crumpled ball at the foot of a nearby chaise where he must have tossed them last night, but he hadn't had the good sense to toss himself down on top of them, and now his neck and back were screaming in agony.

He needed a bath, a cup of tea, and his bed, but there was only the dimmest glow of light coming from the glass doors behind Basingstoke's desk. The house was silent, with even the servants still abed. It couldn't be later than four or five in the morning, then.

An instant later, the mantel clock chimed four times, confirming it.

Well, then. Unless he wished to rouse Basingstoke's servants from their beds and demand a carriage—a course of action that would endear him to precisely no one—he'd have to content himself for now with the chaise and a glass of Basingstoke's very good brandy. Not quite the thing, drinking brandy in the wee hours, but it would pass the time, and help take the sting out of his neck.

He rose and stumbled across the room, muttering curses under his breath, fetched a glass from the sideboard, and shifted Basingstoke's crystal liquor decanters about until he found the brandy. After a fortifying sip he turned to make his way back to the chaise, but paused when he reached Basingstoke's desk.

A half-finished letter lay on top of it, and four or five pages of crumpled paper were scattered on the floor beneath it, dark blots of ink staining the pages.

Ah, yes. Miss Thorne. How could he have forgotten Miss Prudence Thorne?

He never forgot a pretty face, and not many ladies in London could lay claim to Miss Thorne's dainty little nose, the soft, pretty curve of her chin, the wide, hazel eyes, and the unusual golden-brown shade of her hair that put him in mind of warmed honey.

There was only one lady in all of England with that hair and those eyes, but for all the sweet softness of her face, she had the devil's own disposition.

There was no forgetting *her*, that was certain.

Miss Prudence Thorne. The daughter of Major Thomas Thorne, who'd lost a hefty sum of money to him at Lord Hastings's ball last season. Miss Prudence Thorne, dear friend of the Duchess of Basingstoke, and evidently her guest in London, and likely for the shooting party that would take place at Basingstoke's country house early next week.

Miss Prudence Thorne, who despised him with the heat of a thousand suns.

Teasing her had been the only pleasant part of his evening. Alas, he hadn't succeeded in provoking her into a passion, though it had been a near thing, that fiery temper of hers simmering just underneath the surface, the faint red flush of it tinting her white skin.

Really, the lady did herself no favors by keeping such a tight rein on herself. It would be glorious when her control finally snapped. He only hoped he'd be there to witness it.

Rather a fetching creature all around, Miss Thorne.

She made no secret of the fact that she loathed him, of course, but so far, her disgust had been of the quiet, implacable kind. For all her other innumerable flaws, Miss Thorne was not a tantrum thrower. She hadn't thrown anything at all, and though he knew her tongue was layered with barbs, the lady had limited herself to pinched lips and icy stares.

Unlike Selina, who could take a lesson in self-control from Miss Thorne, but then there was really no comparing the two ladies. Selina never experienced a single emotion that wasn't motivated by selfishness, greed, or spite. Even her hatred of him was a product of jealousy and wounded pride.

Miss Thorne, though . . . well, perhaps he'd earned her dislike.

Despite what the gossips whispered about him behind his back, he *did* have a conscience. He simply didn't pay much attention to its squawking. But he had experienced a twinge or two of regret over that wager with Major Thorne last season. He wasn't much given to self-reflection, but it had niggled at him, like a flea burrowing under his skin.

It hadn't been quite right, that wager. He'd been out of sorts that night, bored and antsy at once. Balls during the season always made him so, with all those predatory gazes crawling over him, the marriage-minded mamas sizing him up as a potential husband for their simpering daughters, measuring and weighing him as if he were a cut of beef.

It was all Hasting's fault, really. If his bloody ball hadn't been such a deadly bore, Jasper would never have had to resort to the cardroom in the first place. He preferred to limit his wagering to White's, or to St. James's gaming hells. If he'd been at one of his usual haunts, like the Pidgeon Hole or Mrs. Leach's, he wouldn't have sat down to cards with Major Thorne at all. It didn't take much to deduce that the major wasn't accustomed to wagering.

He didn't usually trifle with gentlemen who didn't have money to lose. It wasn't sporting.

But he hadn't been in a sporting mood that night, and in the end, he'd taken some thousand pounds or so off the man. Or had it been more than that? The devil of it was, he'd made up his mind to forgive the debt, which was really rather generous of him—heroic, even. Major Thorne was dreadful at cards, yes, but he was a fine old gentleman, and Jasper wasn't in the habit of ruining fine old gentlemen.

But his fits of heroism were fleeting things, and he'd forgotten all about the blasted wager until he'd received a bank draft from Thorne, paying all but five hundred pounds of the debt, with his vowels for the remainder.

Was that why Miss Thorne had appeared in London so suddenly? Had her father sent her here to negotiate the repayment of the remainder of the debt? She hadn't had the air of a lady who intended to beg a favor from him—quite the contrary—but neither did he believe she'd come all the way from Wiltshire of all places just to visit the Duchess of Basingstoke.

They were dear friends, yes, but no one came to London in *August*, for God's sake.

He glanced back at the desk, at the unfinished letter on top, the crumpled balls of paper underneath it.

He shouldn't. He really shouldn't. It was none of his concern.

Only it was too late, because he was already striding toward the desk. He stared down at the scattered balls of paper, giving one of them a half-hearted nudge with his toe, the feeble protests of his conscience warring with the inexplicable curiosity he'd had about Miss Thorne since she'd turned up in Basingstoke's theater box at the end of last season.

It was odd, really, that he should find ordinary Miss Prudence Thorne from Wiltshire so fascinating. Perhaps it was the way she glared at him. She did have rather an impressive glare, all narrowed hazel eyes and thick, dark lashes fluttering with fury.

Still, his irrational preoccupation with her notwithstanding, it was none of his business what she'd been writing. Really, he had no excuse for invading her privacy. A proper gentleman would take his brandy, return to his chaise, and wait quietly until a servant appeared.

Right, then. He backed away from the desk, but he hadn't taken two steps toward the chaise before he paused again.

What if Miss Thorne had been writing to her father about the debt? Then it could be said to be his business, couldn't it? Five hundred pounds was a considerable sum, after all. Perhaps Miss Thorne and her father had some sort of scheme afoot, some devious plot to wriggle free of Thorne's obligations. For all he knew, Miss Thorne could be planning to rob him. Surely, he owed it to himself to find out for certain? Why, his very safety could be at risk!

He returned to the desk, snatched up the bundle of

discarded papers from the floor, then made himself comfortable in Basingstoke's chair and smoothed them out one by one before taking up the first one.

Dearest Father, I've arrived safely in—

That was as far as she'd gotten before the sentence ended in an unsightly blob of ink. He laid it aside and picked up the second one, then the third, but they were much the same as the first. A few scribbles followed by an angry ink blot.

The letter on the desk looked more promising, however, so he took it up and began to read. Pleasant journey from Wiltshire, blah, blah, lovely scenery, good roads, something about superior carriage springs and the countryside dressed in golds and greens—a bit of purple prose, that—Freddy's blue eyes, blah, blah, blah . . . the duke's coachman, blah, blah . . .

Good Lord, it was the dullest letter imaginable. He read to the bottom of the page, then tossed it aside with disgust. Not foul plots or schemes, and not a word about the debt or any details about her reasons for being in London.

Bloody disappointing, really. He drained his brandy, leaving the empty glass on Basingstoke's desk with Miss Thorne's tedious letters and made his way back to his corner. He snatched up his coat and lay down upon the chaise, his back shrieking in protest.

What did Basingstoke mean, having such a wretched piece of furniture in his study? The thing was as hard as a slab of marble. The man was a duke, for God's sake. Surely, he could afford a proper chaise?

Still, it was better than the chair, and at least there was a pillow—a stiff, hard little thing, yes, with a tiresome number of tassels, but he thrust it under his head, tugged his coat over himself and squeezed his eyes closed, waiting for sleep to take him.

It was still dark when Prue woke, a vague sense of panic rousing her from a sound sleep.

Something was amiss. She'd left something undone. Her brain chased around in sleepy circles, trying to pinpoint the nameless dread making her stomach churn. Was it something to do with Franny? Had she forgotten to tell her something?

No, that wasn't it.

Her father, then? No, he was safely back at Thornewood. She hadn't yet finished her letter to him, but that was—

Oh, no! She jerked upright, her fingers gripping the coverlet.

The Duke of Basingstoke's study! She'd left his quill lying on his desk, the inkwell uncovered, and a half dozen spoiled papers on the floor! For pity's sake, what had she been thinking, leaving the duke's private study in such disarray, after he'd been kind enough to offer it to her?

She leapt from the bed, snatched up her cloak and shoved her arms into it as she made her way out the bedchamber door and into the darkened hallway, muttering a quick prayer of thanks that she'd had the sense to pay attention when the maidservant had shown her to her room. Otherwise, she might have been wandering the hallways for hours, searching for the staircase.

But she found it easily, and was downstairs in a trice, wincing at the chill of the marble floors under her bare feet as she made her way past the entryway and into the hallway that led to the duke's study.

The door creaked as she pushed it open, and an involuntary shiver seized her as she entered. Goodness, it was cold in here, but it would only take a moment to set the quill and the inkwell to rights and gather up the spoiled papers.

She hurried to the desk, but she stopped short when she reached it.

The crumpled papers were no longer on the floor, but spread out flat atop the duke's desk as if a hand had smoothed them, one on top of the next in a neat pile, with her half-finished letter on top. Beside them stood an empty tumbler with a few dregs of amber liquid pooled at the bottom.

She took up the glass and sniffed. Brandy? She sniffed again. Yes, that was certainly brandy, but who would be drinking brandy in the Duke of Basingstoke's study in the middle of the—

"You're up rather early this morning, Miss Thorne. Did you forget something?"

She gasped and whirled around, her hand reaching instinctively for the neck of her cloak, her fingers tightening around it. That deep, dark voice curled around her again, a touch raspy from sleep this time, but certainly *him*. There was no mistaking that slow drawl, always with a hint of amusement in it, as if he had the most delicious secret and couldn't wait to whisper it into her ear.

Montford, of course. No other gentleman in England spoke as he did.

"I beg your pardon, Miss Thorne." A lean, dark shape detached itself from the chaise on the other side of the room. "I didn't mean to startle you."

The fire had died down some time ago, but she'd left the study door open behind her when she entered, and as he came forward, a dim shaft of light from the hallway fell over his face.

Another gasp tried to tear itself loose from her chest, but this one caught in her throat, lodging there as he sauntered toward her.

The coat, cravat, and waistcoat he'd been wearing last night were nowhere to be seen. He was in his shirtsleeves, the wide-open neck of his white linen shirt exposing the hollow of his throat, a smattering of crisp dark hair peeking out from the layers of loose linen. His head was a mess of tousled dark waves, and the hint of a beard shadowed his jaw and neck.

"Why . . . what are you doing here?" That throaty, breathless murmur wasn't *her* voice, was it? She sounded as if she'd swallowed a mouthful of gravel.

"I fell asleep. I can't say I recommend Basingstoke's study as a bedchamber, if you were wondering. His chaise isn't a bed so much as a medieval torture device."

"I *wasn't* wondering." Not only that, but she'd very much prefer not to discuss bedchambers with him when he looked like . . . *that*. Like a . . . a . . . dear God, he looked like a pirate, with those wild curls and that dark beard, and he was still coming toward her, far too close to her, so close she fancied she could distinguish each infinitesimal hair shading his jaw from the others, could imagine the rasp of them against her fingertips.

Not that she intended to *touch* them. Or him. Certainly not *him*, no matter if her fingers had grown strangely restless, plucking at the folds of her cloak, the thin night rail she wore underneath caressing her heated skin. Even her toes were warming up, the ice melting . . .

She didn't recall backing away, but she must have done, because her backside came up against the desk, her hands curling over the edge of it, the smooth wood pressing into her palms.

"What brings you downstairs so early in the morning, Miss Thorne?" He came to a stop at last, but the wicked smile that curved his lips, the gleam of his teeth in the darkness, was almost as disorienting as those prickles of hair were. "Were you worried about me?"

"I don't know how I could be worried about you, Your Grace, when I couldn't have known you'd fallen asleep down here." Except, of course, that she *had* known it, or at least suspected it. She even had an intimate knowledge of the particular timber of the Duke of Montford's snores.

But if she had realized he was *still* here, nothing in the world could have induced her to venture downstairs. For pity's sake, what sort of gentleman spent the night in another gentleman's study? "I came down to tidy my mess and fetch my—" She broke off with an outraged gasp. There could only be one explanation why her letters were no longer scattered on the floor where she'd left them, but instead spread out in a neat pile on the desk. "You read my letters, didn't you?"

"Could we truthfully call those letters, Miss Thorne? No, I think not. A few illegible scribbles, nothing more. I do compliment you on the creativity of your inkblots, however. I've never seen more handsome inkblots in my life." He gave her a winning smile.

For one dreadful moment her treacherous lips twitched, but she pressed them together into a tight line before they could do anything foolish, like return his smile. "How dare you? Those were *private* letters, Your Grace. You had no business reading them."

"Private?" He snorted. "Ah, yes. Titillating, indeed. I almost felt as though I were listening in on your confessional. I think I enjoyed the "Dear Father" part the most.

Heady stuff, that. Your description of the countryside in her green and gold robes brought a blush to my cheek."

A blush, indeed. The man likely hadn't blushed since he left off wearing short pants. She crossed her arms over her chest. "Are you quite finished?"

"Not quite, no. May I just hint, Miss Thorne, that you really should be thanking me. You left rather a mess in poor Basingstoke's study, and I was kind enough to pick it up for you."

"Thank you? Very well, Your Grace, I'll thank you to stay out of my affairs in the future." She turned to snatch up the letters, and her gaze fell on the empty tumbler. "Have you been *drinking*? At"—she glanced at the mantel clock—"five o'clock in the morning?"

"Certainly not, Miss Thorne. What a scandalous accusation."

"I beg your—"

"I drank that at four o'clock in the morning."

Dear God, had there ever been a more incorrigible man? "You—"

"I do beg your pardon, Miss Thorne, but as much as you seem to wish to keep me here chatting with you, I believe I heard one of the servants stirring. It's past time I took my leave. I don't like to worry my valet, you know. He's rather protective of me."

He returned to the chaise, snatched up a rumpled pile of clothing and strode to the study door. "It is, as always, a great pleasure to see *you*, Miss Thorne." He offered her an extravagant bow, then turned and vanished through the door, the long length of his cravat trailing behind him.

CHAPTER 3

Keep him here, indeed. The man was either daft, in his cups, or both at once. It was nothing to her, of course. The Duke of Montford might get up to whatever nocturnal mischief he pleased without her experiencing a single twinge of curiosity about it.

Prue stuffed her letters in the pocket of her cloak and tiptoed to the door, but paused to peek around it first, in case Montford was lingering in the entryway.

He was gone, thank goodness, and she'd do well to follow in his footsteps before Basingstoke's butler, Trevor, appeared, and she was obliged to explain what she was doing in the duke's study at five o'clock in the morning in her bare feet, with her night rail peeking out from under the hem of her traveling cloak.

She crept into the hallway and was a mere half dozen steps from darting up the stairs to the safety of her bed-chamber when a sudden, mad urge made her pause and glance back over her shoulder.

No. It was ridiculous, not to mention improper, and unnecessary. She started back toward the stairs again, but paused once more on the bottom step, furious with her-self, but unable to make her feet stir another step.

The chaise, where Montford had spent the night . . .

She wanted to see it.

Goodness, what a fool she was! It was utter folly, but the urge had her tight in its grip now, and really, what was the harm in it? It wasn't as if she'd have another chance to see where the devil slept.

Heat blossomed in her cheeks as she retraced her steps back to the hallway, through the study door and past the Duke of Basingstoke's desk to the chaise on the other side of the room, near the fireplace.

It was an ordinary chaise, nothing in the least remarkable about it. Certainly, there was nothing about it to indicate a large duke with impossibly long legs had slept on it the night before, aside from a slightly flattened pillow at one end with a shallow indentation in the center of it where his head must have rested, his tousled curls spread out over the fabric.

She cast a furtive glance around the room, her lip caught between her teeth. No, it was an absurd notion, and she wouldn't give into it. It was out of the question . . . only there was her hand, already reaching for the pillow, like a guilty child intent on snatching up a handful of forbidden sweets.

But even that humiliating thought wasn't enough to keep her from grabbing the pillow, her cheeks on fire as she brought it up to her face, pressed it to her nose, and inhaled.

She couldn't have said what she expected it to smell like—cheroots, perhaps, or brandy and snuff and the heavy, cloying scent of a courtesan's perfume—but to her surprise a faint scent of spice and citrus clung to it. What was that scent? Not the Bay Rum favored by so many of London's fashionable gentlemen, but something else entirely—amber, perhaps, with a hint of orange blossom?

No, it couldn't be. Surely, the wicked Duke of Montford didn't smell of something so innocent as orange blossoms?

She raised it to her nose and inhaled again, the warm, spicy scent flooding through her. It wasn't Albany, another popular scent for gentlemen, as there wasn't a whiff of lavender to it. Did she detect cinnamon, or was that ginger? She raised the pillow for a third sniff, but then froze, appalled at herself.

God above, what was she *doing*?

Was she . . . *sniffing* the Duke of Montford?

A muted shriek left her lips, and she hurled the pillow away from her, desperate to be rid of it, but instead of landing on the chair she'd been aiming at, the dratted thing hit the edge of the table and skittered under the chaise.

Well, this was what came of sniffing a duke, wasn't it?

She dropped to her knees, stuck her arm underneath the chaise and patted about, but she couldn't find the pillow. "Dash it." She pushed the table out of the way, lay down flat on her stomach, and peered under the chaise.

Ah, there it was, right in the middle, just out of reach of her fingertips. She squirmed closer, stretching until she finally caught one of the corner tassels, pinched it between her fingers and dragged the blasted thing out. "There you are, you devil."

She tossed it back onto the chaise and was just sliding the table back into place when a glimmer caught her eye. She drew closer, peering down at the pillow.

There was something shiny caught in one of the tassels.

It looked like . . . an earring? But what would the Duke of Montford be doing with an earring? She took up the pillow, worked the object loose, and held it up to the light spilling in through the doorway to get a better look at it.

It *was* an earring, and not just any earring, either, but

a large, dangly one, set with . . . goodness, were those rubies? Rubies, of that size? No, it couldn't be.

Yet it was. There was no mistaking the deep red stone, winking up at her like a mischievous crimson eye. Dear God, it was enormous, easily the size of the end of her thumb. It was shaped like a teardrop and surrounded by at least a dozen diamonds in a heavy gold setting, and there was a tiny, perfect pearl dripping like a tear from the end.

She stared down at it, her heart pounding hard in her ears. She'd never seen such a magnificent piece of jewelry before, much less held one in her hand. Where did one even wear such a piece as this, and how on earth had it ended up tangled in a tassel on a pillow in the duke's study?

It must belong to Franny. Yes, of course. Such an extravagant piece was entirely fitting for an important personage like the Duchess of Basingstoke. She'd never seen Franny wear these, though, or anything like them, really. Franny's tastes were simple, and this was a dramatic piece, one that demanded attention.

Had Basingstoke purchased the earrings for Franny, intending them as a gift, and then misplaced them? It didn't seem likely. The Duke of Basingstoke wasn't the sort of gentleman who'd be so careless as to misplace a fortune in rubies, and he knew his wife's tastes too well to choose jewels she wouldn't favor.

Perhaps they were from the family coffers then, an heirloom.

Either way, Franny would certainly want it back. A ruby that size was worth a fortune, and that was to say nothing of the pearl and diamonds. What must it be like, to live the sort of life where jewels like this were commonplace? She spread the earring out in her palm, admiring the way the faint light played over the ruby, the deep red center burning like it contained its own private fire.

There was no sense in wondering, because it was no sort of life she'd ever live. No sort of life she'd ever longed for, either, though one couldn't look at such splendid jewels without recognizing what they represented.

Ease, comfort, security. A whole world of experiences that were far out of the reach of a lady like herself.

Freedom. And that . . . *that*, she did long for, had always longed for.

But it was a foolish thing to long for, wasn't it? Very few ladies enjoyed the sort of freedom she envisioned. Why, she may as well yearn for a casket of gold coins, or a castle nestled amongst the clouds, a winged horse, or some other mythical entity.

Wishes that would never be realized.

Meanwhile, the servants were stirring.

She took up the pillow again. There was no second earring caught in the tassels, but when it came to rubies nearly as big as one's thumb it was best to be sure, so she dropped down onto her knees again and peered under the chaise.

Yes, there it was, the second earring, the ruby glimmering faintly. She was obliged to lay flat on her stomach to get it, but at last she managed to grasp the little pearl dangling from the end and slide the earring out from under the chaise.

She rose to her feet, brushed the dust from her cloak, and went to stuff both earrings into her pocket, but one of her thumbs grazed the ruby, and it moved.

Oh, no. Had she loosened one of the stones when she slid it out from under the chaise? She perched on the edge of the opposite chair and prodded carefully at the ruby, testing the setting. That was strange. The ruby itself wasn't loose, but the setting shifted when she pressed down on it.

She leaned closer to get a better look.

How curious. There was a tiny hinge, just at the edge of the setting. She'd never seen anything like it before. Why would there be . . . wait.

These were no ordinary earrings. They were *lockets*, with the rubies set into the lids.

She touched her thumb to the hinge, the locket sprang open, and inside . . .

There was a tiny painting. She brought it closer to her face, squinting down at it. It was difficult to make it out in the dim light, but it seemed to be a portrait of a gentleman, and it looked as if he was—

"Dear God!" She dropped the earring into her lap as if it had bitten her. "God in heaven, is that . . ." She peeked at it again, then jerked back with a gasp, slapping a hand over her eyes. "It *is*!"

The portrait was tiny, but the brushwork was so skilled, so exquisitely done, one could see at a glance what it depicted, and what it depicted was, well, not the sort of portrait one expected to find inside an otherwise innocent-looking locket.

Despite having grown up with no mother, she knew a bit more about the sexual act than most inexperienced young ladies did. Her father had insisted upon it, and had taken it upon himself to explain the mechanics of it, but he hadn't embellished upon the facts, and he certainly hadn't gone into the more, er, exotic aspects of the thing.

What was happening in the painting certainly qualified as exotic.

That was shocking enough, but that wasn't what held her attention.

It was the gentleman.

He was tall and broad shouldered, his bare legs thick with muscle, with a smattering of crisp dark hair that matched the wild mass of tousled curls atop his head.

A familiar wicked grin curved his full lips.

She stared at him, her heart pounding. Unless she was mistaken, he looked very much like . . .

She leapt up from the chaise, rushed over to the duke's desk and lit the lamp with shaking fingers, then held the earring up to the flickering light.

She *wasn't* mistaken.

The man in the portrait looked very much like the Duke of Montford.

Prue tried to fall back to sleep once she returned to her bedchamber, but as it turned out, a naked duke under her pillow was quite enough to ruin her sleep for the rest of the morning.

A portrait of a naked duke, that is.

She'd slipped the earrings under her pillow for safe-keeping, but she spent a restless morning nonetheless, plagued with fitful dreams of a tall, dark-eyed demon with a maddeningly smug grin sneaking his hand underneath her pillow, his soft laugh stirring the loose hair near her ear.

That had been enough to startle her awake and send her scrabbling frantically under her pillow to make certain the earrings were still there. There'd been no drifting off to sleep again after that, and she'd lain awake for the rest of the morning, her arms at her sides, staring up at the blue-striped canopy above and thinking of . . . nothing.

Certainly *not* of naked dukes. One naked duke, that is, but from multiple angles, because there were two portraits, one in each locket, and the second one was even more scandalous than the first.

She rose at last when the clock struck seven, scrubbed the sleep from her eyes with the water in the basin, and dressed, the ruby earrings stuffed into the pocket of her skirt.

She was more than ready to be rid of the cursed things. They were beautiful, of course, but it wasn't at all peaceful, having such costly jewels in one's possession, even without the naked duke.

She would have made a dreadful pickpocket.

The trouble was, what was she meant to *do* with them? Who was she meant to give them to? Regrettably, the answer was obvious. Who else, but the Duke of Montford? It would be the last thing she ever did, of course, as she was sure to expire of embarrassment on the spot.

Indeed, she wasn't certain she could ever look him in the eye again as it was.

No, surely it made more sense to give them to Franny? She could pass them on to Basingstoke, who could then return them to the Duke of Montford. Yes, that would be best. Who was better equipped to deal with a naked duke than another duke, after all?

She didn't like to drag poor Franny into this business, but what else could she do?

Dash it, she'd have been much better off if she'd just left the wretched things where she'd found them! Surely, Montford would miss them soon enough, and come back for them? Perhaps she could just toss them back under the chaise, and forget she'd ever seen them?

But alas, no. What if Montford didn't realize he'd lost them in Basingstoke's study? Why, it could be days before he thought to look under the chaise. One of the

servants was sure to find them before then, and there was
no telling what sort of chaos that might lead to.

No, she had no choice but to hand them over to
Franny, and the sooner she was rid of them, the better.

She hurried from her bedchamber and descended to
the breakfast parlor, where she did her best to look innocent while she waited for Franny to appear, the purloined
earrings burning a guilty hole in her pocket.

"My goodness, Prue, you're up early this morning."
Franny stopped short in the doorway a short time later,
one eyebrow quirked. "Did you not sleep well?"

Certainly, she had. As well as any lady haunted by a
smirking, dark-haired demon. "As well as I ever do when
I'm not at home. But you look fatigued yourself, dearest."
She frowned at the violet smudges beneath her friend's
eyes. "Oh, dear, was Freddy fussing again last night?"

"I'm afraid so. You can't imagine how much havoc
one small infant can wreak, Prue! He has a touch of colic,
and we were up half the night trying to soothe him to
sleep."

"Dear me, that does sound trying. I'm sorry for it,
though you might consider turning him over to his nurse-
maid on occasion." Prue hid a smile behind her teacup,
knowing what Franny would say before she even opened
her mouth. Freddy was a very important personage in the
eyes of his adoring parents.

"Oh, no, I couldn't do that! The poor little mite wails
so piteously unless either Giles or I hold him, and neither
of us can bear to listen to him cry."

"No, of course not." She patted Franny's hand. "Perhaps
a nap this afternoon, then. You're not much use to Freddy
if you're exhausted yourself, you know."

"I know. A cup of tea, if you would, Groves." Franny
nodded her thanks as the footman leapt forward to fill her

teacup and was quiet until she'd finished it. "There. I feel ever so much better now." She turned a sharpened gaze on Prue. "My dearest Prudence, you have quite an odd look about you this morning. Has something happened?"

Prue choked on the sip of tea she'd just swallowed. For pity's sake, how did Franny always *know* when something was afoot? One could never hide a blessed thing from her. It was both impressive and trying in equal measure. "Whatever do you mean? What can have happened between last night and this morning?"

Plenty, as it turned out. She shoved a hand into her pocket and fisted the earrings, the hard edges of the rubies digging into her palm.

"You're a dreadful liar, Prue." Franny's teacup landed in the saucer with a stern click. "Is something amiss with one of the servants? Or . . . oh, no. It's not your father, is it? Is he—"

"No, no, he's very well. It's nothing like that. It's, er, well . . ." Dear God, how to say it? A lady couldn't just blurt out that she had a naked duke secreted away in her pocket, could she? "The Duke of Montford appeared in His Grace's study while I was writing my letter to my father last night."

There. That was a good start.

"Did he? Well, I can't say I'm surprised. He wanders as he pleases, you know." A sly smile twitched at the corners of Franny's lips. "I daresay he was surprised to see *you*."

"He was, I can assure you." Not as surprised as she'd been to see him this morning, however.

"And what did Montford have to say for himself?"

"Oh, the usual absurd things. He demanded to know why Basingstoke hadn't warned him I was coming to London." *Warned* him, as if she were some sort of plague or pestilence. "Really, he's the most infuriating man I've ever come across. I don't know how you tolerate him, Franny."

"I daresay this will shock you, but I'm rather fond of Montford."

"Fond of him!" Prue stared at her, aghast. "How can you be, Franny? He's dreadful!"

"He's not, really, though I'd sooner attempt to persuade a feral cat to make friends with a rabid dog than reconcile you and Montford."

"A feral cat! I do hope you're not referring to *me*."

"Would you prefer to be the rabid dog?"

"I prefer to be neither."

Franny laughed. "Never mind that. What else did Montford say?"

"Let's see. He went on and on about your cook's roasted fowl, of all things, informed me Town is as dull as a tomb, complained that I was lecturing him about missing dinner, pried into my reasons for being in London, and held forth at tedious length about how every young lady in England is on the prowl for a wealthy, titled husband."

"Well, he's not entirely wrong about that last thing."

"Perhaps not, but it's neither here nor there, and I don't care one whit about the Duke of Montford's opinions. I didn't pay attention to a word he said."

"Clearly."

Franny gave her a knowing grin that Prue chose to ignore. "In any case, it wasn't what he *said* that matters. It's what he *did*."

"Well, what did he do, then?"

Did she dare? The earrings were right there, in her pocket.

But Franny looked so pale and tired this morning, and she had such a lot to manage, what with her schemes to see Prue married, and now Freddy's colic. She didn't need yet another thing to worry about. Wouldn't it be best to simply put the earrings back where she'd found them? She could keep an eye on them and see to it they stayed where they were until Montford caught on that he'd lost them and came to fetch them.

Yes, that would be much better than burdening Franny with this nonsense.

"Prue? What did Montford do?"

"Oh, he, ah . . . he fell asleep in Basingstoke's study." The servants would already know that by now, so there was no sense in hiding it, as both Franny and Basingstoke would hear of it soon enough. "On the chaise, in front of the fire. Just as I left, I heard him snoring."

"Snoring! My goodness."

"Indeed. I found him there this morning. I'd forgotten some papers and returned to fetch them, and there he was, in nothing but his shirtsleeves!"

Not that she'd noticed. Much.

Franny glanced at the footman. "Groves, will you go to the kitchens and see if Cook has any more of those apricot tartlets? I do adore her tartlets."

"Yes, Your Grace." Groves bowed and hurried out the door.

Franny waited until he was out of earshot, then turned back to Prue. "You mean to say you came upon the Duke of Montford half-dressed in Giles's study? My goodness, Prue, you have had an exciting morning."

"I'd sooner call it distressing. What does the Duke of Montford *mean*, falling asleep in Basingstoke's study and leaving bits of his clothing flung about?"

Franny's eyes widened. "His clothing was flung about?"

"Well, no, but I, ah . . . I did find one of his gloves

underneath the chaise." Not gloves so much as rubies and diamonds, but the less said about the earrings, the better.

Franny frowned. "What were you doing under the chaise?"

"Nothing! I, er, I dropped a pillow on the floor and had to reach under the chaise to fetch it." Anything else she may have done with that pillow was irrelevant to the story, and thus didn't bear repeating.

"Is that all? Because you've gone as red as a peony."

"Of course, that's all! What else could there be?" Oh dear. Her voice had gone rather shrill.

Franny merely raised an eyebrow, however. "Why, not a thing, Prue, if you say so. Now, what shall we do today? Do you fancy a trip to Bond Street?"

"Shopping? My dearest Franny, when have I *ever* fancied shopping?" She was hopeless with the hats, gowns, ribbons, and furbelows that seemed to fascinate other ladies. "You know how fretful it makes me." Not as fretful as dark-haired, pirate-like dukes in nothing but their shirtsleeves, but fretful enough.

"Yes, but I thought perhaps you might need a few things for this afternoon." Franny gave her a meaningful look. "We're to have Lord Stoneleigh for tea."

Ah, yes. Lord Stoneleigh, speaking of things that made her fretful.

But that wasn't quite fair, was it? It wasn't Lord Stoneleigh *himself* that made her fretful. Just the prospect of marriage to him. She sighed. "Courtships are awkward things, aren't they?"

"Under the circumstances, yes, I'm afraid so. But I think we must strike first, dearest. There aren't many available gentlemen in Lord Stoneleigh's circumstances. London's mamas are already sharpening their claws for him."

"Yes, I suppose they are." Any one of their daughters would likely make him a better wife than she would, too. Was it even fair of her to be considering the marriage, when she was so reluctant?

Franny sighed and reached for her hand. "Now, Prue, there's no need to look like that. It's only tea, not a formal courtship. If you don't like Lord Stoneleigh, we'll find someone else for you."

A brief silence fell, both of them seemingly lost in thoughts neither of them would say aloud.

There *was* no one else.

"You needn't worry, Franny, because I *do* like Lord Stoneleigh." At least, she didn't recall disliking him. She'd met him only once before, when she'd visited Franny in London at the end of last season. Aside from a vague recollection of a chatty gentleman with fair hair, she didn't recall much about the man.

Still, she mustered a smile from somewhere and pasted it on her lips. "Indeed, I don't know how any lady could object to such an, er . . . pleasant gentleman."

Franny studied her for a moment, no doubt seeing at a glance everything Prue was attempting to hide, but all she said was, "I don't fancy a shopping trip, after all. Let's remain at home today, shall we? I've fetched a stack of books from the library I think you'll enjoy, and you can finish your letter to your father. Will that suit?"

"Yes, that will do very well, indeed." Between Lord Stoneleigh and the Duke of Montford's scandalous earrings, a shopping trip to Bond Street might have sent her right over the edge. "Now, I believe you said something about apricot tartlets?"

CHAPTER 4

"May I compliment you on your exquisite mantelpiece, Your Grace? Such fine white marble!" Lord Stoneleigh leaned closer to peer at the medallion carved into the center panel. "It's in the Greek style, I believe?"

The Duke of Basingstoke, who'd already been compelled to accept Lord Stoneleigh's compliments on the tapestry hanging in the entryway, the magnificence of the mahogany dining table, and the splendor of the Aubusson carpet under their feet, merely inclined his head.

"And that mantel clock! Why, it's very like one I keep on my own mantel at home. Very like it, indeed!" Lord Stoneleigh pressed a hand to his chest, as if quite overcome by the glory of it. "Yours is far superior, of course. I don't believe I've ever seen a more handsome mantel clock in my life, Your Grace!"

This extravagant compliment was directed to the duchess, his lordship apparently having given up on the duke. Franny accepted it with more politeness than her husband, but her eyes were wide as they met Prue's, and both ladies were obliged to look hastily away from each other before they gave themselves away with a grimace.

"Thank you, Lord Stoneleigh. You're very kind. Tell me, how do your parishioners do?"

"Very well, indeed, Your Grace." Lord Stoneleigh beamed. "The pews quite overflow of a Sunday. I consider their presence a hearty endorsement of my sermons, and can't help but be flattered by it, as I'm sure you understand, Your Grace."

"Of course. I believe the roof of the church was damaged by all the rains this past spring. Such a lovely building, All Saints Church! Have you any plans to see it repaired?"

"Er, no, not this year, I'm afraid, Your Grace. Next spring, certainly, the weather permitting, of course, though I daresay my loyal parishioners would even brave a leaky roof to attend my Sunday sermons."

He launched into an effusive speech about the devotion of his parishioners and went on at such length Prue stopped listening after a time, lowering her gaze to her lap. She weaved her fingers together into a tight knot and concentrated on the stretch of her skin across her knuckles, but her heart continued to thrash madly against her ribs, like a panicked bird attempting to escape its cage.

Lord Stoneleigh was a good, decent man. He was a vicar, for goodness' sake, and thus presumably a gentleman of sterling character. Neither was he a fool, despite his having waxed poetic about nearly every stick of furniture in the Duke of Basingstoke's drawing room.

He was simply nervous, that was all. It wasn't every day one dined with a duke, and Basingstoke was an imposing figure, and rather frightening, really, until one got accustomed to his blunt manner.

Lord Stoneleigh could even be said to be a handsome man, with his broad shoulders and the gleam of candlelight on his fair hair, and he did have a pair of handsome gray eyes. Not the soft, dreamy gray of foggy mornings, or the smoky gray of slightly tarnished silver, but the cooler gray of stone, or the steely gray of storm clouds, or—

Stop it. His eyes were perfectly fine. They weren't cold or steely. It was merely a trick of the light that made them look so, and then only for an instant.

There wasn't a single thing wrong with Lord Stoneleigh. Not a single thing.

She'd lost count of how many times she'd been obliged to repeat that to herself this afternoon, and it wasn't fair to Lord Stoneleigh, who'd been as cordial as a gentleman possibly could be, with his polite enquiries about her journey to London and her father's health.

It wasn't as if she hadn't known what she was getting herself into, coming here. She'd met Lord Stoneleigh at the end of last season, and he was much as she remembered him to be from her visit then, that is, a tall gentleman with fair hair, though she didn't remember him being quite so . . . talkative?

Not that there was anything wrong with chattiness. Or with Lord Stoneleigh.

No, not a single—

"That's a very fine instrument, Your Grace. Do you play, Miss Thorne?" Lord Stoneleigh nodded toward the pianoforte situated between two windows at the other end of the room. "Perhaps you might favor us with a song, if Her Grace approves it?"

Prue's gaze flew to Franny's, her fingers twitching in alarm. Nothing would put a quicker end to this courtship than her banging about on the pianoforte in her usual tuneless fashion. Her father often said her playing sounded like a half dozen racoons chasing each other across the keyboard.

Now, if Lord Stoneleigh had asked her to hunt, or shoot, or race she might have shown herself to proper advantage. She was a crack shot with a pistol and a bow and arrow, and she could outride any gentleman within a twenty-mile radius of Thornewood.

But those weren't, alas, the sorts of skills that were of much use in a drawing room, were they? She gave him an apologetic smile. "I beg you'll excuse me, my lord. I'm afraid I don't have much of an ear for music."

"No ear? That *is* a pity, Miss Thorne." Lord Stoneleigh shook his head. "Perhaps a stricter dedication to your craft might help? I often advise my parishioners that practice is the greatest weapon against mediocrity."

"You're quite right, my lord. I'm ashamed to say I've rather neglected my music recently." As recently as the last decade or so, that is.

"Not to worry, Miss Thorne. I have a lovely instrument at the parsonage." Lord Stoneleigh patted her hand, then added hastily, "It's nothing so grand as His Grace's, of course, but it's serviceable enough for a novice to practice upon."

Prue gritted her teeth. There wasn't a single thing wrong with Lord Stoneleigh. Not a single thing, only . . . was it really only four o'clock? It felt as though they'd been at tea for hours.

"Perhaps Miss Thorne might play for us another time, my lord." Franny cast an uneasy glance at Prue. "It's quite warm this afternoon, and I'm certain she's fatigued from her journey from Wiltshire."

"Of course. Forgive me, Miss Thorne. I didn't think." Lord Stoneleigh gave her an apologetic smile which warmed up his eyes a degree or two, and for an instant her spirits lifted. Mightn't she grow fonder of him as they became more familiar with each other? He wasn't a *bad* man, after all. No, indeed. There wasn't a single thing wrong with him.

Surely a gentleman with such a pleasant smile might work his way into her heart sooner or later? Perhaps it would all turn out well in the end, and—

"I'd be happy to supervise your practice if you'd like, Miss Thorne. I've been told I'm an excellent instructor, and I flatter myself there's some truth to it."

Or perhaps not.

Not that it mattered, one way or the other. Her toes were already hanging over the abyss. One push, and she'd trip into a courtship. From there it was a direct plunge over the edge, head tumbling over heels, straight into the bottomless chasm of marriage.

She'd never intended to marry. Unlike so many young ladies, she hadn't dreamed about her future spouse, or imagined herself as a wife, but it was her only hope of getting herself and her father out from under a crushing debt, and it wasn't as if there were dozens of wealthy gentlemen eager to wed a penniless bride.

Rather scarce on the ground, those sorts, especially in London.

Lord Stoneleigh was a rare specimen, a pearl in the oyster that was London's marriage mart. That is, he was a man of some fortune and a respectable if modest title who need please no one but himself in his choice of wife. There was no exacting mama who demanded her son marry a title lurking over Lord Stoneleigh's shoulders, and no cantankerous uncle holding his purse strings, his eye fixed on an heiress.

Of all the thousands of gentlemen in England, Lord Stoneleigh might be the only one who'd make both an appropriate and willing match for her.

An enthusiastic match even, if Franny were to be

believed, but then Lord Stoneleigh had been wildly enthusiastic about the mantel clock as well, so it was difficult to tell if his admiration was sincere.

He'd been plain Mr. Robert Luttrell up until a year ago, a second son upon whom the Duke of Basingstoke had just conferred a valuable living in the parish of West Farleigh, where Basingstoke House, the duke's country estate was located.

Since then, however, Mr. Luttrell had enjoyed an unexpected elevation in rank by the convenient death of a distant second cousin. He was now Baron Stoneleigh, and as a man of some consequence and a tidy fortune, he'd confided to Franny that he thought it only proper he find a wife to serve as his baroness and the mistress of his comfortable parsonage.

That he happened to be a friendly gentleman of impeccable principles added to his luster. So, Franny had duly invited Lord Stoneleigh to tea this afternoon, so Prue might get on with the business of making him fall in love with her.

If Lord Stoneleigh offered her his hand, she'd accept it, and considering the alternative—that is, no home at all, once Thornewood was sold—she'd count herself fortunate to get it. West Farleigh was a lovely little village, and Franny and Basingstoke spent a good deal of time at their country estate there. She'd see them often, and life as a vicar's wife would be quiet and peaceful.

There were far worse fates than that, surely.

"I'm afraid you've been cooped up indoors for too long today, Prue." Franny gave her a significant look. "You look a trifle languid. Does she not look languid, Your Grace?"

"Hmmm?" Basingstoke startled, his eyelashes fluttering open as if he'd just woken from a doze. "Did you say something, Your Grace?"

"Yes. I asked if Miss Thorne looks languid to you? It won't do for her to become lethargic. I wonder if some exercise might do her good? Perhaps she and Lord Stoneleigh should take a stroll around the gardens."

"Oh. Oh, yes!" Basingstoke said, finally catching on. "Indeed, Miss Thorne, I must insist you go for a walk at once. The fresh air will perk you right up."

"What a wonderful suggestion!" Lord Stoneleigh leapt to his feet. "Indeed, you must, Miss Thorne. I'm a great believer in exercise, and one can't have too much fresh air, you know. I wouldn't wish you to become ill." He gave the duke and duchess a deep bow, then offered his arm to Prue. "Shall we?"

Prue blinked as all three pairs of eyes turned on her at once, Franny's unmistakably eager, and Lord Stoneleigh's expectant. As for the duke, he looked as if he were about to slip into another doze, but still, a refusal was out of the question.

So, she rose to her feet, a smile stretching her lips, and took Lord Stoneleigh's arm. "Indeed, my lord, a walk sounds lovely."

Yes, perfectly lovely. Lord Stoneleigh was a good man—not a thing wrong with him—yet somehow, as he drew her hand through his elbow and led her away, a hollow space yawned open inside her chest.

Somehow, she couldn't imagine herself ever living for Lord Stoneleigh's smiles, as Franny and her duke did for each other's, but she was back to the cloud-enveloped castles and winged horses she'd been daydreaming of this morning.

She was no longer a child, with a child's starry-eyed

dreams. She was a grown woman now, and there was no sense in wishing for things that could never be.

It was a great pity Jasper had never listened to his grandfather's lectures about the sins of laziness, because if he had, he'd have realized he'd lost the ruby earrings far sooner than he did.

But if he *had* been lazy, it was all the fault of Basingstoke's torturous chair. A night spent tossing and turning upon that villainous contraption was enough to send the most vigorous gentleman directly to his bed for the rest of the morning.

Most of the afternoon as well, as it happened.

He'd awoken at last and was lounging against the headboard atop a mountain of pillows, still blinking the sleep from his eyes when Loftus appeared with a silver tray in his hands. "Good afternoon, Your Grace. May I serve you some tea?"

"You're a prince among men, Loftus." Jasper struggled upright and motioned for Loftus to place the tray upon his lap. "A true gentleman's gentleman."

"That's kind of you to say, Your Grace." Loftus poured the tea, then began bustling about the room, preparing the shaving things and retrieving the clothing Jasper had left scattered about the room when he collapsed into his bed.

He was well into his third cup of tea before he recalled he'd left a king's ransom worth of rubies in the pocket of his coat. "Take care with that coat, Loftus. I've left something in the pocket. Fetch it out for me before you take it away, if you please."

"Yes, Your Grace." Loftus rifled obediently through the pockets, then looked up at Jasper with an anxious frown. "I beg your pardon, Your Grace, but the pockets appear to be empty."

"Nonsense, man. Look in the front right pocket."

"Yes, Your Grace."

Jasper sipped his tea as Loftus searched again, then finally turned the pockets inside out. "I beg your pardon, Your Grace, but I can't find anything."

The earrings were there. They had to be. "Give it here, Loftus."

"Yes, Your Grace." Loftus handed over the coat and stood by silently as Jasper poked into the pocket, but all he turned up were a few bits of lint. "What the devil's happened to them?"

Oh, no. No! He couldn't have been so careless, could he?

He shoved his hands into each pocket, nearly ripping apart the seams, panic gripping his throat as his fingers twisted in the silk lining. No smooth, hard stones, no dangling pearls, no carved gold settings. He delved into the tight corners, pinching and clawing, but it was no use.

The earrings were gone.

Dear God, how—*how*, in the name of all that was holy could he have lost them? It had taken hours for him to win them back from Selina, hours of sitting across from her at that bloody table with sweat trickling down the back of his neck, only to lose them again before the night ended?

What could have become of them? He stilled with his coat crushed between his hands as he retraced his steps from the night before.

Selina had laid down her cards—a ten, a five, and a four.

A decent hand, but not good enough to beat his.

She'd taken the loss with her usual grace. Livid color had flooded her cheeks, then all at once she'd swept her arm across the table, sending the cards and thousands of pounds in jewels scattering in every direction before storming to the dressing room door, flinging it open, and ordering him out of her sight, declaring she couldn't bear to be in the same room with him for one second longer.

He hadn't fancied another hairbrush to the forehead, so he'd done as she bid him, scooping up the ruby earrings and dropping them into his coat pocket, leaving the diamond and sapphire parure on the table. Then he'd made his way to his carriage, sucking in the first deep breath he'd drawn all night as he climbed inside and bid Knapp to take him to Basingstoke's.

He'd still had the earrings when he reached Park Lane. He recalled patting his pocket just to make certain they were there before he climbed out of the carriage.

Could they have fallen out of his pocket at Park Lane? Mightn't he have dropped them in the carriage? "Quickly, Loftus. Go and find Knapp and have him search the carriage at once. I've lost a valuable pair of ruby earrings, and I must have them back."

Loftus's eyes widened. "Yes, Your Grace!"

Unless . . . no, they weren't in the carriage, because they'd been in his pocket when he entered Basingstoke's study. Yes, he distinctly remembered slipping his hand into his pocket to check while Miss Thorne was scolding him about his absence at dinner.

The chaise. Of course! They were likely even now buried in the cushions of Basingstoke's villainous chaise!

That cursed chaise had swallowed his earrings!

They must have slipped from his pocket when he stripped off his cravat, coat and waistcoat and threw them on the chaise. Careless, that. It wasn't quite as bad as laziness, but not far off. Good Lord, perhaps his grandfather was right about him.

"Wait, Loftus!" He pushed the tea tray aside and leapt from the bed. "Where are you going, man? Come back here at once!"

"Yes, of course, Your Grace!" Loftus rushed from the bedchamber door back to the bed, panting. "What can I do, Your Grace?"

"Help me dress, then find Knapp and have him ready the carriage. I must pay a visit to Basingstoke."

CHAPTER 5

Jasper didn't knock when he arrived at Park Lane, but slipped stealthily through the front door, letting out a sigh of relief when he didn't see Trevor lurking in his usual corner.

A good man, Trevor, but he was rather a stickler for order and would insist on announcing Jasper's arrival, and he didn't want Basingstoke looming over his shoulder and demanding to know what he was looking for as Jasper rifled through the chaise cushions.

So, he sidled down the hallway that led to the study like a proper thief, pausing once to glance over his shoulder, but it was well past calling hours, and the house appeared quiet.

At last, some luck. He'd just nip in, find the earrings, and nip back out again without Basingstoke ever knowing he'd been there. The last thing he wanted was to have to explain those earrings to Basingstoke, who was sure to preach at him until blood seeped out of Jasper's ears.

Lectures, he didn't need.

Basingstoke had never been one of Selina's admirers, though he'd been a touch more tolerant of her than

Grantham, who thought her a viper of the first order, and made himself quite a nuisance about it, too.

Not that Grantham had been wrong. Perhaps Jasper would even admit that someday, after the sting of his own stupidity had faded somewhat, but for now, the fewer details his friends knew about his disastrous liaison with Selina, the better.

Now, if only Basingstoke wasn't lurking in his study, all would be—

"Montford!" Grantham was lounging in front of Basingstoke's desk, a glass of brandy in his hand. "It's been an age since I've seen you. Where have you been hiding yourself? I'd begun to think you'd left London for your country estate."

"Well, Montford, here you are at last." Basingstoke looked Jasper up and down, one eyebrow raised. "What took you so long? I've been waiting all day for you to come and beg my pardon for missing dinner last night."

Damn it. Couldn't a man sneak into another man's private study without every duke in London knowing of it? Here were both foxes at once, and the hen house stuffed to the rafters with scandalous rubies. "Beg pardon, Basingstoke. I lost track of time, I'm afraid."

"Yes, very well." Basingstoke glanced behind him, into the corridor. "What's become of Trevor?"

"I haven't the vaguest idea. He wasn't in the entryway." Jasper strode across the room and dropped into one of the chairs in front of Basingstoke's desk, taking great care not to betray himself with even a single glance at the chaise.

"This is rather an odd time for a call, isn't it?" Basingstoke fetched another glass from the tray on his desk, poured out a measure of brandy, and handed it to Jasper.

"I don't see what's so odd about it." Jasper tipped the

glass to his lips and drained the brandy in one swallow. "Grantham's here, isn't he?"

"I came earlier." Grantham eyed Jasper's empty glass. "Thirsty, Montford? Or is something troubling you? Don't tell me Lady Selina is still tormenting you."

"Selina?" Jasper turned to Grantham, startled. He'd broken with Selina more than a month ago, so why was Grantham asking about her *now*?

Unless . . . oh, no. Had Basingstoke found the earrings? Had he and Grantham been sitting here discussing them? Good Lord, he hoped not, because there was no explanation for those portraits that didn't make him look like an utter fool. "Why, er . . . why are you so curious about Selina all of a sudden?"

Grantham snorted. "I wouldn't say curious. Suspicious, yes. Wary, certainly. Downright dubious, absolutely."

Basingstoke gave Grantham a warning shake of his head. "We're only curious about her insofar as she pertains to *you*, Montford. She may go to the devil, otherwise. But you look a bit green about the gills, much as you did when she was pulling your strings."

Pulling his strings? He could have happily lived the rest of his life without *that* image in his head. "I've told you already. I've finished with her."

Whether she was finished with him, well . . . that was another question entirely, wasn't it? He'd got the earrings off her, yes, but he wasn't fool enough to believe that would be the end of it. If Selina were presented with an opportunity to wreak her revenge on him, she'd seize it in an instant.

"That's still the case, then?" Grantham toyed with his glass, but his sharp gaze remained on Jasper. "She hasn't lured you back in?"

"God, no. I've learned my lesson as far as Selina's

concerned, I assure you." He may never take another mistress again, in fact.

Basingstoke eyed him for a moment, then nodded. "I'm glad to hear it, Montford." He reached for Jasper's empty glass. "Another brandy?"

"I may as well, I suppose." He needed a bit of time to figure out how to get two troublesome dukes out of this room. The earrings were certainly somewhere near the chaise. It wouldn't take but a moment to find them.

"So, Montford." Basingstoke poured the brandy and handed the glass back to Jasper. "My wife tells me you did, in fact, turn up for dinner last night. Hours late, of course."

My wife. Basingstoke was fond of those two words and said them as often as he could. Not that Jasper begrudged the man his satisfaction. The Duchess of Basingstoke was a delight, and Basingstoke's tenderness toward her was rather charming.

Pathetic, of course, but charming, nonetheless.

"The duchess is correct. I did come, and much to my shock, I found Miss Prudence Thorne enthroned in the chair behind your desk, behaving for all the world as if she'd just been crowned queen."

Grantham snorted. "I doubt that, Montford. That doesn't sound like her. I've never met a lady less inclined to draw attention to herself than Miss Thorne."

No, but then she didn't need to *try* to draw attention to herself. She'd caught his attention easily enough, and right after the debacle with Selina, too, when he'd vowed to never again be taken in by a pretty face. "Perhaps not, but she's the sort of female a man likes to keep his eye on, all the same."

"She's the sort of female a man *does* keep his eye on,

whether he likes it or not, Montford." Grantham chuckled. "Very fetching, indeed. It's the green eyes."

"They're not *green*, Grantham. They're hazel, and there's nothing so special in *that*. There are dozens of ladies in London with hazel eyes." Not a single pair of them the same shade as Miss Thorne's, but that was neither here nor there. "You might have told me she was in London, Basingstoke. She despises me, you know. She could have crept up behind me and slit my throat with your letter opener."

"Rather messy, that." Grantham took a sip of his brandy. "Bloody, you know."

"Yes, that would have been dreadful," Basingstoke agreed. "I'm rather fond of my letter opener. It was my grandfather's."

Jasper scowled at him. "As it was, she gave me a proper dressing down."

Basingstoke raised an eyebrow. "One you did nothing to deserve, of course."

"Of course not. What's she *doing* here, Basingstoke? No one comes to London in August, for God's sake. She claims she's come to see the duchess."

"I don't know why you're so suspicious of her, Montford. She *did* come to see Francesca."

"I daresay she did, but that's not the only reason. She's come to find a husband, hasn't she?" Not that it mattered to *him*, of course. He wasn't the least bit interested in Miss Thorne's romantic prospects.

Basingstoke took a swallow of his brandy and set his glass aside with a sigh. "Very well, Montford, you've puzzled it out. Miss Thorne has made up her mind to marry, and Franny has found a gentleman she believes will do very well for her. Miss Thorne is in London to meet him, and Franny has high hopes it will lead to a courtship."

Jasper gazed down at his own glass of brandy, his mood turning inexplicably sour. "Who?"

Basingstoke blinked. "Who, what?"

"Who is the gentleman the duchess has chosen for Miss Thorne?"

"I don't see why that matters to you, Montford."

"It *doesn't* matter." Why should it? "It's purely curiosity, Basingstoke, nothing more."

Miss Thorne might not be fashionable, or have much in the way of family or fortune, but she did have the steadfast friendship of the Duke and Duchess of Basingstoke, which was nearly as valuable. He might not care for the lady, but that didn't mean he wished to see her sacrificed to some blackguard. "Not Westview, I hope. The man has half a dozen mistresses stashed a block apart in Wellington Street. Carruthers won't do either, as he drinks to excess—"

"For God's sake, Montford, do you suppose my wife would suggest her dearest friend wed a lecher or a drunkard? I can assure you she's taken the utmost care with—"

"Not Horsley, either. I can't prove it, but I'm certain he cheats at cards."

"I can't help but agree with you there, Montford." Grantham nodded. "No gentleman wins as often as Horsley does unless there's foul play afoot."

"It's not Horsley! Really, neither of you give Francesca enough credit. She's an excellent judge of character."

"If it's not Horsley, then who is it?" Jasper demanded.

"Yes, Basingstoke, do tell," Grantham drawled.

Basingstoke huffed out a breath. "I don't pretend to know why either of you are so determined to know every detail of Miss Thorne's matrimonial affairs, but I'm not about to tell you two gossiping hens all of her secrets. Even if I wished to, I'm not at liberty to . . ."

Basingstoke went on at some length about Miss Thorne's marriage prospects being a sensitive matter, and Miss Thorne being due the courtesy of privacy, but Jasper had stopped listening to him, because something far more interesting than Basingstoke's lecture was unfolding on the other side of the double glass doors behind him.

He nudged Grantham, and nodded at the doors. "Look, Grantham. Just there."

The terrace off of Basingstoke's study led into a small, private garden with a series of stone pathways that wound past a dozen or so tidy rose arbors. While Basingstoke was nattering on, Miss Thorne had wandered into sight from the direction of the south lawn with a tall, fair-haired gentleman right on her heels.

Jasper leaned forward in his chair. The man's face was hidden by an enormous shrub, but it looked like . . . "Luttrell! *That's* the gentleman you've chosen for Miss Thorne?"

Basingstoke stared at him. "How the devil did you work that out?"

"Because, Basingstoke, the two of them are walking together in the garden right behind you!" That was no casual stroll, either. Miss Thorne's cheeks were far too pink for that, and there wasn't a single raised eyebrow or pinched lip in sight.

She looked almost bashful. Miss Thorne, *bashful*! As for Luttrell, he looked as he always did, that is, far too pleased with himself.

Jasper leapt to his feet and hurried to the doors. "For God's sake, Basingstoke, why in the world would the duchess choose *Luttrell* for Miss Thorne?"

"He's not Luttrell now, Montford, but Lord Stoneleigh."

"Stoneleigh? Who the devil is Stoneleigh? I've never heard that name before in my life. That gentleman right there"—Jasper pointed an outraged finger—"is Robert Luttrell."

Basingstoke let out an exasperated sigh. "That's what I'm trying to tell you. He's Lord Stoneleigh now, and has been these three months or more. Do pay better attention, Montford."

"What? You mean to tell me Luttrell's a lord now?"

"Baron Stoneleigh, yes. He inherited the title rather unexpectedly, and a tidy fortune along with it."

Not just a lord, then, but a lord with the means to take a wife.

"Stoneleigh has had his eye on Miss Thorne since he met her last fall. Franny's hoping for a match between them, now that Miss Thorne has made up her mind to wed."

"For God's sake, Basingstoke, you can't truly be considering a *match* between Miss Thorne and Luttrell? Are you mad?" Why, Miss Thorne would eat the poor vicar for breakfast, luncheon, and dinner. She'd flay him alive with that sharp tongue of hers, fricassee him, then bake him into a pie and swallow him whole. "I can't think of any gentleman less suited to Miss Thorne than some puffed-up vicar."

"I don't think Miss Thorne agrees with you, Montford."

Grantham nodded at the window, and Jasper turned his attention back to the travesty unfolding in the garden. Luttrell—or Stoneleigh, or whatever the devil his name was now—had just offered his arm to Miss Thorne, and she . . .

By God, she *took* it, without so much as a glare or a thrust of that stubborn chin. Indeed, she accepted the man's arm with a sweet smile on her face, as if he'd just given her the crown jewels.

What, not one sharp word? Not even a hint of a scowl? Not a single disdainful syllable from those pink lips? Jasper watched as they resumed their stroll, his mouth agape.

"What's the matter with Stoneleigh?" Basingstoke demanded. "And before you claim he's a drunkard, a lecher, or a cheat, Montford, may I remind you he's a vicar?"

"That proves nothing, Basingstoke." The clergy were among the worst scoundrels in England. "I don't claim the man is a blackguard, but he's . . ." How to put this without being rude? "He's a simpering, nitpicking, hypocritical fusspot. He's utterly wrong for Miss Thorne, and will make her life a perfect misery."

Basingstoke blinked at him, and Jasper blinked back.

Had he, er, said all that aloud?

"Well, that's plain enough," Grantham murmured. "While I don't entirely agree with Montford, there's no denying Stoneleigh is a bit of a mushroom, Basingstoke."

"Yes, he bloody is. If he does want Miss Thorne, it's only because she's friends with you and the duchess." He'd gone quite hot in the face, which was odd, as he didn't give a damn who Prudence Thorne married.

"I don't think that's the *only* reason, Montford," Grantham said. "You have *seen* Miss Thorne, have you not?"

Jasper gritted his teeth. "Seen her, and felt the lash of that thorny tongue of hers, too."

"I think you're being a bit hard on Miss Thorne, Montford, not to mention poor Stoneleigh. He seems quite taken with her." Basingstoke joined him at the glass doors, both of them peering out at the couple. "There's not a thing wrong with Stoneleigh. It's a good match, particularly for her."

"That's true enough." Grantham peered over Jasper's shoulder. "Good God, the man can talk, can't he?"

"Rather, yes. He came for tea today, and complimented the furnishings with such tiresome enthusiasm I nearly fell asleep in front of my Grecian fireplace." Basingstoke snorted. "Ladies and their matchmaking schemes, eh, Montford?"

Basingstoke nudged him, but Jasper hardly heard him, as all his attention was fixed on Stoneleigh, who was holding forth on some subject or other, his hands clasped judiciously behind his back, his face stern as he went on, and on, and . . . dear God, still *on*. "Do you suppose he's delivering his Sunday sermon to her?"

Basingstoke's brow furrowed. "It's difficult to tell. Whatever it is, Miss Thorne seems to be attending eagerly enough."

"Bollocks, Basingstoke. She looks as if she's about to collapse from boredom and fall face first into the shrubbery."

Basingstoke opened his mouth, but before he could reply there was a knock on the study door. "Yes, come in."

Trevor entered, looking a bit harried. "I beg your pardon, Your Grace . . . that is, Your Graces. The duchess asks that you join her in the nursery, Your Grace, as it's time for Lord Frederick's bath."

"Is it as late as that? I do beg your pardon, gentlemen, but—"

"Not to worry, Basingstoke. It's time I was off, as I have an engagement tonight." Grantham joined Trevor at the door, pausing to look over his shoulder at Jasper.

"You *are* attending Basingstoke's shooting party, aren't you, Montford?"

"Yes, I'll be there."

"Very good. I'll see you then."

Grantham vanished after Trevor, and Jasper turned to Basingstoke. "Never mind me, Basingstoke. Go and attend to your wife and son. Freddy must have his papa for his bath, mustn't he?"

"Do stay, if you like, and help yourself to another glass of brandy. I won't be long."

"Very well." He *would* stay and help himself, but not to more brandy.

Basingstoke hurried off, and after a hasty bow, Trevor followed on his master's heels.

Jasper waited until both sets of footsteps had faded to silence before he darted toward the chaise. The pillow that had nearly broken his neck last night was still there, but he tossed it aside and rifled behind the cushions and into the gaps between them.

No ruby earrings.

He stood back, panting, and kicked one of the chaise's legs. "Villain! Yield up your treasure, damn you."

But another, more violent search of the chaise didn't turn up the earrings, and neither did a careful examination of the floor near the fireplace.

Had they dropped underneath the chaise, then? He got down on his knees and crawled about, running his hands over the floor, but there was nothing under there.

If the earrings had ever been here, they'd vanished. Had one of the servants found them? If so, then what had since become of them?

He rose from his knees and dropped down onto the chaise, the hard cushions digging into his arse.

Now what?

There was nothing for it. He'd have to confess the whole of it to Basingstoke, ask for his help finding the earrings, and endure the lecture that followed.

Perhaps he'd even listen this time. It had been bloody foolish of him to lose the damn things, almost as foolish as it had been to take up with Selina in the first place.

Even now, he wasn't sure why he'd given into the temptation of her. It wasn't as if he hadn't recognized her for what she was before he'd tumbled into her bed. There'd been no love or even loyalty between him and Selina, no matter how much she insisted otherwise. Indeed, he preferred there not be, as romantic illusions only complicated things.

But what did it matter now? It was done, and he wouldn't be so foolish again. He'd find the earrings with Basingstoke's help and put this entire debacle behind him.

Until then, perhaps he'd have another glass of brandy, after all.

He rose and went to the sideboard but paused at the glass doors. Stoneleigh and Miss Thorne were still in the garden. Stoneleigh was *still* nattering on, and though Miss Thorne was doing her best to hide it, there was nothing genuine about the stiff smile pasted to her lips.

Stoneleigh didn't seem to notice it, but Jasper saw it as plainly as if she'd confessed it aloud. It was the same expression she'd worn when she'd come into the study early this morning and found him still here, and in his shirtsleeves, no less.

He snorted to himself as he poured another brandy. It had been plain to see that Miss Thorne had never before laid eyes on a single strand of male chest hair before this morning. He'd never seen a lady more scandalized in his life. It was a good thing he'd left when he did, or else she might have fallen into a sw—

Wait. He paused, the glass halfway to his lips.

He'd left her here in the study this morning alone, without a single servant as witness.

Basingstoke's servants were an unfailingly loyal group, devoted to their master and mistress. If a servant *had* found the earrings, they would have turned them over to Basingstoke at once, and Basingstoke and Grantham would have given him an earful as soon as he walked into the study this afternoon.

He glanced back at the chaise. Just what had Miss Thorne got up to when she'd been alone in the study this morning? Something she ought not to have, he'd wager.

Outside the glass doors, Stoneleigh had drawn Miss Thorne's hand through his elbow, and he was leading her toward the terrace that led into the library.

Well, how convenient.

The library was just the place for him to have a private chat with Miss Thorne.

He dropped his untasted brandy on Basingstoke's desk and darted out the door and down the corridor to the library. Once inside, he dashed toward a chair in a dim corner of the room, out of reach of the glow of the fire burning in the grate.

He'd just dropped into it when one of the terrace doors opened.

"No, my lord. It's quite alright. There's no need for you to accompany me inside."

Prue hovered in front of the glass door, blocking Lord Stoneleigh from following her into the library. It had taken every shred of her control to hold on to her temper while they'd been walking in the garden, and it wouldn't do for it to snap in the library.

Not with all these heavy books about.

"Such charming bashfulness, Miss Thorne!" He bowed over her hand, his lips grazing her glove. "Your modesty does you credit."

"Thank you, my lord." She pasted a bright smile over her clenched teeth and withdrew her hand from his tight grip. "Good-bye."

"Until tomorrow, Miss Thorne." He offered her yet another bow and then wandered off in the direction of the front drive, where his carriage was waiting.

She waited until he was out of sight, then closed the door and threw herself into a chair, dropping her forehead into her hand. Her courtship, such as it was, had just gone from awkward to disastrous.

She'd been startled when he'd launched into a detailed discourse on the evils of wagering, but she'd assumed he was only reciting his next Sunday's sermon to her. It was a bit strange, yes, but she'd have to accustom herself to such things if she was to become a vicar's wife.

As it turned out, it wasn't a sermon at all. It was a warning.

A great many people knew about her father's ill-advised wager with the Duke of Montford, mainly because the *ton* was forever panting over Montford's antics. There'd been enough gossip that the tale of her father's ruination—much embellished, of course—had reached as far as West Farleigh, where Lord Stoneleigh's parish was located.

After carrying on for some time, Lord Stoneleigh had moved on from a general commentary on the evils of wagering to the specific evil of her father's wager with the Duke of Montford. Then in the next breath, he'd hinted it would be best if she didn't spend a great deal of time with her father once they were married.

Oh, he didn't blame the daughter for the sins of the father—he was quick to assure her of *that*—but he was a vicar, after all, and must set the example for his flock.

It was, of all things, the last one she'd expected from him. She couldn't have been more shocked if he'd slapped her.

She raised her face to gaze into the fire. Lord Stoneleigh was right about one thing. There was no end to the evils that wager had brought down upon their heads. Her father—a decent, honorable gentleman— seemed destined to be punished forever for this one mistake.

What was to be done now? Marrying Lord Stoneleigh meant financial security for herself and her father, yes, but at what cost? Was she meant to turn her back on the only parent she had left, the parent she adored, who'd taught her to ride and shoot, and who'd loved her with the tender devotion of two parents after her mother had died?

All this, on the command of a husband she hardly knew?

She watched the flames dance in the grate, her heart sinking. Her every instinct urged her to flee London, to return to Wiltshire before Lord Stoneleigh's visit tomorrow, but there was nothing to return to. The land was already gone, and it was only a matter of time before the estate was sold as well.

Thornewood would no longer be their home, then. Not then, and not ever again.

There was no going back. There was nothing for it but to go forward, straight into Lord Stoneleigh's parsonage, with its fine piano and glorious mantel clock.

Straight into Lord Stoneleigh's arms . . .

A shudder seized her, as if a cold, enormous hand had clamped down on the back of her neck and was shaking her until her teeth rattled in her—

"I never would have taken you for such a shameless liar, Miss Thorne."

Prue jerked upright as a man detached himself from a chair on the other side of the room and sauntered toward her, a smirk on his lips. The Duke of Montford, of course. Who else? The man seemed to be always lurking around the next corner, then turning up at the worst times, like a bad penny.

Thank goodness the tears prickling behind her eyes hadn't yet had a chance to fall. She couldn't think of a single thing more humiliating than weeping in front of the Duke of Montford.

Although seeing him naked was close.

"Such a sweet-faced young lady, too." He threw himself into the chair opposite hers, his long legs sprawled out so the tip of his boots brushed the hem of her cloak. "I confess you had me fooled. It's your eyes, I think. No one would ever suspect so many secrets could lurk in those innocent hazel depths."

"I have no idea what you're talking about, Your Grace." She jerked her skirts back, tucking her hems tightly around her feet. "I'm no liar."

At least, she hadn't used to be.

"No? But I distinctly recall you telling me you came to London only to visit the duchess. You specifically said you weren't hunting for a husband, yet not two days after your arrival, I find you cavorting in the gardens with Lord Stoneleigh."

"Cavorting!" She'd never cavorted in her life. "I most certainly was *not*—"

"But it's not the cavorting that's so shocking. Shocking

enough, mind you, but not as shocking as your coming all the way from Wiltshire only to squander your chances of an advantageous match on a pincushion like Lord Stoneleigh."

"Lord Stoneleigh is *not* a pincushion." Or was he? In truth, she didn't know what Montford meant, but it didn't sound like a compliment. "He's a respectable gentleman."

Montford snorted. "A respectable pincushion, perhaps. Really, Miss Thorne. You sell yourself far too cheaply. You could do much better than Stoneleigh. You might have a viscount, with your pretty face."

"My affairs are none of your concern, Your Grace." Dear God, but the man was enough to drive a lady to violence. "Surely you have better things to do than spy on me and my . . ." Wooer? Her suitor? No, she couldn't quite force either of those words from her lips. "My . . . Lord Stoneleigh."

Oh, dear God, that was much worse, and naturally Montford immediately seized on it.

"*Your* Lord Stoneleigh? Is he yours already, and you only just arrived? Well done, Miss Thorne! I offer you my sympathies, er, I mean, my congratulations. But you're quite right. I didn't come here this afternoon to pry into your affairs. I came in search of some property I've lost."

"Property? What prop—" Oh, no. The earrings! She'd never put them back under the chaise! Between one thing and another, she'd completely forgotten them.

How she could forget she had a fortune in rubies stashed away in her pocket was rather a mystery, but she and Franny had spent most of the morning chatting, then she'd finished her letter to her father, and afterwards she'd retired to her bedchamber for a nap. By the time she woke, it was time to dress for tea with Lord Stoneleigh.

"I seem to have misplaced a rather remarkable pair of ruby and diamond earrings. The last time I recall having them was in Basingstoke's study last night. I'd assumed they'd slipped from my coat pocket when I was sleeping, but it's the most curious thing, Miss Thorne. When I searched the chaise, I didn't find them."

"Oh, dear. That's, er . . . quite unfortunate, Your Grace." Had there been just the tiniest quaver in her voice?

"Yes, isn't it? It's almost as if they've vanished. I can't account for it." His dark eyes roamed over her face, and for one dreadful moment she was certain he could see the guilty flush scalding her cheeks. "I don't suppose *you* happened to see them?"

Those cursed earrings had been worrying her since she found them under the chaise this morning, and now, at last, she could be rid of the dratted things. All she had to do was take them out of her pocket, hand them over to Montford, and explain she'd found them under the chaise last night and had taken them up for safekeeping, and that would be the end of it.

They were right there, within easy reach of her fingertips. A mere moment would see the thing done, yet she didn't move, only sat there as still as a mouse cowering in the shadow of a cat's raised paw.

All but her twitching fingers, tracing the shape of the stones through the worn pocket of her cloak.

Nothing less than a possible solution to her marriage quandary was right at her fingertips, if only she had the nerve to put it to use.

Did she dare?

She needed time to *think*, but there was no time. Montford was waiting. Either she confessed to having taken the earrings, or she kept quiet, and seized the opportunity that had slid from his pocket directly into her waiting hands.

It was a mad scheme, foolhardy, risky in the extreme, but how could she live with herself if she didn't even attempt it? She'd never let a bit of risk stand in her way before, and this time, her very freedom was hanging in the balance.

Her father was a proud man—too proud, at times. He wouldn't permit any of their friends to help them out of their difficulties. In his view, an honorable gentleman saw to his own debts, and he'd sooner die than accept so much as a penny from any of them.

But if Montford chose to forgive the remainder of the debt, well . . . there was nothing her father could do about that, was there? He couldn't *force* the duke to take his money.

By the strangest twist of fate imaginable, the Duke of Montford was both the cause of all their troubles, and the only one who could help her out of them.

The earrings could well prove their salvation. A bit of clever, er . . . *negotiating* on her part could erase her father's debt, and free her from a marriage to Lord Stoneleigh in one master stroke.

But it was no small thing, to trifle with a duke. Not just any duke, either, but one of the Duke of Basingstoke's dearest friends. The Duke of Basingstoke, who just happened to be married to *her* dearest friend. Mightn't Franny take it amiss, if she stole a pair of earrings from her beloved husband's friend?

No, not *stole*. She was no thief.

It wasn't as if she was going to *keep* them. She only meant to borrow them for a bit longer while she considered what was best to do with them. Surely, that couldn't be considered theft. It wasn't as if she'd plucked them out of

Montford's pocket herself. The earrings had fallen right into her hands, for pity's sake.

That wasn't stealing. It was divine providence.

It was a delicate business, to be sure, but it couldn't be an accident that she suddenly found herself in possession of such unusual jewelry. Surely, the earrings were nothing less than a gift from Fate herself?

Who was *she*, to refuse such a gift?

Really, she'd be doing Montford a favor. It would teach him to take better care of such incendiary trinkets in the future.

"You're thinking very hard, Miss Thorne. I didn't ask you to unravel the mystery of the Sphinx. It's a simple question." He leaned forward, abandoning his sprawl, his gaze so intent on her it was as if he could see every secret hidden in her head, every beat of her pounding heart. "Did you, or did you not see the earrings?"

"I—I did not, Your Grace." Until the words actually left her lips, she hadn't been sure what she was going to say.

He gazed at her for a long time, neither of them moving or speaking, the moment stretching thin between them until at last he broke it, his voice its usual deep drawl, but the hint of amusement was gone, and the smirk had dropped from his lips. "Are you certain of that, Miss Thorne?"

She wasn't certain of anything anymore, but the thing was done, and it was too late to turn back now. "Yes, Your Grace, quite certain."

He didn't believe her. She knew it at once from the slight narrowing of his eyes, the tight press of his lips, and really, why would he? She was a dreadful liar. Perhaps she should have considered *that* before she attempted to deceive one of the most powerful dukes in England.

He rose from his chair, his long, lean body seeming to take days to unfold, until he towered over her, casting an enormous, menacing shadow against the wall behind him. She half expected him to seize her and shake her until his rubies fell from her pockets, but he only stared at her.

And stared, and stared, for so long she wished the chair would swallow her up.

Finally, he offered her a sweeping bow. "Very well, Miss Thorne. If you do happen to come across them, you will let me know, won't you? They're quite valuable."

She gulped. "Yes, of course, Your Grace."

He didn't say another word, only made his way to the library door, but before he went out, he turned and cast her a look that made a shiver dart down her spine. "I *will* have those earrings back, Miss Thorne. One way, or another."

Then he was gone, leaving her alone in the deepening gloom and wondering, now that it was too late, if lying to the Duke of Montford was the biggest mistake of her life.

CHAPTER 6

"Your Grace? I do beg your pardon, Your Grace." A tentative finger tapped Jasper's shoulder. "You have a visitor downstairs in the drawing room."

"Mrrumph." Jasper rolled to the other side of the bed, away from Loftus's bothersome poking. "What time is it?"

"It's seven o'clock, Your Grace."

Jasper peeled one eye open. "In the *morning*?"

"I'm afraid so, Your Grace."

"For God's sake, not my grandfather again." He rolled over onto his back with a huff. He'd lost count of how many times he'd begged the old man to observe proper calling hours, but in this, as in all things, Colonel Cornelius Kingston did as he pleased.

"No, not this time, Your Grace."

"Then toss whoever it is out on his arse at once, Loftus. He may call again at one o'clock, like the rest of the civilized world, the mannerless barbarian."

"I'm afraid that's out of the question, Your Grace." Loftus leaned closer, his voice dropping to a whisper. "It's a *she*, Your Grace. Your caller is a *lady*. A *young* lady."

"A young lady?" Jasper peeled the other eye open.

"What sort of young lady? Christ, it's not Lady Archer, is it?" Selina had never dared venture into Berkeley Square before, but she was now a lady scorned, and there was no telling what she'd do.

"No, Your Grace. I've never seen this lady before."

"I see. Tell me, Loftus. What does this young lady look like?"

Loftus blinked. "Look like, Your Grace?"

"Yes. Is she pretty?"

"I didn't take much notice, but she's pretty enough, I suppose, Your Grace. I believe her hair was some shade of brown, and her eyes some shade of brown, as well, or . . . green, perhaps?"

"I see. Did this brown-or-green-eyed young lady give her name, Loftus?"

"She did not, Your Grace. I did enquire, but she refused to give it to me. I ventured to hint it wasn't yet calling hours, but she insisted upon seeing you nonetheless. She has a rather willful air about her, especially for such a young lady, and she's *alone*." Loftus's lips pinched into a disapproving line at this flagrant disregard for propriety.

Ah, now that *was* interesting. He could only think of one willful young lady with the nerve to appear on the doorstep of a notorious rake, alone, and well before proper calling hours.

Who else could it be, but Miss Prudence Thorne? Despite her nervous denials in Basingstoke's library yesterday, it seemed she did have some business with him, after all. "Did she state the nature of her visit?"

"Not as such, Your Grace. She would only say that you'd wish to see her, as she had something in her possession that belongs to you, and she was certain you'd want to have it back."

Well now, this was becoming more promising with each passing moment.

It was the earrings, of course. Those were two false-hoods she'd told now. Miss Thorne was, it seemed, every bit the shameless liar he'd accused her of being. "Never let it be said I disappointed a pretty young lady, Loftus. Hand me those pantaloons, will you?" He waved a hand at the crumpled pantaloons he'd left in a tangled pile on the floor beside the bed last night.

Loftus gaped at him, aghast. "Oh, but Your Grace, surely you don't mean to wear—"

"Not to worry, my good man. I swear to you I won't venture a toe outside the townhouse. Now, don't fuss Loftus, but do as I ask."

Loftus let out a faint wheeze, but he fetched the panta-loons, shook the wrinkles out as best he could, and held them out for Jasper, who managed to stumble out of his bed and into them without falling over. "Will you have the coat, too, Your Grace?"

"I suppose I'd better. No cravat, though, and no bloody waistcoat. Just the shirt, if you please, Loftus."

"Perhaps just a wee swipe with the hairbrush, Your Grace—"

"No time at the moment, Loftus." If Miss Thorne was foolish enough to appear on his doorstep at such an absurd hour, then she might take him as he came. "You may deck me out in violet satin later, if you please."

Loftus wrung his hands, but he did as he was bid and pulled the limp shirt over Jasper's head, then held up the coat so Jasper could shove his arms into the tight sleeves. "There. See, Loftus?" He clapped his valet on the shoul-der. "As good as new."

"Yes, Your Grace."

He made his way down the stairs, through the entryway, and down the corridor into the drawing room.

And there, wearing a serviceable brown morning dress that did nothing to hide a rather lovely, rounded backside, stood Miss Thorne, studying the gilt clock that dominated the mantel. It was a monstrous French thing, with a naked cherub perched on the back of a vine-draped wagon pulled by two snarling leopards.

"Ugly as sin, isn't it? But alas, it was a gift from my grandfather, so there it stays."

She whirled around, startled, but she recovered her composure quickly, throwing her shoulders back and folding her hands in front of her. "Good morning, Your Grace."

"I'm not certain I'd call it *good*, Miss Thorne, but interesting, certainly."

Had Loftus said her eyes were green, and her hair brown? The man was blind. Anyone could see her eyes were *hazel*—more gray than green this morning—and her hair that distinctive, rich shade of golden brown that could only be referred to as *caramel*.

One of her slim, impertinent eyebrows rose, because yes, in addition to her sharp tongue, Miss Prudence Thorne had the most impertinent eyebrows he'd ever seen. "You may call it whatever you like, Your Grace. But I'm afraid I've dragged you from your bed. I do beg your pardon."

"It *is* rather early in the morning for a call, Miss Thorne. To what do I owe this unexpected pleasure?"

"Unexpected, yes. A pleasure?" She bit her lip. "I can only hope you'll still find it so once I've explained my reason for being here."

"You mean this isn't just a friendly call?" She didn't intend to simply hand his earrings over to him, then. Of course, it wouldn't prove to be that easy, because there was nothing *easy* about Prudence Thorne.

"No. We're not friends, Your Grace. I've come because I have something of yours in my possession that you wish to have back, and in return, there is something you can do for me."

He was heartily sick of uppity females after that tussle with Selina, yet one corner of his lip was already twitching. It wasn't as if he was *enjoying* this, of course—no gentleman appreciated being toyed with—but at least Miss Thorne was a worthy opponent, and he did like a good scrap every now and again. Already his worst devils were rising up, urging him to battle. "That sounds vaguely like a threat, Miss Thorne."

"Not a threat, Your Grace, but merely a trade. That's all."

Good God, but she had a nerve, waltzing into his home and demanding he negotiate the return of the earrings she'd stolen from him! "I don't understand, Miss Thorne. You already assured me you don't have my ruby earrings. What else could the humble Miss Thorne have in her possession that can be of any interest to the Duke of Montford?"

Oh, she didn't care for that at all. Her face darkened, her expressive eyebrows pulling into a frown. "I do have the earrings. I found them on the floor in the duke's study, under the chaise you slept on."

"Are you saying you *lied* to me, Miss Thorne? How appalling of you." He waved her toward a chair. "Perhaps you'd better sit down and confess your sins."

"No, thank you, Your Grace." She edged away from him, closer to the door. "If it's all the same to you, I prefer to stand."

"Fine. Then let's get right to it, shall we? I told you

yesterday I'd lost a valuable pair of ruby and diamond earrings, and you told me you hadn't seen them." He tsked, shaking his head. "Does a lie fall from your lips every time you open your mouth, Miss Thorne?"

She gave him a cool smile. "Not *every* time. Occasionally one does, when a lie proves useful."

"How refreshingly honest. Very well, then you *do* have my earrings."

"Yes, Your Grace. It's quite lucky I happened to see them, is it not? I can't imagine the fuss that would have ensued had one of His Grace's servants found them, instead."

"Yes, that might have proved inconvenient. You've come to Berkeley Square today to give them back to me, I presume. I'm pleased you've found your conscience at last, Miss Thorne."

"*Give* them back? Oh, no, Your Grace. I'm afraid I can't do that. No, I've come to negotiate the terms for their return."

"Negotiate?" He took a step toward her. "Terms?"

She didn't scurry backward, but held her ground. "Why yes, Your Grace. As fate would have it, we are each of us in possession of something the other needs."

"I see. Just what is it you need from me, Miss Thorne? I confess myself quite curious."

"I imagine you've already guessed, Your Grace. My father owes you a debt, one he can't easily pay. Forgive the debt, and I will return the earrings to you with none of the gossips in London any the wiser."

He stared at her. Was Prudence Thorne *blackmailing* him? For a measly five hundred pounds? For God's sake, she'd marched into the drawing room of one of London's most notorious reprobates—alone, no less—to trade a pair of earrings worth thousands for *five hundred pounds*?

"And if I don't agree to your terms, Miss Thorne? What then?"

"I daresay you don't wish to find out, Your Grace."

For all her bravado, he saw at once by the way her eyebrows shot up that it had never even occurred to her he might refuse. Good Lord, but she was spectacularly bad at this.

"Come, Miss Thorne. If you're going to threaten a duke, then do it properly. Do you intend to expose me to the *ton*? Take the earrings to the scandal sheets?" She'd be better off stealing the damned earrings outright than attempting to blackmail him, but here she stood without seeming to have the least understanding of the sort of trouble she was inviting.

"I—I don't understand, Your Grace. You made it clear during our conversation yesterday that the earrings are of great importance to you, and you wish to have them back. Why would you refuse my offer?"

Why, indeed? He wanted those earrings back so he could wash his hands of Selina for good, and here was a way to have them with very little trouble to himself. It wasn't as if he gave a damn about the five hundred pounds. In the time it took him to sign away the debt, he could be finished with this whole debacle.

And yet, and yet . . .

Was she truly so desperate that she'd risk her reputation—even her very safety—to sneak over here and blackmail a duke? Not that he'd ever hurt her, of course. He was a scoundrel and a cad, not a savage, but she didn't know that. What if he'd been another sort of man? The sort who'd stop at nothing to get his property back? Really, someone needed to teach her a lesson about threatening powerful aristocrats.

If she was so desperate for money, then why not simply steal the earrings?

And if she *was* desperate for money, he wasn't such a fool as to imagine it had nothing to do with her father's wager. What lengths had Major Thorne resorted to, to pay off the initial thousand pounds?

Just like that, the fatal fascination he had for Miss Thorne once again reared its ugly head, not twenty-four hours after he'd been certain her lies had cured him of it forever. "Tell me, Miss Thorne. Does Basingstoke know you're here?"

"No!" Her chin shot up, her hazel eyes sparking. "Neither does the duchess, and I prefer to keep it that way. Once you and I have concluded our business, I will return to Wiltshire at once, and you may believe me when I say I won't trouble you again."

Ah, so she intended to beg off from the shooting party, and scamper back off to the country, did she? Blackmail a duke, pocket her ill-gotten gains, and bury herself somewhere in the wilds of Wiltshire. Then what? What would become of her then?

It shouldn't matter. It *didn't* matter. Miss Thorne was nothing to him, only . . .

This mad scheme of hers must be connected to his regrettable wager with Major Thorne. For all his flaws, he wasn't in the habit of reducing elderly gentlemen to penury, or letting their fool-headed daughters endanger themselves by trifling with cold-hearted rakes.

"You forget I haven't agreed to your terms yet. Threatening a gentleman is an ugly business, Miss Thorne, particularly for an innocent young lady like yourself. You're quite sure you wish to go through with it?"

"I don't have any other choice, Your Grace. I can't simply stand by and watch you ruin my father."

"Your father ruined himself when he engaged in a wager he shouldn't have. The first rule of wagering, Miss Thorne, is never to risk anything you can't afford to lose. Your father finds himself in these difficulties because he broke that rule."

Her chin shot up. "I don't deny it, but that's between myself and my father, Your Grace. The only business that should concern you is the business you have with *me*."

"I beg to differ. I'm on the receiving end of your blackmail scheme, Miss Thorne, and thus every part of this business can rightly be said to be my concern."

"Blackmail, Your Grace? I prefer to think of it as a trade."

"Think of it however you like, but the facts are what they are, Miss Thorne. You're demanding money in exchange for returning my own property to me—property that if revealed to the public could prove hazardous to my reputation. Forgive me, but that is the very definition of blackmail. May I see the earrings?"

She blinked. "See them? I didn't bring them with me, Your Grace."

"No? Whyever not? They're rather an integral part of your blackmail plot."

"It's *not* a . . ." She trailed off, drawing in a deep breath. "If I'd brought them, what would have stopped you from simply taking them from me?"

"What stops me from doing whatever I like with you now? It's a question you might better have asked yourself before you left Park Lane this morning. But I'm a gentleman, Miss Thorne. I don't manhandle young ladies, even when they're attempting to extort money from me."

"I thought it best to err on the side of caution, Your Grace, and leave the earrings at home."

"Are you under the impression you're being *cautious*,

Miss Thorne? Very well, then. I congratulate you for going about your blackmail so judiciously. But you've made a grave error, I'm afraid." He leaned closer to her. "Why should I believe you have the earrings in your possession at all, if you can't show them to me?"

"Do you imagine I'd risk coming here at all, if I didn't have them?"

"I've no idea what you'd risk or not, Miss Thorne." He was beginning to get an idea, however, and he didn't like it. Not one bit.

She bit her lip. "I can describe the earrings to you."

"Very well." He took a seat on a settee near the fireplace and waved a hand at her to proceed.

"They're gold, with large, teardrop-shaped rubies, each stone surrounded by a dozen small diamonds, with a single small pearl dangling from the ends."

"Is that all?"

Her brow furrowed. "Is that all? What more do you want?"

"The *paintings*, Miss Thorne. I can only assume you've seen them. Perhaps if you could describe those to me, in detail, I might be persuaded that you do indeed have the earrings in your possession."

"*Describe* them? You can't be serious."

"But I am, Miss Thorne. I'm deadly serious." Someone had to make her understand how foolishly she was behaving, coming here and recklessly tossing down a gauntlet in front of a man who could crush her as easily as snapping his fingers.

Her cheeks went positively scarlet, the pretty blush spreading down her throat and disappearing underneath the absurdly high color of that dreadful gown. "But I—"

"Whenever you're ready, Miss Thorne."

She hesitated, and triumph surged through him. Her

blackmail plot was going to die with a whimper right here and now before she could squeeze a single concession out of him, and perhaps she'd think better of it before attempting such a dangerous trick again.

It went without saying that she wouldn't *dare* describe the—

"You're, ah, standing up in both portraits, and you're . . . in a state of undress."

He stared at her, his jaw dropping open like a door with a rusty hinge. By God, was she really going to go through with describing those portraits? Didn't the girl have any sense at all? "Do you suppose I won't call your bluff, Miss Thorne?"

Her chin hitched up another notch. "You demanded I describe the paintings to you, Your Grace. I'm doing as you bid me."

Very well, then. If she wanted to toy with him, he wouldn't make it easy on her. "A gentleman is said to be in a state of undress when he's in his shirtsleeves, Miss Thorne. That is not the case in those portraits, as I'm not wearing a shirt in either of them."

"You're not in a state of undress so much as . . . not dressed at all."

He settled back against the settee. "Ah yes, I recall now. Do go on, Miss Thorne. Am I alone in the portraits?"

"In the first one, yes."

Yes, the first one was relatively tame, as illicit paintings went. "And the second?"

"No. There's a dark-haired lady with you in the other one. Your mistress, I presume."

His *mistress*! What did naïve Miss Thorne know about his mistress, or anyone's mistress, come to that? She was meant to be an innocent. Then again, she wasn't so innocent she'd hesitated to blackmail him, was she? "*Former* mistress. Do go on, Miss Thorne. What is my former mistress doing in the second portrait?"

There. That should put an end to this nonsense.

She sucked in a breath, the scarlet blush draining from her cheeks, her voice dropping to a whisper. "In the second portrait, the lady is kneeling at your feet, and she's . . . well, she's—"

"Stop!" Before he realized what he was doing, Jasper was on his feet, striding toward her and seizing her shoulders. "That's enough. Not another word, Miss Thorne."

"But you told me to—"

"Because I didn't think you'd dare! For God's sake, blackmail isn't a game!" Damn it, she was shaking. His fingers tightened around her slender shoulders, anger flooding through him, but the devil of it was, he couldn't say whether he was angry at her for being so bloody foolish, or at himself for humiliating her.

He released her abruptly and pointed at the door. "Go back to Park Lane at once, Miss Thorne, and don't ever try such a foolish stunt again, or you can be certain I'll tell Basingstoke all about it."

"But what about the trade? Your earrings—"

"Do what you will with them. Take your tale to the scandal sheets, if you must. That story is worth far more than five hundred pounds." His grandfather would be livid if those scandalous earrings ever saw the light of day, but he'd wager every last penny he had that they never would.

Miss Thorne might play at blackmail, but she'd never go through with it.

She gaped up at him. "*What?* That's all?"

"I don't care for being threatened, Miss Thorne, but if

you insist upon blackmailing a duke, you may as well get your money's worth." He nodded at the drawing room door. "Now go."

He threw himself back onto the settee as she stumbled toward the door, but just as she was about to leave, he stopped her. "One word of caution, Miss Thorne. Take care when you attempt to sell those rubies. They're quite distinctive, and easily recognizable to any jeweler in London. I wouldn't want you to be taken up for theft."

She didn't reply, but fled the drawing room, and a moment later he heard Keating, his butler, usher her out the front door.

Reckless, foolhardy chit! He'd have done better to remain in his bed and have Loftus toss her out, after all. He threw an arm over his eyes, collapsed against the settee, and lay there seething until he heard voices on the street outside and poked his head up again. "Good Lord, what now?"

He got up, went to the window, and peered out, and damned if Prudence Thorne wasn't lingering at the bottom of *his* front steps, in front of *his* townhouse, doing her best to charm *his* grandfather, and making a decent job of it, if the old man's grin was any indication.

Attempting to blackmail a duke was, it seemed, only the start to *her* day.

He let the draperies fall back, marched out into the entryway, and waited, his arms crossed over his chest until his grandfather mounted the stairs and entered the townhouse. "What did she say to you?"

"Who?" His grandfather stopped short, blinking. "Jasper, my dear boy, what are you doing, standing about in the hallway in that . . . that . . ." He waved a hand at Jasper's wrinkled coat and bedraggled pantaloons. "Costume? For God's sake, lad, you look like a pile of soiled linens the laundress left behind."

"Doing? Why, nothing much, Grandfather, just wondering what that hellion was saying to you."

"Hellion?" His grandfather glanced at the closed door, then turned back to Jasper. "What, you mean that young lady I just passed? She's no hellion, lad. She was a sweet little thing. Clever, too. That sort of young lady is worth a dozen of those simpering misses who parade in and out of your bed."

Jasper snorted. Just what every gentleman in London looked for in a lover—*cleverness.*

"This sounds like the start of a lecture, Grandfather. Perhaps you'd be good enough to deliver it while I have my morning coffee."

He turned toward the breakfast room, his grandfather on his heels. "Coffee, Esmond," he barked at the footman, throwing himself into a chair. "What will you have, Grandfather?"

"Nothing for me." His grandfather waved Esmond off. "I dined hours ago."

Jasper drained his coffee in one gulp, ignoring his burning tongue, and signaled Esmond for another cup. "So, Grandfather. To what do I owe the pleasure of your exceedingly early morning visit?"

Pleasure, indeed. He didn't take any pleasure in anything that happened earlier than the late afternoon. His grandfather knew it well, and didn't approve of it, any more than he did any of Jasper's habits. Still, his grandfather was the closest thing he'd ever had to a parent, and one didn't toss one's parent out of one's townhouse, no matter how annoying they might be.

"Not so early I'm your first visitor, by the looks of it. What did that young lady want? It looked as if she was coming from here."

"I haven't the faintest idea." It was closer to the truth than one might think. He couldn't make heads nor tails of Prudence Thorne, but he wasn't about to tell his grandfather the girl had just tried to blackmail him.

His grandfather eyed him. "I wouldn't take kindly to your trifling with a young lady like that, Jasper."

Jasper set his coffee aside with a sigh. For all his wicked ways, he didn't trifle with innocents. Indeed, he should be offended at the mere suggestion, but he didn't have the energy to do battle with his grandfather today. "Is that why you came this morning? To warn me away from innocent young ladies?"

"Not innocent ones, no. I came about that courtesan you've been carrying on with. That dark-haired chit— what's her name? Sienna, or Sophia?"

"Selina. Lady Selina Archer."

"That's the one. Now, you know I don't like to interfere in your business, lad—"

Jasper snorted, and his grandfather's bristly eyebrows lowered.

"You needn't concern yourself with Selina anymore, Grandfather. We're finished."

"Well, I know *that*, my boy."

"Of course, you do." Jasper just managed not to roll his eyes. "Despite having just claimed you don't like to interfere in my business."

Of all the busybodies in London, his grandfather was the busiest. He was likely bribing one of the servants, as he seemed to know every detail of Jasper's life, but he couldn't be bothered to find out which one. "If you already know about Selina, then what are you doing here?"

"Don't take that tone with me, boy." The eyebrows lowered another notch.

"I beg your pardon, Grandfather. I'm, ah, a bit out of sorts."

"Yes, I can see that. I'm here because I happen to know you were with that Lady Sienna—"

"Selina."

"—last night, so I came to warn you away from taking up with her again."

"No need. We're finished for good." Until Selina's next move, that is.

As if Selina wasn't enough to try his patience, now he had this business with Miss Thorne and those bloody earrings. He might not have seen them with his own eyes, but she had them. Either that, or she had a vivid imagination when it came to a gentleman's anatomy.

God in heaven. He could hardly believe she'd had the nerve to describe those paintings to him! If he hadn't heard it with his own ears, he'd never have believed it.

He'd never seen a lady's cheeks burn so red in his life.

"Good. I don't want another of your scandals, Jasper."

Scandals? Who had time for scandals? Between Selina's vows of vengeance and Miss Thorne's thievery, his time was quite taken up as it was. He was only one gentleman, after all. "Not a single scandal, Grandfather."

"Good. Now, I hear Basingstoke's hosting a shooting party at his estate in Kent. Is that so?"

"Yes. It's to be a fortnight of grouse hunting."

"Ah, good. You're leaving for Kent today then, eh, lad?"

"I am, indeed." *Someone* had to keep an eye on Miss Thorne.

"I see, I see." The old man rubbed his hands together, looking pleased with himself. "It will do you good to get out of London for a bit."

It might, at that, and with any luck, perhaps he'd find a way to steal his earrings back from Prudence Thorne.

CHAPTER 7

Basingstoke House
West Farleigh, Kent

It was just past seven o'clock in the morning when Prue slipped out the front door of Basingstoke House, blinking at the pale fingers of sunlight curling over the peaked roof of the stables.

No one else was about. The Duke of Basingstoke's other guests were far too fashionable to rise so early, so she had the entirety of the estate's twelve hundred acres all to herself. She wouldn't need all that, of course—a few dozen acres would do very well for her—still, it was nice to know it was there, all the same.

She lifted the hems of her riding habit and meandered down the pathway, the soft thud of her boots against the packed earth the only sound in the stillness of the morning, but just as the path gave way to the stable yard, she heard the thunder of hooves and the jingle of a harness, and looked up to see an elderly gentleman riding into the yard. He brought his horse up near the barn and attempted, with some difficulty, to dismount.

She paused, studying his profile. Why, it was *him*—the same gentleman she'd met outside the Duke of Montford's townhouse yesterday. There was no mistaking that shock of thick, white hair or the formidable line of his jaw.

He was an arresting figure, dressed all in black, with the proud, upright bearing of a former military officer, and he put her so much in mind of her own beloved father, a sharp pang of homesickness pierced her breast.

"Take care with the reins, Colonel Kingston!" A servant in navy blue livery darted from the stables into the yard, frantically waving his arms. "Colonel! You mustn't attempt to—"

But the man's warning came too late. The white-haired gentleman stumbled as he dismounted, one arm pinwheeling as he lost his balance.

"Colonel!"

The servant rushed forward, but she was closer, and she raced to the gentleman's side, catching his arm before he could topple backwards and keeping a firm grip on him until he'd regained his balance.

"My goodness, sir, you gave me a fright! I do beg your pardon for grabbing you like that, but I daresay a bit of manhandling is preferable to a tumble, isn't it?"

"You, again!" Shrewd, bright blue eyes regarded her from underneath a pair of impressively bushy silver eyebrows. "Where did you come from, girl?"

"Er, the house?" Was this a trick question? "I was on my way to—"

"The last time I saw *you*, you were all alone in Berkeley Square, wandering about the public streets where any thief or scoundrel might have got to you." The silver eyebrows lowered disapprovingly. "Now here you are again, scampering about in the stable yard in the dark. What are you thinking, girl? Don't you have any sense at all?"

The Duke of Montford had asked her that only yesterday, which meant two separate gentlemen had asked that same question of her in the same week. Mustn't that mean the answer was a resounding, no?

The gentleman's tone was gruff, his manner so blunt it bordered on rude. Another young lady might have been offended, but she was accustomed to plain speaking, and offered her interrogator a sunny smile. "I was thinking I'd quite like to ride this morning. This *is* a stable yard, is it not?"

He stared at her for so long she began to squirm, much as she did when she'd been a child on the receiving end of one of her father's lectures, but then he let out a wheezing laugh. "Cheeky thing."

"Colonel!" The servant hobbled toward them, his brow pinched with concern. "Are you hurt?"

"Not a bit, Plunkett, not a bit. This young lady here kept me upright."

"I saw." The servant, who was a good deal older than he'd first appeared and suffered from a pronounced limp, turned to her with a grateful smile. "Quick thinking, miss!"

"Quick thinking and quick instincts, Plunkett. That's the thing, eh?"

"Indeed, we're grateful to you, Miss . . . er, Miss—"

"Thorne." Prue dipped into a curtsy. "Prudence Thorne."

"Well, Prudence Thorne, I beg your pardon for not introducing myself to you yesterday. I'm Colonel Cornelius Kingston, and if there's anything I can do to return the favor, you tell me at once."

"I wouldn't mind having a closer look at your horse, Colonel Kingston, if you don't mind." She was a beautiful bay mare with dainty hooves and a streak of pure white on her forehead. "She's a Cleveland bay, is she not?"

The silver eyebrows rose. "You know horses, girl?"

She reached out to stroke the horse's velvety nose. "Oh, yes. I learned to ride nearly before I could walk. My father is retired cavalry, the 1st Royal Regiment of Dragoons."

"Thorne, you say?" Colonel Kingston and his servant exchanged a glance. "What, you mean to say Major Thomas Thorne is your father?"

She paused her stroking. "Yes. Are you acquainted with him?"

"No, but I know of him. His regiment fought with the Union Brigade at Waterloo. Those boys took an eagle off the French in that skirmish. Your father's a hero, girl."

"He is, Colonel. He is, indeed," Prue replied, beaming.

"Is he here at Basingstoke House with you?"

"No, Colonel. His indifferent health keeps him in Wiltshire, I'm afraid." It wasn't quite the truth, but it didn't seem like the thing to confess that her father had vowed he'd never come amongst the *ton* again after his disastrous wager with the Duke of Montford.

"What, you don't mean to say you're here alone, girl?" The colonel's eyebrows grew positively fearsome.

"Oh no, Colonel. My father would never allow that. I'm here as a guest of the Duchess of Basingstoke."

"The duchess, you say? Well, that's alright, then, I suppose. She's a good girl, the duchess. She took Basingstoke right in hand, and he's much improved for it. Basingstoke is a friend of my grandson Montford, you know."

Ah, so this was the terrifying grandfather Franny had told her about. He didn't look like much of an ogre to her, but then Colonel Kingston might become fearsome, indeed, if he knew about the recent unpleasantness between her and his grandson.

God knew *she* was appalled at it.

Speaking of which . . . she glanced behind her, toward the house. Her lady's maid had mentioned that the Duke of Montford had arrived for the shooting party late last night, and she couldn't be certain he wasn't peeking out his windows right now, watching her.

She was no coward, but she couldn't stomach facing Montford just yet.

"I take it you're acquainted with my grandson, Miss Thorne?"

"Er, well, yes, that is, in a manner of speaking . . ." Fortunately, she was saved from having to say any more, because just then a groom emerged from the stables, a riding crop in one hand and the reins of an enormous black horse woven between the fingers of the other.

"Oh, my." She stared, her breath snagging in her throat. Was that her mount?

Franny had chosen this horse especially for her, for her exclusive use while they were in the country. He was called Sampson, and goodness, but he was a spectacular creature, a vision of equine beauty, with long, graceful limbs and a rippling, coal-black mane.

He was already dancing with impatience, his massive hooves pawing the ground, eager to be gone.

She edged closer, her breath still held. "Oh, my goodness."

"Miss Thorne?" The groom, a man by the name of Cosgrove, waved her over with a smile. "Are you ready for your morning ride?"

"Yes, indeed." Prue waved to the groom, then turned back to the colonel with a smile. "I beg your pardon, Colonel, but Mr. Cosgrove is waiting for me. It was a great pleasure seeing you again." She curtsied, gave the bay mare's nose one last lingering pat, and after a smile at Plunkett, made her way toward the stables, where Cosgrove had brought Sampson up to the mounting block.

Soon enough she was settled on Sampson's back and galloping for the open fields beyond the stables, Cosgrove at her side. Goodness, it almost felt as if she'd never been on the back of a horse before! That wasn't the case, of course—her father was cavalry, after all, and they did keep a few horses—but there weren't any stallions like Sampson to be found on their tiny estate.

This was a horse fit for a duke.

She leaned low over his elegant arched neck, her fingers gripping the reins, hoofbeats pounding in her ears and a magnificent explosion of dust billowing around her, a grimy cloud she inhaled along with each of her panting breaths, fine grit coating her teeth.

It was *glorious*.

Such a rare moment of freedom! Because surely this was what freedom was, the wind whipping color into her cheeks and cooling the sweat at her temples, the horse's broad back surging between her thighs.

Had Lord Stoneleigh ever surged between a lady's thighs?

Oh, dear, now where did that thought come from? It wasn't at all proper to wonder such things, but it must be acknowledged that what she knew of Lord Stoneleigh so far argued against surging of any kind.

But she wouldn't spoil her ride by thinking of him now. Lord Stoneleigh, the Duke of Montford, her father's debt, and the scandalous ruby earrings would, alas, all still be waiting for her when she returned to Basingstoke House.

For now, it was only her and Sampson, flying across

the duke's estate, the ground a blur beneath them, with Sampson's long, powerful legs eating up the distance. His chest was heaving, his lovely black coat gleaming with sweat by the time she reined him into a trot, and then a walk, leaning low over his neck to croon into his twitching ear. "Such a good boy, Sampson! You're a beautiful runner."

"You'll have a good view of Montford Park once we clear this next ridge, Miss Thorne."

"What, the Duke of Montford's estate? I didn't realize it was as close as that."

"It's quite close." Cosgrove came up alongside her, his horse's spotted brown and white coat also damp, and pointed his riding crop toward the tree line. "It's just there, behind those trees."

"As close as that? Why, how wonderful to have a chance to see it from this vantage point. "It's meant to be a terribly elegant house, isn't it?"

"Aye, miss. It's a grand old place, to be sure, and the grounds even more so. Basingstoke and Montford hold a good portion of Kent between them." Cosgrove settled his horse with a twitch of the reins. "There will be fine shooting, if the weather holds." He cast her a doubtful glance. "You don't shoot, do you, miss?"

"Indeed, I do, Cosgrove." Shooting wasn't a sport for ladies, but she'd never been much like other ladies. "I adore shooting."

Shooting, angling, billiards—even fencing, though admittedly she was a novice at it. She'd tried her hand at bare-knuckle boxing, too, much to the delight of her father's friends, who were frequent guests at Thornewood and always encouraged her antics.

She'd even smoked a cheroot once, which had proved

to be one time too many. They tasted of ash, and the dratted thing had burned her bottom lip.

Cosgrove grinned. "You can ride, sure enough. I thought Sampson here might be too much horse for a lady, but I haven't seen many ladies who handle a mount as well as you do."

She grinned back at him, pleased. "If I'd been born a boy, I'd have made an enviable Corinthian." Instead, she was the only child of a military father who'd made the best of his dearth of sons by turning his daughter into a proper hellion.

But not much of a wife, alas. Not much of a friend, either.

She'd have to confess the whole of the dreadful business with Montford to Franny, and the sooner, the better. She'd planned to tell her on the journey from London to Kent—she'd spent the entire morning screwing up her courage—but at the last minute the duke had decided not to ride, and had joined them in the carriage.

But there was no hiding it, especially now that Montford was at Basingstoke House. He was sure to tell Basingstoke she'd taken his earrings, if he hadn't already. Truly, it would be a relief to unburden herself to Franny. She despised secrets, and was dreadful at keeping them, and she couldn't stomach lying to her dearest friend.

Of course, there was every chance Basingstoke would take offense and send her back to Wiltshire at once, and that . . . well, she may not be madly in love with Lord Stoneleigh, but the threat of ending up right back where she'd started was enough to shake some sense into her.

It wasn't as if there was anything *wrong* with Lord Stoneleigh. There wasn't. Not a single thing. Goodness knew London had a great deal worse to offer in the way of husbands. He just wasn't the sort of gentleman who was likely to find her eccentricities charming.

But then, there'd never been much chance she'd find a gentleman who would.

If ever there was a lady unsuited for marriage, it was her, a natural result of being raised by a gruff, military father. She was a crack shot, yes, but that wasn't likely to get her far with the fashionable gentlemen of London. They'd all expect her to draw, play, and sing as other ladies did, and to have at least a rudimentary knowledge of dancing, at the very least.

Indeed, she'd be lucky to get Lord Stoneleigh. It was a great pity she hadn't acknowledged that truth *before* she'd made that disastrous proposal to Montford. Oh, why had she been so foolish as to attempt to blackmail a duke? In hindsight, it hadn't been such a wise idea at all.

Fortune didn't, as it turned out, favor the bold.

It didn't matter that she'd asked for far less than the earrings were worth. Blackmail was blackmail, regardless of the amount. The moment she'd mentioned her father's wager, she'd sealed her fate.

It wasn't like her to misread a situation so drastically, but that walk with Lord Stoneleigh had left her in a panic, and she'd been all muddled in her head when Montford had confronted her about the earrings.

The whole thing had been a disaster, from the moment she'd lied to him about the earrings until the moment his butler had slammed the townhouse door behind her, the force of it nearly knocking her clean off the top step and into the shrubbery on the other side of Montford's wrought iron railing.

It had never even occurred to her that the Duke of Montford wouldn't care a whit if all of London saw him . . . saw his . . . well, perhaps the less she dwelled on his masculine bits and pieces, the better. It certainly hadn't gotten her anywhere so far.

Not only had she failed in her blackmail attempt, but if she'd correctly interpreted that gleam in his dark eyes when he'd dismissed her from his townhouse yesterday, she'd also enraged him, and likely earned herself a powerful enemy. The best she could hope for now was that he had as short of an attention span for vengeance as he did for his mistresses.

She'd feel better once she confessed her foolishness to Franny, but that wouldn't undo the damage she'd done. The best she could hope for now was that Lord Stoneleigh's objections to her father would soften as time passed.

Until then, she'd do her best to be a kind, proper wife to him—

"Shall we go on, Miss Thorne? I believe Her Grace is expecting you for luncheon."

"Yes. I'm ready." She tapped Sampson with her crop and came abreast of Cosgrove's horse, a gentle mare named Domino, and they set out at an easy trot, their horses' tails swishing lazily at insects as they made their way over the next ridge and Montford Park came into view.

She gasped. "My goodness, how lovely!"

"Aye, miss. Aside from Basingstoke House, there's not another estate in Kent to equal it."

"No, I should think not." Of course, the Duke of Montford must have an impressive estate—he *was* a duke, after all—but she hadn't realized how far short her imagination had fallen from the reality until she was looking down upon the house from above.

It was a sprawling estate, but settled so perfectly into

its surroundings it put her in mind of an exquisite, creamy pearl nestled into a jewel box of bright green silk.

A valley lay between them and the park, one so lush and green it looked from this distance like a velvety swathe of baize rather than the coarse brown it should have been, given Kent's dry, hot summer. It must have been fed by a hidden spring or some such, or perhaps a duke's grounds simply didn't wilt, no matter what the weather.

Perhaps they didn't dare.

The house itself sprawled across the peak of the next rise, above Basingstoke House, which was nestled into the valley directly below them. Montford Park was a masterpiece of elegance done in a warm, cream-colored stone, and no doubt it was as lovely inside as out. Why, if she lived there, she'd hardly dare touch her fingertips to the wallpaper, or set so much as a toe upon the carpets. How did one accustom themselves to such luxury? "Such classical lines! I believe it's in the Palladian style, is it not?"

Cosgrove opened his mouth to reply, but before he could utter a word, the quiet was shattered by the explosion of a gunshot coming from the forest behind them, the deafening crack ripping through the air, tearing a gaping hole in the calm afternoon. The ball shot past her, terrifyingly close to her head, buzzing by her like a deadly insect, disturbing the air by her ear as it whizzed by. "What in the world? That sounded like a gunshot!"

But no, it couldn't be. It was still several days shy of the twelfth of August. The Duke of Basingstoke wouldn't permit shooting on his grounds before the season began.

Yet there was no mistaking the sound of a sudden, single discharge like that, the echo of it ringing with such deafening insistence she slapped her hands over her ears.

"Some halfwit is out here shooting . . . whoa, Sampson."
The horse, startled by the blast, was dancing nervously
beneath her. "For pity's sake, they might have killed
someone!"

"Damned fools!" Cosgrove jerked on Domino's reins.
"They're behind us, near the edge of the forest. Quickly,
Miss Thorne. Down the hill."

Sampson was pawing at the ground, his massive
hooves tearing the sod to shreds, and she laid a hand on
his neck to steady him. "There, it's alright, boy."

But it wasn't alright, not in the least, because all at
once Sampson let out a shriek that set all the hair on her
neck quivering. He lurched underneath her, nearly sending her toppling backward from the saddle, but she seized
his mane at the last minute, clutching desperately at the
coarse hair as he bolted down the hill with her bouncing
atop him, her legs jerking wildly as her feet tore loose
from the stirrups.

"S—Sam . . ." She tried to cry out, but her throat had
gone so dry with panic she couldn't catch a breath. The
ground flew beneath her in a sudden, dizzying rush, a
blur of green and brown and pounding hooves, too
quickly for her to think or even take a breath, time
enough only to sink her fingers as deeply as she could
into Sampson's thick mane and hold on, hold on as
tightly as she'd ever held onto anything, her knuckles
going white with the strain.

Because if she fell—dear God, if she fell . . .

A cracked skull, her head split open, her brains splattered over the hillside like the guts of a rotted pumpkin?
Broken legs, a broken back, a broken neck? Or all of
them at once, the possibilities spreading out before her
in a ghastly smorgasbord of tortured limbs as Sampson

flew down the hill, still lost in a wild panic, as if the devil himself were after them.

The reins. She'd lost the reins. They must be dragging behind them!

If Sampson's feet became tangled in the reins, if he slipped on the shifting rocks, if *she* slipped from the saddle that was sliding and bouncing beneath her with each of Sampson's terrified strides, she was finished.

Dear God, what would become of her father then? And what of Franny? She simply couldn't leave her brains smeared all over Franny's hillside! Her friend would never recover from such a ghastly sight, and it would quite spoil the duke's southern view.

Hold on. There was nothing for it but to *hold on* until Sampson either reached the bottom of the hill—an end point that seemed impossibly far away still—or he wore himself out.

Hold on, that was all she had to do. She could manage it, she was a skilled rider, and experienced with horses, but her teeth were rattling in her head, her backside thumping with one agonizing crunch after the next against the hard saddle beneath her, her arms aching, burning with fatigue already, and the hill was endless, the bottom of it miles away, and Sampson, a stallion who lived to run showed no signs of slowing—

"Runaway horse! Runaway horse!" The shout echoed from behind her, Cosgrove's voice, hoarse with fear, but she didn't turn to look, *couldn't* turn away from the sight of the hill unfolding before her, the hill that would prove her undoing, the valley beyond it a green ribbon in the distance she could just glimpse between Sampson's flattened ears.

Oh, why was it so far away still? Surely, Sampson's wild chase had begun hours ago? Days ago? Her fingers were so numb she could no longer feel them, and Sampson's mane was slipping from between them, one hair at a time, slipping, despite her struggles to hold on, hold *on*, her legs shaking, the grip of her thighs around the saddle slackening—

"It's alright, Sampson, you can stop now. It's alright, boy." She leaned as close to the horse's head as she dared, her words falling from numb lips, the wind still roaring in her ears, snatching her whisper and sending it whirling into the abyss, only . . .

Had Sampson's ears twitched at the sound of her voice?

"That's it, boy, listen to me. You're alright, there's nothing to fear." She babbled on and on, not even knowing what she said, but by some miracle her voice was calm, steady, and—another miracle—Sampson was listening to her!

"Calm, boy, calm."

Everything around her faded to silence then—the roar of the wind, the thunder of hooves, the shouts coming from behind her, even the shuddering of her own heart in her chest.

It was only her and Sampson and the low, breathless words falling from her lips.

CHAPTER 8

"Bloody *hell*, Hodge! What the devil are you firing at?" Jasper spun toward his manservant and pushed the end of the still-smoking shotgun away from him. "You might have blown my head off! For God's sake, man, do I look like a grouse to you?"

"I didn't—forgive me, Your Grace!" Hodge turned wild eyes on him. "I didn't have my finger anywhere near the trigger! The damn thing exploded!"

Jasper raised an eyebrow, and poor Hodge, already pale with shock, went another degree paler as the curse escaped his lips. One didn't curse at one's master, particularly when one's master was the Duke of Montford. "Er, I mean, the weapon discharged unexpectedly, Your Grace!"

"It's a bloody Manton, Hodge. They don't just explode without warning."

Or not often, at any rate.

"Yes, Your Grace." Hodge gave him a miserable nod. "I'm terribly sorry, Your Grace."

Jasper sighed. Hodge had only just entered his employ a month earlier, and he hadn't yet gotten over his terror of dukes. The man was bound to be a nervous wreck this next week, as no fewer than three dukes were attending Basingstoke's shooting party, along with a few marquesses, a handful of earls, and a stray viscount or two.

And one Baron Stoneleigh, damn the man.

"Never mind it, Hodge." Jasper was tempted to peer down into the barrel—not the wisest course of action, as a thing that had exploded once might certainly do so again—but instead he took the gun from Hodge and laid it on the ground with the barrel pointed toward the trees.

"I—I do beg your pardon, Your Grace." Hodge was still babbling and wringing his hands. "I swear I never got near the trigger—"

"Yes, alright, Hodge. Calm down, will you?" He'd wondered if Hodge might be too high-strung to act as a proper attendant for the shooting party, and now he had his answer. "There's no need for hysterics. I don't believe you've shot anyone. No harm's been done—"

"Help! Runaway horse! Runaway horse!"

Jasper jerked around as the panicked shout rang out across the meadow, drowning out the echo of the gunshot. "What the devil? What bloody horse?" It was still early, and they hadn't seen another soul all morning.

"There, Your Grace!" Hodge pointed a shaking finger toward the crest of the hill ahead of them, the remaining blood in his face draining like water through a sieve.

Jasper whirled around just in time to catch a flutter of movement and a familiar, craggy face in profile. One of Basingstoke's grooms, Collins, or Cartwright—he'd seen the man around the stables—had just sent his mount careening down the side of the hill, the horse's white tail streaming out behind him.

"Damnation. Secure the gun, Hodge, then ride back to Basingstoke House and find the duke. Tell him there's been an accident. Quickly, man!" Jasper sprang up into the saddle, sank his boot heels into Phoenix's flanks, and they were off with a lurch, leaving Hodge behind to fumble with the rifle.

This wasn't good. Hodge's rogue shot might not have hit anyone, but if the horse that had bolted had thrown himself over the edge of that hill and into the void, only the most skillful horseman would be able to control him.

Anything less, and someone was certain to end up hurt.

Or worse, dead.

He paused for half a second at the verge of the crest, and there was Collins, or whatever the groom's name was, struggling down the hill, but making a slow enough go at it, his terrified horse balking at every step of the steep decline and threatening to send them both crashing to the ground.

And yes, damn it, far ahead of him, streaking down the hillside as if the hounds of hell were riding his heels, was an enormous black mount, churning up the ground as he tore along in a blind panic, huge, muddy clumps of shredded earth flying off the backs of his hooves.

And atop him . . . good Lord, was that a woman? By God, it was!

A *lady*, perched on that giant of an animal's back? A lady in a navy-blue riding habit, the hems of her skirts flying in the wind, her matching hat lying crumpled in the dirt some lengths behind her, a wild cloud of hair sailing out behind her like a whirlwind.

Jasper charged after her, shooting past the groom in half a dozen long strides straight down the side of the hill, leaning low over Phoenix's neck, urging her onward, the two of them gaining on the lady with every stride until he was close enough to see . . .

Devil take it!

She'd lost the reins! God above, how was she even still seated? Nine out of ten riders would have fallen off as soon as the horse threw himself down the side of the hill, but here was this lady, hardly wider than a walking stick by the looks of her, seated through nothing more than sheer force of will, her hands clutching the horse's mane, and her thighs, well . . . he had rather a lot of experience with the strength of a lady's thighs, but he'd never seen anything like this.

The lady could *squeeze*, by God.

But this was no time to admire her thighs. As strong as she was, she'd tire soon. Meanwhile, her horse showed no signs of slowing, and it was a *long* hill, and so steep from here it appeared nearly vertical, until it leveled off before it dipped down into the valley beneath it.

"Come on, girl!" He braced his own thighs hard against Phoenix's sides and leaned lower over her neck, triumph shooting through him as she responded to him at once, springing forward, not a bit of fear in her. "That's it! Good girl! Come on!"

The black horse was fast, but Phoenix was faster, gaining on the other horse in steady degrees, but the reins trailing in the dirt threatened at every moment to trip him up and send the lady sailing right over his head. Another length, and he might be able to grab them, or failing that, he could position Phoenix in front of the stallion and stop them that way—

"You're alright, Sampson. It's alright, boy."

How he could even hear her over the crack of the wind whipping past his ears he couldn't say, but there it was, soft and sweet, the murmur of it a continuous drone beneath the roar of pounding hooves.

She was talking to the horse—no, *crooning* to him, as if she were singing a lullaby.

Her tone was soothing, calm—*calm*, when one wrong move on her part would send her hurtling to the ground, the horse's hooves likely coming down on top of her, splitting her skull or breaking her neck—yet somehow, she was calm, and even more incredible, now that the horse's initial panic had lessened, he appeared to be *listening* to her, his pace slackening just enough for Jasper to get Phoenix in front of them and ease them down from a hell-for-leather dash into a controlled gallop.

It took time, but slowly, bit by bit the black horse's pace slackened, until at last he joined Phoenix in a steady trot near the bottom of the hill, Jasper keeping his own horse back a bit to allow the stallion some space while the lady guided him to a stop.

When they halted at last, he leapt from Phoenix's back and strode over to her, his heart a heavy drumbeat in his chest, because, by God, that had been *close*, far too close.

He reached the stallion, laid a hand on his foaming neck, and looked up into a face gone so colorless he might have believed she was evaporating into a mist before his eyes, that is, if it hadn't been for her red mouth, a smear of blood at the corner of her lip. "Are you hurt, Miss Thorne?"

Because, of course, it was *her*. He'd known it even before he saw her face, because who other than Prudence Thorne could end up in such a scrape, and still manage to come out of it unscathed? The lady might be hopeless at blackmail, but damned if she couldn't talk a runaway horse safely down the side of a mountain. "Miss Thorne? Can you hear me?"

She glanced down at him, but she didn't reply. Her golden-brown hair was a tangled mass of windblown curls around her white face, her eyes dark, the hazel swallowed up by her pupils.

He reached up to her. "Here. Take my hand, and I'll help you down."

She didn't appear to hear him, but sat frozen atop her mount, her hands still clutching his mane as if she wasn't certain they'd actually stopped. When she did reach out at last, it wasn't to take his hand. Instead, she laid her palm flat against the stallion's damp neck and bent close to his ear. She whispered a few words Jasper couldn't hear, then she slid from the saddle, her boots hitting the dirt with an unsteady plop.

But she didn't remain on her feet for long.

She stood there for a moment, swaying, and then her legs buckled beneath her, and without a sound, she sank to the ground and lay there, unmoving, seemingly dead to the world as her horse lurched around her, his big hooves dangerously close to her slender limbs.

"Miss Thorne!" A swoon, or was she hurt, after all? Every instinct screamed at him to scoop her up into his arms at once, but her mount was far from calm, his eyes still rolling in his head, showing white, and there was no guarantee he wouldn't bolt again. If Miss Thorne should be in the way of his hooves when he did, or if one of her limbs became tangled in the reins . . .

"Here, boy. Come on." He approached the big stallion, getting between the horse and Miss Thorne's prone body, his hands out in front of him, one eye on her and the other on those massive black hooves. By some miracle she'd made it down the hillside without breaking her neck, and he wasn't going to let the horse trod on her now.

Fortunately, the horse was already exhausted by his efforts to get down the hill. He didn't attempt to bolt again, but remained still long enough for Jasper to snatch up the reins and lead him over to Phoenix. "There, that's it. Good boy."

Phoenix gave a sympathetic snuffle, which calmed the stallion enough that he was willing to stand quietly with her while Jasper rushed back to Miss Thorne, falling to his knees beside her.

There was no blood to speak of, and no grotesquely mangled limbs. "Miss Thorne?" He ran his hands over her arms and legs. No obvious breaks, and no broken skin or swelling, but he didn't like the look of her.

She was too pale, too still.

He slid his arm carefully under her shoulders and gently lifted her up so she was draped over his lap. No, no blood, but she was as limp as a boiled shrimp. Where the devil was Collins? He turned toward the hill to find the groom still struggling to coax his mount down the slope. Damnation, but the man was only halfway down—

". . . smell of orange blossom."

Startled, he glanced down at Miss Thorne. "I beg your pardon?"

"Orange blossom, and . . ." Her eyes were closed, her brow furrowed. "Amber, I think, but I'm not certain. I've never smelled the scent before."

He blinked down at her. Amber, and orange blossom? Was she describing his cologne? "It's amber and orange blossom, with a hint of cinnamon. I have it made up for me at Truefitt and Hill."

"Mmmm." A dreamy smile curved her lips. "It's lovely."

She thought he smelled lovely? Pleasure rushed through him, and for the first time in God knew how long, he didn't know what to say. "I—well, thank you, Miss Thorne."

At the sound of her name her long, dark lashes parted, and she gazed up at him with a pair of unfocused eyes.

Hazel eyes. Yes, they were certainly hazel. Not green, not brown, not gray, but hazel. There'd been a time he would, if pressed, have said her eyes were an unremarkable brown, but he couldn't recall now how he could have thought so, when they were nothing so much as a mossy chocolate color, and this close he could see the starburst around her pupils was the same honey gold as her hair.

It was only a swoon, then, and no wonder. If that was the worst that came from this misadventure, they could all consider themselves lucky. But she was dead white still, her face utterly drained of color but for that smear of blood where she'd bitten down on her lower lip. What looked to him like a thousand hairpins were caught in the mess of waves scattered about her head like a tangled halo, and her navy riding habit was streaked with dirt.

"Your Grace?" The clouds had cleared from her eyes, and a frown was tugging at her lips. "I'd be grateful, indeed, if you'd be so good as to unhand me."

"Not just yet." He brushed her hair back from her face and prodded gently at her temples, then trailed his hands down either side of her neck. Purely for medical purposes, of course.

"W—what are you doing?" Her eyelashes fluttered, her throat moving in a nervous swallow. "There's no need for, er . . . *that*."

"I beg your pardon, Miss Thorne. Just checking for fatal head injuries, but your skull seems to be intact. Lucky, that."

"Lucky for *you*, yes. It would have been rather inconvenient if I'd died of a head injury sustained after you *shot* at me, wouldn't it?"

Ah, there was that jagged tongue. "Nonsense. I never shot at you." Hodge had, but it hadn't been intentional, and he'd missed, in any case, so he'd just as soon keep his servant out of it.

"No? How strange, because birdshot flew so close to

my head I daresay I'll never again regain the function in my left ear."

"That *is* a shame." He grinned down at her, nearly giddy with relief. "Though I can't help but just hint an injury that silenced your tongue would have been a great deal more useful."

Her hazel eyes flashed, and she rose up onto her elbows, ready to do battle despite having nearly broken her fool neck not ten minutes ago. "As apologies go, Your Grace, that one leaves rather a lot to be desired."

"Indeed. But perhaps you'd better lie back, Miss Thorne. You've had a dreadful shock."

But Miss Thorne didn't lie back. Miss Thorne wasn't much inclined to do anything she was told to do, regardless of whether it was for her own good, or not. "You *are* aware, are you not, Your Grace, that grouse season has not yet begun?"

"Of course, I'm aware." What did she take him for? Every self-respecting gentleman in England knew grouse season began on August twelfth, and not a moment sooner.

She raised an eyebrow. "It's August *eleventh*, Your Grace."

"This may surprise you, Miss Thorne, but I'm perfectly able to read a calendar. I've even been known to tell time, on occasion. Shocking, but there it is."

"I see. Then I'm left to assume you imagine the rules that govern the rest of England don't apply to you. It's not an uncommon assumption among dukes, I'm afraid."

"You may assume whatever you like, but the truth of the matter is that the shotgun malfunctioned. I do apologize for the mishap. I'm very sorry I frightened you."

She bristled at the word. "Nonsense. You never frightened *me*. You frightened Sampson."

"Yes, well, be that as it may, it was your neck at risk,

and I regret that most sincerely. May I help you to your feet, Miss Thorne?"

"I don't need any help, thank you, Your Grace."

That was not the case, as it happened. As soon as she tried to gain her feet she swayed, and would have fallen down again if he hadn't caught her. "Steady there, Miss Thorne."

She pushed his hands away. "I said I don't need—"

"Yes, I heard you, but we both know that's nonsense." Without further ado, he swept her up into his arms and marched her toward his horse.

"Your Grace!" Predictably, she began to kick and squirm like a fish on the end of a hook. "What do you think you're doing?"

"I should think it was obvious. I'm carrying you to my horse, Miss Thorne, whereupon I will ride with you back to the house before you get yourself into any more trouble."

"No, indeed, Your Grace. You must let me down at once. I'm perfectly able to ride."

"No, you're not. You're trembling all over. Now stop arguing, and do as I tell you."

"Do as you tell me? Why, how dare—"

"Enough." Jasper strode over to Phoenix, lifted Miss Thorne into the saddle, and before she could offer any more protests, he swung up behind her and put a hand on her hip to steady her. "Hush, Prue. Your fussing is unsettling the horses. Hasn't poor Sampson suffered enough for one day?"

He couldn't have said whether it was his use of her Christian name or his appeal on Sampson's behalf that silenced her, but she didn't say another word as Collins made it to the bottom of the hill at last, panting. He took Sampson's reins from Jasper, then turned an admiring look on Miss Thorne. "There aren't more than a dozen men in England who could've got Sampson down that hill without injury."

Jasper couldn't argue with that. The lady could *ride*, by God. He'd never seen a more skilled horsewoman in his life. The chit put half the men in England to shame. "Yes. That was well done, Miss Thorne."

He might have paid her a different compliment. He might, for instance, have told her she had the prettiest hazel eyes he'd ever seen, and it would have been nothing but the truth, but somehow, he knew nothing else he could say would please her half as much.

She didn't reply, but the tension drained from her, her stiff body turning softer, pliable, relaxing by degrees until she was leaning against him, her back pressed against his chest.

They made their way back to Basingstoke House thus, with Phoenix plodding along steadily beneath them, and Prudence Thorne balanced on the saddle in front of him, her lush bottom nestled between his thighs.

CHAPTER 9

"The Duke of Montford tried to *shoot* you?" Franny was pacing from one end of Prue's bedchamber to the other, wringing her hands. "That's why your horse bolted? Because Montford *fired* on you?"

Something of that sort *may* have slipped from Prue's lips, yes. She may *possibly* have uttered a few other phrases that weren't strictly true, as well, like "showers of birdshot," and "murderous rampage." "Well, there's a chance he didn't precisely . . . that is, he *claims* his shotgun malfunctioned, but—"

"Prudence Thorne." Franny ceased her pacing and turned to face Prue with her hands on her hips. "Tell me the truth this instant."

Dash it, the tips of her ears were heating, just as they always did when she was burdened with a guilty conscience. "Oh, very well, if you must know. There's a chance—a mere sliver of a chance, mind you—that it was an accident."

"Thank goodness." Franny let out a long sigh and dropped onto a silk settee. "I confess I thought it unlikely Montford would make an attempt on your life. Now, if y*ou'd* shot *him* . . . yes, I might have believed that. It would have made more sense."

"*Me*, shoot the Duke of Montford? Shame on you, Franny. Why, I'd never do anything so drastic as that." Though it couldn't be denied shooting the Duke of Montford would solve a great many of the problems plaguing her. Still, the crown tended to frown upon murdered dukes.

Franny patted the space beside her on the settee. "Come, sit down. I imagine you're still shaking after that charge down the hill."

Her knees were a touch wobbly, but she eyed the pale gold silk settee and shook her head. "I can't."

"What? Whyever not?"

"Because I'm covered in dust and dirt, and I don't want to spoil your settee." Prue pointed a dramatic finger at the pale gold carpet under her feet. "Look there! I've already left grass stains on your carpet."

"Never mind that." Franny caught her by the wrist and tugged her down onto the settee. "Giles is forever wandering about in here head to toe in dust and dirt, just like every other Duke of Basingstoke before him."

"Yes, but His Grace owns the furnishings, and may destroy them if he pleases. That's the difference." Still, the settee was a lovely fluffy one, and sinking down upon it was rather like being embraced by a cloud. Now that she'd succumbed, she may never get up again.

"Perhaps I shouldn't have chosen Sampson for you." Franny sighed again. "One of the mares in the stables might have been a safer choice, but I know you prefer a challenging mount, and I couldn't resist your having a chance with him."

"Oh, I'm so glad you did! You mustn't blame Sampson, Franny. He's a wonderful horse. The two of us got along brilliantly until the poor thing was startled by the gunshot."

"Still, I wish I'd considered—"

"Hush. You couldn't have known the Duke of Montford would take it into his head to wander about the grounds with a shotgun before grouse season begins." Really, Montford seemed to court trouble.

"I saw you come flying down the hill from my sitting room window." Franny turned back to Prue, her eyes glistening. "The descent seemed to go on for hours."

Prue reached for her hand. "Oh, my dear. I'm so sorry you were frightened."

Franny took a shaky breath. "I can't imagine how you managed to hold on for so long."

"Sheer terror, I think. I grabbed Sampson's mane just as he bolted, and I swear my fingers just froze there. I'm surprised I didn't come away with a handful of black horsehair."

"Montford charged down the hill after you in a rather heroic fashion." Franny cast her a measuring glance from the corner of her eye. "He risked his own neck for your sake, Prue."

"Heroic! The Duke of Montford wouldn't know heroism if it clubbed him over the head. Imagine my shock when I regained my senses and found *him* hovering over me like a vulture intent on a meal." Though it must be acknowledged she didn't know of many vultures with such lovely dark eyes, or such an enticing scent.

Amber, orange blossom, a hint of cinnamon, and underlying it all, leather and the musky scent of clean, male sweat. Whoever would have thought a gentleman's scent could be so alluring—

"A vulture! Come now, Prue, that isn't fair. He was quite careful with you, and from the window it looked as if he behaved like a perfect gentleman. That is, as perfect a gentleman as Montford ever is."

Dash it, there went the tips of her ears again, burning with guilty heat. "I suppose he could have done worse." She slumped against the back of the settee. "I'll thank him for his assistance this evening, I promise." She wouldn't even mention that if it hadn't been for his carelessness with his shotgun, she never would have found herself in such a predicament to begin with, no matter if it *was* the truth.

"Good. That's the proper thing to do." Franny nodded as if satisfied, but a sly smile was twitching at her lips. "It was rather sweet, the way he leapt from his horse, fell to his knees beside you, and—"

"It wasn't nearly as dramatic as you make it sound, Franny." She'd been unconscious at the time, yes, but the Duke of Montford wasn't the sort of man who'd fall to his knees for any lady, least of all one like *her*.

Especially not after what she'd done. She glanced at the wardrobe, where she'd tucked the ruby earrings inside one of her reticules.

"No? Because from the window, it almost looked as if he gathered you into his arms."

"Gathered me into his arms, indeed. I don't know why you insist on painting Montford as some sort of dashing romantic hero. All of London knows the man's an unrepentant scoundrel." Though he *had* been surprisingly tender with her, his fingers so gentle when he'd touched her, like the softest breath.

"Yes, well, we all know how reliable London's opinion is. They used to refer to Giles as Helios, if you recall."

"Well, to be fair, Basingstoke does have rather a look of the sun god about him—"

"I don't deny Montford has his flaws," Franny went

on, holding up her hand to silence Prue. "But he has a
kind heart, in spite of it all. He's a hero in scoundrel's
clothing, if you will."

Prue shook her head, but a smile rose to her lips. She'd
wager her last penny Montford was precisely what he
appeared to be, that is, a rake down to the marrow of his
bones, but since Franny had fallen in love with Basingstoke, she persisted in thinking the best of everyone.

It was rather sweet, really. Misguided, of course, but
sweet.

The ugly truth was that men—particularly wealthy,
aristocratic men, with the possible exception of the
Duke of Basingstoke—were selfish, arrogant creatures,
and Montford along with them. "When I told Montford
the blast had nearly deafened me, he said it was a pity
the birdshot hadn't injured my tongue and silenced me
forever."

Franny choked on a laugh. "No, he didn't!"

"I assure you, he did. Not quite what you'd expect a
hero to say, is it?"

"Not at all. Why, he's no better at holding his tongue
than you are, the wicked man."

"No, but since he and I are both here, and I'm destined
to endure his presence, I suppose it would be wise of me
to make the best of it, as I have no wish to spoil your
shooting party. I'll behave, I promise it, Franny."

It was a trifle late, as promises went. Once again, her
gaze was drawn to the wardrobe.

"I daresay it will be easier for you to keep that promise
than you think. Montford isn't nearly as bad as you imagine him to be."

"I've no doubt of it, Franny." That wasn't *quite* true, but surely, the Duke of Montford must have some redeeming qualities?

It was true enough he hadn't wasted any time coming down the hill after her. He'd even beat Cosgrove to the bottom. And perhaps she *had* felt a moment of relief—a brief moment, that is, so brief as to be insignificant—when she'd come to and found him leaning over her, those hypnotic dark eyes fixed on her face.

He'd apologized for the mishap, as well, and he'd appeared sincere when he expressed his regret at having frightened her, but she didn't wish to dwell on that, as those were the sorts of troublesome details that might make it difficult for her to continue to dislike him.

It was much easier if she disliked him, and he disliked her heartily in return. Indeed, it was a bit puzzling that he'd come down the hill after her at all. She bit her lip and glanced guiltily at her friend. "Franny, I have something I need to tell you."

"Yes?" Franny had risen to her feet and was considering the dinner gown the maid had set out for Prue. "This is pretty. Will you wear it tonight? My garnet bracelet will look nice with it."

Oh dear. This was going to be harder than she'd thought. "Um, Franny—"

"I have a pair of garnet earrings that match the bracelet."

"I've done something dread—"

Franny turned to smile at her. "Lord Stoneleigh won't be able to take his eyes off—"

"Franny!" Prue blurted out. "I, ah . . . I've made a terrible mistake, one I regret extremely."

Franny turned away from the gown, her eyebrows drawing together. "Goodness, you've gone quite red. What have you done?"

"I—I found something in Basingstoke's study the other night."

Franny blinked. "Is that all?"

If only it was! "No, I'm afraid not." Prue rose, fetched the earrings from the wardrobe and dropped one of them into Franny's hand. "I found these earrings. They're rather remarkable ones. At first, I thought they were yours."

"My goodness." Franny held up the earring. "No. I've never seen them before in my life. That's a very fine ruby, is it not? It's not paste, that's certain, not with that fire. But they're not the sort of jewels I prefer. They're beautiful, of course, but a bit much for my tastes."

"Yes, I know that now. They're, ah, they belong to the Duke of Montford. You recall I told you he fell asleep on your chaise the other night, and that I found one of his gloves underneath it the following morning?"

Franny looked from Prue's face to the earring in the palm of her hand. "It wasn't a glove, after all?"

"No. It was these earrings. They slipped from his pocket when he removed his coat."

"Why, that foolish man! What was he *thinking*, carrying jewels like this in his pocket? It's a miracle he wasn't robbed!"

Well, in a sense he had been robbed, by *her*. Robbed, and then blackmailed. Oh, dear. She really had been awfully unfair to him. "I daresay he'd just come from wherever he got them. When he burst into the study, before he realized it was me sitting at the desk, he said something about Basingstoke never guessing where he'd just been—"

Franny gasped. "Lady Selina!"

"Who?"

"Lady Selina Archer, Montford's mistress. Or Montford's former mistress, I should say." Franny plucked the other earring out of Prue's hand. "Yes, these look like something she'd wear."

"Oh. Is she very beautiful?" Of course, she must be. Montford himself was . . . well, he was quite—that is, Montford wasn't the sort of man who'd settle for anything less than London's most alluring ladies, that was all.

"Yes, very beautiful in that dramatic way Montford seems to prefer, but with a hardness to her, much like these stones. Goodness, I do hope he isn't starting up with Selina again. There was a most spectacular scandal when he broke with her, you know."

Prue *didn't* know, nor did she want to, only, well, perhaps there was just the tiniest little niggle of curiosity in her breast. "What happened?"

Franny lowered her voice. "Montford was reportedly quite smitten with her at first—well, as much as Montford's ever smitten with anyone. Their affair went on for months, much longer than his usual entanglements. Indeed, Giles was quite worried about Montford for a while."

"Why should he be worried?" Surely, Montford was scoundrel enough to manage his mistress? It wasn't as if this Lady Selina Archer was his first, or his last.

"Lady Selina has the face of an angel, but beneath those silky dark curls and big blue eyes lurks a nasty disposition. Montford found it out soon enough, of course— they always do. But you see, Selina fancied herself the next Duchess of Montford, and she was furious when he broke with her." Franny shook her head. "I don't know why every lady always imagines she'll be the one to catch Montford, when no one ever has before."

"But why was it such a scandal when they parted?" After all, aristocratic gentlemen took and then discarded mistresses every day, and no one in London ever blinked at it.

"Oh, *that*. He had the misfortune to be standing in front of a window when he finished with her, and she happened to have a rather heavy silver hairbrush in her hand at the time. She hurled it across the room at him."

"My goodness! Did it hit him?"

"I'm afraid so. That is, it glanced off his forehead and smashed into the window behind him, shattering it."

"No!"

"Yes, indeed, and if that wasn't bad enough, poor Lord Arthur happened to be driving past at the time in his barouche with the top down, and the hairbrush . . ." Franny trailed off, wincing.

"Oh, no. Don't say it hit *him*, too!"

"It did hit him. He nearly lost an eye, and I'm afraid Montford got the blame for it, though he didn't do anything but duck. Montford does tend to get the blame for such things. I don't deny he's an unrepentant scoundrel, but it wasn't his fault that time."

She was no admirer of Montford's—far from it—but that did seem a trifle unfair. "I daresay that cooled his ardor for Lady Selina quickly enough."

"I think his ardor was well cooled before that, but yes, shattered glass and a bleeding head wound does put a damper on one's passions, does it not? I can't think why in the world he'd agree to see her again, especially to retrieve these." Franny studied the earrings. "I'm certain they were costly, but Montford's always been generous with his mistresses. Why not just let Selina keep them?"

"Er, well, they're not the usual sort of bauble, Franny."

"No, indeed. I've never seen such large rubies before."

"No, I mean . . ." How to put this? "They're not just rubies, Franny. They're lockets, and there are portraits inside them." Prue took the earrings back and sprung the clasp on one of them. "See for yourself."

Franny took the locket and peered down at the portrait. "Is that . . ." She jerked back with a gasp, slapping a hand over her eyes. "Dear God, it *is*!"

Prue sprung the clasp on the other earring. It was a mistake, because as soon as she caught sight of the tiny portrait tucked inside, she was unable to tear her gaze away. "Is that really . . . do, ah, do ladies really do that to . . . to gentlemen?"

Franny blushed up to the roots of her hair. "Er, well, there are certain acts a gentleman . . . that is, sometimes a lady will . . . oh, for pity's sake! Very well, then. Yes, a lady might occasionally do, er . . . *that* to a gentleman, if he enjoys that sort of . . . attention."

"He does seem to be enjoying it. The way his hands are . . ." Prue cleared her throat.

"The gentleman, Prue." Franny looked up. "He looks quite a lot like—"

"The Duke of Montford. The Duke of Montford in a state of . . ." She was going to say *undress*, but what was the use of mincing words?

Montford was as naked in the paintings as the day he was born.

"No dress," Franny finished.

"But surely this can't be accurate." Prue reached for the earring that revealed in rather vivid detail a certain private part of Montford's anatomy and held it up, her brow raised. "If you take my meaning."

"I don't have the faintest idea if it's accurate or not, but I will say it's . . . well, I've only seen the one, but it's quite . . . it's not entirely out of the realm of possibility that it *is* accurate."

"How remarkable." A bit puzzling proportionally, however, given a lady's anatomy.

Franny let out a groan and buried her scarlet face in her hands. "For pity's sake, Prue, *why* did you have to show these to me? How will I ever look Montford in the eye again?"

"I don't know! I wish I'd left the troublesome things under the chaise where I found them."

"His grandfather will go *mad* if he finds out about these." Franny worried her lower lip. "It's not as if naughty earrings would be Montford's first scandal, but it would be a sensational one, and his grandfather reacted badly to the hairbrush incident. He's a friend of Lord Arthur's, you know."

"I beg your pardon, Franny. I should have told you the truth at once, but I didn't want to trouble you with this business, especially after I saw the portraits."

"Indeed, you should have done, but I can understand why you might not wish to discuss them." Franny peeked at the earring again, then snapped the locket closed with a grimace. "Did you say you found these the night Montford fell asleep in the study? That was days ago. Why haven't you given them back to him?"

"Because I . . . I . . ." Prue covered her face with her hands. God in heaven, what a fool she was. "I've made a dreadful mistake, Franny."

Franny's fist closed, trapping the earring inside. "I think you'd better tell me everything."

Prue hardly had a chance to open her mouth before the entire story was pouring from her lips. Her misgivings about Lord Stoneleigh, her anxiety for her father, and finally, with much stammering and a few tears, her blackmailing the Duke of Montford.

Franny didn't speak until Prue had talked herself

hoarse, and even then, she showed remarkable restraint, saying only, "I understand your hesitation about Lord Stoneleigh, but if you don't like him, Prue, then you mustn't marry him, no matter how dire the situation with your father is. We'll think of some other solution. You know Giles and I would be happy to give you the money."

"No, Franny. You're very kind, but my father won't allow it." Even if *he* would accept their help, *she* wouldn't. Accepting money from a friend was the quickest way to end a friendship, and she couldn't bear to lose Franny. She'd never be able to pay it back, in any case, so it was out of the question.

"As to Montford, I confess I don't quite understand how you got from finding the earrings to blackmailing a duke." Franny shook her head. "It isn't at all like you to behave so, er . . . rashly."

Prue let out a long sigh. "Stupidly, you mean?"

"Well, since you said it yourself, then yes. What were you thinking, Prue?"

"I *wasn't* thinking. I let myself get worked up into a state until it seemed like the only solution, and the next thing I knew, I was on his doorstep."

"I suppose we'd better turn the earrings over to Giles. He'll give them back to Montford, along with a blistering lecture, and there's nothing Montford detests more than a lecture. Oh, dear. I do hope there's not a row between them."

Franny held her hand out for the other earring, but Prue hesitated. The last thing she wanted was to be the cause of a rift between Montford and Basingstoke. "I think it's best if I make this right with Montford myself."

Franny raised an eyebrow. "Are you certain?"

Hardly, but she'd made this mess. She couldn't burden

poor Basingstoke with the whole, ugly business. "Yes. If I can't resolve it with Montford, then we can always ask Basingstoke to intervene."

"Very well." Franny took her hand and pressed the other earring into her palm. "If you think that would be best."

Best? She'd forfeited any claim to that days ago, but she nodded with a decisiveness she didn't feel, and slipped the earrings into her pocket.

CHAPTER 10

"Nice shot, Montford." Grantham followed the progress of the red billiard ball as it rolled across the baize and dropped into a corner pocket, then turned and slapped Jasper on the back. "Well done! It's fortunate your shot this morning wasn't as accurate, eh?"

"Quite fortunate, yes." Basingstoke leaned a hip against the table. "My wife wouldn't have taken it kindly if Miss Thorne had returned from her morning ride riddled with birdshot."

"I told you already, it was an accidental discharge." Jasper set his cue aside and dropped into a chair with a grunt. "I never fired on Miss Thorne." A gentleman didn't shoot a lady simply because she'd blackmailed him, for God's sake.

She didn't truly believe he'd fired *at* her, did she?

"Of course, you didn't, Montford." Grantham glanced at Basingstoke with a frown, then abandoned his own cue and joined Jasper in front of the fire. "I beg your pardon. I was only jesting, but that was in poor taste."

"Never mind, Grantham." Jasper slumped in his chair. Dinner hadn't yet begun, but already his head was pounding so relentlessly streaks of bright light were pulsing behind his eyelids, and his skull felt as if it were shattering into jagged pieces. "Perhaps it would be best if I had dinner in my bedchamber tonight."

"Come now, Montford, there's no need to banish yourself to your bedchamber." Basingstoke took the chair beside Grantham's. "No one believes you actually meant to do Miss Thorne an injury today. It was an unfortunate incident to be sure, but in the end, no harm was done."

No harm, no. Miss Thorne was perfectly well, and would live on to torment dozens of other unlucky gentlemen with her forked tongue, as he'd been reminding himself all day.

It had worked, at first. But once she was safely inside the house and his heart had ceased its thrashing about, he found himself replaying the chilling scene over and over again in his mind—the stallion's tail a black streak behind him as he flew over the crest of the hill, and Miss Thorne jolting like a ragdoll on top of him, clinging to his mane as if her life depended on it.

Because it *had*.

One misstep on the horse's part, or an instant's inattention on Miss Thorne's, and it would have ended differently. "She might have broken her damned neck."

"Yes, but you saw for yourself that Miss Thorne's neck is entirely intact." Basingstoke gave him a baffled look. "I don't deny it was a near thing, but you seem to be taking it rather badly."

"You do," Grantham agreed. "It's not like you, Montford."

· "Indeed, it's not, because I'm a rake and a scoundrel, a man devoid of all proper feeling, a man of no tenderness or sensibility. Is that what you mean to say, Grantham?"

Grantham's eyebrows shot up. "No. Not at all, Montford."

· Damn it. How had that slipped out? This was what

came of lying about in his bedchamber all afternoon, imagining a dozen different conclusions to this morning's fiasco, all of which ended with Miss Thorne in a twisted, lifeless heap on the ground.

That wasn't *all* he'd imagined, however. No, there'd been that other, er . . . matter. A dream, nothing more, only he'd been awake at the time, so—oh, very well then, it had been a daydream, a perfectly harmless bit of erotic fantasy not unlike others he'd indulged in, though admittedly never after a near tragedy before.

The lady in today's sensual flight of fancy had hazel eyes, and long, caramel-colored curls, and she'd driven him to such a fever pitch of desire he'd been obliged to take matters into his own hands. Pathetic, really, that a notorious rake like himself should be compelled to find his pleasure alone in his bedchamber.

Now in addition to being disgusted with himself, he'd turned all maudlin.

He glanced at the mantel clock, which had just chimed. Good Lord, was it really only nine o'clock? He was bloody exhausted, but there was no sense in returning to his bedchamber, as it would only exacerbate this moody fit he'd fallen into. "Let's finish the game, shall we? It's my turn." He rose to his feet before either of his friends could say a word and retrieved his cue. "You're down by six, Grantham."

Grantham and Basingstoke exchanged another glance, but after a moment of puzzled silence, they rose and joined him at the billiards table. "If something is amiss, Montford," Grantham began, "you can confide—"

"Don't be absurd, Grantham. Nothing's amiss." Nothing a night's sleep wouldn't cure. Why, he'd be as fit as ever tomorrow. "Are we playing, or not? If so, then let's get on with it."

They resumed the game, but a strained silence had fallen over them, and they might have gone on that way if Grantham hadn't decided it would be a grand idea to bring up the one topic guaranteed to turn Jasper's dark mood even darker still. "How does Miss Thorne get on with Lord Stoneleigh? Do you predict a match, Basingstoke?"

Jasper fumbled his cue, and his ball went wide. "Damn it, Grantham, you just cost me the game."

"Indeed, that was a spectacularly bad shot, Montford." Basingstoke twirled his cue between his fingers. "May we take that to mean you have a specific interest in Miss Thorne's marriage prospects?"

"Take it however you bloody well like, Basingstoke."

Grantham tutted. "Come now, Montford, don't be cross. What difference does it make to you who Miss Thorne marries?"

"None whatsoever. It's no business of mine." Miss Thorne might marry whomever she liked without him batting an eye. "As long as it's not Stoneleigh."

Very well, then. *Nearly* whomever she liked.

"Then I have bad news for you, Montford." Grantham leaned over the table to line up his next shot. "Stoneleigh took Miss Thorne for a walk around the lake this afternoon."

"What? You mean to say Stoneleigh is *here*, at Basingstoke House? What the devil is he doing *here*?" The last thing any shooting party needed was a bloody vicar.

Basingstoke frowned. "He *lives* in West Farleigh, Montford. You do recall I bestowed the living on him?"

"He and Miss Thorne appeared quite cozy this afternoon." Grantham sent the ball careening across the baize with a stroke of his cue. "Quite cozy, indeed."

Cozy? Oh, he didn't like the sound of that. "Stoneleigh

could never make a lady like Prudence Thorne happy. Of all the gentlemen in England, he's the last one I'd choose for her."

Basingstoke shrugged. "Be that as it may, Montford, Miss Thorne must wed, and Stoneleigh is offering. Or he will be, soon enough."

"That's good. She hasn't any time to waste. Damn it." Grantham cursed as his ball went wide of the pocket. "Your turn, Montford."

Jasper turned to Grantham. "What the devil does *that* mean?"

Grantham blinked. "Well, Montford, it means you take your cue, aim it at your ball, and try and hit—"

"Not *that*, Grantham. I mean what you said about Miss Thorne. Why should she be in such a rush to marry that she's forced to accept a mushroom like Stoneleigh?"

Basingstoke hesitated, his gaze meeting Grantham's. "It's nothing you need worry—"

"Bollocks." Jasper dropped his cue onto the side of the table and turned on his friends, his chest suddenly gone as tight as a fist. "The two of you have been casting significant glances at each other all evening. You're like a couple of gossiping maiden aunts with a naughty secret."

Basingstoke winced. "Very well. Perhaps I should have told you earlier, but Francesca promised Miss Thorne, and I promised Francesca I wouldn't divulge—"

"Just get on with it, will you, Basingstoke?" He'd had a bad feeling about Miss Thorne's sudden desire to marry ever since she'd appeared on his doorstep with those blasted earrings, and now a chasm of dread was opening in the pit of his stomach.

"Major Thorne is ruined, Montford. That wager . . ." Basingstoke shook his head. "He's sold off all of his land to a neighboring squire already, and his estate is next."

"Sold his estate?" Jasper fell against the billiards table, all his limbs going slack at once. "Why didn't anyone tell me?" Or perhaps the better question was, why hadn't he figured it out himself? He'd suspected from the start that Major Thorne's pockets were too shallow to meet his obligations. He should have known Thorne would be forced to resort to something like this.

"Thorne's proud, Montford. He won't accept help, nor does he want his financial difficulties to become fodder for *ton* gossip. Miss Thorne confided in Francesca only under the strictest promise to keep the matter quiet."

Thorne wouldn't accept help, meaning he wouldn't allow Basingstoke or any of his other friends to pay off his debt. *That* was why Miss Thorne had come to him with her mad blackmail scheme. She'd never be able to persuade her father to accept five hundred pounds, but if the debt simply disappeared, there'd be nothing Thorne could do about it.

The earrings in exchange for erasing the debt.

It all made perfect sense. If he'd been in her place, he'd have blackmailed him, too. Except he'd refused her, hadn't he? He'd sent her away, thinking himself very ill-used, and now she'd be obliged to marry a smug, conceited, self-righteous fusspot of a vicar!

Damnation, but this was a disaster. He must see her at once and tell her he'd changed his mind, and would be perfectly delighted to be blackmailed, after all. He'd also have to find a way to do something about the property they'd already lost. Perhaps he was every bit the unrepentant scoundrel all of London said he was, but he wasn't going to put an honorable old fellow like Thorne out of his home.

Not Thorne's daughter, either, no matter how much of a tart-tongued hellion she was.

"Your Grace?" A footman appeared in the doorway. "The duchess requests your presence in the drawing room to escort the guests into dinner."

"Thank you, Hobbes." Basingstoke set his cue in the rack. "Come, gentlemen. We mustn't keep the duchess waiting."

Jasper trailed after his friends, wincing as the brighter light in the hallway pierced his throbbing skull.

He only had to get through dinner, then he'd see to setting things right with Miss Thorne. It was a matter of a few hours only. As long as bloody Stoneleigh could refrain from offering his hand to Miss Thorne during dinner, all might still be well.

His optimism lasted for approximately two minutes, which was how long it took to walk the dozen or so steps from the billiard room to the drawing room. Once there, he paused on the threshold, a hiss escaping his lips.

There, standing to one side of the fireplace with a proprietary hand on Miss Thorne's arm stood Lord Stoneleigh, a satisfied smirk on his lips. On the other side of Miss Thorne stood his grandfather, his cane in his gnarled hand and his thick mane of white hair brushed neatly back from his face.

As for Miss Thorne herself . . .

He blinked, then blinked again.

The dusty, bedraggled Miss Thorne of this afternoon was gone, and in her place was another Miss Thorne, one he couldn't recall ever having seen before, with pink cheeks, her golden-brown hair tied back into a sleek chignon fastened with a green velvet ribbon. She was dressed in a modest gown, the color of which made him think of forests and grassy knolls. It wasn't fashionable, but it brought out the green in her eyes, and the plain style suited her.

No wonder Stoneleigh looked so bloody pleased with himself. Judging by the possessive grip he had on her arm, he considered Miss Thorne to be already *his*. And the way he was gazing at her, with that ridiculous mooning, besotted expression.

Jasper stifled a snort. Good Lord, hadn't the man ever seen a pretty face before?

"There you are, Jasper my boy!" His grandfather's hearty voice boomed across the room, and Jasper tore his gaze away from Miss Thorne to see the old man waving him over. He shuffled across the room to his doom, a stiff smile pasted on his lips. "Good evening, Grandfather. How are you, sir?"

"Eh, well enough, for an old man. Better now that I've found Miss Thorne."

Yes, any gentleman would be better for having found Miss Thorne, especially in that gown. It was strange, that he should find her plain green gown so alluring when he was accustomed to dining with ladies wearing the finest silks, their ears and throats dripping with magnificent jewels, but somehow the modest garnet necklace and earrings she wore put even his rubies to shame.

"Don't stand there gaping at the lady, Jasper." His grandfather nudged him. "Offer Miss Thorne your greetings."

Was he gaping? "I beg your pardon, Miss Thorne." He bowed over her hand, and a faint hint of honeysuckle tickled his nose. "I do hope you've recovered from your unfortunate misadventure this morning"

She offered him a graceful curtsy. "I have indeed, Your Grace. I'm very well, thank you."

She certainly *looked* well, with that dark green ribbon

woven into the locks of her thick hair, her lips an arching bow of enticing red in the soft, creamy skin of her face. She smelled it, too, with the scent of honeysuckle wafting around her.

Honeysuckle, of all things. It was the last scent in the world he would have imagined would suit her, sharp-tongued as she was, but she wore it as easily as she did her pretty green gown, the scent clinging to her skin like an old friend.

"Allow me to express my thanks to you, Your Grace, for your solicitous attention to Miss Thorne this morning." Stoneleigh offered him an ingratiating bow. "I didn't see it myself, being much occupied at the church today, but I heard all about the frightful incident with Miss Thorne's mount. Really, my dear Miss Thorne, you must attend more assiduously to your safety."

His dear Miss Thorne! Who did Stoneleigh think he was, addressing her so familiarly? And to make such a point of thanking Jasper, as if Miss Thorne were Stoneleigh's exclusive responsibility! The man was an upstart, a popinjay—

"I can't imagine why Miss Thorne would choose to ride such an enormous beast of a horse. The creature's a bit wild, I think." Lord Stoneleigh gave a delicate shudder. "If I'd known she'd take it into her head to do something so foolish, I would have made certain—"

"Indeed, my lord, you're quite mistaken about Sampson." Miss Thorne frowned at Stoneleigh. "He's not wild in the least. The duchess herself chose him for me, and she would never put me on a horse she didn't think I could manage."

"There, it's all right, Miss Thorne. You've had a shock today, and I daresay you're still not entirely recovered from it." Stoneleigh patted her hand as if she were a small child. "Had I been here, I would have put a stop to it, I assure you, Your Grace."

Assure *him*, would he? Stoneleigh could take his assurances and stick them in his cassock. He opened his mouth to say so, but before he could get a word out, Stoneleigh was off again, apparently only having just warmed to his subject. "I don't presume to find fault with the duchess—no, indeed, far from it, for a wiser, more gracious lady I can't imagine—but I can't help but just hint that I think a nice, sedate mare would have been a better choice for a lady of Miss Thorne's skills."

Now that was one step too bloody far, by God. A man might shake his head over Miss Thorne's sharp tongue, but there wasn't a single soul in England who could fault her horsemanship.

"Nonsense, man." His grandfather turned on Stoneleigh, his eyebrows fierce. "Miss Thorne's an excellent horsewoman. She knew what she was about. If she hadn't, she wouldn't be standing here now. She'd be laid out in a pine box."

Jasper winced. Between his grandfather's bluntness and Stoneleigh's fussing, what had promised to be a pleasant house party was turning into a toasty sojourn in one of Dante's circles of hell.

"One shudders to think of it, does not one, Colonel Kingston? But I daresay Miss Thorne won't have much time for riding in the future, will you, my dear Miss Thorne?" Stoneleigh gave her a fond look, but he didn't wait for her to answer. Instead, he turned a wide, toothsome smile on Jasper and his grandfather. "At least, so I flatter myself."

That was too much, right there. "Now see here, Stoneleigh—"

They were interrupted by the duchess, who pronounced

the dinner served, and the company began to move toward the dining room, Lord Stoneleigh squiring Miss Thorne with the assiduousness of a shepherd with a particularly wayward sheep.

Jasper was seated farther up and on the other side of the table, too far to overhear their conversation, but he observed that Lord Stoneleigh scarcely closed his mouth throughout the entire meal, while Miss Thorne scarcely opened hers.

As for himself, he scarcely looked at anyone but *her*, his gaze catching and holding on her face. It was a bright face, vivid and expressive, with sharp, intelligent eyes and a quick, mobile mouth.

Or it had been, until Stoneleigh got ahold of her.

She looked neither left nor right, but kept her gaze on her plate, her expression dull, and her shoulders slumped as if she'd grown too weary to hold them straight. She was doing her best to hide her distress, but she wasn't much of a dissembler. She was making a poor job of it, but Stoneleigh chattered on and on without waiting for her to reply, and without seeming to find anything amiss.

Which for him, there wasn't.

No, it was all going rather well for *him*. Never mind if Miss Thorne was wilting before their very eyes, like a flower crushed under a boot heel.

A peculiar pang pierced Jasper's chest, and everything else—the mishap with Sampson, his ruby earrings, the blackmail, and his newfound understanding of Miss Thorne's deplorable circumstances all faded to the back of his mind.

The gentlemen lingered over their port for a blasted eternity, but when at last they filed into the drawing room to join the ladies, Jasper made a point of hanging back.

When he passed Miss Thorne, he paused long enough to drop a small, folded note into her lap.

She startled and jerked her head up, her gaze meeting his.

"Tonight," he whispered, and passed by her without looking back.

CHAPTER 11

Meet me in the billiards room once the house is quiet to discuss the earrings.

He'd signed it simply *M*, but even that scrawled letter wasn't necessary, as it wasn't likely Prue would soon forget the sound of the Duke of Montford whispering *tonight* to her when he'd passed by her in the drawing room this evening.

If it hadn't been for the note, she might have thought she'd imagined the whole encounter, for he took no notice of her at all after he'd tossed it into her lap. The evening had spun into an endless eternity, but Montford hadn't looked her way again, not even once.

She may as well have been invisible.

Not that it mattered. Why, she'd hardly even noticed it, and in any case, he might have spent the whole of the evening gazing into her eyes, and she still wouldn't have met him in the billiards room tonight. Of course, she wouldn't. Only the most naïve, credulous sort of female would agree to meet an unscrupulous scoundrel of a duke in a deserted billiards room in a remote part of the house, and at night, no less!

Then again, she *had* attempted to blackmail the unscrupulous scoundrel of a duke, so perhaps it was too late to get missish about a clandestine meeting. Either way, it hadn't stopped her from unfolding and refolding the note so many times the seams of the paper were beginning to tear.

The house was quiet, with everyone long since slipped into slumber, dreaming the dreams of the innocent. But not *she*. No, not she, for all that she was exhausted from that torturous dinner. She should have gone straight to her bed, but instead here she was, still in her dinner gown, perched on the edge of the chair in front of her dressing table with Montford's note clutched between her fingers, eyes wide open and her stomach in knots.

But then, she wasn't innocent, was she?

She'd stolen a pair of ruby earrings from a duke, attempted to blackmail him, and hidden the whole sordid tale from Franny. She was far from innocent, and now she was obliged to face the devil, and beg his pardon for her sins.

The devil, or the Duke of Montford. Same thing, really.

Even now he might be downstairs in the billiards room, watching the door, waiting for her to appear. A shiver tripped down her spine at the thought of his long, lean figure sprawled in a chair, because Montford never simply sat, but always sprawled, his muscular legs in their tight breeches stretched out in front of him, dark eyes half-closed and his full lips twisted into that familiar smirk, the firelight behind him casting his flickering shadow against the wall . . .

Oh, dear. She was becoming overwrought.

Perhaps it would be best just to get the thing done instead of sitting here fretting about it. She may be a thief, a liar, and a blackmailer now, but she drew the line at spinelessness.

She tossed her cloak over her dinner gown, then with one furtive peek outside her bedchamber door, she crept into the hallway. Her gaze skittered left and right as she made her way down the stairs, but there was no one lurking in the dim corridors, and not a soul to be seen on the staircase or in the entryway.

Not Montford, nor anyone else.

She paused as she reached the last step, shivering in the chill, and pulled her cloak tighter around her neck. The silence was so thick it made her ears ring. Perhaps Montford had changed his mind?

But as she made her way down the hallway toward the billiards room, an odd clicking sound made her pause. It sounded like . . . yes, there it was again, the click of a cue striking a billiard ball, and then the muted roll of the heavy ivory ball over the thick baize.

Someone was awake, then.

She tiptoed closer and peeked around the edge of the open door. The room was dim, lit only by a few sconces and the banked fire in the grate, but there was enough illumination for her to see the Duke of Montford leaning over the table in his shirtsleeves and waistcoat.

He'd been a trifle out of temper this evening—or, if one wished to be truly accurate, he'd been as irritable as a snarling dog, snapping at everyone who ventured to address him. When he wasn't biting his dinner companions' heads off, he was glowering at Lord Stoneleigh, those dark brows of his lost under that thick lock of hair that lay over his forehead. More than one guest at the table had looked askance at him, most particularly his grandfather.

But he didn't look snarly *now*. A less perceptive lady might even make the mistake of thinking him harmless. His hair was tousled, as if he'd been dragging his fingers through it, and his cravat was undone. The long folds of linen hung limply around his neck, leaving the smooth, olive skin of his throat bare.

Oh, no. No, no, no. This was a mistake. Of all the people tucked under this roof, he was the last one she should be meeting in a dimly lit, deserted room. It wasn't fair, really, that such a dastardly gentleman should be so shockingly handsome. It would be ever so much easier to pinpoint the scoundrels if only they looked the part.

No lady with any sense would trust herself alone with a man who looked like *that*.

Slowly, she backed away from the doorway, but before she could reach the safety of the hallway, the deep rumble of his voice stopped her.

"Going somewhere, Miss Thorne?"

She froze, her eyes flying to his face.

She'd withstood any number of heart-stopping moments in her life. There'd been that time she'd taken a pair of scissors to her hair and poor Mrs. Braddock, their housekeeper at Thornewood, had fainted dead away at the sight of her shorn head. Or that time she'd ripped the seat of her breeches attempting to jump her horse over a fence, and a crowd of the village lads who'd been watching had seen her bare bottom.

But nothing—*nothing*—could have prepared her for the tension that sparked between them the moment their gazes locked. His eyes, already so very dark, went jet black, and his lips curled into a slow smile. "Do you always wear your cloak when you play billiards?"

It was no concern of his what she did, and she opened her mouth to say so, but the cutting rebuke never made it past her lips. "Are we going to play?" was what emerged instead. That might have been fine—it was a valid question, after all—but her voice was so low and breathy, warmth flooded her cheeks.

He straightened up from the billiards table and rested a hand atop his cue. His dark gaze roved over her, but he didn't answer her question. Instead, he said abruptly, "Did you enjoy yourself at dinner this evening, Miss Thorne?"

Dinner? What did dinner have to do with anything? But if he even had to ask if she'd enjoyed herself, she must have put a better face on the evening than she'd imagined. "It was fine, Your Grace."

"So, it's to be Luttrell, is it? A loquacious sort of gentleman, Luttrell, but he *does* seem taken with you." His eyes narrowed on her face. "As taken as he was with the fried artichoke bottoms, at any rate. He divided his time between gazing at them and gazing at you."

For pity's sake, who did the man think he was, making such an observation about another gentleman's attention toward her? "I didn't notice, Your Grace, and I confess myself surprised that you *did*. I can't see that it has anything to do with you."

If he noticed her outrage, he paid it no mind. "Luttrell is well enough, I suppose, though not the most exciting gentleman—"

"He's Lord Stoneleigh now, not—"

"Ah, so you're angling for a title, then? As I said once before, you underestimate your charms, Miss Thorne. You've the face of a viscountess, at the very least."

The face of a viscountess, indeed. What nonsense.

"I'm not angling for anyone at all, Your Grace." It was

both a lie and the truth at once, but really, it was too much, having to stand here and submit to his impertinent questions when she wouldn't be obliged to marry at all if it weren't for that blasted wager.

"Yes, you said so when I asked you that first night in Basingstoke's study, but you seem to have changed your mind since then. Otherwise, you wouldn't have spent all evening flirting so outrageously with Luttrell."

"I wasn't—" She broke off, sucking in a breath before she lost her temper entirely and cracked one of the pool cues over the Duke of Montford's head. "Whatever my interest in Lord Stoneleigh might be, Your Grace, it isn't any business of *yours*."

He shrugged. "True enough, I suppose."

"You can be sure I've no intention of explaining anything to do with my marriage prospects to—"

"Do you fancy a game?"

Game? What game? What in the world was he talking about *now*? "I don't . . . what do you mean?"

"A *game*, Miss Thorne." He nodded at the billiards table. "Do you fancy one?"

"What, a game of billiards?"

"Do you have some other game in mind? If so, do tell." He leaned a hip against the table, a faint smile teasing at the corners of his lips. "I'm open to suggestions, Miss Thorne."

That smile was . . . well, no man should have a smile like that, wicked and teasing at once, and goodness knew Montford deployed it like the weapon it was, with the slow curl of it starting at the corners of his lips before it had its way with the rest of his mouth.

It didn't coax a shiver from *her*, of course, or leave a spray of gooseflesh on *her* skin.

"You seem to me to be a lady who enjoys games,

Miss Thorne, but perhaps you don't play billiards? Forgive me if it was an ill-considered invitation. It slipped my mind for a moment that most ladies don't."

"I don't believe a single thing has ever slipped your mind, Your Grace." He was good at playing the thoughtless rake, but he didn't fool her. Anyone who cared to look into his eyes could see he possessed a keen intellect. For all his desultory manner, there was little that escaped his notice.

"I'm flattered, Miss Thorne, but you give me too much credit." He fetched another cue from the rack and held it out to her. "Come. There's no one about to see you, and you've no need to be wary of me."

"*Wary*?" Her ripple of laughter seemed louder than it should in the quiet room. "Do you suppose I'm frightened of you, Your Grace?"

He eyed her for a long moment, then murmured, "No, I think not. But if you're reluctant, then perhaps a wager might tempt you into a game?"

There was that smile again, as dark as his eyes. He was the devil's own minion, luring her into sin, and she didn't trust him any more than she would Satan himself. Her father had been taken in by that mesmerizing smile, and just look where that had landed them. "I don't wager."

"No? Why is that, Miss Thorne?"

"Because I don't have anything I can afford to lose. You said yourself that was the first rule of wagering, Your Grace—never risk anything you can't afford to lose." It was nothing but the truth, but this was a man who'd given his mistress rubies as large as a baby's fist. A duke with that much wealth at his fingertips wasn't likely to understand her reasoning. No doubt he'd find it comically provincial.

But he didn't laugh. He merely gazed at her, a strange

expression on his face. She couldn't read it, but he'd certainly never looked at her in quite that way before. "Is something wrong, Your Grace?"

"No." He looked away, clearing his throat. "Normally I'd applaud your restraint, Miss Thorne, but in this case, the wager can only help you. You have something in your possession that belongs to me, and I'm willing to make a considerable sacrifice to get it back."

"If you truly wanted it, Your Grace, you might have had it by now. Only yesterday you told me I might do whatever I liked with those earrings. What's brought about this sudden change of mind?"

"I'm weary of these games. I want those earrings back in my possession at once before they're lost, or worse, they miraculously find their way back to Lady Archer."

Lady Archer! Well, she hadn't even thought of *that*. Some blackmailer she'd turned out to be. "I'm not as unscrupulous as you seem to think, Your Grace." Then again, hadn't she already proved herself to be a thief, and an extortionist? It stood to reason he'd think her a lying, unrepentant schemer, as well.

"You say so, Miss Thorne, but you've done rather well for yourself up to this point, haven't you? Do you have the earrings with you?"

"Yes."

"Very good. Then let's start negotiations, shall we?" He regarded her for a long moment in silence, his eyes glittering. "The wager I propose is a simple one. If I win, you will return the earrings to me. If you win, I will forgive your father's debt. Not just the remaining five hundred pounds, but the whole of it."

She stared at him. Surely, he couldn't be serious? "But that's fifteen hundred pounds!"

"Yes, I'm aware of that, Miss Thorne."

Had the man gone mad? "You mean to say, Your Grace, that you'd risk fifteen hundred pounds on a single game of billiards?"

He shrugged, his expression giving nothing away. "I don't see why not."

She stared at him, her heart slamming against her rib cage. One game of billiards, and she could come away with enough money not only to keep their estate, but also reclaim the property they'd sold.

It sounded too good to be true, which meant it likely *was*.

Why should Montford offer her such a chance? Of course, fifteen hundred pounds was a mere pittance to him. He likely wagered double or triple that amount on a casual game of cards at White's every evening.

"Well, Miss Thorne? The night marches on."

How could she possibly agree to a wager with him after she'd scolded her father so mercilessly for his own wager with the man? Then again, how could she say no? If she won, their future would be secure, and there'd be no need for her to marry Lord Stoneleigh. Such an opportunity wasn't going to come her way a second time.

Unless . . . mightn't there be some trick to it? Montford had made quick work of her father. Mightn't he do the same with her? "Let me see if I understand you correctly, Your Grace. You're risking fifteen hundred pounds on a wager after I've offered to return your earrings to you simply for forgiving the five-hundred-pound debt? Do I have that right?"

"You do indeed, Miss Thorne, but you've forgotten one thing. In order to get the fifteen hundred pounds, you have to *win* at billiards."

"And if I lose?"

"If you lose, you'll return my ruby earrings to me, and I will consider this matter closed."

Of course, he thought he'd beat her easily. He'd said it himself—most ladies didn't play billiards, and the few who did weren't likely to offer much in the way of a challenge to a gentleman like him, who must play frequently.

But she wasn't like most ladies. There was a chance she could beat him at billiards, particularly as he wouldn't be expecting her to be any good. Still, it all seemed too easy. "A day ago, I offered to return your earrings if you forgave the remainder of my father's debt. You declined, but now you're proposing an exchange that is far more advantageous to me than the one you refused. I can't think of any reason you should do so."

"It's quite simple, Miss Thorne. You attempted to *blackmail* me before. I don't give into threats, no matter how charming the extortionist is. A wager, however, is a matter of honor between gentlemen—or in our case, a gentleman and a lady."

Dear God. Only a duke would draw such a costly distinction. "Your honorable wager is costing you an extra thousand pounds, Your Grace."

He smiled. "Only if I lose, Miss Thorne."

"Which you're certain won't happen, I take it." His pride, alas, might cost him even more than his scruples before the game was over.

"I'm willing to take the risk, yes. I want those earrings back in my possession, and you happen to have them. The fifteen hundred pounds brings you to the table, but it's still a great deal less than what the earrings are worth. I don't intend to lose our game, Miss Thorne, but if I do, the fifteen hundred pounds is yours. You have my word on it."

The word of a scoundrel, yes.

Still, for all his questionable behavior, the Duke of Montford *was* a gentleman. He'd consider an unpaid debt a stain on his honor. She could trust him in this, if not in anything else, and goodness knew the earrings weren't doing her any good languishing in her pocket.

She was going to return the earrings to him no matter what happened. She had everything to gain, and nothing to lose.

It was the perfect wager.

"We haven't got all night, Miss Thorne. Do you accept the wager, or not?"

She raised her face to his, a thrill rushing up her spine at the look of anticipation in his dark eyes. Strangely enough, the two of them weren't so different. "Very well, Your Grace. I accept your wager."

CHAPTER 12

Miss Thorne was still wearing her dinner gown.

The same dinner gown that turned her eyes from hazel to a soft, inviting green. The dinner gown that clung to every curve and skimmed every sleek hollow. The dinner gown with that maddening green velvet bow that tied just underneath the swell of her bosom.

Which was all very well, of course, because he was a gentleman, not some lecherous savage. It was perfectly fine. Why, once they started the game, he'd hardly even notice her gown, or her green eyes, or her curves, hollows, and bosom.

Jasper carried on with this lie right up until the moment she stripped off her cloak and tossed it over the back of a chair, her dark green skirts swirling around her ankles as she marched across the room to inspect the billiard cues. She selected one, then turned to face him, the cue in her hand and a cool smile on her lips. "Shall we begin, Your Grace?"

Begin? How could he begin when she was wearing *that*?

He'd admired the gown at dinner, but he hadn't appreciated the full hypnotic power of it with Stoneleigh hovering over her as if she were a porcelain doll on the verge of shattering. Now, with the firelight behind her outlining her shape, there was no overlooking the way the forest green silk clung to every inch of her.

The gown was outrageous, a torment, a scandal! What did she mean, wearing such a shocking garment? Oh, at first glance it appeared plain enough, but the simplicity of it—the very lack of the usual busy trimmings meant a gentleman's eye had no place to land other than on *her*. The bare skin of her arms and shoulders, the sweet, creamy swell of her bosom . . . dear God, he hardly knew where to look first.

He'd never seen a more diabolical frock in his life.

"Is something wrong, Your Grace?" She was frowning at him, a fetching little wrinkle between her brows. "If you've changed your mind about the wager—"

"No!" He tore his gaze away from the maddening wisps of her loose hair, the firelight gleaming on the golden strands and flickering over the long, slender line of her neck. He wouldn't get another chance to undo the mess he'd made with that wager with her father, so he'd simply have to keep his gaze averted from that . . . that mockery of a gown.

Especially that fiendish little bow tied under her bosom. "Of course, I haven't changed my mind, Miss Thorne."

"If you're certain."

"Quite certain." He nodded at the billiards table. "After you. You have played billiards before, have you not?"

"Once or twice, yes." A little smile twitched at the corners of her lips. "Cues or maces, Your Grace?"

"I prefer cues, but I shall defer to you." He offered her a bow.

"Cues are acceptable to me, with chalk, of course. How many points wins the game, Your Grace?"

For a lady who'd only played once or twice before, she appeared to have a solid command of the rules. Could it be that Miss Thorne was a mountebank? It would be just as well if she were, as it would make it easier for him to lose this game without attracting her suspicions. "Twenty-one points. One game, one winner, and no regrets. That means no weeping or other histrionics if you lose, Miss Thorne."

"Histrionics?" She threw back her head in a laugh. "Do you take me for a sore loser, Your Grace?"

Her laugh caught him off guard, but when he glanced at her, her eyes were shining and her color high, and despite himself, his lips twitched. Ah, the lady was a competitor, it seemed. They had that in common, then.

"You, a sore loser, Miss Thorne? No, I think not. A sore winner, perhaps." She laughed again, and this time he made no effort to hide his smile. This game was costing him fifteen hundred pounds, so he may as well enjoy it. "I await your pleasure."

She cast a critical eye over the table, and then without further ado she bent to her task, lining up her cue behind the plain white ball. With one practiced stroke she sent it rolling across the baize, where it hit the red ball with a smack, then dropped neatly into a side pocket. "Hazard."

He jerked his gaze from her backside to her flushed face. Good Lord, but this game was shaping up to be worth every penny he intended to lose. "You have exceptional form, Miss Thorne."

"I . . . thank you, Your Grace." She looked away, another flood of color surging into her cheeks, and dear God, was there ever a lady who had a more charming, bashful blush than Miss Thorne laboring under a compliment?

"I have exceptional aim, as well." She gave him a

knowing little grin, as if she were laughing at some private amusement. "That's three points to me, Your Grace."

Any qualms he might have had about maneuvering her into a game vanished like a puff of smoke at the sight of that smile. He hadn't truly understood how much the wager with her father had been plaguing his conscience until now, but it was oddly satisfying, putting everything back into its proper place again.

He took up his cue and with one quick strike his ball shot across the baize. It hit her ball, which disappeared into a corner pocket. "Hazard, Miss Thorne."

"But alas, only worth two points." She shook her head in mock sympathy. "Pity, Your Grace."

"Don't become too cocky, Miss Thorne. We've only just begun playing."

But the game went on much as it had started, with Miss Thorne piling up points, every confident strike of her cue a cannon or a hazard. He was right on her heels, always only a point or two behind, but growing increasingly distracted by the glorious sight of Miss Thorne stretching and bending over the billiards table. It did wonderful things to her pert little backside, which he'd become a trifle obsessed with.

This, right here, was the reason ladies shouldn't be encouraged to play billiards. It was hardly fair, when they had such an advantage over any gentleman who was suffering from the indignity of increasingly tight pantaloons.

On and on it went, with Miss Thorne growing ever more fetching as she forgot herself, the long locks of her hair escaping her chignon and brushing her shoulders, that damned gown rippling around her with her every twist and arch of her body, the firelight turning the silk a deep, seductive emerald green that perfectly matched her eyes.

By the time she was within three points of winning the game, he'd discarded his cravat and waistcoat and was obliged to mop at his forehead with his handkerchief after her every turn.

"It's your turn, Your Grace." She straightened from the table, her smile fading as her gaze landed on him. "Are you unwell? You look a bit warm."

Oh, he was warm, alright. Warm, as hard as stone, and so light-headed from the inconvenient rush of blood to his nether regions he was beginning to feel a bit wild. "Yes, yes, I'm perfectly well, but I'd be grateful indeed, Miss Thorne, if you could manage to hold your tongue while I take my turn."

Her brows shot up, but she retreated a few steps to give him room. "Why, of course, Your Grace."

He bent over the table, blinking at the arrangement of the balls. He was one judicious stroke away from potting both her ball and the red ball, a winning hazard that would give him the game, and by God, it was tempting, as he wasn't a man who enjoyed losing.

But in this case, a loss was a win.

He leaned over the table and lined up his shot, intending to pot his ball, but to hit it hard enough that it smacked into the red one before it fell into the pocket for a losing hazard, a three-point loss.

But that wasn't what happened. Perhaps the pent-up lust racing through his veins threw him off, or perhaps he aimed correctly by mistake—he didn't make a habit of intentionally losing at billiards, after all—but his ball rolled just a shade to the left of the red one and dropped into the pocket without touching it.

Damn it. They were tied now, at twenty points each. Still, all Miss Thorne had to do was sink her ball, and the game would be over, the debt hanging over her head gone, and her home restored to her.

A tidy night's work, all told.

"It's your turn, Miss Thorne." He nodded at the table. "One shot finishes it."

She cast a careful eye over the baize and leaned over the table, lining up her shot with her usual exquisite care, her form as perfect as ever, and with a graceful stroke of her cue, sent her ball spinning across the baize and heading straight for the pocket, just a little farther and it would—

Miss? Hell, and damnation! She'd missed the shot! Her ball struck the red one, then fell into the pocket with a final, hollow thud that marked the end of the game.

For an instant, neither of them said a word, but then she straightened up from the table, looking dazed. "I—I can't believe it."

He was still staring at the table in shock. "Neither can I." It was the perfect shot! All the stars had been aligned, and all the angels weeping. How could it have *missed*?

She remained still for some time, her gaze fixed on the red ball sitting atop the baize, her throat working, until at last she turned to him with a forced smile. "I . . . well, that's it, then. Well done, Your Grace. You're a worthy opponent."

Well done? This was a bloody disaster. How was he going to come up with another scheme to return the fifteen hundred pounds to her without arousing her suspicions?

"That leaves the matter of the earrings, I suppose." She hurried to the chair where she'd tossed her cloak and snatched it up, rifling through the pockets. When she turned to face him again, the earrings were pooled in the center of her palm, the firelight catching at the jewels and making the rubies flash with red fire.

She was gazing down at the jewels, an odd expression on her face. Not covetousness, but . . . relief, almost, the opposite of Selina's expression when he'd given the earrings to her, with that flash of pure, naked greed in her eyes. The first thing Selina had done when she got her hands on them was assess the size of the rubies and judge the weight of the gold in her palm.

"Here you are, Your Grace."

She held them out to him, and he took an instinctive step backward.

He didn't want the cursed things back.

Everything that had happened these past few months—the regrettable wager with Major Thorne, the ugliness with Selina, Miss Thorne's desperate attempt at blackmail, and the secrets, all the shameful secrets he'd kept from his grandfather and his friends . . . somehow, that small pile of glittering stones in her palm had come to represent the worst of what he was.

He could hardly bear to look at them, much less touch them, but what could he do, besides take them? He crossed the room with reluctant steps, but when he reached for them, she closed her fist, trapping the earrings inside.

"Wait, Your Grace."

If she'd asked him to give the rubies to her, he would have done so in a heartbeat. How might she look, with jewels glittering at her throat and ears? Not rubies, though. No, not rubies for Prudence Thorne. Emeralds, perhaps. Yes, emeralds would look lovely on her, the vivid gleam of the stones coaxing out the deep, lush green of her eyes.

But she didn't ask. Instead, she met his gaze without flinching. "I want you to know how much I regret taking these from you. I never should have done so. When I found them, I intended to return them to you at once, but . . . well, I shouldn't have taken them in the first place, nor should I have blackmailed you." She took his hand, pressed the earrings into his palm

He closed his fingers instinctively around them, then shoved them into his pocket. "Miss Thorne—"

"It was very wrong of me, and I beg your pardon," she said, then turned to go.

He didn't plan on stopping her. He certainly didn't plan on touching her. If he'd been in his right mind, he would have bid her a terse goodnight, then breathed a sigh of relief that he hadn't given into the temptation of touching her.

Prudence Thorne wasn't the sort of woman a man touched on a whim.

She was the sort of woman a man could drown in.

But he was already turning her toward him, drawing her closer, his fingers clasped gently around her wrist, her impossibly soft skin gliding under his thumb, and she was so close he could taste her scent, honeysuckle rushing over his tongue with every breath he drew.

She didn't resist when he urged her closer, nor did she protest when he lowered his mouth to hers, but only gazed up at him with darkened hazel eyes, her lips soft and open with wonder.

He couldn't do anything else then but take her mouth in a dizzying rush of desire. She let out a soft gasp when his lips brushed hers, her warm breath a maddening drift over his lips, but she didn't draw away, and he let his hand settle on the back of her neck, a low moan tearing from his throat as he coaxed her with gentle strokes of his tongue to open to him.

Her plush lips parted on a sigh, and God, her mouth was like silk, warm and smooth and sweet against his.

He slid his hand down her back in a slow caress, the dark green silk gliding under his palm, and settled it on the curve of her hip, his other hand caressing the soft, secret skin of her neck, his fingers tangling in the loose locks of her hair, his need for her rising higher with every panting breath shared between them, heat thrumming in his belly.

Had he thought he could kiss her sweetly, chastely? Had he thought he could kiss her once, and let her go? Then he was a fool. The moment he touched her, he wanted more—all of her—every sigh and moan, her long, slender legs wound around him, his hands tangled in her hair, her body trembling for him—

He let out a defeated groan, then summoned every shred of his self-control and set her gently away from him. "We can't. . . . Go upstairs, Miss Thorne. *Now*."

She was still for a heartbeat, her fingers pressed to her swollen lips and her eyes wide, then without a word she turned and fled, leaving him alone in the darkness, his harsh breath tearing from his chest and his lips on fire with the taste of her.

He was still for a long time after she'd gone, unmoving, the ruby earrings heavy in his pocket, but when he came back to himself, the room was dark, and the last few coals in the grate had collapsed into ashes.

Miss Thorne's cloak was still draped over the back of the chair.

She'd left it behind.

He caught the earring up in his fist and studied the pearls dangling from the ends of each ruby. They weren't large pearls, but they were lovely, perfect ovals with that luster only pearls could boast, and subtly beautiful in the way the finest pearls were. He gazed down at them, at the dying firelight playing over them, making them glow like stars.

He couldn't give her emeralds, but he could give her these. Not because they were valuable, or because he owed them to her, or because tonight had left him, for reasons he didn't understand, with a tiny tear inside his heart.

But because they were beautiful, and he wanted her to have them.

He turned them over in his hand. The pearls were secured only by a thin gold loop. It wouldn't take much to pry the circlet open and slide them free . . .

He didn't give himself a chance to think about it, but hurried across the room and down the corridor to Basingstoke's study, where he rummaged about in the desk until he found the letter opener. It was a crude, blunt instrument for such a delicate task, but it took only a few twists with the tip of the opener to create a space in the tiny gold circle.

One by one, he slid each of the pearls free, then he replaced the letter opener in the drawer and bounded back down the corridor to the billiard room, the pearls clutched in his fist.

He snatched up Miss Thorne's cloak and slid the pearls deep inside one of the pockets, then folded the cloak neatly over the back of the chair where she'd left it.

Then he stepped back, his breath rough, and closed his eyes.

Yes, this was right. The pearls belonged with her.

He turned to leave the billiards room but paused at the door and looked back over his shoulder. Perhaps it was risky, leaving a cloak with pearls in the pocket in Basingstoke's billiards room, but if Miss Thorne missed the cloak and came back downstairs for it tonight, it would appear odd if it weren't here.

So, there it would stay, until she came for it.

He blew out the last lamp, then turned and left the room, leaving the cloak draped over the back of the chair, the pearls like a tiny pair of secrets, hidden inside.

CHAPTER 13

The Glorious Twelfth dawned with an unseasonable blast of cold air and a thick cover of menacing dark clouds that threatened a deluge at every moment, but the weather hadn't dampened the company's enthusiasm for the day's sport. Footsteps had been echoing in the hallway outside Prue's bedchamber door even before the sun rose, the servants scurrying about to do their masters' bidding.

She stretched her aching limbs and rubbed a hand over gritty, burning eyes. She'd drifted to sleep in the wee hours of the morning after subjecting her pillow to numerous bouts of desperate pummeling, only to wake up to her humiliating defeat at billiards last night.

The Duke of Montford had held her in the palm of his hand from the moment he'd challenged her to a game in that deep, husky voice, right up until he'd pocketed the ruby earrings.

It wasn't that he'd cheated her. It wasn't *his* fault he could turn even the least susceptible lady's knees to jelly with nothing more than that smoldering dark gaze of his. Really, all it had taken was a few quirks of those full, handsome lips, and she'd been as foolish as every other lady who sighed over his charms.

Well, perhaps not *quite* as foolish. She hadn't wagered anything she couldn't afford to lose, but to think she'd had Thornewood right in the palm of her hand, only to see it slip from her fingers with one fumbled thrust of a cue!

It was *maddening*.

There was nothing to be done about it, however. She'd played her best, she'd lost, and now Lord Stoneleigh awaited. She glanced at the window, listening to the raindrops patter against the glass, the water trickling toward the sill in rivulets, and let out a sigh.

She didn't love Lord Stoneleigh. She was *never* going to love Lord Stoneleigh. In fact, with every hour she spent in his company it seemed less likely she'd even grow to *like* Lord Stoneleigh.

How in good conscience could she possibly marry the man? Didn't he deserve a wife who loved him? Or at the least one who could tolerate his presence for more than five minutes at a time? It was true the man didn't notice her aversion to him, but surely, he'd catch on after a year or two of marriage—

"Miss Thorne?" There was a brisk knock on the door. "Miss Thorne, are you awake?"

"Yes." Prue struggled free of the coverlet she'd been hiding under and sat up, resting her back against the headboard. "Come in, Maria."

The door opened and Maria bustled in with a tea tray balanced on her arm, a torrent of cheerful words already flowing from her lips. "Good morning, miss! It's a wild one out there today, and as cold as a witch's heart, too."

"It doesn't seem as if it's put anyone off the shooting

party. The entire house has been awake since dawn by the sounds of the commotion this morning."

"Oh, aye, miss. The gentlemen are as eager as ever, though they'll have a right time of it, in this weather. Here you are, miss." She set the tray on the side table and hurried toward the wardrobe on the other side of the room. "Will you have your blue gown today? I think it's your warmest—"

"No, that won't do for scrabbling about in the bushes." What a pity she couldn't wear breeches, as she did at Thornewood! It would be so much more comfortable than dragging her heavy skirts about, but she didn't dare push propriety quite that far. "I suppose I'll have to have my riding habit, Maria."

"Your riding habit!" Maria turned to stare at her, the blue day dress over her arm. "What, you mean to say you're going to *shoot* today?"

"Of course. It is a shooting party, isn't it?" Why shouldn't she shoot, if she wished to? She could handle a shotgun as well as any gentleman.

"But I . . . begging your pardon, miss, but ladies don't shoot."

"This lady does. I've accompanied my father and his friends on dozens of shooting adventures. I'm actually quite a good shot, Maria."

"If you say so, miss." Maria gave her a doubtful look, but she turned away to rummage through the wardrobe and came out with Prue's rather worn riding habit in her arms. "Here we are."

Maria helped her into her habit, then Prue sat at the dressing table and drank her tea while Maria brushed out her hair and pinned it in a heavy coil at the back of her neck. "Right, miss. That should keep it out of your eyes."

"It's perfect. Thank you, Maria." Prue abandoned the

empty teacup on the tray and turned to the maidservant with a half-hearted smile. Yes, she'd squandered her only chance to rescue her father from debt and her own prospects were grimmer than ever, but Basingstoke's magnificent grounds awaited. That was something, at least.

Maria held out Prue's hat, shaking her head. "It's a bit crumpled, I'm afraid."

"Oh, dear. It is, isn't it?" Unfortunately, her hat had fallen victim to that mad dash down the hill yesterday. Sampson must have trod on it, because the brim was quite squashed, and the jaunty little feather rather bent, but it was the best she had, and so it would have to do. She jammed it down on top of her head and rose from the dressing table. "There. I'm ready."

Maria followed her to the bedchamber door, wringing her hands. "You will be careful today, won't you, miss?"

"Certainly not, Maria!" Prue tucked her gloves into her skirt pocket and gave Maria a wink. "What fun would that be?"

Maria frowned. "I wouldn't like you to do yourself an injury, miss."

"There's no need to worry, Maria," Prue called over her shoulder as she dashed through the bedchamber door into the hallway. "I'm not apt to shoot myself, I promise you!"

She closed the door behind her and made her way downstairs to the breakfast room, where she found Franny alone at the table with a half-finished cup of tea in front of her. She looked up when Prue entered. "Good morning!" She eyed Prue's riding habit, a rueful smile rising to her lips. "Ah, so you do intend to shoot today? I wondered if the weather would put you off."

"No, indeed." Prue paused in the doorway. "Unless you object to it? I won't go if you'd rather I didn't."

"No, not at all. I might have known a little drizzle wouldn't deter you."

"Perhaps your husband might not like it." Prue dropped into the chair opposite her friend, her spirits flagging at the thought. "Does Basingstoke object to ladies shooting?"

"Not in the least. I told him you're fond of shooting, and he said you're welcome to come." Franny glanced toward the door and lowered her voice. "Did you have a chance to resolve that business with Montford last night?"

"I did, yes. Montford has his earrings back." One of them was satisfied, at least.

"What about that other matter? Is he likely to create a fuss about it?"

"You mean, does he intend to have me taken up for blackmail? No. The matter is closed. You needn't worry anymore Franny, I promise you. I'll tell you everything when we return this afternoon."

Well, perhaps not *everything*. She raised a hand to her lips. They felt tender still, swollen. She wouldn't tell Franny about the way her heart had leapt in that breathless instant before Montford's lips met hers, or describe to Franny the way his eyes appeared as dark as midnight itself in the firelight, or confess that she'd dreamed of his kiss, and woken to the taste of it lingering on her lips—

"Thank goodness!" Franny let out a breath. "I daresay Montford was happy to—"

She was cut off by masculine voices and the tread of heavy boots in the hallway, and a moment later Basingstoke strode into the room, with the Duke of Grantham on his heels.

"Good morning, ladies!" Grantham offered each of

them a bow. "Miss Thorne, I'm delighted to hear you're joining our shooting party today."

"Thank you, Your Grace."

"I expect we'll be off soon, my love." Basingstoke smiled down at Franny, tweaking one of her curls. "Blount is gathering the shooting party in the courtyard by the stables. Will you come see us off?"

"Of course." Franny set her teacup in the saucer and rose to her feet.

Prue got to her feet just as a particularly violent gust of wind arose, rattling the windowpanes and sending a torrent of raindrops battering against the glass. "Perhaps I'd better go and fetch my cloak. I'll be out in a trice."

She was halfway up the stairs when she recalled she'd left her cloak in the billiards room the night before. She hurried back down, retracing her steps from last night, and yes, there it was, draped over the chair where she'd left it. She snatched it up, then made her way out to a small stone courtyard connected to the stables by a narrow pathway.

Gentlemen crowded about, all of them in their finest shooting costumes, along with a motley collection of spaniels, retrievers, and pointers, all yapping excitedly, and at least two dozen servants weighted down with leather game bags.

"Quite a spectacle, isn't it?" Franny asked, appearing at her elbow.

"A glorious spectacle, yes."

"Speaking of which . . ." Franny nodded over Prue's shoulder, her blue eyes twinkling. "Here's Montford."

Prue turned, and her heart shot into her throat.

The Duke of Montford had just strolled into the court-yard. He was wearing a bottle green frock coat, with a gleaming black top hat arranged over his tousled curls. A servant trailed after him, but Montford carried his own leather bag, the strap slung over his broad chest and the bag at his hip, and he wore a pair of leather spatterdashes up to his knees, laced over a pair of shockingly tight buff breeches.

Goodness, there went her knees again, trembling like jelly. Could any lady ever be ready for such a sight as that? One glance was more than enough. She'd take care not to risk another for the rest of the day.

Not that he'd pay her any mind, of course. He likely hadn't given their kiss last night a second thought. He'd kissed dozens of ladies, all of them fashionable and beautiful. Why, he'd probably laughed himself silly over her clumsy kiss as soon as she'd left the billiards room last night.

He paused on the edge of the gathering, his gaze roaming over the crowd. When he caught sight of her, his lips curled in a wicked smile and he came toward her at once, pausing only to nod at his companions as he crossed the courtyard. "Good morning, Miss Thorne."

"Your Grace." She gave him a brisk nod, but already she could feel her cheeks warming.

Those breeches . . . dear God, they were positively scandalous.

"You're awake rather early for a lady who was so late getting off to her bed last night." His gaze swept over her, taking her in from the tips of her boots to the top of her head. "Er, Miss Thorne, are you aware that your hat is a bit dented?"

"Yes. Perfectly aware, Your Grace." No doubt he thought her poor little hat very amusing, but she wouldn't let such a silly thing as a flattened hat spoil her chance to join the shooting party.

He didn't laugh at her, though, but only gave her a

grave nod, his dark eyes roaming over her face. "I thought you might bear me a grudge after our game last night."

"Not at all, Your Grace. I told you, I'm not a sore loser."

"No, but I don't believe you enjoy losing to *me*, Miss Thorne."

No, dash it, she didn't, but she'd bite her lip bloody before she'd admit it. "Nonsense, Your Grace. You think yourself much more important than you are."

He grinned. "Very well, then. It's kind of you to come see the shooting party off."

"See you off? No, indeed. I'm here to shoot, of course."

"Shoot?" He'd taken her arm to follow the rest of the party down the pathway to the stables, but now he came to an abrupt halt, his good humor vanishing in an instant. "You can't mean to say you intend to join the shooting party?"

"Certainly, I do." For pity's sake, what was so shocking in that? Ladies occasionally joined the fox hunt without civilization collapsing in on itself. Why should shooting be any different?

"No, Miss Thorne. It's out of the question. I forbid it."

"*You* forbid it?" She'd never been fond of the word "forbid," and to hear it fall from his too-handsome lips was like a spark dropping into a pan of gunpowder. "I beg your pardon, Your Grace, but you have no authority to forbid me anything at all. I will do as I please."

She would have marched on by him, but he caught her elbow, his brows lowering in a scowl. "The devil you will." He marched her over to Basingstoke, who was conferring with his gamekeeper. "Basingstoke? We have a problem."

"For God's sake, Montford, we haven't even left the stable yard yet. How can we have a problem already?"

"We won't be leaving the stable yard at all if we don't tend to this first."

"A moment, Blount, if you would." Basingstoke turned to them with a sigh. "Yes? What is it, Montford?"

"Miss Thorne is under the impression she's accompanying the shooting party today. Kindly tell her she isn't, and we can be on our way."

Prue's hands curled into fists. "How *dare* you presume to think you can order me about, you arrogant, presumptuous—"

Basingstoke held up a hand, and she trailed off into silence. A good thing, too, because the next word about to fall from her lips was "arse."

"I don't see why Miss Thorne can't join us. She regularly shoots with her father at home, and knows the rigors involved. She's a crack shot, too, Montford. You should see—"

"No, I shouldn't see, and I won't, because she isn't coming with us." Montford crossed his arms over his chest, his dark green frock coat pulling tight at his wide shoulders.

And here it came again, the word "arse," burbling up in her throat, clawing its way into her mouth—

"What's your objection, Montford?"

"She's not . . . she can't . . ." For an instant, Montford seemed not to recall why he objected so strenuously, but then he turned a baleful glare on her and pointed a finger at her skirts. "She doesn't have the proper clothing. Look at her! She'll slow us all down with those heavy skirts, her hems catching on every tree and shrub! She'll scare the grouse away with all those yards of wool dragging after her."

Why, the nerve of the man, using a lady's riding habit

against her! "I do beg your pardon, Your Grace. Would you prefer I wear breeches, instead?"

"Now you mention it, Miss Thorne, I would quite like to see—"

"Never mind, Montford." Basingstoke shot him a quelling glance. "Really, I don't see what all the fuss is about. We'll take the shooting brake and make up for any lost time that way."

"Please don't make any special arrangements on my account, Your Grace." Prue glared at Montford. "I'm quite accustomed to walking in skirts, and perfectly happy to do so."

"I've no doubt of it, Miss Thorne, and you needn't ride if you don't wish to, but we'll bring it along, so any of the party that does choose to ride may do so. Now then, does that satisfy you, Montford?"

"No, Basingstoke, it doesn't." Montford stalked off toward the stables, and spent the short time required to ready the shooting brake huffing under his breath, as if every bird on the Duke of Basingstoke's twelve-hundred-acre estate was sure to fly away during the brief delay.

"Goodness, Montford is out of temper this morning, isn't he?" Franny murmured, taking Prue aside to straighten her hat. "You did say you came to an agreement last night?"

"We did." Hadn't they? Montford had his earrings back, and she . . . well, she wasn't going to Bridewell for blackmailing a duke, which was more than she deserved. "At least, I thought we had."

"How strange." Franny glanced at Montford, who was still fuming. "Whatever is the matter with him, I wonder?"

"I haven't the faintest idea, but I'm resolved not to pay any attention to him for the rest of the day."

"That's probably for the best." Franny gave her crooked

hat one final tilt, then gave up and leaned closer, her voice swelling with suppressed laughter. "Otherwise, you might be tempted to shoot him."

As it happened, she *wasn't* tempted to shoot Montford, mainly because he kept far away from her for the entire day. She felt his dark, brooding gaze on her more than once, but every time she attempted to catch his eye, he scowled and looked away.

By the time the afternoon arrived she was, however, tempted to injure *herself*. Just something trifling—a turned ankle, perhaps—but bad enough so she might escape what had turned into a truly wretched outing.

She was soaked to the bone within the first hour. By the second hour, the coarse wool of her riding habit had rubbed every inch of her skin raw. One of her boots sprang a leak, and the poor little feather in her hat was clinging desperately to its soggy bit of ribbon.

If it had only been the dreadful weather, she could have borne it. It was hardly her first wet shooting party. This was England, after all. Neither would a day spent tramping up and down hills and through heavy under-brush have troubled her much, though it was a good deal more exhausting than she'd anticipated to drag a stone's worth of skirts behind her with every step.

Montford had been right about that, drat him.

But in the end, what had truly worn her spirit down to a thin, feeble thread was Montford's obvious displeasure in her presence. The weight of that disapproving glare cut through her until she felt like a pale imitation of herself, a weary, bedraggled ghost moving silently through the dripping trees.

But she kept on as the afternoon waned, her legs

wobbling with fatigue and her finger shaking on the trigger of her borrowed shotgun. Montford might scowl at her as much as he pleased, but she wouldn't give him the satisfaction of knowing he'd been right.

And there was one bright spot in the day. Colonel Kingston had remained by her side for most of the morning, chatting cheerfully. He was charming company, and the amusing tales he told of his time in His Majesty's Army were quite diverting.

When at last they finished their sport and turned back toward Basingstoke House, the colonel climbed into the brake and patted the seat beside him. "Come, Miss Thorne, take pity on an old man's weary bones, and keep me company."

Perhaps the colonel was truly weary, or perhaps he'd only resorted to the brake to give her an excuse to ride without losing her dignity, but by that point, she no longer cared. She joined him and they rode along, chatting companionably about her father and Thornewood, and the quiet life they lived in Wiltshire.

They were halfway to Basingstoke House when Blount stopped the party and gestured to a small, rocky area surrounded by a thin stand of oak trees. "We've had good luck with the grouse here the past two seasons, Your Grace, if the gentlemen—and the lady—wish for one last foray."

Prue *didn't* wish for one last foray, but she could feel Montford's gaze on her once again, and her pride wouldn't permit her to rest while the gentlemen shot. So, she dragged herself from the brake and drew her cloak as tightly as she could around her shivering body.

The beaters came forward to rouse the game, and she raised her shotgun and took aim, but just as the grouse began to flee their cover, the sky opened and released a heavy torrent of rain upon them, and her hat chose that moment to admit defeat. The brim collapsed, and a deluge of cold rainwater water flooded into her eyes, blinding her just as a frantic flutter of wings churned through the air.

A half a dozen shots rang out at once, and her own gun jerked back hard against her shoulder, the recoil stunning her. Had she shot? She lowered the muzzle, dazed. A metallic odor flooded her nose, and a thin curl of smoke drifted from the barrel.

"Man down! Man down!"

The shots were still echoing around them when the shout went up, half a dozen men, all of them shouting at once. Her rifle fell from her nerveless fingers and tumbled to the ground. She backed away from it, the gentlemen's cries ringing in her ears.

"It's Montford! Montford's been shot!"

Footsteps thundered past her as the men all raced toward Montford, rainwater flying from their coats, their boots splashing in the muck. The rain was falling in sheets now, pounding the ground around her. She blinked against it, her gaze locked on the man in the bottle-green frock coat at the center of the melee, his black top hat lying on the ground beside him.

Montford.

She'd shot the Duke of Montford.

CHAPTER 14

"Jasper, my boy, your backside looks like a plate of braised beef tongue."

Heavy footsteps shuffled across the floor, interspersed with the muted thud of a walking stick. A moment later a pair of feet and a gnarled hand gripping a familiar gold lion's head appeared in Jasper's sightline, and his grandfather's shadow fell over him. "Good God. You've done it this time, haven't you, lad?"

"*I've* done it? Do you suppose I shot *myself* in the arse?" Jasper was lying on his stomach on his bed, his head resting on his arms, a mountain of pillows wedged under his hips, and his bare arse on display to anyone who happened to stroll through the door.

"Eh, well, better a shot to the backside than one between the eyes."

"No, it bloody *isn't*." He usually made it a point not to curse in his grandfather's presence, but a load of birdshot to the arse had a way of loosening a man's tongue. "At least a shot between the eyes is quick."

"That's so. It'll kill you, though." His grandfather dropped into the chair beside the bed with a sigh. "Bit of a drawback, that."

"I'm going to die anyway—slowly, of humiliation. That hazel-eyed hellion blasted a half dozen holes into my backside!"

"I know it, lad. I saw it happen. Remarkable shot, really. Not one in a hundred men could have done it so neatly. The lady's a markswoman."

Jasper craned his neck to scowl at his grandfather. "She missed the damned bird and shot me instead! How the devil is that remarkable?"

"She didn't miss, lad. She got the grouse, too, but you didn't notice it because you were on the ground by then, howling like a banshee." His grandfather shook his head. "I don't know that I've ever heard you howl like that before."

"Yes, well, I daresay you'd howl, too, if you'd been shot." Jasper shifted on the bed, wincing. Christ, it felt like his arse was on fire. "I warned Basingstoke not to bring Miss Thorne out this morning." He'd been right all along, and now he had the arse to prove it.

"What was that all about, lad? Why were you so insistent she not go out today?"

"Because only yesterday she was nearly killed in a riding accident! For God's sake, has everyone but me forgotten about that? I didn't want to see her shot, any more than I wanted to see her neck broken!"

His grandfather stared at him. "You mean to say you were concerned for Miss Thorne's welfare, lad? *That's* why you objected?"

"Yes! That is, it's nothing to do with Miss Thorne, of course. I would have been as concerned about any lady in such a situation."

"Well, I'll be damned," his grandfather murmured.

"But did Basingstoke listen to me? No! By all rights it should be *him* lying here with an arse full of birdshot."

His grandfather made a strangled noise that sounded suspiciously like a smothered laugh. "Now, lad, there's no need to take on so. The doctor says it's not a serious wound. You'll be as good as new soon."

Not soon enough. When he'd set out this morning he'd had a fine-looking arse—more than one lady had remarked on it—and now instead of a charming dimple in his left cheek he'd have scars, thanks to Prudence Thorne. It had taken the chit a single afternoon to destroy one of the prettiest arses in England. "She shot me on purpose."

"That's not fair, Jasper. Miss Thorne never meant you any harm. I've never seen a lady more upset than she was this afternoon. It was an accident. No visibility with all that rain, you know."

"Bollocks. You just said she's a markswoman." Prudence Thorne could ride, and she could shoot. God help them all if she ever got hold of a fencing foil. "I'm telling you, Grandfather, she was waiting all day for a shot at me. When she got my poor, vulnerable arse in her sights, she took it."

His grandfather chuckled. "Aye, the girl's got pluck, doesn't she?"

"*Pluck*? Is that what you'd call it?" For God's sake, if she'd aimed just a little higher, he'd be lying here with his brains leaking onto his pillow. "She wanted her revenge on me, and she bloody well got it."

A brief silence fell, and when his grandfather spoke again, his voice had gone dangerously soft. "Revenge? Revenge for *what*, lad?"

Hell, and damnation. "Er, nothing. Pardon me, Grandfather, but I'm feeling a bit faint—"

"Why should Major Thorne's girl want revenge on you?" His grandfather rapped the floor with the tip of his walking stick. "Best to just confess it now, lad, for I'll find it out one way or another."

That was true enough. God knew the old man had eyes everywhere. He made it his business to know everything about Jasper, from the flavor of tarts he favored at his breakfast table to the flavor of the tarts he favored in his bed.

His grandfather would find out about his wager with Major Thorne. There was little doubt of that, yet that wasn't the reason a confession was hovering on the tip of his tongue.

Or not the *only* reason.

His conscience, usually so reliably silent, had been pricking at him ever since that damnable wager with Thorne. A proper gentleman would have forgiven the debt from the start. At the very least, when Miss Thorne came to him with the earrings, he should have realized how desperate she was, and permitted himself to be blackmailed. If he'd only done as she asked the first time, his perfect arse dimple might still be intact.

Prudence Thorne was a termagant of the first degree, yes—a hellion, a menace who should be forbidden from ever wielding another weapon—but he couldn't quite convince himself all the blame for the chaos between them could be laid upon her shoulders.

Or he *hadn't* believed it, until she'd shot him in the arse.

"Jasper? I asked you a question."

"Yes, alright. I sat down to cards with Major Thorne at Lord Hasting's ball at the start of last season, and he lost a sum of money to me."

"Ah. A large sum, I take it?"

"For Major Thorne, yes. Fifteen hundred pounds. I never should have agreed to play so deeply with him in the first place. He can't afford it, and Miss Thorne has borne me a grudge ever since."

"I see. Is that all?"

"Not exactly, no. That day you met Miss Thorne on the street outside my townhouse, she'd come to ask me to forgive the remainder of her father's debt, and I—I refused."

"Oh, Jasper."

Jasper winced. His grandfather's voice was heavy with disappointment, and rightly so, but it wasn't as if Miss Thorne was blameless in this thing. His grandfather might not be quite so impressed with her pluck if he knew she'd stolen his earrings and tried to blackmail him with them.

But the less said about the earrings, the better. Mention of them would lead to all manner of uncomfortable questions, and the answers would give his grandfather an apoplexy. "Miss Thorne's only other way of settling the debt is to marry a gentleman of means, so the Duchess of Basingstoke arranged for Lord Stoneleigh to court her, and—"

"Stoneleigh? What, you mean that fool of a vicar? That popinjay is Miss Thorne's suitor?" His grandfather's thick white brows lowered. "Good God, lad, is it any wonder she shot you?"

Perhaps not, when one looked at it that way, but he wasn't to blame for Stoneleigh, at least. "I *told* Basingstoke Miss Thorne is too good to be cursed to a lifetime of marriage with Stoneleigh! I *told* him Stoneleigh is a devil hiding under a vicar's cassock! I don't know what Basingstoke's thinking, encouraging a lady like Miss Thorne to throw herself away on a buffoon like—" He broke off when he noticed his grandfather was staring at him. "What?"

"Nothing at all, lad, only you've gone to a good deal of trouble on Miss Thorne's behalf. A good deal of trouble, indeed."

Heat rose into Jasper's cheeks until his face was as hot as his arse. "I didn't do it for *her*," he muttered, his reply muffled by the pillow covering his face. "I did it to save *myself* from a guilty conscience, that's all."

"Very well, but you haven't absolved yourself yet, lad. Miss Thorne's father still owes you a debt, doesn't he?"

Yes, he bloody did, but not for lack of trying on *his* part. How the devil had Miss Thorne managed to snatch defeat from the jaws of almost certain victory at billiards last night? He'd never come across a more contrary woman in his life. "He does, yes."

"Then your copybook is still smudged, lad."

"Not for long. I'll forgive the debt. Between that and the birdshot lodged in my arse, I believe I can consider myself absolved of any obligation to Miss Thorne."

With the debt forgiven, she could rid herself of Stoneleigh. Beyond that, she was no longer his concern, and not a moment too soon. It was just as well she'd shot him, as it had snapped him out of his preoccupation with her.

It would be one thing if he merely despised her, or didn't. Lusted after her, or didn't. Admired her, or didn't. He could dismiss her from his thoughts easily enough, then. But the trouble with Prudence Thorne was, she didn't fit into any of the proper categories.

What was a man meant to do with a woman like that? It was bloody exhausting, trying to work it out. Well, he was done with it. From now on he'd simply wash his hands of her and save his sympathies for the poor devil who ended up marrying her.

Now that was settled, there was nothing left to do

but take a nap. He gave his pillow a few good whacks to plump it up and buried his face in it, closing his eyes. "Shall we talk again later, Grandfather? I find myself rather fatigued. Blood loss, I daresay—"

"You're going to marry Prudence Thorne."

Jasper peeled one eye open. Odd, but it had almost sounded like his grandfather had said he was going to *marry* Miss Thorne. "I beg your pardon?"

"Miss Thorne, lad. You're going to marry her."

Strange. He understood the words, but they made no sense when put together in that order. Perhaps he'd already fallen asleep and was having a nightmare. He peeled the other eye open. "One more time, if you would."

"You heard me, Jasper. I like the girl. She's got spirit."

"Spirit?" Jasper forgot his injury entirely and jerked up, only to fall forward on his face again with a hiss. Damn it, but that hurt, like a swarm of bees all stinging his arse at once. "She has a temper, and she's a bloody good shot. Only a fool would marry such a woman."

"A lady of courage like that, a lady of sense? She'll do you a world of good. She'll be the making of you, lad. Prudence Thorne is worth a thousand Lady Archers."

For an instant Jasper's mind went utterly blank, but then he let out a laugh—a peculiar one, rather high-pitched. "That's very good, Grandfather! A very good jest, indeed!"

"I'm not jesting, lad." His grandfather's smile was gentle, and he gave Jasper an affectionate pat on the back. "Prudence Thorne is going to be the next Duchess of Montford."

It was the gentleness that did it. The old man wasn't the tender sort. If he was patting and smiling, then he meant what he said. Jasper gaped at him, his mouth opening and closing like a fish's before, at last, he squeaked, "You want me to marry the lady who *shot* me?"

"Yes. A bit awkward, that, but it was an accident, you know. Why, the two of you will laugh about it in a few years' time."

"In a few years' time, she'll have murdered me!"

"Take care not to give her reason to, lad, and I daresay you'll survive."

Jasper stared at his grandfather in horror. Dear God, the old man was entirely in earnest.

This was bad. So very, very bad. Bad enough he was having trouble catching his breath. "I didn't think to marry for some years yet, Grandfather—"

"You didn't think to marry at all, you mean. Come, Jasper, let's be candid with each other. I'm perfectly aware you don't wish to marry, just as you're perfectly aware you must do so, regardless of your wishes. You have a duty to your title to produce an heir. A *legitimate* heir."

"But why are you so insistent I marry *now*? I've only just reached my twenty-eighth year. There's plenty of time yet, surely?"

"It's nothing to do with your age, lad. It's about finding the right lady. Miss Thorne is . . ." His grandfather paused, and when he spoke again, his voice was rough. "She puts me in mind of your mother."

Jasper stilled. "M-my mother?"

"Aye. You don't remember her, lad, but Eugenia was a lively one."

His grandfather almost never spoke of Jasper's mother. He had only the haziest memories of her and his father—her dark eyes, and her lips warm on his forehead when she leaned over his bed to kiss him goodnight. His father's strong arms around him, tossing him into the air then catching him again. The scent of orange blossoms . . .

And laughter. So much laughter.

He'd gone to live with his grandfather right after they died, and he used to spend hours staring up at their portraits, a lost little boy in his grandfather's silent portrait gallery, concentrating so intently on their faces, determined not to forget them—

"Eugenia never let your father get away with a thing." His grandfather sighed, and there was a world of grief in the sound. "He grew to love that about her."

That was . . . well, he didn't know quite what to say to that. "But you can't truly think Prudence Thorne is the right lady for me. She *shot* me!" Why did his grandfather keep overlooking that?

"On the contrary, Jasper, I'm convinced she *is* the right lady for you. You don't see it yet, but she's the lady you've been waiting for."

"She won't have me." Of course, she wouldn't, so there was no need to panic. The parson's mousetrap hadn't snapped closed just yet.

"Find a way to see to it that she does. You have a winning way with the ladies."

"Not with Miss Thorne. She despises me."

"No, she doesn't. Far from it, lad." His grandfather braced his hand on his walking stick, heaved himself to his feet and shuffled toward the door, but he paused when he reached it. "You've had your share of scandals, boy. I don't deny it. But you're a good lad at heart, and you deserve to be happy. Search inside yourself, Jasper, and you'll see I'm right about this."

Jasper spent a long time after his grandfather left staring at the length of headboard in front of him. It was an

Italian monstrosity, with all manner of whorls and figures carved into the dark mahogany.

He reached out to trace one of the curves with his fingertip.

For years the *ton* had been whispering about the day his grandfather would lose patience with him and cut him off without a penny. He didn't need his grandfather's money, of course—he was a duke, and the sole heir of his father's title and fortune.

But it wasn't about the money. It never had been.

He and his grandfather didn't see eye to eye on most things, and he knew his grandfather was disappointed in him. Not that he blamed the old man for it. He'd been a wastrel since he'd been sent down from Oxford for brawling, and in the ten years since, he hadn't done much to redeem himself, so perhaps he'd earned his grandfather's disappointment.

But his grandfather was the only family he had. The only family he'd ever had. Since he was a boy, it had only ever been the two of them, and the thing was . . . if you failed the one person in the world who cared the most about you, the only person who'd been there from the beginning, who knew all your flaws and weaknesses and still believed in the goodness of your heart . . .

If you failed that person, then what did you have left?

He had to marry sooner or later. His grandfather was right about that. It wouldn't be a love match no matter whom he married, so why wouldn't Miss Thorne do as well as any other lady? She'd blackmailed him and shot him, yes, but even then, she was still far from the poisonous viper Selina had been.

It wasn't as if his life would change much once he was married, either. He'd go on mainly as he had before, and Miss Thorne would be free to do the same.

He abandoned his contemplation of the headboard and reached for the bell. Loftus must have been hovering close by, because he was at Jasper's bedside in an instant. "What can I do, Your Grace? Are you in pain? Shall I fetch the laudanum?"

"No, Loftus. Help me to dress, will you?"

Loftus gasped. "Oh, but Your Grace! You mustn't—"

"I'm not looking forward to it any more than you are Loftus, but there's something I must do, and it can't wait. Now, help me to dress, won't you?"

"Of course, I will, Your Grace." Loftus threw back his shoulders. "Of course, I will."

CHAPTER 15

"You haven't spoken a single word in the last hour, Prue. I don't believe I've even seen you twitch." Franny laid aside the sheet music she'd been reading and turned to Prue with a frown. "You're beginning to make me quite nervous."

"Imagine how much more nervous you'd be if I had a shotgun in my hands." Prue attempted a laugh, but it disintegrated into a pitiful sniffle on her lips. "Oh dear. That isn't funny, is it?"

After today, nothing may ever be funny again.

They'd returned from the ill-fated shooting party hours ago, Prue hatless and wild-eyed and Montford laid in the brake, his face white and twisted with pain. Franny had assessed the situation in one glance, and whisked Prue off to her private music room, ordering Trevor not to admit anyone aside from her husband.

Prue had fallen onto a settee, shivering with cold and shock, and had scarcely moved a muscle since. Every part of her was numb, from her fingertips to the soles of her wet feet.

"It was an accident, dearest." Franny rose with a sigh

and joined Prue on the settee. "A consequence of wretched weather and poor visibility, nothing more."

Prue only nodded in reply. Another sob was lurking on the end of her tongue. If she opened her mouth, it might escape.

"An accident," Franny repeated firmly, giving Prue's hand a brisk pat. "Everyone in the shooting party said so."

They had, yes, only . . . had it been an accident? She'd been so *angry* with Montford when they'd left that morning, so baffled by his behavior. How could a man kiss her so sweetly one moment, then shout at her in front of two dozen aristocratic gentlemen the next?

She'd been beside herself after that scene in the courtyard, so distressed she scarcely knew which way was up anymore. Wasn't it possible her subconscious had taken matters into her own hands? Mightn't it be the case that her subconscious was a wicked, murdering villainess?

Even if her subconscious was innocent, and it truly had been an accident, it couldn't be denied that a great many *accidents* seemed to occur whenever she and the Duke of Montford were together. Lost rubies, blackmail schemes, runaway horses, random shootings.

Perhaps Fate was trying to tell them something?

"Montford is going to be perfectly fine," Franny offered, when Prue still didn't speak. "The doctor assured us he would be."

"I know." She had to scrape the words up from her raw throat. Most of the birdshot had only grazed Montford, not punctured his flesh. His injury was painful, certainly, and it would take weeks to fully heal, but he wasn't in any danger.

"This won't look nearly so dire tomorrow, I promise you." Franny touched her cool fingertips to Prue's cheek and rose to her feet. "I'm off to bed. Might I suggest you come up, as well? You're still too shaky and pale for my liking."

No doubt, but there was no rest to be had in her bed-chamber. Still, she managed a half-hearted smile for her friend. "You go on. I won't be far behind."

She stared into the fire for some time after the door closed behind Franny, but it was too quiet. So very quiet, the silence giving her too much space to ruminate over the utter disaster she'd made of everything since she'd arrived in London.

What sort of lady came to Town to be courted by a baron, and instead ended up nearly killing a duke? If she hadn't already been convinced that she wasn't destined to marry, then she certainly was *now*.

Of course, there was no longer any question of her marrying Lord Stoneleigh—not after the brake had arrived at the front entrance of Basingstoke House with poor Montford laid out along the seats in the back, the buff-colored breeches that had done such credit to his long, muscular legs splattered with blood.

As soon as Lord Stoneleigh heard the tale of Montford's accident, he couldn't get away from Basingstoke House quickly enough. He hadn't spared even so much as a glance for her, nor had he taken any leave of her, though that omission was rather a leave-taking in itself, wasn't it?

As Franny had said once before, bleeding wounds did tend to put rather a damper on one's passions. Not that Lord Stoneleigh had ever felt any true passion for her, any more than she had for him. It was for the best he'd gone. She never would have been able to bring herself to marry him.

So, she was—somewhat inexplicably, considering all that had happened—right back where she'd started, before she'd left Wiltshire. Well, nearly so. She'd since blackmailed and shot the Duke of Montford in the back-side. If blackmailing a duke didn't land her in Bridewell, shooting one certainly might.

So, rather worse than where she'd started.

Perhaps it would be for the best if she returned to Wilt-shire, before she made another blunder. Franny would object to her leaving so abruptly, but deep down she'd be relieved to see Prue go. Goodness knew she wasn't doing either herself or anyone else any good remaining here.

Yes, she'd speak with Franny tomorrow morning. She rose to her feet and dragged herself toward the door, weary down to her bones, but as she made her way down the hallway toward the staircase, she paused in the doorway of the billiards room.

It was dark, the grate cold, but she entered anyway, shivering at the chill in the air as she approached the billiards table and took up one of the balls, running her fingers over the smooth surface.

Did Montford believe she'd intended to shoot him? When her shot struck him, tearing into his flesh, did he think, even for an instant, that she'd *meant* to hurt him? That she was taking revenge for her father's wager, or her loss to him at billiards last night?

Or did he imagine it was their kiss that had offended her? Oh, that was a wretched thought, unbearable—

"Have you come for another game, Miss Thorne? One would think you'd have learned your lesson by now."

She whirled toward the door, her heart vaulting into her throat. A tall, broad-shouldered shadow was leaning against the door frame, as if she'd conjured him from her imagination alone. His face was cast in darkness, but the dim light from the hallway behind him caught the gleam of disheveled dark curls, the grim curve of his lips, the lazy arrogance with which he lounged in the doorway.

"I—I—aren't you meant to be in bed?" For pity's sake, the man had been *shot* only hours earlier! What was he doing, prowling about when he'd just suffered a load of birdshot to his backside? "Why are you downstairs?"

"Are you not pleased to see me, Miss Thorne?" He straightened from his fashionable slouch and came toward her—no, *stalked* toward her, like a predator who'd spied his next meal, and was already salivating with the anticipation of sinking his teeth into it.

She retreated a step, even as she cursed herself for her cowardice. "If you're looking for the Duke of Basingstoke, he isn't here. He's retired for the evening."

A soft laugh floated toward her from the darkness. "I didn't come for Basingstoke, Miss Thorne. I came for *you*."

Oh, dear God, here it was, the consequences of her foolishness, creeping from the darkness and looking much taller, sturdier, and more forbidding than she'd ever seen him look before. "I, ah, I beg your pardon, Your Grace, for, er . . . for—"

"Shooting me in the arse?"

She winced. "Well, yes. I hope you know I didn't mean . . . I never intended to . . . the brim of my hat collapsed, you see, and the water splashed into my face. Rather a lot of water, in fact, and I'm afraid I pulled the trigger, er . . . accidentally."

He drew closer, a dark chuckle on his lips. "That's an extraordinary story, Miss Thorne."

"It's not a story, Your Grace." She raised her chin. "It's the truth."

"Perhaps so, though you must allow it looks suspicious, given our history. Stolen jewels, blackmail, secret wagers." He tutted, shaking his head. "You lead a rather dangerous life, Miss Thorne, for an innocent young lady from Wiltshire."

Not so dangerous she wished to tangle with *him*, however. "Stay where you are, if you please, Your Grace." Without thinking, she darted around to the other side of the billiards table, putting it between them, her fingers tightening around the heavy ball in her hand. A bit melodramatic, perhaps, but at least her voice hadn't been shaking.

Much.

He paused in his pursuit, surprise flashing across his face. "For God's sake, Miss Thorne, I'm not going to *hurt* you. What sort of man do you take me for?"

"An angry one." She was grateful for the darkness, as her cheeks were so hot, they'd undoubtedly gone scarlet. Goodness, when had she become such a coward? "What is it you want from me?"

He approached the table, but he didn't venture any closer, only plucked up one of the billiard balls. "I had a rather unexpected visit from my grandfather this evening." His long fingers curved around the ball as he weighed it in his hand. "I believe you and he have become rather friendly, have you not?"

"We have, yes." That had been one of the worst things about the, er . . . mishap this afternoon. She *liked* his grandfather. Colonel Kingston was a proud, stately old gentleman. A bit gruff, yes, but charming in his own way, like her father was.

And this afternoon he'd watched her shoot his only grandson.

"You've made quite an impression on him." He tossed the billiard ball up in the air and caught it again as if it weighed no more than a feather. "I can't say I've ever seen him as determined as he was when he came to see me in my bedchamber this evening."

"I beg your pardon, Your Grace, but I don't see what this has to do with me." Nor did she wish to, by the look of him. He was polite enough, but there was something dark underlying his calm, as if he were holding onto his temper by the slimmest thread.

"You may beg all you like, Miss Thorne, but I'm afraid it's much too late for that. You've made your bed, and now you'll be obliged to lie in it. Or perhaps I should say, we'll both be obliged to lie in it, *together*."

Lie in bed, together? For one wild moment, an image flashed behind her eyelids. The Duke of Montford as he'd been in the painting, every inch of his body on glorious display, from his smooth, olive skin to the crisp, dark hair dusting his chest, his flat, taut belly, as well as the other . . . anatomical curiosities.

She swallowed. "Together?"

"That's right, Miss Thorne. Together, until death parts us."

The words bounced about inside her skull, slamming into each other with an ominous crack, but even as her ears rang with them, they made no sense. He couldn't possibly be saying what it sounded like he was. "I don't . . . *what*? What in the world do you mean?"

"My grandfather is what you might call an eccentric, Miss Thorne." He tossed the ball up in the air and caught it again without ever sparing it a glance, his dark gaze never leaving her face. "The sorts of things that would rightly anger another man—things like a young lady shooting his grandson, for instance—don't necessarily have the same effect on him."

Was that a good thing? She worked over his words in

her spinning head, but try as she might, she couldn't make sense of them. "I don't understand."

"No, I don't imagine you do. If you'd had the least idea what you were getting us both into, I daresay you would have been more careful, and held your tongue rather than ingratiating yourself with him. It *is* possible, isn't it, Miss Thorne? For you to hold that impertinent tongue of yours?"

She crossed her arms over her chest, nettled. "On occasion, yes. Is it possible for you, Your Grace, to speak plainly? Or did you come here tonight to play games with me?"

"You wish me to speak plainly?" He dropped the ball onto the baize and leaned over the table, his hands braced on the sides and those dark, dark eyes fixed on her face. "Very well, Miss Thorne. Plainly speaking, I've come in search of you tonight to offer my hand to you."

His *hand*? She must have misheard him, because when a gentleman offered a lady his hand, that meant . . . no, it was out of the question, impossible—

"You look puzzled, Miss Thorne. Permit me to explain. My grandfather is, as I said, eccentric, and instead of being angry with you for today's stunt, as anyone in their right mind would be, he admires your *pluck*." He spit this last word out from between clenched teeth.

"Pluck," she repeated faintly. "But I—"

"I'm not finished, Miss Thorne. He so admires your pluck, in fact, that he's decided you'd make me an ideal bride. A lady such as yourself—a lady of such courage, such spirit, such extraordinary mettle is, according to my daft grandfather, the only lady in London who can possibly manage his devil of a grandson."

With every word from his lips her mouth had gone drier, until, instead of making words, her tongue flopped about uselessly like a fish caught on an angling line. Try as she might, she couldn't get a single intelligible word past her lips.

"What, nothing to say *now*, Miss Thorne? Not a single word? May I take your uncharacteristic silence as acceptance of my hand, then?"

That loosened her tongue quickly enough. "Of course, you may not! For pity's sake, Your Grace, this is utter madness! Why didn't you simply tell your grandfather *no*?"

A strange expression crossed his face then, one she couldn't read. "That, Miss Thorne, is far easier said than done."

He could only mean one thing by that. "He holds your purse strings?"

"In a manner of speaking, I suppose, but this isn't about money. My grandfather has wished for some years now for me to find a suitable bride, and this time I've made up my mind not to disappoint him."

"But I'm *not* a suitable bride! I'm not fashionable, I have no money, no family, no connections—"

"Ah, but you have something other ladies don't have, Miss Thorne."

What? Whatever elusive quality he imagined she possessed she almost certainly did *not*. "What would that be, Your Grace?"

His lip curled. "*Pluck*."

Oh, for pity's sake. "Nonsense. That doesn't make me a suitable bride for a *duke*."

"In my grandfather's eyes, it does. He's set his heart on you, Miss Thorne."

"But *you* haven't! I should think that would make a difference to him."

He shrugged. "I have to take a wife sooner or later. It may as well be you."

"One would think, Your Grace, that you'd choose a wife with more care than a coat or a new pair of boots." But then *he* hadn't chosen her at all, had he? His grandfather had.

"Permit me to be perfectly clear, Miss Thorne. This isn't a romance. A marriage between us would be a business arrangement, nothing more. We'll fulfill our obligations as the Duke and Duchess of Montford, but otherwise, we'll lead entirely separate lives."

My, how tempting! What lady could possibly refuse such a tender offer? "You're a *duke*," she said again. If she repeated it enough times, perhaps she could make him understand. "If I marry you, I'll be a *duchess*."

"That is the way it generally works, yes."

"But I don't *want* to be a duchess!" God above, if ever there was a lady who wasn't suited for such a grand title, it was *her*.

He snorted. "Don't be absurd. Every young lady wants to become a duchess."

"No, you don't understand! I'm not . . . I can't . . ." She wasn't elegant, she didn't care for drawing, company, gossip, or fashions. She didn't play, sing, paint, sew, or embroider, and she was a fish out of water when it came to performing in the drawing room.

Even more to the point, she didn't care for the Duke of Montford. "I don't even *like* you."

Oh, dear. Perhaps she might have said that with a trifle more kindness, or at the very least, not quite so *loudly*. But Montford only smirked. "Nor I you, I assure you, Miss Thorne, but why let a small thing like a deep and abiding mutual antipathy get in the way of a marriage between us?"

Why, he was as mad as his grandfather was! It seemed as if neither of them had the least intention of putting a stop to this scheme, so she'd have to do it for them. "No, Your Grace. I can't—indeed, I won't marry you. Not under any circumstances. So, you may tell your grandfather you offered your hand, and I refused you."

With that, she came around the side of the billiards table, intending to sweep by him and out the door, her head high, but he caught her wrist as she passed. "Just a moment, Miss Thorne. We haven't finished talking."

"Yes, we have." She tugged on her arm, but while he remained gentle, he also didn't let her go, instead drawing her closer, and goodness, he was tall—her head barely reached the center of his chest. The scent of orange blossom, amber, and a hint of brandy enveloped her, and all at once, she couldn't get away from him quickly enough. "Let go of me, Your Grace."

"Not just yet, Miss Thorne. I freely admit I have no wish to marry you—I've no wish to marry at all, come to that—but my grandfather has made his wishes clear. He's forcing my hand, and so, I'm forcing yours. It's that simple."

"Forcing! Don't be absurd, Your Grace. You can't *force* me to marry you."

"No? Your father still owes me five hundred pounds, Miss Thorne. I can call in that debt anytime I choose. Now, for instance."

"But he doesn't have it!" Dread tightened her chest and writhed like a serpent in the hollow of her stomach. "We . . . we don't have it."

She met his gaze, but instead of the triumph she expected to see, his eyes were bleak. "You came to London determined to save your father and your home with an advantageous marriage. Would marriage to me really be so much worse than marriage to Stoneleigh?"

She squeezed her eyes closed. "I—I don't know."

She'd never been less certain of anything in her life, yet how was she to find her way out of it? She no longer had a pocketful of scandalous jewels to bargain with. Her father couldn't pay the five hundred pounds until they sold Thornewood, and once they did, where were they meant to go? They'd have no home, no money.

She was caught, and there would be no scheming her way free. Not this time.

"Think about it, Miss Thorne. If we marry, you need never worry about money again, and you'll enjoy a great deal more freedom as the Duchess of Montford than you ever could as plain Miss Thorne."

Freedom. That magical thing, as elusive as turreted castles and winged horses. Her mind seized on the word, held it tight.

"I'll give you until tomorrow to give me your answer." Montford released her and stepped back, offering her a stiff bow. "Until then, good night."

Then he was gone, melting back into the shadows, leaving her alone in the cold room, his words echoing in her head.

CHAPTER 16

It had been nearly a year since Prue had first laid eyes on the Duke of Montford, and she hadn't enjoyed an entirely restful night since.

Tonight, the last night she would spend at Basingstoke House was no different. She lay in the dark for hours, arms flung wide atop the enormous bed like a beached starfish. It was the most decadent bed she'd ever lain upon, so wide she couldn't reach the sides even with the most determined stretch, but it seemed one could remain sleepless in a grand bed as easily as a humble one.

She gave up at last, abandoned the bed, and curled up into the window seat with the coverlet pulled tightly around her shoulders. Her window looked down on the south garden, the full moon casting its bright rays over the roses, the silvery beams trickling over the vivid bursts of color.

Bright scarlet, buttery yellow, sunset pink, and creamy ivory.

She drew her knees up to her chest, shivering a little in the chill, and rested her temple against the cool glass. Tomorrow was her wedding day.

Tomorrow, she would become the Duchess of Montford.

Her father wasn't pleased about it. He'd arrived at Basingstoke House yesterday afternoon looking like a thundercloud, ready to bundle her into their ancient carriage and drag her straight back to Thornewood before she could "put herself into the hands of that ruinous scoundrel, Montford."

His words, not hers.

She didn't blame him for it. Despite her father's modern notions about female capabilities, from the moment she'd been born he'd watched over her with the eagle-eyed protectiveness with which all fond fathers did their daughters. To blame him now would be to blame him for loving her too much, and that she could never do.

Fortunately, Colonel Kingston had taken him in hand. She had no idea what the colonel had said to soothe her father's ruffled feelings—the most he'd confided to her was that the colonel had spoken plain sense, one military man to another—but eventually her father had given her his reluctant blessing.

And so, here she was, mere hours away from becoming a duchess.

Goodness, how *strange* that sounded.

After the ceremony, she and Montford would remain in Kent only long enough to enjoy a small, private wedding breakfast, then they would leave for London, and Montford's lavish townhouse in Berkeley Square.

What they would do once they arrived there . . . well, that was anyone's guess really, but presumably they'd each of them get on with the business of pursuing their own lives. Montford had made it clear this was no love match, but merely a marriage of convenience. She had every expectation he'd go on in much the same way he'd done before their marriage, though one would hope he'd be a trifle more discreet about it.

That thought made her chest tighten with a curious pang, but she took care not to dwell on it. How had Montford put it? They'd made their bed, and now they'd be obliged to lie in it, together.

But there were worse things than becoming a duchess, and it must be acknowledged that since she'd accepted his proposals, Montford had been exceedingly polite to her.

Excruciatingly polite.

Theirs would be a courteous marriage, if nothing else.

But there was no sense in worrying over those things she couldn't control. Instead, she would focus on the ways in which her marriage would benefit herself and her father. It would take the burden of debt from their shoulders, as well as the burden of any future financial worries. Then there was Thornewood, her beloved home, which would soon be restored to them.

She might go back to visit it at any time she wished.

But most of all, she thought about freedom. In the end, she'd turned out to be dreadfully selfish, because it was that promise above all the others that had swayed her in favor of the marriage.

Oh, she wasn't so foolish as to believe marriage was her winged horse, her cloudy castle turrets. Marriage never was, for a woman. Any lady of sense recognized that marriage would take far more from her than it gave in return. If anything, most women were more constrained after their marriage than before it, husbands upon the whole being troublesome, demanding creatures.

But then most women didn't marry a duke.

She and Montford had an understanding. Neither of them would seek to curtail the other's freedom. They would each be at liberty to do as they pleased—within reason, of course. And if it sounded a bit lonely, and not much like a marriage at all, the disappointments she endured would be well worth the opportunities she'd receive in exchange.

The trick would be in having the courage to seize them.

She returned her gaze to the garden below her window, to the deserted stone pathways dotted with marble benches, the peaked roof of the stables visible above the spindly aspen trees that bordered the lake. They were young trees yet, their pale bark glowing in the moonlight, but they'd be beautiful one day, with their fluttering leaves soaring into the sky.

London wasn't going to welcome her.

The *ton* was sure to disapprove of their new duchess, an unfashionable upstart from goodness only knew where—some tiresome country village or other. Such an ordinary lady, too, without any accomplishments to speak of, and not even very pretty.

There was only one way she could have caught the elusive Duke of Montford's eye.

By shooting him in the backside, of course.

No doubt the *ton* was already whispering about her, but that scandal was sure to explode with a vengeance once she arrived in London. It would be difficult once it did, and she didn't anticipate Montford would help her much.

So, she'd have to make her own way through it, and there was only one thing to be done in such a situation as that—only one way to manage such overwhelming censure coming from every corner of London.

It was quite simple, really.

She'd survive only if she made up her mind right here, and right now, not to care one whit about any of it. Let the tongues wag, if they must, because cringing and cowardice would only encourage more abuse.

She was giving up a great deal for this marriage, just as every woman before her had done, and by God, she'd seize every little bit of freedom that came her way in return, because she would have *earned* it.

She didn't have to answer to the *ton*, nor did she have to answer to Montford.

She would answer to no one but herself.

She was Prudence Thorne, and Prudence Thorne she would remain, even in the face of the *ton*'s scorn and disapproval. She wouldn't allow herself to be erased once she became the Duchess of Monford.

That was all.

It didn't seem as if she remained in the window seat for long after that, gazing down upon the silent, moonlit grounds, but she must have done, because when she came to herself again it was to the soft chime of the mantel clock.

It chimed twelve chimes, then came the hush after the echo of the ringing faded away.

Her wedding day had arrived.

She remained where she was, her arms wrapped around her legs and the coverlet draped over her shoulders, watching as the moon's glow began to fade and the sun rose over the stable roof, tinting the sky a glorious rosy pink.

The day would be a fine one. Surely, that was a good omen?

"Prue?" There was a tap on the door, and Franny's voice drifted in from the corridor outside her bedchamber. "Are you awake?"

She was indeed, and had been for days. "Yes. Come in, Franny."

Franny opened the door and peeked around it. "You're already out of bed."

Prue rose from the window seat with a smile. "Yes. I couldn't sleep."

"Nervous, I daresay. All brides are anxious on their wedding day."

That was what everyone claimed, yes, but it didn't make much sense to Prue. Surely the wedding was the least of her worries. It was the marriage itself that terrified her.

"You needn't be, you know," Franny went on. "Montford's a dear soul, despite what London may say about him, and Giles and I will be there to help if things should go awry."

Franny and Basingstoke had intended to remain in the country until the end of the month, but once Prue informed Franny of her betrothal, she'd insisted on throwing a ball in honor of the new Duchess of Montford. It would take place in two weeks, and Franny was returning to London at once to plan it.

Prue smiled at her friend and took her hands. "You've been so very good to me, Franny, so patient with all of my, er . . . blunders and mishaps. I daresay you'll be pleased to see me safely wed at last."

"Nonsense. You do know that the more tumultuous the courtship is, the happier the marriage will be, do you not?"

"Is that what they say? I've never heard it before."

"It's what *I* say, dearest, and I offer my own marriage to Basingstoke as proof, though to be fair, we never had a proper courtship. It was more of a skirmish, really, rather like one of the brawls one sees in the pit at the theater. It was all perfectly wretched, I assure you, but you see how I delight in him now. It will be the same for you, you'll see."

Delight, in Montford? That didn't seem likely, but it was unseemly to abuse one's husband on one's wedding day, so she merely smiled again. "Then I'll have nothing else to wish for."

Franny patted her cheek, then turned and threw open the door to the wardrobe. "Now, which of these gowns have you decided on?"

Prue had hardly given a wedding gown a thought, but once she'd accepted Montford's proposals, Franny had appeared in her bedchamber with a half dozen housemaids on her heels, each of them carrying one of Franny's own gowns in their arms. She'd commanded Prue to choose one for her wedding gown and wouldn't hear any arguments to the contrary.

It wasn't as if Prue could marry a duke wearing her worn riding habit and old cloak, after all.

Franny had dozens of gowns that might serve as a wedding ensemble, but after much discussion, they'd narrowed it down to two. One was a pale yellow silk with a full, flowing skirt. It had a sumptuous train, and yards of extravagant embroidered lace at the neck and sleeves and in a panel down the front of the bodice and skirts.

The other was much simpler. It was a creamy ivory color of the thinnest, finest linen imaginable, with a scooped neck, a pleated train that fell in an elegant drape from the shoulders, and long sheer sleeves that ended at the wrists in a wide band of the prettiest lace Prue had ever seen. It was so delicate it looked as if the gentlest of breezes would scatter it like dandelion fluff.

She joined Franny in front of the wardrobe, reaching out a finger to touch the yellow silk. "I hardly know which to choose. They're both so pretty." Except, no, that wasn't the truth at all. The trouble was, the gown she ought to choose wasn't the gown she wanted.

The yellow silk was much grander than the simple ivory gown, and thus far more appropriate a garment in which to wed the Duke of Montford.

But it was the other one she wanted.

The ivory gown was perfection, an utter dream of a gown, from the graceful lines to the exquisiteness of the linen to the restrained lace at the wrists. It was almost painfully simple, but the beauty of it arose from that very simplicity. Even as she fingered the fold of yellow silk, she couldn't tear her gaze away from it.

And she may as well begin as she meant to go on . . .

"The ivory." She turned to Franny, an inexplicable shyness falling over her. "It must be the ivory."

"That's the one I would have chosen for you." Franny squeezed her arm, then removed the ivory gown from the wardrobe and laid it carefully on the bed. "What shall we do for a veil?"

Prue glanced toward the window, thinking of the creamy white roses, so lovely in the silver moonlight, then turned back to Franny and said decisively, "No veil at all, but just a few of the white roses from the garden. Will that do?"

Franny smiled. "I think that will be perfect."

"Alright there, Montford?" Grantham was lounging against Basingstoke's desk, his narrowed gaze fixed on Jasper as if he were ready to leap up at any moment and tackle him around the knees.

"Here, Montford." Basingstoke handed him a small glass of brandy. "A bit of courage for you, just in case."

Jasper took the glass and set it on the desk without tasting it. "There's no need to get me sotted, Basingstoke. As for you, Grantham, do stop hovering over me, if you please. I promise you both I'm not going anywhere."

Though perhaps they might be forgiven for thinking he'd bolt, as he'd once declared he'd sooner seek his coffin than he would the next Duchess of Montford.

"You're taking this all rather well, Montford," Grantham said, swallowing his own brandy. "I expected a great deal more wailing and gnashing of teeth."

"And at least one escape attempt," Basingstoke added.

"If I didn't intend to go through with marrying Miss Thorne, I wouldn't have offered her my hand at all." As it was, he'd made rather a mess of the proposal. A gentleman did not, in the best of circumstances, bully and threaten a lady into marrying him.

If anyone should flee, it was Miss Thorne, but he hadn't seen her running down the drive, so presumably she hadn't crept out a window yet.

"It's nearly time." Basingstoke snapped his watch closed, replaced it in his coat pocket, and took up the discarded glass of brandy, which he once again offered to Jasper. "You're quite sure, Montford?"

"Yes, I'm sure." It wouldn't do for Miss Thorne to catch a whiff of brandy on his breath while he was speaking his wedding vows.

"I'll have it." Grantham took the glass and downed the contents in one swallow. "All this talk of weddings and brides and marriage is rattling my nerves."

"It'll be you next, Grantham," Basingstoke warned. "When the time comes, do try and do it with a bit more grace than Montford or I, won't you? At least one of us should get through it with our dignity intact."

Grantham snorted. "I may never do it at all, and certainly not anytime soon. I'm in no rush to marry, I assure you."

Basingstoke pointed at him with his brandy glass. "You've just cursed yourself, Grantham. Make no mistake, you'll be married by this time next year."

Grantham thumped his glass back down on the desk. "Bollocks."

"Basingstoke's right, Grantham. I said the same, and look at me now." Jasper gave his jacket a tug and straightened his top hat. "The ladies have their way in the end." Though to be fair, it was *him* who'd insisted upon marrying Prue, not the other way around. If it had been left up to her, he'd have been back in London more than a week ago, and very much an unmarried scoundrel still.

It was a strangely disconcerting thought.

"It's not the lady you need to worry about, Montford. It's her father." Grantham grimaced. "I half expected him to challenge you to a duel when he arrived yesterday."

"He didn't look particularly pleased, did he?" God knew what Major Thorne must be thinking. Likely that Jasper had compromised his daughter, and his grandfather was forcing him to marry her.

"Eh, Thorne will come around, Montford." Basingstoke slapped him on the back. "You're making his daughter a duchess, after all."

"Thorne doesn't care for titles any more than his daughter does." The fact that he was a duke wouldn't have saved his skin, but his grandfather had had a word with Thorne, and the man had arrived at the dinner table last night in a better humor. Still not pleased, mind you, but no longer on the verge of doing Jasper an injury.

So, that was one crisis averted. Lucky thing, too, as

nothing cast a pall over a wedding so much as a dead groom.

But despite all the chaos, things appeared to be well underway this morning. Loftus, who lived for such occasions of sartorial splendor, had outfitted him in black breeches—*not* pantaloons, no, indeed—and a black coat and top hat, then in a frenzy of creative inspiration had decided on a pale gold embroidered waistcoat, finished with a double row of gold buttons.

"Right, then, shall we, gentlemen?" Basingstoke straightened his cuffs and turned toward the door, adding over his shoulder, "If you get the urge to bolt, Montford, just say so. Grantham and I will subdue you."

But Jasper was perfectly calm as they made their way to the small, private chapel in the western corner of the estate grounds. Perhaps he was like one of those birds who remained in their gilded cage even after the door was thrown open, suddenly paralyzed by the freedom they'd longed for.

Or perhaps he was just reconciled to his fate. Whatever the reason, there was no need for any unbecoming violence on either Basingstoke or Grantham's part, because he passed over the threshold of the chapel without as much as a murmur of defiance.

It was a beautiful place, with a pair of white marble columns flanking the doorway, and another set of columns on either side of the recessed altar. The wall behind it was done in elaborate gilt scrollwork, the pattern repeating on the high-domed ceiling above.

Hundreds of events had taken place here—hundreds of weddings, baptisms, and funerals. More than a dozen generations of Basingstoke dukes and their families had marked the most important occasions of their lives in this chapel. If all the bridegrooms that came before him could make it through their own wedding ceremonies without bolting or casting up their accounts, then he could do the same.

The chapel was quiet as they all waited for the bride to arrive. Jasper looked over the small party of his dearest friends gathered in the pews, and an unexpected pang gripped his chest. His grandfather was right in the front, his gloved hands folded over the handle of his walking stick. He smiled as his gaze met Jasper's, and he was so clearly bursting with joy it was impossible for Jasper to look at him and believe marrying Prudence Thorne could be a mistake.

Soon enough, there was a stir at the door of the chapel. Prue entered, one hand on Franny's arm and the other on her father's. They paused on the other side of one of the columns so Prue might receive her father's blessing, but he couldn't see her face, only the flutter of a white skirt as a soft breeze drifted through the door.

But in the next instant, everything—the columns, the gilded ceiling, the light pouring in through the half-moon window above the altar, and even his grandfather's encouraging smile faded at the edges of his vision.

The chapel went still, everyone holding their breath as Prue emerged from behind the column and began to walk down the aisle.

He'd imagined he'd be stoic as she came toward him, unmoved, but his heart was beating in a wild tattoo against his ribs, his palms were damp, and his eyes . . . good God, why were his eyes stinging?

He caught his breath when she stopped in front of him at last. He'd always admired her, had always thought her uncommonly lovely, but when he gazed at her now there was something else there, pressing under his breastbone, something more than admiration. He couldn't have said what it was, but it felt like . . . wonder, almost, as if he'd just seen her for the first time.

She was breathtaking, and despite all her finery, somehow still utterly herself. This was the same Prudence Thorne who scolded him for reading her private letters; the same Prudence Thorne who'd stolen his earrings, blackmailed him, and then begged his pardon so sweetly when she'd returned them to him.

She was the same Prudence Thorne he'd kissed, who'd kissed him back without reservation, her cheeks flushed pink in the firelight.

She wore a simple white gown of a linen so soft and fine it looked as if she were wrapped in a cloud. She wore no veil, and no jewels—no ornamentation of any kind, aside from a few creamy white roses in her hair that put him in mind of the pearls he'd slipped into the pocket of her cloak, and since then, had seemingly disappeared.

But *she* was here, standing before him, and without thinking, he reached for her, took her chin between his thumb and forefinger, and tilted her face up to his. "Beautiful," he whispered, and was rewarded when a wash of color climbed into her cheeks and the corners of her lips turned up in a shy smile.

He didn't remember much after that. He must have repeated his vows, and he recalled hearing the same vows spoken back to him in her soft voice, her lips moving, the morning sun from the window above them caressing the white rose petals in her hair.

CHAPTER 17

A man's wedding night was, as it turned out, rather trickier than Jasper had anticipated it would be. A deflowering was a straightforward business, after all, with only one objective, and thus it should have been as easy as sneezing, or snapping his fingers.

It was the solemn duty of every conscientious bridegroom to perform a thousand different tender services on behalf of his innocent bride on their wedding night, but downing three tumblers of brandy before venturing into her virginal bedchamber wasn't one of them.

To be fair, they were small tumblers, but that was due to Loftus's judiciousness rather than to any restraint on Jasper's part.

Even so, one could argue it was two glasses too many.

Perhaps two and a half.

It wasn't as if he'd *meant* to drink three tumblers of brandy. He'd been in good spirits when they left Basingstoke's estate early in the afternoon. He'd acquitted himself rather well at the wedding, and he had every reason to believe he'd do himself credit in the marital bed. One of the few advantages of being a rake was an intimate familiarity with a lady's needs, and it didn't go amiss that his blushing bride had already seen the most startling part of his anatomy.

Or a painting of it at least, but it was quite a good likeness.

But as their carriage rolled along the dusty roads between Kent and London, the daylight slipping by degrees into a deep violet twilight, he was assailed by an unexpected twinge of doubt. By the time the carriage came to a stop at his townhouse in Berkeley Square, the twinge had turned into such a riot of nerves it felt as if he'd swallowed a swarm of bees.

It was the "virginal" part of the business that did him in, though it must be acknowledged the "wife" bit didn't help.

"May I assist you into your banyan, Your Grace?"

"Banyan?" Jasper forced his forlorn gaze from the bottom of his empty brandy glass to Loftus, who was standing beside him with the banyan in his hands, wearing the familiar, infinitely patient expression that indicated he'd been waiting for some time. "Oh, yes. I suppose so."

"Very good, Your Grace." Loftus pried the empty glass from Jasper's fingers, set it on the tray and slid the heavy silk banyan over his arms. "There. May I assist you with anything else, Your Grace?"

"Er . . ." Surely, there was something else? "Is, ah, is the duchess in her bedchamber?" For God's sake, what an absurd question. Of course, she was. Where else would she be? Why, she was likely laid out in the bed with the coverlet pulled up to her chin, quivering with fear.

"Yes, Your Grace, I believe so. Shall I go and have a word with Mrs. Stritch, just to be certain?"

"Mrs. Stritch?" Jasper blinked. "Who the devil is Mrs. Stritch?"

"She's the duchess's lady's maid, Your Grace. You sent word to Mr. Keating from Basingstoke House, ordering him to appoint a lady's maid for Her Grace."

"Ah, yes. I forgot." He'd asked Keating to hire an older, stern sort of lady, someone who could be relied upon to keep an eye on his duchess, and from the quick glimpse he'd gotten of Mrs. Stritch, it looked as if Keating had done as he'd asked. The woman was gaunt and bony, steely gray from head to toe, and properly terrifying. "Please do ask Mrs. Stritch if . . . if the duchess is prepared to receive me."

Receive him? He cringed. If Loftus noticed this unfortunate choice of words, he didn't show it, but merely bowed, his expression neutral. "Yes, Your Grace."

As soon as Loftus turned his back, Jasper snatched up the decanter, poured a small measure of brandy into his glass and drank it down in one swallow. The sensible part of his brain let out a faint cry of dismay, but reason was no match for panic.

What did he know about bedding a virgin? Not a blessed thing. He knew even less about bedding a wife, but he had a vague notion it wasn't at all the same sort of thing as bedding a mistress, which was a loud, carnal, sweaty, even acrobatic affair. Surely, a gentleman wasn't meant to behave with such shocking savagery with his *wife*?

Damn it, why hadn't he thought to ask Basingstoke about how to manage it? Basingstoke's own duchess seemed rather fond of him, so he must have done a decent enough job of—

"Mrs. Stritch informs me that Her Grace awaits your pleasure, Your Grace."

His pleasure? Alas, another unfortunate choice of words.

Loftus's gaze landed on the empty brandy glass in Jasper's hand. "Perhaps the sooner the better, Your Grace."

Jasper scowled at him. "Yes, alright, Loftus. You may go."

"Yes, Your Grace." Loftus went, closing the bed-chamber door behind him.

Right, then. Time to bed his wife. Jasper threw his shoulders back and tightened the tie of his banyan. Really, he was being ridiculous, making such a fuss over it. It wasn't as if he didn't know what he was doing, for God's sake. A mistress wasn't a wife, no, but presumably they shared the same anatomy.

He strode to the door that connected his bedchamber to Prue's, tapped his knuckles against the wood, then tapped harder, taking care to make his knock as com-manding as possible.

A feeble knock wouldn't do, in these circumstances.

"Yes?" Prue's voice drifted through the door. "Come in, Your Grace."

He simply had to take care to be mindful, and above all, gentle. It wouldn't do to allow himself to become too inflamed with his animal passions. A gentleman didn't fall upon one's innocent wife like a ravening animal—

"Good evening, Your Grace."

He froze just inside the door, his mouth going dry. The room was dim, no doubt in deference to Prue's modesty, but a dozen or so candles had been lit, their gentle light casting the bedchamber in a golden glow. She was standing in front of the fireplace in a flowing white night rail, her hands clasped modestly in front of her. The flickering flames behind her revealed and then hid the outline of her body by turns, as if playing a game of hide and seek, and her hair . . .

He bit back a groan.

That glorious hair he'd spent so many weeks admiring had been gathered into a loose plait, tied at the end with a white ribbon and draped over one of her shoulders. The muted light danced over it, turning the gilded threads the color of golden treacle.

One tug on the end of that ribbon and those thick locks would spill about her shoulders in a loose, golden-brown waterfall. He could touch it, tangle his fingers in it, raise each shining strand to his lips—

"Is something amiss, Your Grace?" Prue's smile faded, her brow puckering uncertainly.

He'd been silent too long. He was already making a mess of this, damn it. "I . . . no. You look . . ." He cleared his throat. "Just lovely." The word wasn't enough, not nearly enough, but the extravagant compliments that usually fell from his lips with such practiced ease utterly failed him.

Yet it seemed to be enough for her. "Thank you, your . . . thank you, Jasper," she murmured, a delicate flush rising in her cheeks. She didn't say anything more, but just stood there plucking at the folds of her night rail, as if waiting for something.

Him. She was waiting for *him*. He was the *husband*, for God's sake, and meant to take matters in hand. He closed the door behind him with a quiet click, then crossed the bedchamber and took her hands in his, squeezing her fingers to stop their trembling. "There's no need to be nervous," he murmured, meeting her gaze. "I'm going to take care of you, Prue."

He meant it. God, he'd never meant anything as much as he meant those words, but men and mice might make their plans one moment only to see them go awry in the next, and already the brandy and her nearness were making his head spin.

Mindful, and above all, gentle . . .

He reached for her, stroking his fingertip down her long, thick plait before catching the end of the white ribbon in his fingers. "May I?"

She nodded, her gaze never leaving his face as he tugged the ribbon loose and let it flutter to the floor, then unwound the plait until her hair hung like a golden curtain over her shoulder. "So beautiful," he murmured, running his fingers through it. "I've always thought so."

"You have?" She let out a nervous laugh. "I never would have guessed."

"Yes." He wound one of the thick locks around his finger, fascinated by the way the light danced over it. "So many colors, and so soft. Softer even than I imagined it would be."

She flushed. "You . . . you imagined it?"

"Mmmm." He brought the lock of hair to his mouth, desire flooding his belly at the tickle of those soft strands against his lips, the faint scent of honeysuckle. "I think you'd be surprised at what I've imagined, Your Grace."

"Oh." The pale skin of her throat moved in a swallow.

"Come with me." He took her hand and led her to the bed, easing her down with a gentle hand on her shoulder. "Lie down."

He paused beside the bed and slid the banyan over his shoulders, then dragged his shirt over his head. Her cheeks went scarlet at the sight of his bare chest, and he followed the enchanting blush as it drifted down her throat and vanished under the narrow ribbon that trimmed the neckline of her night rail.

Just how far did that delightful blush go? He wanted

nothing more than to find out, to lay all that perfect pale skin bare and follow that enticing wash of color with his hands and lips, but she was trembling already, and he'd promised he'd take care of her.

All in good time. "May I join you?"

She nodded, catching her lower lip between her teeth as her gaze roved over his chest, and he smothered another groan as he joined her on the bed, propping his head on his hand to take in the sight of her laid out on the bed beside him. She was watching him from under half-lidded eyes, her skin flushed and her hair scattered across the pillow, gleaming in the firelight.

Good Lord, what had he ever done to deserve such a beautiful wife? Something stirred to life inside his chest at the sight of her, the ache of it both painful and sweet at once. "I want to touch you. Will you let me?"

She gave him a hesitant nod, but still she stiffened a little when he reached for her, her eyes flying open, but he only laid a hand on the sweet curve of her abdomen. Her skin was warm underneath the thin muslin of her night rail, her chest moving up and down with her quickened breaths.

She gazed up at him as he brushed a few stray strands of hair from her forehead, her eyes dark and mysterious under their fluttering lids, her enlarged pupils crowding out her irises so only a sliver of hazel remained.

"I'm going to kiss you now." He lowered his head and let his lips hover over hers, giving her a chance to pull away, but she didn't, and the magical moment before their lips touched went on and on until the tension between them drew as thin as a thread of silk.

A groan tore from his chest as their lips met, hers parting so sweetly under his, it sent a wave of heat roaring through him. How strange, that kissing her should be so familiar, as if he already knew the shape of her lips, had memorized her sweet taste, had spent a lifetime, his entire lifetime kissing *her* . . .

"Prue," he whispered against her lips. God, but he wanted to take that trembling mouth hard with his until neither of them could think of anything but each other's taste, but his control was already slipping, his skin on fire and his cock straining between his thighs.

He wanted more—all of her—but it was too soon, too much at once, so he held back, brushing his mouth over hers again and again, desperate for the taste of her. She arched into him, the hardened tips of her breasts pressing into his bare chest, her fingers sinking into his hair to urge him closer, her tongue creeping out to touch his.

He groaned, his head swimming, lost to the desire pounding through him, his mouth hot against hers. "God, yes, sweetheart, so good." He slipped his leg between hers, tangling their limbs together, the warm, tempting hollow between her legs pressing against his thigh. She was so sweet, so close, and he was getting lost in her, his cock aching to sink into that tempting heat.

Need to be careful with her . . . go slowly . . . a proper gentleman, not a ravening animal . . .

But he was losing the battle, his control slipping, his chest heaving with his panting breaths as he toyed with the loose neckline of her night rail. His hands shook as he dragged it lower, trailing his lips over her neck, then burying his mouth in the warm, fragrant hollow of her throat, tasting the pulse that fluttered wildly under the soft skin there.

"*Jasper*." She caught a handful of his hair, tugging him closer, a murmured plea on her lips. She wanted him, was straining against him and opening her legs to make room for him in the warm cradle of her body, her thighs moving restlessly against his hips.

He slid her night rail up to her knees, caressing the bare skin of her calf before sliding his hands up to her waist, squeezing her there, his fingertips brushing her hip as he reached to cup her backside, and press her closer to him. There was no way she couldn't feel how much he wanted her, his cock hard and his hips moving gently against her, but instead of pushing him away she wrapped her legs around his waist to pull him closer, a strangled cry on her lips. "I want . . . Jasper, please."

"So eager." He thumbed one of her nipples, his lips parting as it hardened, the dark blush pink of it visible through the thin muslin of her night rail. "Shall I kiss you here?"

"*Yes*." She sank her fingers into his hair, dragging his head lower, a sharp cry falling from her lips when his mouth closed over her nipple. He suckled the rigid peak and caressed it with the tip of his tongue until she was clutching at him, and he was ready to explode just from the sight of her, her mouth slack with pleasure, whimpers and pleas falling from her lips.

"So passionate, Prue. I love watching you." He trailed his fingers over her belly, pausing to press a kiss there before he slid his hand underneath the hem of her night rail, easing it up, up, up, then over her head with one quick tug, his breath catching when every pale, quivering inch of her bare skin was revealed to him. "You're so beautiful, sweetheart."

He struggled out of his breeches and pressed a lingering kiss to her lips as he slipped his hand between her trembling thighs.

"Oh, oh." She moaned, her neck arching, and he stroked her gently, coaxing her with soft murmurs until she grew damp, her honey coating his fingers and her hips rising and falling with the movement of his hand.

He was desperate for her, desire pounding through him. He shifted to kneel between her legs, spreading her wider with a gentle nudge of his hips. He pressed the tip of his swollen cock to her entrance, an agonized groan tearing from his lips at the silky wet heat of her.

He allowed himself one restrained thrust, then froze when she sucked in a breath.

"Oh!" Her gaze flew to his, her eyes wide.

She was slick with arousal, but so small, so tight.

Too tight. "Shhh. It's alright. I've got you." He stilled his hips, pausing to stroke her again, rubbing and circling her tiny bud with his thumb until she was slick and open, and she began pushing back on his hand.

"Yes, that's it." God, it was so good, so good. He slid the tip of his cock inside and she gasped again, her thighs tightening around him, her big hazel eyes locked on his face with an expression of pain and pleasure at once, her jaw tight, but her lips soft and open still, her eyelids fluttering over dark, liquid eyes.

He leaned down to press a tender kiss to her lips. "If you need me to stop—"

"No!" She grabbed his upper arms and locked her legs around him. "Don't stop. It's . . . I'm alright."

Was she? God, he didn't know, but her thighs were like a vice, holding him tightly, her exquisite heat wrapped around him, her hips meeting his every thrust, and then in the next breath it was too late to stop. Her breathless cries filled his ears, her fingernails sinking into his back as she convulsed around him, and he let out a defeated groan, throwing his head back as his climax seized him, his back bowing as the tight knot of pulsing heat at the base of his spine unraveled in waves of dizzying pleasure.

A moment later, it was over, and he fell onto the bed, dazed. Prue remained flat on her back beside him, her chest heaving with her uneven breaths, but otherwise, she didn't make a sound.

Had he hurt her? Did she want him gone? She was so still, so quiet, the silence stretching on until a cold, hard kernel of dread lodged itself under his breastbone. "Prue?"

She let out a sigh and turned toward him with a soft, dreamy smile. "It does fit, after all."

For an instant, he wasn't sure what she meant, but then he remembered the painting, and an unseemly shout of laughter sneaked past his lips. "It does indeed, and rather nicely, at that."

The dread dissolved then, and he reached for her and wrapped one arm around her waist. With a gentle hand on the back of her neck he turned her into him, tucking her face against his chest. She didn't resist, and they remained that way, her breaths becoming deep and even as the candles guttered, and the fire burned down to embers in the grate.

CHAPTER 18

Jasper's warm body was curled around Prue, the dusting of crisp hair scattered over his bare chest tickling her cheek. It was quite late, the sun a bright halo around the closed draperies, fingers of light curling around the edges, trying to push the heavy silk aside so they might peek inside, but her husband slept on, his breathing deep and even.

She lay still, listening to his slow, steady breaths for some time before she could resist no longer, and rose up onto her elbow to gaze down at him.

Her breath caught at the sight. He'd thrust the coverlet off sometime in the night, and the soft folds were draped around his hips, leaving a bounty of smooth, bare olive skin spread out before her like some delectable feast.

Goodness, he was handsome. Beautiful, even, with his silky dark hair in tousled waves over his forehead, his full, sensuous lips relaxed in a sleepy pout. She reached out a tentative hand and traced the line of his neck with her fingertips, her teeth sinking into her lower lip at the fascinating sight of his pulse fluttering against his bare throat.

She edged closer, staring at it, mesmerized. What

would it taste like? Did she dare dip her tongue into that tempting hollow to find out? She leaned closer, her lips parting against her shallow, panting breaths, and pressed the tip of her tongue into that intriguing dip, sighing at the warm glide of his skin under her lips, the faint taste of salt and soap against her tongue.

He let out a low groan and she jerked away, her cheeks heating as her gaze flew to his face. He was awake, but he didn't move or speak, only gazed up at her with dark, hooded eyes. So, she reached for him again, tracing her tongue around the shell of his ear before biting down on the lobe.

"Ah." He caught the back of her neck, his strong fingers sliding into her hair as the hoarse groan fell from his lips, and pleasure surged through her. A kiss, a caress could make him cry out for her touch? Would it truly be as easy as that, to make her husband want her?

She dragged her hand down his chest, watching his face as she lingered to stroke the crisp, dark hair there with light, teasing fingers. His breath caught at the caress, his muscles twitching under her palms, and she moved lower, licking and teasing his hot skin until she reached the thin line of dark hair under his navel, following it with her tongue until the trail disappeared under the crumpled edge of the coverlet . . .

She got no farther. A deep, throaty growl tore from his chest, and in one heart-stopping instant he'd surged up and tumbled her onto her back against the bed, his mouth descending on hers in a savage kiss.

Oh, yes. *Yes*. This was what she wanted. His mouth, his tongue, his shuddering breaths, the weight of his powerful body over hers, their legs tangling and his fingers gripping her hips, holding her against him as he kissed her, his lips open, his mouth wet and needy and willing, but she only got only a fleeting taste of his desire before he jerked his head away with a gasp, and rolled away from her.

She lay there, stunned. What had happened? Had she done something wrong? "Jasper?"

He didn't reply, and a well of emptiness opened up in the pit of her stomach, so deep and cold she shivered. "Jasper, are you—"

"I beg your pardon, Your Grace, but I've an engagement this afternoon." He grabbed her hand and raised it to his lips, pressing a careless kiss to her knuckles, then he tossed the coverlet aside, slipped out from underneath it, and marched across the bedchamber, gathering up his discarded clothing as he went.

"An engagement?" Why would he arrange an engagement the morning after his wedding night? It didn't seem likely, unless . . . well, he *had* made a point of saying they'd each pursue their own activities once they were married.

It seemed he meant to start right away.

"I'm afraid I may be gone for a good part of the evening, as well. If I don't turn up by dinnertime, do feel free to dine without me." He dropped a quick kiss on her forehead and chucked her under the chin. "I'll come and bid you good-bye before I leave."

Before she could say a word in reply, he was gone, the click of the door closing between them somehow deafening, the echo of it lingering far longer than it should have.

She lay still in her bed for a long time after he left her alone, a confusion of blurry images unspooling behind her eyelids. Jasper kissing her, his lips tender against her heated skin. Jasper touching her, his hands so gentle, so careful, as if she were precious, his deep, hypnotic voice whispering in her ear, telling her she was beautiful, and the low groan that had spilled from his lips when he'd found his pleasure.

It had been magical.

It was what every lady dreamed of, wasn't it? Her handsome new husband, gazing at her as if she'd hung the very stars in the sky? How her heart had soared with hope in that moment, and in the toe-tingling, breathtaking bliss that followed! He'd so overtaken her senses that she'd begged—yes, actually begged him to . . . well, at the time she hadn't known quite what she'd been begging for.

But he had, and he'd given it to her, bringing her to the heights of pleasure, his arms wrapped around her, his sweet kisses gentling her as the ecstasy had melted into warm waves of bliss, her heart slowing its frantic pace and a delicious languor overtaking her.

Those moments with him had been amongst the loveliest of her life, but this morning it had disintegrated into nothingness like the last hazy remnants of some wonderful, impossible dream that fled at sunrise.

He'd pulled away from her, his face shuttered, his gaze guarded, and dear God, the awful silence that had fallen between them after he'd jerked away from her had unfolded with such agonizing slowness, as if she were hanging off a sheer cliff's face, waiting to plunge to her death as she lost her grip, one fingertip at a time.

She didn't know how it was meant to be between a man and a woman, but a lady didn't need to be a courtesan to know this morning hadn't been the way it ought to have been.

What had happened? It had all gone wrong, somehow, only she didn't know how, or why. She must have done something she oughtn't to have done. Was a proper wife not meant to initiate lovemaking? Should she not have kissed him? He'd seemed pleased with her attentions at first, but it must not have been the right thing, after all.

Oh, if only she hadn't woken him! If only she'd remained as she was, with his strong arm curled around the curve of her waist and the steady thump of his heart under her ear. He might still be here then, and she'd have nothing else to wish for, any unanswered questions between them fading into silence with their mingled breath.

But it was too late now. Already, she could hear him stirring on the other side of the connecting door, and while a foolish part of her hoped he'd change his mind and return to take her into his arms once again, the other part of her—the part that knew better—feared he'd never cross the threshold between their two bedchambers again.

Her heart sank all the way down to her bare toes at the thought, but it wasn't as if Jasper had promised her romance and kisses, and nights clasped in his arms. He'd made it clear from the start this was to be a business arrangement, nothing more.

She'd known what she was getting herself into with this marriage. She'd made her decision with her eyes wide open, and she wouldn't snivel over it now, no matter if she had hoped—

Well, it was neither here nor there now, was it?

If Jasper intended to leave her to her own devices, then she'd do well to make certain she had her own pursuits to fill her days. She rose from the bed and slipped her night rail over her head, but just as she was about to cross the room and ring the bell for the servant, she paused, her gaze falling on the bed.

Was that . . . but no, surely not. It didn't make sense.

She hurried across the room to one of the windows and jerked the draperies back, blinking as light poured into her bedchamber, then strode back across the room and tore the coverlet off the bed with a sweep of her arm.

But with one glance, her suspicions were confirmed.

There was no blood. Not a single, precious drop. The sheets were a perfect, pristine white. She dropped down on the edge of the bed, stunned.

She only knew of two reasons why that would be the case. The first was that she'd come to her husband's bed with something less than the strictest purity, which was most certainly not the case, whereas the second . . .

Dear God, was it possible that her marriage hadn't been consummated?

It had hurt a bit when he'd entered her, yes, but it was the merest twinge, and not at all the sundering she'd feared after she'd seen the portrait of Jasper without his clothing.

She was no stranger to the laws of physics, after all.

But *how*? How could such a thing have happened? Jasper was meant to be an infamous rake! Surely, he must realize it? But if he was aware of the, er . . . blunder, why hadn't he said anything to her? Even more to the point, why had he fled her touch this morning? One would think a husband would make it a point to properly deflower his new wife.

Instead, he'd fled her bed as if she had the plague.

It didn't make any sense. For pity's sake, a thing like an accidentally virginal wife wasn't likely to grow less awkward the longer one waited to address it, was it?

Rather the opposite.

She'd have to ask him. Goodness, what an awkward discussion *that* was sure to be! But they were man and wife now, and if it was as she suspected, it was rather a drastic oversight.

She rose from the bed, her instinct to go to him at

once, but she froze as she drew near the connecting door. No, she couldn't do it. She simply couldn't bring herself to go to him after he'd fled her bedchamber this morning like a criminal fleeing the gibbet.

He'd said he'd come and bid her good-bye before he left for his engagement. It would simply have to wait until then. Perhaps pride was a sin, but she gathered the wounded remnants of hers around her and turned away from the door with a jerk of her chin.

But what was she meant to do with all the lonely hours of the long day that now stretched before her? She'd imagined she'd be occupied with Jasper this morning, but she was at liberty now, and she didn't intend to squander her first day in London sulking in her bedchamber over her hard-hearted husband.

No, she'd begin how she meant to go on.

She strode toward the pretty little writing desk in the corner of her bedchamber, jerking the draperies open as she went, her spirits lifting a little as sunlight poured through the glass.

There was a neat stack of paper in the top drawer of the little desk, along with a freshly trimmed quill, and in a lower drawer there was a lovely crystal inkwell filled to the brim with black ink.

She sat down, took a fresh sheet from the drawer, and dipped her pen. Yes, this was very good. Already she felt better, just from having the pen in her hand.

She bent over the paper and began to make out her list, putting Angelo's Fencing Academy at the top. It would be the easiest of her goals to pursue, as Mr. Angelo was perfectly willing to instruct ladies in the art of fencing. Gentleman Jackson's Boxing Academy was next door to Angelo's, and while she didn't have much interest in learning to box, she'd quite like to have a peek inside, just to see what all the fuss was.

Underneath Jackson's, she wrote Joseph Manton's Shooting Gallery. Now that one was going to prove more difficult, as ladies were not welcome at Manton's. They were forbidden outright at Tattersalls, but she wrote it underneath Manton's all the same. It merely required a bit of creativity to find her way around the rules. Perhaps Colonel Kingston would be willing to help her in her endeavors.

It was excessively trying that she would be reduced to subterfuge at all. Aside from Angelo's, nearly every venue was forbidden to her, no matter if she was more than proficient enough to hold her own among the gentlemen. It seemed fashionable ladies of the *ton* were meant to occupy themselves primarily with gossip and shopping—

Ah, but that reminded her! At the bottom of her list, she scratched out the name Madame Laurent, and beside it, Bond Street. Madame Laurent was Franny's modiste. Franny couldn't sing Madame's praises highly enough, and she assured Prue that Madame Laurent would be thrilled to have another duchess on her client list, regardless of whether or not that duchess might have a *singular* taste in fashion.

There! She laid her pen aside and reread her list.

Yes, it would do for a start. As she grew more accustomed to London, she was certain to find other things she'd like to try.

Oh, if only she'd allowed her father to accompany her to London, as he'd wished! How he would have loved to join her on her adventures! But she needed to find her own way first, so she'd begged him to return to Wiltshire for now, with promises to call him to London soon.

Until then, perhaps she could persuade Franny to—

"Good morning, Your Grace."

Prue jerked around in her chair, surprised to find that Mrs. Stritch, her new lady's maid, had entered the bed-chamber while she'd been busy with her list. "I don't believe I rang the bell."

"No, Your Grace." Mrs. Stritch gave her a thin smile. "But I came to see if you required anything from me. It looks as if it will be a fine day, and I was certain you wouldn't want to waste it lying about in your bed-chamber."

Well, how . . . helpful, if a bit curious, given last night was her wedding night. If ever a lady deserved a bit of a lie-about, it was then. Still, she'd never had a lady's maid before. Perhaps this was how they went on.

She let it go and gave Mrs. Stritch a sunny smile. "There is one thing you can do for me, Mrs. Stritch. Have you seen His Grace this morning? I need a brief word with him before he leaves."

Mrs. Stritch was gathering up the discarded coverlet Prue had left on the floor. "His Grace left the house an hour ago, Your Grace."

"What, he's gone *already*?" He'd left without saying a single word to her, after he'd promised he'd bid her good-bye? It must be a terribly important engagement, for him to leave in such a hurry.

Or perhaps he didn't have an engagement at all, and simply wanted to be out of the house and away from her. Perhaps he'd gone off to White's, where all the aristo-cratic gentlemen who wished to escape their wives went. "Did he leave a message for me?"

"Not that I'm aware, Your Grace. Mr. Loftus, his valet . . ." Mrs. Stritch paused for an instant with the coverlet bundled in her arms, her gaze lingering on the bed, but then she returned her attention to Prue. "I beg your pardon, Your Grace. As I was saying, Mr. Loftus, His Grace's valet, said only that His Grace had an appointment this afternoon, and would be away from the house for most of the day."

"I see." But she didn't see, not at all. Or perhaps she *did*, all too clearly.

"I've ordered a bath for you, Your Grace. Shall I see to your clothing for the day while we wait for the servants to bring it up?"

"Certainly, though I'm afraid there aren't many clothes to choose from yet. I haven't had time to see the modiste, but there's a gray day gown in the wardrobe that should do for today." It was one Franny had given her, to hold her over until she could have some clothing made up. It was a bit simple for a duchess, but it was a lovely, soft heather gray, and Prue adored it.

Mrs. Stritch ventured into the wardrobe, but a moment later there was a muffled gasp, and she emerged looking positively scandalized, the gray gown in her hand. "I do beg your pardon, Your Grace, but surely you can't mean *this*?"

Prue raised an eyebrow. Mrs. Stritch was holding the neck of the gown between her thumb and forefinger, looking for all the world as if she were holding a feral raccoon in her hand instead of a perfectly acceptable day gown. "Yes, that's it."

"Oh, but Your Grace, this won't do at all! Why, I don't like to think what the other fashionable ladies in Bond Street will think if they see the Duchess of Montford appear amongst them wearing *this*!" Stritch shook the gown, outraged.

Prue didn't care one whit what the fashionable ladies thought of her, but she pasted a careful smile over her gritted teeth. "That's quite alright, Mrs. Stritch, as I have no plans to shop today."

Stritch cast another venomous look at the gray gown, her lips tightening, then said, "Perhaps if Your Grace would be so good as to tell me your plans for today, we might find an appropriate gown for you to wear."

"Very well. I do intend to go to Bond Street, but not to shop. I thought I'd call in at Angelo's Fencing Academy, to see if I might arrange to take fencing lessons with the master. I've always wanted to learn to fence, you see. I might just peek in at Gentleman Jackson's, as well."

"Gentleman Jackson's," Stritch repeated faintly, clutching her throat as if she were about to swoon. "Angelo's Fencing Academy?"

"Yes. Is there something amiss, Mrs. Stritch?" Prue eyed the woman steadily, waiting. Odd, but she had the strangest inkling Mrs. Stritch might not do as her lady's maid, after all.

Mrs. Stritch drew herself up and placed a bony hand on her even bonier breast. "I beg your pardon, Your Grace, but as you're new to London, I fear it would be remiss of me not to just *hint* that there are certain behaviors considered highly inappropriate for young ladies, and most certainly for young duchesses—"

"That will be all, Stritch."

Stritch stared at her. "I don't understand, Your Grace. Do you no longer require my help in dressing?"

"I no longer require your help at all, Mrs. Stritch. You are dismissed from your position."

Mrs. Stritch positively goggled at her, then all at once the thin veneer of respect she'd pasted on fell away entirely. "Why, you vulgar little upstart. You can't dismiss me. The duke won't allow it. He chose me specifically to keep an eye . . ."

Mrs. Stritch trailed off, but it was too late by then.

"Keep an eye on me?" Had he, indeed?

Well then, even more reason to let Mrs. Stritch go. "I am the Duchess of Montford, Mrs. Stritch, and I may dismiss you as I please." Prue jerked her chin up. Underneath her bravado she was shaking, but it seemed London was going to test her mettle right away, and meekness would get her nowhere.

And while it *was* rather presumptuous of her to dismiss her lady's maid not even a full day after she became the duchess, she would not employ a servant she didn't trust. London was going to be difficult enough as it was. The last thing she needed was Mrs. Stritch hanging over her shoulder, subtly scolding her at every opportunity and then reporting her failings back to Jasper.

How dare he assign a servant to spy on her, as if she were a wayward child! His Grace was in for a rude awakening if he imagined she'd permit such high-handed behavior!

No, indeed. It wouldn't do. The woman had to go, and now. "Shall I call one of the footmen to see you out?"

Mrs. Stritch gaped at her for another moment, then she tossed the gray gown onto the bed, turned on her heel, and marched across the room and through the door, the hems of her skirts flying in an outraged arc behind her.

Prue flinched as the door slammed closed. "Well, that settles that. I do hope she doesn't intend to ask for references."

She returned to her desk and sat for a bit, waiting until her nerves were steady once again, and there'd been plenty of time for Mrs. Stritch to gather her things and leave the house, then she'd—

Thump!

What in the world? Was Stritch lingering in the hallway? She jumped to her feet and thrust open the door, a tirade worthy of a duchess building in her throat.

But it wasn't Stritch. Instead, A young woman with an unruly mop of curly dark hair stuffed under a cap two sizes too big for her head was in the hallway, struggling with a coal hod. She wore a drab blue gown with an enormous apron over it, and when she looked up and saw Prue watching her, all the color drained from her face. "Y-Your Grace?"

"Hello." Prue ventured farther into the hallway. "What is your name?"

The girl's mouth opened, then closed, then opened again. Finally, she blurted, "It's Sarah, Your Grace."

Prue hid a smile. What would this girl think if she knew the Duchess of Montford was nearly as nervous as she was? "Very well, Sarah. Would you be so kind as to help me dress today? Mrs. Stritch is no longer in my employ, and I find myself rather suddenly in need of a lady's maid."

The girl glanced behind her, then back at Prue. "Me, Your Grace? Y-you want *me* to help you dress?"

"I don't see why not. You do know how to button a dress, do you not, Sarah?"

"Aye, mum—I mean, yes, Your Grace."

"Very well then, we'll start with that, shall we?"

"Yes, Your Grace." Sarah took a few hesitant steps into the bedchamber, and her gaze fell on the gray gown lying on the bed. A timid smile rose to her lips. "Oh, how pretty, Your Grace!"

"I think so too, Sarah." Prue smiled back. "I think so, too."

CHAPTER 19

He had nothing to feel guilty about. Not a single, blessed thing.

His marriage—all twenty-seven hours of it—was going precisely as he'd intended it would. So, while it may have appeared to an uninformed observer as if he'd sneaked out of his own house this morning, that was most emphatically *not* the case.

He had an engagement, that was all. It was a perfectly ordinary thing, for a gentleman to have an engagement, and if he *was* a trifle early—or perhaps more than a trifle—it was only because it was unforgivably rude to keep one's friends waiting.

There was nothing amiss in that. Punctuality was a virtue, and virtues often required sacrifice. So, if he *had* hurt his new wife's feelings when he'd rebuffed her innocent attempts at seduction this morning—if he *had* left her alone and forlorn in her bed, her face as white as the bedsheets—it *wasn't* because he was alarmed by the rush of tenderness that had overwhelmed him when she'd kissed him.

Not at all.

It had all been in pursuit of the virtue of punctuality—

"Montford? Is that you?" Basingstoke paused halfway across the dining room at White's, then hurried forward, his eyebrows raised. "My God, man, are you *early*? We've been meeting every Wednesday for years now, and I don't believe that's ever happened before."

"Never." Grantham followed after Basingstoke, his eyes narrowing as he took Jasper in. "And looking so well, too. Quite elegant indeed, Montford."

Oh, my yes, he was elegant! His cravat was flawless, every strand of his hair was in place, and there wasn't a speck of lint anywhere on his person. He was the very image of a fashionable gentleman of the *ton*, freshly wed and without a care in the world.

Because that was what he *was*, and it was only proper he should look the part.

So, instead of forbidding Loftus to fuss over him as he usually did, today he'd remained quiet while he was brushed, pressed, fluffed, and outfitted to perfection. Loftus, sensing an opportunity, had even managed to squeeze him into his new plum morning coat, the one with such fashionably tight sleeves Jasper had refused to wear it before today.

"We might have canceled, Montford." Basingstoke gave him a searching look. "A man has only one wedding night, after all. Ideally, at any rate."

"Yes, aren't you meant to be cozied up to your new bride, Montford?" Grantham signaled the footman. "Coffee, if you would, Dempsey. I didn't expect to see you for another fortnight at least, Montford."

"It's a marriage, Grantham, not an infectious disease. I see no reason to banish myself to my home simply

Anna Bradley

because I've now got a wife." An enchantingly beautiful wife, with the sweetest lips he'd ever kissed and the softest skin he'd ever had the pleasure of caressing.

Of course, that was neither here nor there.

"Indeed? How singular. If I'd wed as ravishing a creature as the new Duchess of Montford, I wouldn't leave her bedchamber for the rest of the year." Grantham eyed Jasper over the edge of his coffee cup. "So, Montford. What are you *doing* here?"

Jasper gave him a scowl that would have cowed a lesser man, but Grantham being Grantham, he only grinned. "I'm here, Grantham, because we have a Wednesday morning engagement, and I intend to go on with my life much as I did before I married."

Basingstoke snorted with such violence he was obliged to cover his face with his serviette. "Montford, you poor, blind fool," he finally gasped. "You've no idea what you've gotten yourself into, have you?"

For God's sake, the sight of those two smirking faces was enough to put him off his roasted lamb. "I have no idea what you're on about, Basingstoke, nor do I wish to, so you may keep your chortling to yourself."

"Very well, Montford. All jesting aside, then, how does your duchess do? Is she quite well?"

Ah, now there was a question. But how to answer it? He sliced into his lamb with such savagery his knife screeched against his plate.

Perhaps he should begin by explaining that he hadn't the first idea how his duchess was, because he'd been so anxious to escape her embrace, he hadn't exchanged more than a dozen words with her this morning. Or, failing that, he could describe how he hadn't taken a moment to bid her good-bye, even after he'd promised he would.

Or maybe he should make it simple, and confess that while he was rather an expert at offending his mistresses and earning their unending wrath, he didn't have the first idea how to make a wife happy—

"Alright, Montford. Let's have it out, shall we?" Grantham set his coffee aside with a sigh. "Something is troubling you. How are we meant to help you if you don't tell us what it is? Come, you'll feel better when you've unburdened yourself."

"You're not meant to help me at all, because I don't need any help. It's kind of you to offer, Grantham, but I don't know what advice you think you can give me. You're nearly as useless as I am when it comes to marriage."

"That's true enough, but surely Basingstoke here has some precious words of wisdom to impart." Grantham considered Basingstoke for a moment, then shook his head. "Odd, really. I predicted you'd make a hopeless husband, Basingstoke, but you're surprisingly good at it."

"If I'm good at it, Grantham, it's because I happen to be madly in love with my wife." Basingstoke leaned back in his chair, a soft smile playing about his lips, just as it always did when he mentioned his duchess. "Marriage is a pleasure when one is married to a lady one loves. At the risk of sounding sentimental, gentlemen, love makes all the difference."

A pang rose in Jasper's chest, and he turned his gaze away.

Love was all very well, of course, for those who knew how to do it properly.

Like Basingstoke, for instance. His love for Francesca had made him a better man, yes, but even before he'd met Francesca, Basingstoke had shown the most tender love and care for his mother and his three sisters. The capacity for love had always been there, inside him. It had simply expanded to include Francesca when he'd fallen in love with her.

And hence, a fairy tale was born.

But there was no fairy tale waiting to unfold inside Jasper. He hadn't had a mother or sisters to help smooth his rough places. Any lady who made the mistake of rubbing up against him was sure to find herself sliced to ribbons on his jagged edges.

It was one of the reasons he hadn't wanted to marry.

As husbands went, he was sure to be a perfect disaster, and so far, he'd exceeded even his own low expectations of himself. He'd abandoned his sweet wife of a single day because her innocent caresses made his chest ache as if it were cracking open, and all manner of unfamiliar things had begun leaking out of the gap.

And that—*that* wouldn't do.

Even if he wanted to love Prue, he didn't know how to go about it. He'd make a mess of it, just as he had this morning, and soon enough Prue would grow to despise him, just as Selina and every one of his mistresses before her had done.

Only it would be worse, because underneath Selina's hard veneer there was only emptiness. There was nothing there to love.

But that wasn't true of Prue. As lovely as she was, Prue's true beauty wasn't in her face, but in the world of treasures hidden inside her heart. He could sense it in every word she spoke, feel it in her every glance, see it in every shift of emotion in those beautiful hazel eyes.

And he didn't know how to touch any of it.

There was no softness inside him, no tenderness. If anything, Basingstoke's advice would be less useful to him even than Grantham's, because Basingstoke spoke as a man who knew how to love.

Jasper set his knife aside, his appetite deserting him. "There's nothing amiss. My duchess is perfectly content. I'm perfectly content." Loftus was perfectly content, and Keating and Mrs. Stritch, and every bloody person in his entire household was perfectly content, damn it, or as content as they'd ever be. "It's all going swimmingly, I assure you."

"Is it? That's good news, Montford." Grantham sipped his coffee. "You're quite sure there's nothing you wish to discuss?"

"Of course, I'm sure. Now the wedding is past, I daresay we'll settle into a perfectly agreeable routine. We won't live in each other's pockets, but we both agreed that would be the case before we wed. Prue and I both prefer it that way."

"I'm pleased to hear that, Montford, though there'd be no shame in it if it weren't going quite as swimmingly as you say." Basingstoke's gaze was steady. "If that *did* happen to be the case, I would hope you'd confide in us."

Jasper gritted his teeth. "You may wax on about love as much as you like, Basingstoke, but routine is just as important to a marriage. Routine, and obedience. Wifely obedience, that is." Dear God, what was he saying? "For all that my grandfather insists Prue is a lady of spirit, I daresay she'll settle down quite nicely now that we're—"

"Montford! Back in London at last, eh? How d'ye do?"

Jasper jumped. He'd just begun to warm to his subject, and might have gone on about Prue's burgeoning docility for the rest of their meal if Lord Rowell hadn't appeared at his elbow. "For God's sake, Rowell, where did you come from?"

Rowell, who was perfectly harmless, but perhaps not the brightest of London's noblemen, gave him a guileless smile. "From Angelo's. I saw your wife there. Very pretty, indeed. Well done, Montford!"

His wife? At Angelo's Fencing Academy? Surely not. "You've made a mistake, Rowell. I just left my wife in Berkeley Square."

"Indeed? But the lady arrived in a carriage bearing your crest, and I could have sworn I heard Angelo call her 'Your Grace.'" Rowell's eyes widened. "You don't suppose there's another lady running about London claiming to be the Duchess of Montford, do you?"

It didn't seem likely, did it? "What did this lady look like, Rowell?"

"Rather tall, with light brown hair. Pretty, like I said. Lovely green eyes."

Hazel. *Hazel* eyes, but there was no denying it did sound like Prue. What the devil did she *mean*, sneaking out of the townhouse and wandering about London without him? "Tell me, Rowell. What was this pretty, green-eyed lady doing at Angelo's?"

Rowell blinked. "Why, fencing, of course. She's not bad either, Montford. Quick on her feet, you know, and not a bit of hesitation in her. It looked as if she'd handled a foil before. She nearly disarmed Lord Quincy—"

"Lord Quincy!" Jasper went still, everything but his fingers, which went so tight around his wine glass, the stem snapped off in his hand.

"Oh, good Lord," Grantham muttered under his breath.

"You mean to say, Rowell, that *my wife* is at Angelo's at this very minute, fencing with the Earl of Quincy?" If there was one man in London one couldn't trust with one's wife, it was that scoundrel, Quincy. By God, if the man so much as grazed a hair on Prue's head, he was going to bloody kill him.

"Er, yes." Rowell cast an uneasy glance at Grantham. "That is, she was when I left—"

"I beg your pardon, gentlemen." Jasper rose to his feet and tossed the broken bits of his glass onto the table, a red haze descending over his eyes. "I believe I'll pay a visit to Angelo's."

The first thing he saw when he brought his phaeton to a stop outside Angelo's was a dark green carriage with a familiar gold-and-green crest emblazoned on the door. If that weren't enough to convince him, his own coachman, Norris, was sitting on the box.

By God, Rowell had the right of it. His wife, the Duchess of Montford, was even now inside Angelo's, foil in hand, sparring with that villain Quincy, the very last man in all of London he wanted anywhere near his precious . . . er, that is, anywhere near his wife.

With any luck, she'd slice the devil's head off.

"Norris! What in God's name is going on? Where is the duchess?"

"Your Grace!" Norris nearly toppled from the box in his haste to get down. "I beg your pardon, Your Grace! I didn't think you'd approve, but Her Grace was quite insistent—"

"It's alright, Norris. I don't blame you." For God's sake, Prue must have lost her senses! "Where is she?"

"Inside, Your Grace."

"Not alone, I hope?" Surely, she wouldn't go as far as that?

"Oh, no, Your Grace! I insisted Bryce accompany her."

"Good man, Norris." Bryce was one of the brawnier footmen in his employ, and unfailingly loyal. Servant or not, he wouldn't tolerate any nonsense on Quincy's part. "Wait here, Norris. Her Grace and I will be right out."

"Yes, Your Grace."

Jasper marched through the front entrance, anger and worry stirring his blood to a boil in his veins, but as soon as he was through the door, he stopped short.

"Good afternoon, Your Grace." Bryce, who was standing to one side of the center of the room, offered Jasper a respectful bow, but he wore an odd expression on his face—yes, decidedly odd, and one Jasper had never seen there before.

He was smiling. Bryce, the most stoic of all his servants, was *smiling*.

"I don't see what's so bloody funny, Bryce." There was nothing amusing about a runaway duchess. "What the devil are you smirking at?"

"I beg your pardon, Your Grace, but . . . look at her." Bryce nodded toward the center of the room where a crowd of gentlemen had gathered around a pair of combatants who were circling each other. "With a bit of practice, the duchess could become a sword master . . . er sword mistress, that is."

"Good Lord, you mean the duchess is displaying?" It was impossible for him to see what was happening in the center of the room with so many people in his way, but the occasional clash of steel and the excited murmurs of the crowd indicated a bout was in progress.

"Out of my way, damn you." He shoved through the bodies until he reached the front of the crowd, ignoring the irritable protests that rose in his wake, and there, in the center of the room, her gray gown half obscured by the padded white practice sleeves on her arms, was his wife, a rapier in her hand, and she was . . .

By God, she was leading Quincy—because it *was* Quincy, the scoundrel, just as Rowell had said—on a merry chase, giving him quite a time of it, lunging and parrying, her feet a whirlwind of motion as she advanced and retreated. She was a novice, certainly, but she had perfect balance and an athlete's understanding of how to control her body and use her quick, light frame to its best advantage.

She was . . . good Lord, he couldn't take his eyes off her. She fought cleverly, every thrust and riposte sharp but spare, with no waste of energy or movement, and she was innately graceful, just as she'd been when she'd brought Sampson safely to the bottom of the hill at Basingstoke House. He felt the same surge in his chest as he'd felt that day, an unfamiliar flood of some warm emotion he couldn't quite identify, but it felt a bit like . . .

Wonder. Pride. Damned if he wasn't *proud* of his wife.

Still, he couldn't permit her to expose herself to the leering gaze of every bloody blackguard in London. Already the *ton*'s tongues would be wagging out of their heads when word of the dueling duchess reached London's drawing rooms.

It was time to put an end to this.

He searched for the familiar face of Henry Angelo in the crowd, and found him soon enough, near the rack that held the foils. Back through the crush of bodies he went, until he was close enough to Angelo to speak without being overheard. "End it," he muttered curtly in the man's ear. "Now."

"Of course, Your Grace." Angelo stepped forward and with three sharp claps of his hands, put an end to the bout. "Well done, Your Grace! Gentlemen, Her Grace, the Duchess of Montford."

A round of enthusiastic applause went round the room, and Prue, her cheeks flushed a fetching pink from both the exercise and pleasure, executed a charming little curtsy.

Now that the show was over the crowd began to disperse, but as Jasper made his way toward Prue, he saw that Quincy lingered in the center of the room with her. He was speaking to her—speaking to *his wife*, and smiling down at her, and there was that red haze again, swimming in front of his eyes.

He strode forward, putting himself between Quincy and Prue. "What do you think you're doing, Quincy?"

There was no mistaking his tone for a polite enquiry, and behind him, Prue gave a little gasp. "Jasper! What are you—"

"Well, Montford. Caught up with your wife at last, did you?" Quincy snickered. "I don't see what the fuss is about. None of the other gentlemen would spar with the duchess. No doubt they feared you wouldn't approve. So, I volunteered. I couldn't let the lady languish on the sidelines, could I?"

"Yes, you're every inch the gallant hero, aren't you, Quincy? But you needn't worry yourself about *my* wife. Indeed, I'll thank you to keep away from her from now on."

"Jasper!" Prue gasped again, outraged. "For pity's sake—"

"Possessive, aren't you, Montford? I can't say I blame you." Quincy turned to Prue with a smile, and took her hand and raised it to his lips. "Your new duchess is . . . quite something."

Jasper growled—actually *growled*, which was not a thing he'd ever done before, or ever expected he'd do, least of all over a woman.

But Prue was no mere woman. She was his *wife*, and he knew better than to trust Quincy anywhere near her.

But Prue *didn't* know. Not yet, at any rate.

But she would, and the sooner, the better.

CHAPTER 20

The Duke of Montford wasn't pleased.

Not with Bryce, the footman who'd accompanied Prue inside Angelo's, or Norris, the coachman who'd driven her there. Not with Mr. Henry Angelo, who'd welcomed her into his fencing academy with a bow and the offer of a practice foil, and not with Lord Quincy, who'd so graciously agreed to partner her in a bout.

But of all the people the Duke of Montford was displeased with this afternoon, he was the most displeased with *her*.

He hadn't said a single word since he'd barked at poor Norris to take them back to Berkeley Square, and aside from the grip of his fingers around her wrist as he'd bundled her into the carriage, he hadn't touched her. He hadn't even deigned to look at her, but kept his gaze focused steadfastly out the window, his jaw so tight it looked as if it would shatter if he dared exhale a breath.

Prue sneaked another sidelong glance at him from the corner of her eye, waiting with her hands clenched in her lap for him to say something—*anything*—but the silence between them stretched on, the only sound the rattle of the carriage wheels as they made the brief trip down Bruton Street to Berkeley Square.

By the time Norris brought the carriage to a stop at the townhouse, she'd grown so exasperated with him she ignored him when he attempted to hand her down from the carriage. What did he mean by tracking her to Angelo's after leaving her on her own on the first day of their marriage, and dragging her out the door as if she'd done something unspeakable? It wasn't as if she'd been caught in some sort of shocking scandal.

It was a fencing lesson, for pity's sake! Surely, it didn't warrant such a fuss as this?

As soon as they entered the house she went toward the stairs, intending to sweep up them in a dignified silence, but Jasper stopped her with a hand on her arm. "A word in my study, if you would, Your Grace." He didn't wait for her to answer, but turned on his heel and strode down the corridor, leaving her to trail after him as if she were one of his hunting dogs.

Very well, then. If His Grace wanted to talk, then he had quite an earful awaiting him.

He was at the sideboard when she entered the study, pouring a measure of brandy into a tumbler. "Sherry?" he asked, holding up an empty glass, his other hand hovering over one of the bottles.

"Brandy, if you please." It looked as if she was going to need it.

He didn't argue, but poured her a glass of brandy and handed it to her, then nodded at a chair. "Please do have a seat, Your Grace."

She did as he bid her, flouncing over to a settee in an injured silence. He didn't join her, choosing instead to pace silently in front of the fireplace. Just as she was ready to scream with frustration, he turned to her at last and said, "It's not wise, Prue, for you to be seen in the company of a gentleman like Lord Quincy."

"Lord Quincy?" Was *that* what this was about? "You mean to say you caused that dreadful scene at Angelo's because of Lord Quincy?"

"No, Your Grace. I *interrupted* the scene *you* were making at Angelo's by accepting the attentions of a scoundrel like Quincy."

For pity's sake, who cared about Lord Quincy? "I went to Angelo's to *fence*, Your Grace, not to court the attentions of some random gentleman." Still, it hardly seemed fair to attack the poor man, whose only sin seemed to be partnering her in a bout when all the other gentlemen refused. "Besides, Lord Quincy appears to me to be a perfect gentleman—"

"But he *isn't* a perfect gentleman, Prue!" The words exploded from him like a pistol shot, shattering the quiet between them. "He's as wicked a rake as London has ever seen."

My, that was rather the pot accusing the kettle, wasn't it? "Perhaps he's heard I have a weakness for rakes," she muttered.

"I beg your pardon?"

"Er, nothing. You were saying?"

"He'd like to make you think he's a proper gentleman," Jasper went on, his dark brows drawn into a scowl. "It's easier for him to insinuate himself into your good graces that way."

Her good graces? Why, what nonsense! What use could she possibly be to the Earl of Quincy? She didn't have anything to offer the man. "That seems unlikely, Your Grace. Why should Lord Quincy care about insinuating himself with me?"

Jasper had begun pacing again, but at that he turned

to face her, his expression incredulous. "You can't be serious. You're the *Duchess of Montford*, Prue—"

"Yes, I'm aware of that. If you recall, we were married only yesterday. You needn't speak to me as if I'm a child, Jasper."

He drew in a deep breath. "I don't think you're a child, Prue, but neither do I think you understand what it means to be the Duchess of Montford. The entire *ton* will be watching you now. Some of them are harmless enough, but others . . . well, at the very least they'll gossip about you, but there will be those who bear you ill will and will actively try to hurt you."

"I see." As absurd as it seemed, she'd seen too much of the *ton* to doubt him entirely. The worst among them didn't even need a reason to hurt someone, but wreaked havoc for the mere sport of it. "And you believe Lord Quincy is one of these?"

"I *know* he is. If you doubt me, then ask the Duchess of Basingstoke for her opinion of him. She'll say the same."

"But why should Lord Quincy wish to hurt me?" It all seemed a bit far-fetched. "I never laid eyes on the man before today."

Jasper swallowed his brandy in one gulp and set the empty tumbler down on the mantel. "Lord Quincy is friendly with Lady Archer. Even if he doesn't wish you any harm, *she* does, and he'll do her bidding, I assure you."

Lady Archer, the dark-haired lady in the portrait, Jasper's former lover. Oh yes, Franny had told her all about Lady Archer's vindictiveness. "Very well, I take your point, though I can't quite see why Lady Archer should wish me ill. I've got nothing to do with her."

"For God's sake, Prue, of course, you do! You married

me, didn't you? That's more than enough to earn you the enmity of a vindictive viper like Lady Archer."

"Why should it? You broke with her months ago. She threw a hairbrush at you, and it went out the window and hit poor Lord Arthur!" Surely, that was more than enough to put an end to any affection between them, unless . . .

Was Lady Archer still in love with Jasper? Did she want him back, and consider Prue her rival? A bitter laugh hovered on her lips. If that was the case, then she could likely have him for the taking. That disaster this morning had shattered any remaining illusion she might have cherished that her husband wanted *her*.

"Good God, but that story has made the rounds, hasn't it?" Jasper dropped into the chair beside her and dragged a hand through his hair. "She threw the hairbrush at me *after*, when it finally dawned on her she was never going to become the Duchess of Montford. Now here *you* are, in her rightful place. At least, that's how she'll see it."

Wait. Franny had said something about that, hadn't she? Something about Lady Archer having her heart set on becoming the next Duchess of Montford? Now here was Prue, a girl of no name, no money, no fortune, and no fashion, usurping the place of one of London's great beauties.

Yes, perhaps that *would* be enough to earn her Lady Archer's enmity. "But it's not as if Lord Quincy knew I'd turn up at Angelo's this morning. Why, no one even knows we've returned to London—"

"Everyone knows." Jasper's tone was flat. "They knew before we even arrived in Berkeley Square."

"Very well, but my point is, it isn't as if Lord Quincy could have had any ill intent toward me this morning. He merely happened to be there when I came in, and—"

"Quincy's an opportunist who took quick advantage of

the situation today to ingratiate himself with you. He'd think nothing of befriending you if he thinks he has something to gain by it, regardless of whether it damages your reputation. You can be sure he's already reported the whole of your encounter back to Selina. Even now she's likely weaving her web, waiting for her prey to venture close enough that she can snap it up and make a meal of it."

Spiders, web, and prey? It all sounded a bit melodramatic, but it wasn't as if she had any desire to become friends with Lord Quincy, so there was no sense in arguing the point. If Jasper didn't like the man, then she'd simply keep away from him. "Very well then, Your Grace. I promise you I won't have anything to do with Lord Quincy in the future."

There. That had been easy enough.

She rose to her feet, but Jasper caught her wrist and urged her back down into her chair. "I'm not finished, Your Grace. At least half the men at Angelo's who cheered you on with such enthusiasm today also aren't gentlemen. I can assure you the moment you set foot outside the door, they all scurried off to White's or Boodle's to gossip about seeing the new Duchess of Montford fencing at Angelo's."

Ah, so they'd be gossiping about her, would they? Carrying tales to every corner of London, whispering to all their acquaintances that the Duchess of Montford was . . . what? What could they possibly say of her? That she wished to learn to fence? What was the harm in that?

She shrugged. "I don't care."

Once again, she rose to leave, but he tugged her back down into the chair again. "What do you mean, you don't care?"

"Precisely what I said, Jasper. Let them talk, if they

must. They'd likely do so anyway, no matter what I do. Am I meant to abandon all my interests merely because the *ton* doesn't approve of them? Why, I've never heard of anything so ridiculous. I don't care if they do gossip about me."

"*I* care, Prue." He grasped her hands in his. "I won't have every gossip in London whispering about you behind your back!"

"If you wanted a wife the *ton* would approve of, then you should have chosen a different lady, one who likes to spend her days shopping, gossiping, and dressing in the latest fashions. But that's not me, Jasper. It never was."

"Listen to me, Prue. You've no idea how vicious they can be."

"What are you saying, Jasper? What is it you want me to do?" But she already knew, didn't she? She could already feel his words gathering in the empty space between them—

"I want your promise that you won't go to Angelo's again."

She stared at him, her chest going so tight she couldn't catch her breath, but then the anger rose inside her, swelling and pushing until the word trapped in her throat spilled over her lips. "No."

"No?" He gaped at her, as if he thought he'd misheard her.

"No," she repeated, raising her chin. "I won't promise you any such thing. My answer is no."

If she promised this, Angelo's would only be the beginning of the concessions he'd demand of her. Next she'd find the *ton* didn't approve of her shooting at Manton's or visiting Tattersalls, or that they were gossiping about her riding hell for leather in Green Park of a morning, or snickering over her unfashionable clothing, or the thousands of other things she wished to do that duchesses weren't meant to do.

It would never end, and soon enough the Prudence Thorne she'd always been would be swallowed up by the Duchess of Montford. She'd already promised herself she wouldn't allow that to happen. Indeed, she couldn't allow it, because if she did, then what would become of her?

"I do beg your pardon, Your Grace, but I'm not going to change my mind." She snatched her hands from his grip and rose to her feet.

He made no move to touch her again, but when she reached the door, his low voice stopped her. "You're not to go to Angelo's again, Prue. I forbid it."

Her hand froze on the doorknob. There it was, the word she'd been dreading. "You tried to forbid me something once before, Jasper, on the day of the shooting party at Basingstoke House. Do you remember?"

"Remember?" He let out a harsh laugh. "How could I forget? You shot me for it."

No, she hadn't. That shot had been an accident. What she *had* done was go on to do precisely as she'd intended from the start, which was to join the shooting party. And while it was true that she might better have listened to him in that one instance and remained behind, it hadn't made her any fonder of the word "forbid."

Not from anyone's lips, but least of all his. "Yet knowing that, you still think it's wise to attempt to forbid me something I want?"

"I wasn't your husband then. I am now. Surely, you aren't going to attempt to persuade me it makes no difference?"

Slowly, she turned to face him. "No, indeed. It makes all the difference."

"Good." He rose to his feet with the casual confidence

of a man who considered the matter closed. "I'm pleased to find we both agree—"

"Agree? Oh, no, Your Grace. I'm afraid you misunderstand me. Have you forgotten that when you offered me your hand, you made it quite clear we would each pursue our own lives? Because I can assure you, I have not."

"No, I haven't forgotten, but that's not what I—"

"You promised me freedom. I believe your exact words were that I'd enjoy a great deal more freedom as the Duchess of Montford than I ever could as plain Miss Thorne. Do you recall that?"

"I recall it, yes, but that's not what this—"

"I took you at your word, Your Grace, and I intend to enjoy the freedoms I was promised when I agreed to become your duchess. Or do you mean to withdraw your promise now? Are you a man of your word, Jasper, or are you a liar?"

His jaw ticked, but he remained silent.

"Ah. I see how it is. When you spoke of freedoms, you meant only your *own* freedoms. You imagined you'd do exactly as you pleased, while I . . . what, Jasper? Sat about the townhouse and waited for you? What a pity you didn't say so when you offered me your hand. Now, if you'll pardon me, Your Grace—"

"Not quite yet, Prue." He sauntered toward her, his eyes dark and his lips pressed into a tight line. Oh, he was angry, so angry, but she stood her ground as he got closer and closer, pressing her into the doorway, his hands coming up on either side of her face, caging her in. "Perhaps I haven't made myself clear."

She gazed up into his handsome face, her knees nearly buckling from the delicious scent of amber and orange blossom, but she wouldn't back down in this. "On the contrary, Your Grace, you've made yourself perfectly clear. You think because you're my husband now, you can forbid me whatever you wish."

He caught a loose lock of her hair and tucked it back behind her ear, his fingers grazing her cheek, making her shiver. "That's generally how it works, yes. You did promise obedience in your wedding vows, if you recall."

"And you, Your Grace, promised to live in love and peace with your wife, but alas, there will be no peace between us if you attempt to curtail my freedoms."

He gazed at her for a moment, a wry smile at the corners of his lips. "Such a willful, stubborn wife," he murmured, dragging his fingers down her neck. He followed them with his lips, pressing a chain of light kisses from just under her chin to the hollow of her throat.

She caught her breath, grasping his shoulders to steady herself. "D-do you think to seduce a promise to stay away from Angelo's from me, Your Grace?"

He leaned away from her, his eyebrows rising. "Is that what you think?" He dragged his thumb across her lower lip, his eyes darkening when she parted for him. "It's nothing so diabolical as that. Perhaps I just want you, Prue. Perhaps I'm enamored of my willful, stubborn wife."

If it hadn't been for the way he'd turned away from her this morning, she might have believed him. Even a man as practiced at seduction as Jasper couldn't feign such a dark, heated gaze, such ragged breaths, and . . . were his hands shaking?

But no, it couldn't be a coincidence he was overcome with desire for her *now*, when she'd just refused him the promise he sought. The timing was suspect, to say the least.

Still, even that might not have been enough to convince

her he'd use his, er . . . masculine wiles to manipulate her, but this was what Jasper *did*, wasn't it? He charmed ladies, and he did it so well he was accustomed to always having his own way.

But not this time. Not with *her*. "I find that difficult to believe, Your Grace."

"It's the truth, Prue." He caught her chin and turned her face up to his. "You may trust me, wife, when I say I *burn* for you." He nuzzled the arch where her neck met her shoulder, then his mouth drifted to the sensitive skin behind her ear. "If I believed taking you to my bed would persuade you to give me your promise, I'd do so in a heartbeat."

She squeezed her eyes closed, her fingertips digging into his shoulders. If anything could persuade her, it was *this*—the dizzying pleasure of his mouth on her skin, his tongue teasing, the bristle of his emerging beard tickling her neck. "Nothing can persuade me."

"Is that a challenge, Your Grace?" He brushed a soft kiss over her lips, the warm drift of his breath a sweet caress over her heated skin. "It sounds like one."

"Perhaps it is." She tore her mouth from his. "What say you to a wager, Your Grace?"

"A wager?" He drew back, searching her face. "You can't be serious."

"On the contrary, I'm quite serious." A breathless moan tore from her throat as his lips skimmed over her collarbones, her head falling back against the door. "What are you prepared to risk, Your Grace?"

"Whatever I must," he murmured against her skin. "I won't have the *ton* slandering my wife."

She pushed against his chest, his heart thudding underneath her palm. "Very well, Your Grace. Franny's ball is in ten days. If you fail to secure my promise by then, then you will abandon this nonsense about forbidding me from visiting Angelo's."

"Hmmm. And if I take you to my bed before then?"

"Then I'll abide by your wishes, and the subject will never again cross my lips." The subject of *Angelo's*, that is. She hadn't promised not to hire a private fencing master.

Still, a wager was a wager, and her promise to give up Angelo's burned on its way up her throat. It was absurd she should have to give up anything at all, and this time it wasn't merely a handful of scandalous rubies, or even her father's unpaid debt.

Those things had mattered to her—of course, they had—but they weren't so precious she'd been afraid to risk losing them.

Her freedom was another matter entirely.

But someone had to teach the Duke of Montford a lesson, didn't they? He must be made to understand he wouldn't have his way in everything, or else they'd never have any peace between them. Surely, she had nothing to fear? Men were far more likely to become victims of their passions than ladies. Why, he'd likely give up this nonsense long before Franny's ball.

"I only wish to protect you, Prue. You don't yet understand how quickly London can become a prison of its own, once the *ton* has you at its mercy."

He drew back to gaze at her, his dark eyes so serious she had a brief moment of misgiving, but she shrugged it off. As long as she didn't care what the *ton* whispered about her, she could never be at their mercy. "Do we have a wager, Your Grace?"

"Indeed," he drawled, his gaze lingering on her mouth. "Let's begin now, shall we?"

He reached for her, but she slipped under his arm and skipped out into the hallway, turning back to him once she was safely out of his reach. "Oh, Your Grace? There is one other thing I should tell you."

He leaned a hip against the doorframe, a grin twitching at his lips. "Yes? What is it *now*?"

"Nothing terribly shocking. I only thought you should know I've dismissed Mrs. Stritch."

"*Dismissed* her?" He straightened from his slouch, his brows lowering. "Whatever for?"

"She didn't suit. Rather uppity, you know, and a bit too *meddlesome* for my tastes. Curious behavior indeed, for a servant. Don't you think so, Your Grace?"

"Prue—"

"Not to worry, Jasper. I've taken care of it. She's gone now."

"For God's sake, Prue—"

"Oh dear, you don't sound pleased. I'm very sorry, but I knew you wouldn't want me to be burdened with a lady's maid I don't trust. Isn't that right, Jasper?"

She didn't give him a chance to say anything more, but turned to make her way up the staircase, leaving him staring after her.

CHAPTER 21

Seducing his wife should have been the easiest thing in the world, but then history was rife with things that *should* have occurred, yet never did.

That scrap with the American colonists, for instance. Surely, Britain should have triumphed there? It was a bloody humiliating loss, that was certain, but not as humiliating as a duke infamous for his conquests who couldn't manage to bed his duchess.

What use was it being a wicked rake, if he couldn't even lure his own wife to his bed?

"Prue! Open up at once!" He paused in his pacing to rap his knuckles on the door between their bedchambers. "It's hardly sporting for you to hide in your rooms in this cowardly way!"

Nothing. His only answer was a profound silence.

"If I'd realized you intended to hide in your bedchamber for the next ten days, Prue, I never would have agreed to this ridiculous wager!" He resumed his pounding, attacking the door with such violence it was a wonder it didn't splinter to bits under his fist. "Really, Your Grace, I would have thought you'd disdain such a shoddy ploy as this. I took you for a far more ferocious competitor!"

There. That should do it. There was no way his fierce wife would allow such aspersions to be cast upon her courage. He pressed his ear to the door, waiting for the thud of angry footsteps approaching, but there was nothing but a faint shuffling sound, and the door remained firmly closed.

"I know you're in there, Prue. I can hear you moving about. Come out of there at once and give me a chance to seduce you, damn—"

"Jasper? For pity's sake, what in the world are you shouting about? I could hear you all the way from the entryway!"

He whirled around, and there in the open doorway that led from the corridor into his bedchamber stood his wife, blinking at him in astonishment. "Where in God's name did you come from?" He looked from her to the closed door between their bedchambers and then back to her again. "More to the point, where have you *been*? It's only just past dawn!"

She snorted. "It's nine o'clock, Jasper. The sun rose a full three hours ago."

"As I said, only just past dawn." He eyed her, crossing his arms over his chest. She was dressed in a fetching peacock-blue frock, a matching blue hat perched atop her golden-brown curls. To look at her, one would never guess she could have been up to any mischief, but he'd discovered quickly enough that the appearance of innocence meant precisely nothing when it came to his wife. "Where in God's name have you been this early in the morning?"

She may appear to be the picture of ladylike innocence, but the truth was, the Duchess of Basingstoke was a slippery one. It was rather too bad he'd devoted all his energy to becoming a wicked rake, because he would have made an excellent spy. If the last few days had proved nothing else, they'd revealed his heretofore hidden talents for eavesdropping, lurking in hallways, listening at closed doors, and muffling his footsteps so he might sneak about without being detected.

He'd drawn the line at picking locks, but only just.

Still, sneaking about like a thief, in his own house! A man's home was meant to be his castle, damn it, but it seemed that was only the case up until the moment he acquired a wife.

Or, no. Perhaps that wasn't quite true. A gentleman and his wife might happily share a castle, but only insofar as his wife wasn't a stubborn, hazel-eyed termagant, and far too beautiful and tempting for her own good. Such a wife could transform a man's castle into a torture chamber in the blink of an eye.

Not that Prue made herself unpleasant. She didn't scold him, or complain, or argue, nor did she subject him to the barbed tongue that lurked inside that sweet mouth.

No, it was far worse than that.

Instead, she made herself utterly, diabolically irresistible. She was everywhere, and always with a smile on her delectable lips, flirting and teasing him, or casting him heated glances from under heavy eyelids. She was driving him mad, her every move, her every breath, her every cursed flutter of long, dark eyelashes a delicious torment. If her intention had been to reduce him to a blithering fool, she'd succeeded most admirably, and their wager had hardly begun.

It had been four days. Four long, torturous, lust-addled days. Yesterday, she'd laid her hand on his arm, and his cock had surged to instant, aching attention.

His *arm*, for God's sake!

And now—*now*, she was gaping at him with wide, hazel eyes, as if he'd lost his wits! "Well, Your Grace? I asked you a question. Where have you been? You're meant to be in your bedchamber in the mornings!"

How the devil was he meant to seduce her if he couldn't *find* her?

"Am I, indeed? Well, no one informed *me*. I left my bedchamber hours ago." Her chin rose. "And if you really must know, Jasper, I was at Tattersalls."

"*Tattersalls*?" Ladies didn't go to Tattersalls, ever. It was sacred ground, the exclusive province of London's fashionable gentlemen. "My God, how in the world did you manage that?"

She shrugged. "Colonel Kingston arranged it."

"Ah. Of course, he did." He might have known his grandfather had a hand in it.

A fond smile crossed Prue's lips. "As it happens, the colonel is a great friend of Mr. Tattersall."

Oh yes, his grandfather was great friends with every-one in London. No doubt the old man was also behind Prue's infamous visit to Manton's Shooting Gallery ear-lier this week. At this rate, she'd be holding court in the bow window at White's before the month was out.

God only knew what the *ton* would make of this latest escapade to Tattersalls, especially after the commotion the incident at Manton's had caused. She'd made her visit well after the gallery had closed for the day, but of course everyone had got wind of it nonetheless, and some of London's more conservative gentlemen had complained bitterly about Manton's hallowed halls being defaced by the presence of a lady.

Others, though, had merely laughed at it, and professed themselves delighted with the Duchess of Montford's daring. That was typical of London's reaction to their new duchess. Half the *ton* insisted she was quite mad, while the other half maintained just as stubbornly that she was merely a charming eccentric, and a lady of uncommon spirit.

Spirit. That word kept coming up in relation to his wife, didn't it?

Whatever one might think of Prue, one thing was certain.

The Duchess of Montford had caused a sensation in London. Not because she fenced, or shot at Manton's, or assessed horseflesh at Tattersalls with an eye any gentleman in London would envy, and not because she dressed differently than the other aristocratic ladies.

No, it was because she wasn't afraid of them. Their gossip, their whispers, their viciousness—she wasn't afraid of any of it. She did as she pleased, and never troubled herself over what people said about it.

"There's no need for you to stand outside my bedchamber door shouting, Jasper." Prue pinched her lips into a prim line. "You might have knocked like a civilized gentleman, you know, rather than raving like a bedlamite."

"I did knock! I've been knocking for the better part of an hour! And if I am a bedlamite, it's *you* who's driven me mad!"

"An *hour*!" She stared at him. "You mean to say you've been outside my door for an hour, bellowing like an angry bull?"

"I beg your pardon, Your Grace." Jasper drew himself up with a sniff. "I don't *bellow*. I'm a duke, for God's sake." Though to be fair, this was precisely the sort of situation that might reduce the sanest of gentlemen to undignified bellowing. "And if I *did* bellow, it was only because I was certain I heard you shuffling about on the other side of the door."

"For pity's sake, Jasper! The shuffling you heard was Sarah. Some new gowns I ordered from the modiste arrived this morning, and I bid her to make room for them in my wardrobe. Dear God, you've likely frightened her to death!"

Prue turned and rushed down the corridor to her bedchamber. He went after her—he was getting into that bedchamber, one way or another—but he came to an abrupt halt behind her when she froze in the doorway.

"Oh, Sarah! There, it's alright now, you poor thing." Prue cast a furious look at him over her shoulder, hissing, "Look what you've done, you awful man."

"What did I do?" He edged past her into the bedchamber, before someone thought to bolt the door against him again. "Why, not a blessed thing, only . . . oh. Damn it."

The little dark-haired housemaid Prue had taken for her lady's maid was cowering in the corner, her face streaked with tears. She let out a little shriek when she saw him and darted around to the far side of the bed. "I— I beg your pardon, Your Grace, but he just kept going on and on, and I didn't know what t-to *dooo*!" The last word rose to such a high-pitched wail it was all Jasper could do not to slap his hands over his ears.

"There now, don't cry, Sarah. Why don't you go downstairs and have a cup of tea and one of Cook's special apple tarts? No, it's alright, you may come out this way. His Grace is going to go and stand by the wardrobe, and he won't stir an inch, I promise you." Prue shot him a murderous glance and pointed to the wardrobe on the opposite side of the room. "Don't move an *inch*, if you please, Your Grace."

God above, such an almighty fuss, and over nothing. Other dukes weren't subjected to such indignities when they attempted to bed *their* wives—he was almost certain of it. Still, he did as he was bid, before Prue made up her mind to toss him out of her bedchamber.

Sarah gave him one last fearful glance, then she darted across the bedchamber, taking care to keep a wide berth between them, and vanished down the corridor, still whimpering.

"Well, Jasper?" Prue shut the door behind her and turned to face him, her eyes blazing. "What have you got to say for yourself?"

What, indeed? "Er . . . is that a new frock, Your Grace?"

Prue rolled her eyes. "Yes, it's new. Don't try and change the subject from your appalling behavior, Jasper."

"Me? Of course not, Your Grace." He crept closer. "It's just that I've never seen you in that color before."

She'd been to the modiste last week, and since then a succession of new gowns had made an appearance, most of them in the jewel tones she favored, a rainbow of rich blues, bronzes, and deep reds, but the predominant color in her new wardrobe was green in every shade imaginable, from emerald to juniper, and jade to a soft, heathery sage.

She favored green, and he favored it on her, but he'd make an exception for this particular shade of peacock blue, which turned her eyes a lovely blue green, like a summer pond dappled with sunlight. Then again, she could be wearing a flour sack, and he'd still want her.

He crept closer still, half expecting her to flee as poor Sarah had done, but she remained where she was until he was close enough to touch her. "It's quite fetching on you," he murmured, toying with one end of the ribbon that secured the matching hat under her chin. "May I?"

She huffed out a breath, but a smile was tugging at the corners of her lips. "You're utterly shameless, Jasper."

"Mmmm." He tugged on the ribbon and the bow came undone. "If that's so, then it's entirely your fault, Your Grace."

She arched an eyebrow. "It's *my* fault you shouted at my lady's maid and made her cry?"

"Of course, it is." He removed her hat, a flimsy straw affair with a white feather and a bit of peacock-blue ribbon. It wasn't the least bit titillating, as hats went, and thus shouldn't have reduced him to breathlessness, yet here they were.

"I never used to shout at housemaids." He tossed the hat onto the bed. "But I've quite lost my wits since I made a certain hazel-eyed hellion my duchess."

"What nonsense. I'm not a—"

"Hush." He pressed his fingertips to her lips, smothering a groan at how soft they were, how pliant. "I'm sorry I made Sarah cry. I'll beg her pardon, I promise you. *Later*." He took her hand and drew her gloves off, one finger at a time, pressing his lips to each dainty pink fingertip as he bared it. "At the moment, I have another urgent matter to attend to."

One way or another, this ridiculous wager had to end. Before he left this room, he intended to secure her promise she'd never again return to Angelo's.

"Is that so?" She moved her hands to his chest and he stiffened, but she didn't push him away, only rested them there, her palms flat and warm over his shirt, her sweet, plush lower lip caught between her teeth.

God, that pout. Did she have any idea how desirable she was? He tangled his fingers in her hair and dropped a teasing kiss on the corner of her mouth. "Do be careful with that lip, Your Grace." He gently freed it from her bite, his own lips parting as he rubbed the pad of his thumb over that soft, pink skin. "I may have a use for it."

"Oh." She darted a shy look at him from under her lashes with those huge, blue-green eyes, as if she were waiting for him to kiss her.

He opened his mouth against her throat and let his tongue dart out to taste her, and she let out a soft little whimper as his mouth drifted over the silky skin of her neck. When he reached her mouth he teased his tongue over her lower lip, nipping and sucking at it. "Open your mouth for me, Prue."

She let out a soft sigh as she parted for him, her fingers curling into his shirt, holding on. "Your mouth is . . ."

He drew back a little and smiled down at her, his head suddenly dizzy. "Yes?"

"Your lips are so much softer than I remember."

Jasper wanted to sink to his knees. *She'd thought about his lips?*

He touched his mouth gently to hers at first, nibbling and teasing his tongue along the seam of her lips, but when she opened to him and brushed her tongue against his he surged inside with a groan. "You taste so good, Prue. I can't get enough of you."

He held her face in his hands and kissed her over and over again, his mouth soft and then desperate, his hips tight against hers, his cock at full attention. "I laid awake for hours last night, thinking about kissing you, touching you."

Her gaze caught and held his, her tongue darting out to touch the corner of her lip where his mouth had just been, and good God, his entire body exploded with heat at the sight. He couldn't take his eyes off her. She was the most beautiful thing he'd ever seen, with that wicked little tongue flicking over her lips.

He dragged the flat of his palm down her throat, pausing to feel the jump of her pulse against his skin. He wanted her, more than he'd ever believed it was possible to want anyone. "I want to see you," he murmured, trailing his fingertip over the narrow band of velvet that trimmed the neckline of her bodice.

She nodded, her darkened gaze never leaving his face as he reached behind her to loosen the buttons of her gown one by one, his fingers clumsy, until he'd freed her from the last fold of her peacock-blue gown, leaving her in only her shift.

He stood back to take her in, his mouth going dry at the sight of her smooth, pale skin, the tempting shadows of her nipples under her thin, white-linen shift. "So pretty, Prue," he whispered, sliding the backs of his fingers down her neck to her breasts. He plucked at her nipples with his fingers, brushing his thumbs over the peaks, a groan tearing from his throat as they hardened into tight points for him. "Does that feel good, sweetheart?"

"Yes." She curled her fingers into his shirt, her breath coming in rough little pants. "*Yes.*"

He slid his hands down her body, pausing to squeeze her waist before catching a handful of her shift in his fist. He dragged it up, over the long, slender line of her legs and inched his fingers underneath it, his knuckles brushing against her thigh, his palm hot against the sweet curve of her belly.

She trembled against him, her forehead dropping to his chest as he circled his fingertips over her skin, drawing closer to the warm, needy place between her thighs with every sweep of his hand until at last—*at last*—he touched her core, caressing her gently. "I want to kiss you here, Prue."

She gasped, her thighs trembling as he delved between

her folds, his fingertip pressing against the hot, slick center of her. "I want to taste you right here. Will you let me do that? Will you let me taste you?"

She let out a choked whimper, and it was all the answer he needed.

Jasper caught her in his arms, but the bed was miles away, so he lowered her onto the top of the writing desk nearby and slid between her thighs, his desperate cock jerking at the press of her soft, warm core against him. "Hold on to me," he whispered, then he dropped to his knees, nuzzling his face against her thigh. "Do you touch yourself here, sweetheart? Between your legs? Have you ever caressed that sweet little bud until you bring yourself pleasure?"

"Ah!" She gasped at the first touch of his tongue, just the lightest caress, hardly more than a breath, and God, he could listen to her hungry whimpers all night. He wanted to keep her right on the edge of this desk with her legs open to him until she was writhing for him, her throat hoarse from crying out.

But as soon as he tasted her, every thought—the wager, Angelo's, her promise—emptied from his head until there was no holding back, nothing for him to do but give her what she needed.

She arched her back with a desperate, panting little whimper that went straight to his cock. He teased her quivering bud, circling and stroking with the tip of his tongue, his fingers curled around the backs of her thighs to hold her wide open to his mouth so he could feel the vibration of her every gasp and moan against his tongue.

"Jasper!" She threw her head back, reaching down to twist a hand in his hair and hold him against her as she shuddered through her release. He stayed with her as she peaked, then brought her down with long, gentle strokes of his tongue until the tension drained from her body, and she sagged against the desk with a sigh.

He collapsed against her, pressing a kiss to her thigh. He was aching for his own release, his cock pulsing with every heartbeat, throbbing with need. One or two strokes was all it would take, yet he hesitated, his fingers hovering over the buttons of his falls for an instant before he drew them away again.

Not this time. Not after *that*, when it had been so perfect between them.

Once his breathing had calmed, he gathered her into his arms and laid her gently on the bed, pausing only to trace her mouth with his fingertips before he slipped through the connecting door, leaving her with fluttering eyelids and a dreamy smile on her lips.

It was only after he'd closed the door behind him that he remembered.

The wager. He'd forgotten all about the wager.

CHAPTER 22

As mad as Prue's wager was, it did have one redeeming feature. By the time the evening of Basingstoke's ball arrived, Jasper no longer cared that she'd won it.

Such was the power of thwarted desire, he no longer cared about much of anything aside from getting the damned ball over with, so he could admit defeat, withdraw his edict against Angelo's, and take his wife to his bed.

Damned if he could remember why he'd ever objected in the first place.

He marched from one end of the entryway to the other, one eye on the black pumps Loftus had shined to a blinding gloss and the other on the stairs. He'd nearly worn the marble smooth as he waited for Prue to descend from her apartments so they might be on their way to Basingstoke's ball.

Ten minutes, fifteen, a lifetime—

Thud.

He jerked his attention to the staircase, his heart leaping from his chest only to crash back down again with a despairing whimper. It was only Keating, with Jasper's gloves, hat, and walking stick in his hand. "Good evening, Your Grace."

"Good evening. Thank you, Keating." Jasper shoved his hands into the gloves and plopped the hat on top of his head. "You didn't happen to see any sign of the duchess while you were upstairs, did you? It grows late."

"No, Your Grace. Her Grace is dressing."

"*Still*?" How long did it take to put on a silk gown? "What the devil is she doing, harvesting the cocoons herself? Extracting the silk threads and spinning them into a ball gown?"

Keating blinked. "No, I don't believe so, Your Grace, but if Your Grace wishes it, I can go upstairs and see if—"

"No, never mind, Keating." There was no sense sending poor Keating off on some wild chase. One madman in the house was quite enough. "It's just that we're meant to be at Basingstoke's by ten, and it's already—"

He broke off as a warm, musical sound reached them from an upstairs corridor, drifting down the stairs like a handful of tossed rose petals.

It was Prue, and she was laughing.

God, when was the last time he'd heard her laugh? Had he *ever* heard her laugh as she was now, in such an unrestrained burst of joyful sound? He could have remained at the bottom of the staircase all night, just listening to her. How had he not realized how still and silent his home had been, before she came?

"The duchess has a lovely laugh, does she not, Your Grace?"

Jasper smiled. "She does indeed, Keating."

Prue had a lovely *everything*, from her laugh to her wit, her sharp tongue to her beautiful hazel eyes. He turned his gaze up to the top of the stairs, his heart thrumming with anticipation, but he wasn't prepared for the sight of her when she appeared above him, her cheeks flushed pink, her hair gleaming golden brown in the light from the chandelier above.

He watched as she descended, dazzled, a thousand confused thoughts whirling through his head at once, but one stood out from the rest, and it was the only one that mattered.

There was, quite simply, no other woman like her, and by some miracle, she was *his*.

She was wearing a new gown, a deep, emerald-green one he hadn't seen before, the silk swirling around her like jewels when she moved, the color so deeply saturated it was nearly a living thing, and cut perfectly to her lithe figure, lovingly emphasizing every inch of the long, graceful lines of her body.

The gown put him in mind of the simple green one she'd worn to dinner on the second night of the shooting party at Basingstoke House. That had been the first time he'd seen her in evening dress, and he couldn't tear his gaze away from her then, any more than he could now.

It didn't matter what she wore. That drab, brown cloak, her worn, navy-blue riding habit, or the matching hat with a hoof print in the center and that poor, limp little feather.

It wasn't about her clothing at all. It was just *her*.

He waited for her to reach the bottom of the staircase, and never before had a mere dozen steps taken such a torturous eternity, but at last she stood before him, her small, gloved hand slipping into his. "Good evening, Your Grace."

He bowed over her hand, his lips skimming her glove, the faint hint of honeysuckle that clung to her tightening his stomach. He forgot Keating's presence entirely then and reached up to cup her face in his palm. "You're lovely, Prue."

She searched his face, the flush deepening to a vivid rose in her cheeks, but whatever she saw in his return gaze made her lips curve in a shy smile. "Thank you, Your Grace."

"Shall we go?" He tucked her arm into his. "I'll never hear the end of it from Basingstoke if we're late."

Keating stood at the open door, beaming. "I wish you both a pleasant evening, Your Graces."

"Thank you, Keating." Jasper led Prue out to the carriage and waited for Norris to close the door behind them and ascend to the box before taking her into his arms. "You realize it's the night of Basingstoke's ball, do you not, Your Grace?" His eyes closed as the wisps of hair at her temples brushed his chin, her scent floating around him.

God, it was almost painful, how badly he wanted her.

"Is it, indeed?" She let out a soft laugh. "I knew there must be a reason Sarah insisted upon lacing me so tightly tonight."

At the mention of her lacing, he made a heroic attempt not to let his gaze drop to the creamy swell of her bosom spilling from her low bodice, the generous display of decolletage the one concession Prue had made to the demands of fashion in her choice of gown.

But it was no use. He may as well have resisted looking at the sunrise, or a velvety black sky studded with stars. He reached for her, tracing his fingertip over the narrow band of velvet ribbon, skimming the warm skin of the upper swell of her breasts. "Despite her humble beginnings, Sarah has turned out to be an excellent lady's maid."

She caught her breath at his touch, and his gaze flew to her face. The interior of the carriage was dim, the only illumination the flickering light from Curzon Street as they passed, but he could see her eyes—a dark, mysterious green tonight—fixed on him.

"Our wager is at an end." He caught her hand and pressed a kiss to her palm. "Not a moment too soon. I've never lived through a longer ten days in my life. It felt like an eternity."

She lowered her gaze, toying with the buttons on his coat. "It did, didn't it?"

"Did it to you, as well? I never would have guessed it. It seemed as if you could go along quite happily as we had been for at least another year or so."

She laughed. "A year? Goodness, no."

"I can see now I was doomed from the start." When it came to his wife, he was hopeless at wagering. Hopeless at seduction, too. He'd never had any trouble either at the gaming tables or in the bedchamber before, it was true, but then, he'd never before made the grave mistake of trifling with his duchess.

His stunning, exquisite, enticing, maddening duchess.

But despite the past ten days of frustration, her wager had turned out to be a stroke of pure genius. If it hadn't been for the wager, he never would have spent all that time alone in his bed, thinking about her and missing her. It had given him the time he needed to come to his senses and reach the conclusion he should have reached from the start.

The fencing at Angelo's had never really been about fencing at Angelo's, just as her visit to Tattersalls, the shooting at Manton's, or her ride on Sampson that day at Basingstoke House had been about any of those things.

They weren't merely things she *did*. They were who she *was*.

She'd tried to explain it to him, that day he'd dragged her away from Angelo's, when she'd told him if he wanted a duchess who'd spend her days shopping and gossiping, then he should have married another lady.

Why had it taken so long for him to understand what she meant? Unless it was that, for a rake who'd spent a good portion of his adult life bedding one lady after another, he hadn't ever spent much time talking to any of them.

Listening, either.

In the end, all she'd asked from him that day was for the freedom to be who she was.

And he'd refused her. He could no longer remember why, now.

His wife was extraordinary. Why in the world should he wish to make her otherwise?

"I have a gift for you, Your Grace." He touched her chin, tipping her face up to his. "May I bring it to your bedchamber tonight?"

"I think you'd better, yes." She laid a hand on his cheek, her gaze growing serious. "I—I've missed you, Jasper."

He caught her hand and pressed it to his lips. "I missed you, too."

But as the carriage rolled through the dim streets of London, her hand still clasped in his, he knew it was more than that.

It was love. He'd fallen in love with his wife.

"It's, ah, it's terribly crowded, is it not?" Prue cast a nervous glance over the mass of fashionably dressed people crowding the ballroom, her stomach lurching, then turned her gaze to Franny. "So many people."

The ballroom blazed with light, the harsh glare playing over what seemed to be hundreds of people, all of them dressed in the height of elegance, the ladies in extravagant silk gowns, their fingers, wrists, ears, and necks flashing with colorful jewels.

And a great many of them had their curious gazes pointed at *her*.

Perhaps this ball hadn't been such a wise idea, after all. "I thought everyone was meant to be at their country houses. Doesn't the *ton* hunt in September?"

"Generally, yes, but they're curious about you, dearest." Franny squeezed her hand. "They've all come to see the mysterious new Duchess of Montford for themselves."

"You mean to say they've given up their grouse hunting so they might hunt duchesses, instead?" She attempted a laugh, but it set the butterflies in her stomach aflutter again, and a wave of nausea gripped her.

She would not cast up her accounts. She would *not*.

Not with all those prying eyes on her at once.

"I'm no friend to *ton* gossip, as you know, Prue, but it must be said that you *have* rather earned something of a name for yourself." Lady Diana, Basingstoke's eldest sister gave Prue a mischievous smile. "The *ton* has worked themselves into a passion over you. I don't believe I've ever seen the like of it before."

A *passion*? Goodness, that sounded ominous. "I can't think why. They're sure to be disappointed when the mystery is dispelled at last."

"No, they won't be," Jasper said at once. "How could they be?"

"Why, how gallant you are, Montford." Lady Diana grinned. "I never thought I'd see the day, but then marriage does seem to agree with you."

Jasper bowed. "My lady."

"I'll grant you it is a bit of a crush, but surely that's a good thing? This way you get it all over with this evening."

Franny patted her hand. "That's why you agreed to the ball in the first place, isn't it?"

"My dearest Franny, I wouldn't say she agreed so much as you badgered her into it." Lady Diana gave her sister-in-law an indulgent smile before turning to Prue, her blue eyes sympathetic. "It looks dreadfully intimidating, doesn't it? But really, there's nothing at all to be anxious about, I promise you, Prue. The tongues in London are forever wagging over one thing or another. It means nothing."

Were all the tongues in London wagging about her, then? "I don't understand why any of them are interested in me at all. I'm dreadfully dull."

"Dull!" Franny chuckled. "My dear Prue, you're far from dull."

"Indeed." Lady Diana delicately cleared her throat. "You *did* shoot your husband, after all, Prue. That's, ah . . . well, it's rather the sort of thing that catches the *ton*'s attention."

"And in the arse, no less," Basingstoke added with a smirk.

"I didn't!" Prue protested, looking between them. "That is, I *did*, but I never meant—"

"Giles!" Franny scolded, turning to her husband. "Hush."

Basingstoke grinned. "I don't see what all the fuss is. Why, there must be dozens of people in London who are overjoyed Montford was shot in the arse."

Jasper rolled his eyes. "Listen to your wife, Basingstoke, and hush."

"I never shot my husband!" Prue announced, and goodness, it felt good to get *that* out.

Every eye turned toward her. "Er, I'm afraid you *did*,

in fact, shoot me." Jasper smiled down at her. "I still have the scars to prove—"

"I did shoot you, yes. *Accidentally*. But you weren't my husband, then." Is that what the *ton* thought? That she was some crazed wife who'd gone after her husband with a shotgun?

"Very well, then. You shot the Duke of Montford." Lady Diana cocked her head, considering it. "I'm not certain if that's better or worse, especially as you married him directly afterwards. Then there was that incident at Angelo's—"

"It wasn't an incident!" For pity's sake, why did everyone insist on making such a fuss over that? "I went to a fencing academy to fence. There's nothing so shocking in that, surely."

"I believe I heard something about you going to Tattersalls, as well? I daresay that would have ruffled a few gentlemen's feathers." Basingstoke shook his head. "Not that I see a thing wrong with it, mind you."

"I don't see why ladies should be forbidden to shoot at Manton's, or to go to Tattersalls." Lady Diana tossed her head. "Franny says you've got an excellent seat, Prue. Better than most gentlemen, and that you know a great deal about horses."

"Perhaps, but I daresay that won't redeem me with the *ton*."

"They simply don't know what to make of you, dearest." Franny squeezed her hand again. "That's what the ball is for. To take the shroud of mystery away. Once it's gone and they find you're a regular duchess, there will be nothing left for them to gossip about."

"But she *isn't* a regular duchess," Jasper said. "There's nothing ordinary about my wife."

The pride in his voice was unmistakable, and it should

have reassured her, but the knot in her stomach twisted another notch tighter. Oh, what had she been thinking, imagining she could ever be a proper duchess? She didn't belong here. "I, ah . . . I believe I'll visit the ladies' retiring room."

"I'll come with you," Franny said, catching up her long, blue silk train.

Prue stopped her with a hand on her arm. "No, indeed. I'm quite alright, and you must stay and see to your guests."

Jasper caught her arm, his brows drawn. "If you're unwell, we'll leave at once—"

"No." They couldn't leave less than an hour after they'd arrived. It would only cause more gossip. "No, I'm quite well, I promise you. Just a bit warm. I won't be long."

She didn't give Jasper a chance to protest further, but hurried off in the direction of the ladies' retiring room, desperate to be alone for just a moment, so she might take a deep breath and gather herself together without every eye upon her.

But she'd no sooner turned the corner and was hurrying down the corridor that led to the ladies' retiring room than she heard hurried footsteps behind her. She pasted a smile on her lips and turned, imagining she'd find Franny on her heels, but the lady following her wasn't Franny.

It was Lady Selina Archer.

Prue froze in the middle of the corridor, her feet suddenly locked in place. How strange, that she should have so instantly recognized Lady Archer. She'd only ever seen a tiny painting of her, and there were dozens of blue-eyed, dark-haired ladies at Franny's ball.

But she knew her at a glance, and the expression on that beautiful face sent a chill darting down Prue's spine.

"Ah, the Duchess of Montford, at last." Lady Selina's lovely, red bow lips curled upward in a smile as jagged as shattered glass. "I've quite longed to meet you since you arrived in London, Your Grace."

"I can't imagine why, Lady Archer." Prue's voice was cool, composed, but underneath her show of calm she was trembling. What was Lady Archer doing here? Franny hadn't invited her tonight, that was certain, which meant the woman had risked incurring the wrath of the Duke and Duchess of Basingstoke by coming to their home without an invitation.

There could be no innocent reason for that.

"Can't you? But we have so very much in common, Your Grace! Surely, we have just dozens of things we might talk about between us." Lady Archer let out a tinkling laugh, like icicles hitting a glass window.

Prue raised her chin. "I beg your pardon, but we haven't a single thing in common."

Lady Archer tossed her head back with another of those strange laughs, her dark, silky curls cascading down her back. "But of course, we do, Your Grace! We have Montford."

We have Montford. *We . . .*

"Oh, dear. You didn't know." Lady Archer gave a pitying shake of her head. "I do so hate to shatter your girlish illusions, Your Grace, but you must have known Montford wouldn't be satisfied with an awkward country girl like you for long."

She was lying. Both Franny and Jasper had warned her about Lady Archer, about the grudge she bore Jasper, and about the woman's vindictiveness—

"There's hardly a whiff of the country about you now, is there? Why, you look almost like a real duchess! Still, underneath it all, you're just a nobody from some tedious little village in . . . oh, dear. Montford told me, but I've forgotten. Is it Wiltshire?" Lady Archer ran a cold eye over Prue's emerald-green gown. "Alas, even the costliest silk gown can't hide everything."

She traced a bejeweled finger around the plunging neckline of her own scarlet satin gown, and that was when Prue noticed it. A heavy gold necklace of magnificent rubies flashing with a deep, crimson fire, each stone surrounded by diamonds, with tiny pearls dangling from the ends.

Lady Archer noticed her stare, and triumph flashed in her dark blue eyes. "Do you like it?" She raised a hand to her throat and caught one of the rubies on the end of her fingertip. "Montford gave it to me just this week. A reunion gift, of sorts. The rubies do catch one's attention, do they not? But of course, they're not merely rubies. There's a great deal more to them than meets the eye."

Tiny portraits hidden inside the ruby lockets . . .

Jasper, every inch of him gloriously bare, and the other one, with Lady Archer on her knees before him, his hands in her dark hair—

Prue squeezed her eyes closed, but there was no escaping it, nowhere she could look that she didn't see it, and now here was this necklace with its half-dozen massive rubies, hiding . . . what? Portraits of Jasper with this poisonous woman in his arms, their limbs tangled together and his lips on hers, kissing her, touching her—

"Montford's very wicked, is he not? But perhaps you're not as shocked as you should be at his antics, hmmm, Your Grace? You're not quite the innocent you'd have all of London believe."

"What?" Prue's jaw felt tight, rusty. "What did you say?"

Lady Archer gave an exaggerated shrug, but her blue

eyes were gleaming. "I only mean you weren't as pure as a sweet little country lass should be when you came to your husband's bed."

Cold fell over Prue then, so icy it stole her breath. She couldn't breathe, she couldn't *breathe*—

"Did you truly think Montford wouldn't notice?"

The pristine white sheets, the morning after their wedding night . . .

A gasp tore from Prue's throat as panic descended on her in a numbing fog. There was only one way Lady Archer could know such a thing, only one way—

"Oh, yes, Montford told me all about it. The *ton* doesn't yet realize what a whore you are, but they'll find it out soon enough." Lady Archer sneered, all pretense of politeness dropping away from her, leaving nothing but spite in its place. "I wonder what they'll think of their favorite then?"

Lady Archer went on, a torrent of words falling from those red, red lips, words piling atop each other, each one uglier than the last, so many words they might have drowned Prue, but she could no longer hear them over the roaring in her ears.

Tonight, Jasper had told her she was lovely. He'd held her in his arms, and told her he missed her, and she . . . she'd *believed* him.

A curl of anger rose in her belly, and *yes*, it was good, because it was that little flare of rage that broke the strange hold Lady Archer had on her, and she fled back down the corridor the way she'd come, but it was as if it weren't even her any longer. It was another lady, a duchess in an emerald-green silk gown, her footsteps echoing in the corridor as she ran, vestiges of Lady Archer's mocking laugh swirling around her, clinging to her hair and her skirts like the poisonous haze rising from a witch's cauldron.

She didn't go back to the ballroom. She couldn't. There was no way she could face all those staring eyes. She slipped into the Duke of Basingstoke's study instead, and curled up on the settee in front of the cold fireplace.

It was the same settee on which Jasper had slept on her first night in London, the same settee under which she'd found the ruby earrings. She sat there with her emerald skirts billowing around her like a green silk cloud, her arms closed around the stiff little pillow with the fringe of tassels, the one that had once smelled of amber and orange blossoms.

He found her there some time later, an hour later, perhaps, or perhaps a dozen hours. By then, word that Lady Archer had somehow slipped uninvited into the Duke and Duchess of Basingstoke's house had found its way into the ballroom.

Jasper tried to speak to her, in the study and in the carriage on their way home, his voice growing increasingly panicked when she didn't respond to him and didn't raise her eyes even when he begged her to please, please look at him.

It wasn't that she *wouldn't* look at him, it was that she *couldn't*, because she was just so very, very tired, so she turned her face away when he tried to take her in his arms. "I'm fatigued, Your Grace. Please let me go."

He released her, his hands dropping away.

She left him without another word, and went up the stairs to her bedchamber, where she sat on the edge of her bed until the fire went out, and the room was plunged into darkness. Sarah appeared at some point and tried to speak to her, but Prue didn't say a word in response, so she relit the fire and left again, closing the bedchamber door behind her.

Prue never stirred from her place on the edge of the bed.

There was no sound from Jasper's bedchamber next door until long after the house had gone silent, but eventually she heard footsteps, and Jasper's low voice, speaking to his valet.

Only then did she move.

She rose to her feet, crossed the room to the door that connected her bedchamber to her husband's, and with one quick twist of her fingers, she shot the bolt home.

CHAPTER 23

In the summer of her sixth year, Prue had fallen in love with a young boy named Charles Crofton. He had golden hair and brown eyes, and he was a sweet-tempered lad who, despite being older than she was, had tolerated her adoration with all the patience that could reasonably be expected of an eight-year-old boy.

But alas, Charles hadn't loved her in return. He'd gone off to Eton that autumn without a backward glance, breaking her tender, six-year-old heart. She'd been so distraught she'd spent the whole of one morning languishing tragically in her bedchamber before she'd given it up with a shrug and gone off riding with her father.

But there were broken hearts, and then there were *broken hearts*.

The first sort was of short duration, and as sweet as it was painful. The second, though—*that* was a shattering so complete one couldn't breathe for it, sharp claws sinking into the tender pink flesh of her heart, slicing and shredding until there was nothing left but blood and pulp, and it was easier just to give up breathing entirely.

This was the second kind.

Alas, her chest insisted on continuing to rise and fall,

her lungs perfectly indifferent to the death throes of the heart. There was nothing for it, then, but to lie upon her back and stare at the canopy over her head, and wait for . . . something.

What, she didn't know. A reason to stir from her bed, maybe. Some sort of impetus that would move her in one direction, or the other.

It came sooner than she expected.

The bedchamber door cracked open, and Sarah peered around the gap. "Your Grace? May I serve you some tea?"

Prue didn't want any tea, but Sarah had poked her head in twice before already, and she couldn't quite make herself send her away a third time. It wasn't as if she could lie in her bed for the rest of eternity, in any case. "Yes, I suppose tea will do. Come in, Sarah."

Sarah darted through the door, the tea tray rattling in her hands. She set it on the table beside the bed, arranged the tea things, then poured a cup and handed it to Prue. "Here you are, Your Grace. I've brought some of those scones you like, as well."

"Thank you, Sarah." Prue's stomach lurched at the thought of the scones, the stomach being for the most part in sympathy with the heart, but she took the tea, raised the cup to her lips, and made an attempt to choke it down.

Meanwhile, Sarah busied herself with gathering the cast-off remnants of last night's ballroom finery, which were flung about the room in shameful disarray. She'd been desperate to rid herself of every stitch of it, and had torn it off piece by piece as soon as she'd gained her bedchamber, leaving her gloves, ribbon, shoes, and reticle lying where they fell.

All but the emerald gown. She'd taken more care with that. She'd likely never wear it again, but it was too beautiful to ruin, so she'd draped it over the back of a chair.

Sarah paused beside it now and reached out to caress a fold of the skirt before turning to Prue. "The ball last night didn't go as you'd hoped it would, Your Grace?"

It was so far short of the horror of last night that Prue nearly laughed, but the urge died before a sound could pass her lips. "No. I'm afraid I don't have much luck with balls, Sarah." Her mistake had been in thinking Lord Hasting's ball at the end of the last season would prove to be the most miserable she'd ever attended.

"Oh, dear. I'm sorry, Your Grace." Sarah hesitated, glancing from the dress back to Prue again. "What will you do?"

That was the question, wasn't it? If Sarah had asked her that last night, she wouldn't have had an answer, but one thing about a broken heart was that it made sleeping impossible, and when one didn't sleep, one had plenty of time to think.

London had made a coward out of her, because the only thing she wanted, the only thing that didn't make her chest seize with panic to think of it, was to leave London behind. She wanted to be in the country, to lose herself there, far away from Jasper and the *ton*, and far away from having to be the Duchess of Montford.

For a time, at least.

Her first instinct was to flee to Thornewood, but as much as she longed to see her father, a visit home so soon after her marriage would lead to all sorts of questions she couldn't answer.

No, Thornewood would have to wait.

But there was one other place she could go.

Montford Park, Jasper's country estate in Kent.

She'd only ever seen it once, and then from a distance. She'd never even set foot inside, but when she'd closed her eyes last night, there it had been, dancing behind her eyelids as if it were calling to her.

There'd been no mistaking the house, set like a perfect creamy pearl into the green valley surrounding it. It didn't make sense, really, that she should feel so drawn to it, except that it was as close to the cloud-enveloped castle she'd dreamed of as any place she'd ever seen.

She replaced her half-empty teacup in the saucer. "I fancy a visit to the country, Sarah. I think it would do me a world of good to get out of London and breathe some fresh air."

The *ton* would gossip over her precipitate departure, of course, but then they were already gossiping, weren't they? There was nothing they could say that could hurt her anymore, because the worst had already happened.

"Help me to dress, won't you, Sarah? Then have one of the footmen fetch a trunk from the attics, will you? You can begin packing while I speak to His Grace." She couldn't simply vanish from Berkeley Square without Jasper's approval.

Surely, he wouldn't force her to remain in London? He, of all people, must understand she couldn't stay here. It had been him who'd warned her how vicious the *ton* could be, how quickly London could become a prison when they had you at their mercy.

She should have listened to him. How naïve she'd been, but then how could she ever have imagined a woman as malicious as Lady Archer?

She'd never seen anything like the spite in those blue eyes, or heard anything as hateful as the laugh that had followed her as she'd fled down the hallway. How could Jasper bear to be in the company of such a woman?

But then Lady Archer was very beautiful. She wouldn't have believed a thin veneer of beauty over such a cold, wicked heart could ever be enough for him, but then perhaps she'd never really known Jasper at all.

A heaviness descended over her, pressing down upon her, the weight of it settling over her heart, but she pushed the coverlet aside and submitted quietly as Sarah dressed her and brushed out her hair.

There was nothing for it then but to square her shoulders and face her husband.

It was quite early still, not yet seven o'clock, but there was no answer to her knock on the connecting door. So, she made her way from her bedchamber down the corridor to the staircase, then down the stairs into the silent entryway. The house was still and somber, almost as if they'd gone into mourning, but Keating was stationed in his usual place in front of the door.

"Good morning, Keating. Do you happen to know where His Grace is?"

Every proper butler knew all the household's secrets, and God knew there was no butler more proper than Keating. No doubt he'd heard the tale of last night's disastrous ball from the other servants, but he was no gossip.

"Good morning, Your Grace." Keating offered her a bow, his face as impassive as ever. "His Grace is in his study."

"Thank you, Keating." Prue did her best to ignore the writhing nerves in her stomach as she made her way down the corridor to the closed door of Jasper's study. There was no reason for her to feel anxious or ashamed. She'd done nothing wrong. Still, she was obliged to draw in a deep, steadying breath at his summons before she dared open the door.

He was sitting behind his desk, doing . . . well, nothing that she could see. There was a stack of letters at his elbow, but he wasn't reading them, nor was he writing, and he didn't appear to have glanced at *The Times*, which lay in perfectly creased folds on the corner of his desk.

But when she entered, he shot to his feet. "Prue!"

"Good morning, Jasper."

He hurried out from behind the desk. "I didn't want to wake you after . . . after last night, but I've been going half mad, waiting to talk to you. You must listen to me, Prue. Last night—"

"I didn't come to discuss last night, Jasper." There was very little left to say, really. Lady Archer had said it all. "It doesn't matter anymore."

"It *does* bloody matter, Prue. It's the only thing that matters." He dragged a hand through his hair, setting the dark, silky locks on end. His clothing was disheveled and his eyes bloodshot, as if he hadn't slept any better than she had.

And oh, how it hurt to see him this way, and how unfair it was that after all that had happened, she still couldn't harden her heart against him! It should have been the easiest thing in the world simply to turn her back on him, but it didn't work that way, did it?

The heart would continue to love, despite it all.

Because that was what this was, wasn't it? Somehow, in the midst of all their arguments, between the earrings and the wagers and the blackmail and the birdshot, she'd somehow fallen in love with her husband.

What a fool she'd been, to ever have imagined it would be otherwise. For weeks now, all of it, every moment between them—even at the start, when she'd loathed him as the man who'd ruined her father—even then, it had all been leading to this.

She'd wanted him from the very first.

How could she not have realized it would end here?

"Tell me what she said to you, Prue." Jasper's hands

covered her shoulders. "Whatever it was, whatever Lady Archer said to you, I promise you, it was a lie."

"She was wearing a ruby and diamond necklace. She said you gave it to her."

"I did give it to her. I don't deny it, but there are no portraits hidden in the necklace, Prue. They're—"

"It's not about the portraits, Jasper. She, ah . . . she said you just gave her the necklace this week. A reunion gift, she called it." She let out a short laugh, but there was no humor in it. It felt as if it had been ripped from her very soul.

"She's lying, Prue. I gave her the parure with the matching earrings and necklace months ago, before you came to London."

Perhaps he was telling the truth. It did make sense that he would have given Lady Archer the jewels as a set, and it certainly wasn't difficult to imagine Lady Archer lying about such a thing. Perhaps he was as innocent as he claimed.

But there could be no innocent explanation for Lady Archer to have such an intimate knowledge of what had passed in their bedchamber on their wedding night. Someone must have told her that Prue hadn't come to her marriage bed an innocent.

Who could it have been, if not Jasper? And if he had told Lady Archer such a thing, mustn't it be because he believed it himself?

". . . must have said something else. There has to be more to it than this."

She turned back to Jasper, dazed. He was saying something to her, something about Lady Archer and how easily she lied, but all she could hear was Lady Archer's voice in her head, calling her a whore.

Oh, God, the mere thought of it made her stomach roil with nausea. She couldn't bear to think about it, or about Lady Archer and everything she'd said. Not yet. Now, all she wanted was to escape this house, this city, this man.

"I—I want to go to Kent, Jasper. To Montford Park."

He blinked. "Montford Park?"

"Yes. I need . . . I want to get out of London for a time."

"Yes, I think that would be wise. We can go at once, this afternoon—"

"No, Jasper." She shook her head. "I want to go alone."

He swallowed, all the color draining from his face. "You mean, for good? You mean to go and *live* at Montford Park?"

She stared at him, startled, but it was a moment before it dawned on her what he meant.

He was asking if she was leaving him.

Perhaps she should. She could remain in the country then, and never again return to London. It wasn't as though she'd ever yearned for a glamorous life in town, or longed to take her place among the fashionable *ton*.

She could remain in Montford Park, taking care to visit her father or Franny on those occasions when Jasper came to the country. They would likely be rare enough.

It would be easier that way, for both of them.

But she wouldn't do it. That was the coward's way out. As Jasper had said once before, they'd made their bed, and now they'd have to lie in it.

She'd known from the start it was unlikely she and Jasper would ever be as Franny and Basingstoke were, that their marriage could ever become a love match. She'd married him knowing it would likely prove to be one of convenience.

Or, at best, friendship.

She'd hoped for so much more. Yes, she saw that now with a clarity that made her wonder how she could ever have so fooled herself, but she'd married him regardless, knowing it might come to this.

And she wouldn't go back on her word now. For better or worse, she was now the Duchess of Montford, and she couldn't simply turn her back on the promises she'd made and pretend otherwise. "No, Jasper, not to live. I just need a bit of time to myself, away from . . . everything."

"How long?" He gripped her hands, looking panicked. "How long will you be gone?"

"A month, perhaps?" The truth was, she didn't know. However long it took to fall out of love with her husband and regain her equilibrium, so she might live with him again without falling into despair. "I can't say for certain, but I will come back, Jasper. I promise it."

For a moment, it looked as if he would argue. He opened his mouth, but he said nothing, merely shook his head, then dropped her hands and stepped away from her, his arms falling stiffly to his sides. "If this is truly what you want, Prue, then I won't keep you here."

"It is what I want. For now, at least." As for the future, their future, who could say? Time would tell, as it always did, but until then, the years before them were shrouded in a deep, impenetrable fog, like a boat lost at sea.

"Very well. Norris will take you. I'll have a word with Keating and instruct him to see the carriage readied. You'll take Sarah with you?"

"If I may, yes."

"Of course."

For an instant they stood there staring at each other, as though each of them were waiting for the other to speak, a thousand unsaid words swelling between them, but there was nothing left to say, was there? So, Prue turned for the door, but before she could open it, he stopped her.

"Prue?"

She paused at the door but didn't look back. "Yes?"

"I . . . I'll miss you."

Oh, that was . . . she wasn't ready for it. Tears flooded her eyes, and there was nothing left then but to flee the study before he saw them. She rushed into the corridor, and from there into the entryway, hardly aware of where she was going, other than *away*—away from him and that little break in his voice when he'd spoken.

She stumbled up the stairs, aware of Keating's troubled gaze on her back. All she wanted was to get to her bedchamber, where she might fall across the bed and let the tears she'd been holding back since last night have their way with her.

But when she reached Jasper's bedchamber door, she paused.

No one was inside. Jasper hadn't followed her from the study, and she'd seen his valet, Loftus, passing through the entryway on his way to the kitchens when she'd come down the stairs earlier.

Before she left, there was one thing she wanted, and . . . oh, God, it was so foolish, and in the end, it was sure to break whatever was left of her heart, but she couldn't stop herself.

She glanced around her, but there was no one about, and with one quick turn of the knob she was inside Jasper's bedchamber.

Strange, but she hadn't ever been in here before. The one time they'd made love, he'd come to her.

Or perhaps not so strange, given what she now knew about Lady Archer.

She took a few hesitant steps inside, looking around

her as she went. It was a luxurious room, as befit a duke, with a thick, sumptuous blue and green carpet on the floor and draperies in a heavy, darker green silk.

She ventured a few steps farther, smothering a gasp when she peeked around an open doorway into an inner chamber and caught sight of his bed. It was enormous, the four carved posts supporting a massive wooden canopy with matching carvings, the entire thing drowning in swathes of green and blue figured silk.

She quickly backed out again. She hadn't sneaked in here to gape at Jasper's bed. Indeed, it would have been better if she'd never seen it at all.

She'd come for something else.

There it was, near two tall windows, between a large mirror and a cabinet with a lavish, blue-and-gold porcelain washing basin with a matching ewer on top.

Jasper's dressing table.

She tiptoed across the room like the worst sort of thief and paused in front of it. The usual things were scattered across the top—a hairbrush and comb, a hand mirror, and a few shaving things laid carefully atop a piece of blue velvet cloth to dry, but she gave them only a cursory glance, her gaze caught on a cut glass flask with a silver stopper.

She reached for it, removed the stopper, and brought it to her nose.

Orange blossom and amber flooded her senses, and she squeezed her eyes closed so she might drown in it, letting her memory take her back to the moment when she'd first inhaled it, the morning of her second day in London, when she'd sneaked back into the study after Jasper left so she might sniff his pillow.

So silly of her, to have done such a thing, but even more so to have done it without recognizing at once that a lady who wished to know how a gentleman smelled must have more than a passing interest in that gentleman.

She'd been lying to herself from the very start.

But even that was not quite as silly as what she was doing *now*.

It didn't stop her, however, from reaching into the bosom of her dress, withdrawing her handkerchief, and scenting it with a few droplets of the cologne.

She brought the handkerchief to her nose and inhaled. No, not quite.

Perhaps just another droplet, or two—

"Your Grace?"

"Oh!" She whirled around, a little shriek on her lips, the bottle of scent still clutched between her guilty fingers. It wasn't Jasper, thank goodness, but it was the next worst thing.

His valet, Loftus, was standing in the doorway, staring at her as if she'd quite lost her wits. "May I help you, Your Grace?"

"Oh, I . . . forgive me. I just wanted to . . . oh, dear." She fell silent, her cheeks on fire. How in the world could she possibly explain what she was doing in Jasper's bedchamber, rummaging among his personal things? "I, ah, I'm leaving for the country today, and I thought I might just . . . that is, I thought perhaps I could—"

"I understand perfectly, Your Grace." Loftus smiled, his dark eyes kind. "Allow me to help you." He came toward her, reached for her handkerchief, and held it to his nose. "No, that won't do. Perhaps a few more drops?"

Another rush of tears pressed behind her eyes at his thoughtfulness, but he pretended not to notice as he drizzled another half dozen drops of scent onto the bit of linen and brought it to his nose again. "Yes, that's much better. That should last for some time. Will this do, Your Grace?"

He held the handkerchief out to her, and she took a watery little sniff. "Yes, that's just right, isn't it? You're, ah, you're very kind, Mr. Loftus."

"Think nothing of it, Your Grace." He smiled sweetly at her and gave her a formal little bow. "I'm pleased I could assist you. I wish you a pleasant journey."

"Thank you." She couldn't quite smother the little sob that caught in her throat as she stuffed the handkerchief in her pocket, then turned and darted through the connecting door, closing it behind her and leaning against it, tears streaking her cheeks.

"Your Grace?" Sarah was piling folded clothing into a trunk, but she looked up at the sound of the door closing, and her face fell at the sight of Prue's tears. "Oh, no. Has something happened, Your Grace? Are we not to go to Montford Park, after all?"

"No, we're to go this afternoon, Sarah. Make sure to pack enough for at least a month, won't you?"

"Yes, Your Grace."

Prue left Sarah to the clothing and retreated to her writing desk, where she scrawled a quick note to Franny. She'd leave it with Keating on the way out, with instructions to take it to Park Lane.

After that, there was nothing for her to do but wait.

The time passed quickly, more quickly than it should have done, and soon enough she and Sarah were waiting in the entryway for the servants to load the trunks into the traveling coach. To her surprise, Jasper emerged from his study and waited in the entryway with them.

When the time came for them to go, he took her hand in his, his warm fingers cradling hers, and pressed a chaste kiss to her cheek. "Take care of yourself, Your Grace."

And that was all.

In the next instant, she and Sarah were tucked into the coach and rolling down Curzon Street. "We're on our way at last, Your Grace," Sarah said, turning to her with an encouraging smile.

Yes, they were on their way, just as she'd wanted.

Yet in that moment, with Jasper's kiss still burning her cheek, leaving Berkeley Square felt like the worst thing that had ever happened to her.

CHAPTER 24

"His Grace is not at home."

"Not at home? Do you take me for a fool, Keating? It's nine o'clock in the morning. Of course, he's home. Stand aside, man, and let me through."

Jasper raised his head, passing a hand over his gritty eyes. The house had been as quiet as a tomb since Prue's carriage had disappeared around the corner of Curzon Street. He'd stood on the front steps of his townhouse watching it go, and might have remained there for hours longer if Keating hadn't appeared in the doorway and urged him to come inside, out of the rain.

So, he'd done what any man whose entire world had collapsed would do.

Retired to his study and closed the door behind him.

Not that hiding would do him any good now. The past that he'd never much troubled himself over, the past he hadn't ever bothered to regret, had caught up to him at last, and with a vengeance. How arrogant he'd been, to imagine it never would. Looking back now, he hardly recognized the man he was before Prue came into his life.

It seemed incredible that only hours ago he'd been waiting for the moment when Basingstoke's ball would be over, and he could spend the night with Prue wrapped in his arms. How had everything fallen apart so quickly, and so completely?

"I beg your pardon, Colonel Kingston, but I must insist you take your leave at once."

Ah, his grandfather. He might have known. He'd made a point of asking Basingstoke and Grantham not to come until he sent for them, but he'd forgotten to send word to the one person in London most likely to appear on his doorstep and attempt to force his way inside.

There was some sort of scuffle in the entryway, and Keating's voice rose. "Colonel Kingston! His Grace left specific instructions that he is not at home to visitors!"

He *had* left specific instructions, yes, but since when had specific instructions ever done anything to prevent his grandfather from doing precisely as he pleased?

"I'm not a visitor, Keating, I'm his *grandfather*. He's always at home to *me*. Now, begone with you."

Footsteps echoed in the corridor, the raised voices drawing closer. "His Grace was quite adamant that he not be disturbed."

"I'm warning you, Keating, I *will* see my grandson, one way or another. It would be a great pity if I were forced to behave in a manner unworthy of a gentleman, and physically remove you from in front of that door."

If the morning hadn't been bad enough, now it sounded as if a brawl between his grandfather and his butler was brewing outside his study door, and he didn't like Keating's chances. He dragged himself to his feet to save poor Keating from a pummeling, but before he could take two steps toward the door, an outraged shriek came from the corridor.

"Colonel Kingston! You mustn't—"

That was as far as Keating got before the study door flew open. "I must, and I have."

There on the threshold stood his grandfather, red faced and panting, while poor Keating peered over his shoulder, wringing his hands, the usually neat tufts of his brown hair standing on end. "I do apologize, Your Grace, but the colonel is quite insistent that he—"

"You may as well let him in, Keating." Jasper waved a weary hand. "There's no stopping my grandfather once he's made up his mind to something."

"You heard His Grace, Keating." Colonel Kingston jerked his coat back into place with a huff. "Close the door on your way out."

Keating didn't move, but looked to Jasper, waiting. "It's alright, Keating. You may go."

Keating shot one last baleful glance at his grandfather before scurrying off down the hallway, muttering under his breath.

His grandfather waited until Keating was gone and the door closed behind him before he strode across the room. "There's mischief afoot, lad," he announced, dropping into one of the chairs on the other side of Jasper's desk. He frowned as he took in Jasper's wrinkled clothing and disheveled hair. "Foul mischief indeed, by the look of you."

"I haven't slept." Loftus had coaxed him out of his coat and cravat, but otherwise he was still dressed in his evening clothes from two nights ago. He hadn't bathed, and a two day's growth of dark beard shadowed his cheeks.

There hadn't seemed to be much point in fussing over his appearance.

There didn't seem to be much point in doing anything at all.

"I see that." His grandfather settled himself in the chair, his shrewd blue eyes fixed on Jasper's face. "So, what's all this fuss I hear about Basingstoke's ball, eh?"

"You needn't pretend you don't already know the whole sordid tale, Grandfather." His grandfather hadn't attended the ball—he despised balls and had no patience for the *ton*—but even so, the old man had probably heard the whole story before Jasper and Prue had even made it back to Berkeley Square after the ball.

The bushy silver eyebrows rose. "Perhaps I do know, but I'd rather hear it from you, Jasper."

Good God. The last thing he wanted to do at the moment was repeat the whole ugly business to his grandfather, but he'd just as soon the colonel had the truth of it, without all the *ton*'s embellishment. "Let's just say that Lady Archer swore she'd have her revenge on me, and now she has."

He should be furious with her, and so he would be. At some point, the pale shadow of the rage he could feel licking at his veins would burst into a conflagration, and God knew what would happen then. One way or another, her ladyship would pay for what she'd done to Prue.

But at the moment, he was too disheartened to be angry. There was no space inside him for anything but grief.

His grandfather grunted. "Eh, well, I can't say I'm surprised at it. Her sort always does, one way or another. Lord Arthur mentioned something about a scene at Basingstoke's, but he didn't have the whole of it. What did she do, then?"

What, indeed? He didn't even know himself. Only Prue and Selina knew what had really passed between them, and despite his pleas, Prue had refused to divulge a word about it to him. "Lady Archer appeared at Basingstoke's ball—uninvited, of course. We don't know how she managed to get past the footmen."

"She's as slippery as a snake, that's how." His grandfather learned forward in his chair, blue eyes blazing. "And? What did she want, lad?"

"The same thing Selina always wants—to cause trouble." And God knew she'd done a masterful job of smashing everything to bits.

She'd likely been laying out her schemes ever since the ball was announced, biding her time, and waiting for her chance. Which would have been nothing more than a nuisance, if she'd confined her antics to *him*. But Selina had always had finely honed instincts about how to wreak havoc and had quickly singled out the one person she could hurt the most.

Prue.

"It seems Selina's intention was to humiliate Prue by reminding everyone at the ball of our affair." Not that anyone was likely to forget it anytime soon, after that incident with the hairbrush. "She was wearing the ruby and diamond necklace that a great many people recognized as one I gave her when we were . . . er, when I was her protector."

He braced himself for his grandfather to launch into a litany of recriminations regarding Jasper's foolishness in taking up with Selina in the first place, but the old man only said, "What else?"

"I have reason to know Prue also recognized the necklace." Recognized it, and assumed, as of course she would do, that another half dozen scandalous paintings were hidden inside the ruby lockets.

"Yes, alright, but the duchess is no fool. She isn't one to fall apart over a ruby necklace. There's more to this than that, lad."

"Of course, there is, but your guess as to what is as good as mine. Prue wouldn't tell me what Selina said to her, but you can be sure every bloody word out of Selina's mouth was a lie."

A lie, a sneer, a laugh—God, he could picture every moment of how it must have unfolded, and the thought of Prue having to endure one of Selina's rages made his stomach clench with pain and fury. "At the very least, I know she told Prue I've returned to her bed. She claimed I'd only just given the necklace to her this past week, and that I called it a 'reunion gift.'"

Yes, that would be exactly the sort of lie Selina would tell, and it made his stomach turn.

"That woman's a pure devil," the colonel muttered. "Still, it can't be as bad as what you're imagining."

Yes, it could be. "It's bad enough that Prue's left for Montford Park."

"Left?" His grandfather stared at him. "What, you don't mean to say she's *left you*, Jasper?"

Had she left him? She'd insisted she was coming back, but it felt . . . well, it felt very much like she'd left him. "I don't know." His hands clenched into helpless fists. "She promised she'd return, but I'm not sure if she . . . I don't know. I don't know anything anymore."

"Hell, and damnation, lad." His grandfather shook his head. "But surely you can explain to the duchess that whatever that viper said to her is nothing but a bald-faced lie? She won't take Lady Archer's word over yours."

"No." Prue wouldn't easily have credited any of Selina's lies, because, despite everything, his wife had more faith in him than he deserved. "But there had to have been something, some lie or tale so convincing Prue had no choice but to believe it to be true."

His grandfather frowned. "Yes, that's likely so. You've no idea what it was, eh?"

"No. Unless Prue chooses to confide in me, I may never know."

But whatever it was, he knew this. It had struck at the very center of Prue's heart.

It had hurt her badly. So badly she'd crept off to Basingstoke's study without a word to him or Franny, like a wounded animal. Her face, when he'd found her there, curled up on the settee, the look in her eyes . . . dear God, would he ever be able to unsee the pain in those hazel depths? Could he ever forget—

"Listen to me, Jasper. You need to go after the duchess at once. Nothing good will come of her being alone at Montford Park. Those lies are like an infection in the bloodstream, lad. The longer it goes unchecked, the worse it will become."

"She doesn't want me, Grandfather." Prue hadn't accused him of anything. Not a single harsh word had crossed her lips, but her pain was in her every glance, her every dropped gaze, in the way she couldn't bear to look at him, her bolted bedchamber door. "She went because she wishes to be away from me."

"That may be, lad, but that's not what she needs."

"It's precisely what she needs!" The fury that had been hovering just out of Jasper's reach since last night suddenly sank its razor-edged teeth into his throat. "Now do you understand why I didn't wish to marry? Because I knew this was what would come of it! I knew I could never be a proper husband, and now Prue will be the one who suffers for it."

His grandfather stared at him, white faced. "Jasper—"

"Prue is the Duchess of Montford now, Grandfather! She will remain the Duchess of Montford for the rest of her life, and there's not a damned thing she can do to escape me. Don't you see? She believes I've betrayed her—"

"But you *didn't* betray her, Jasper! This isn't your fault. If it were, you know very well I wouldn't hesitate to take you to task for it, but you're not to blame. Not this time."

He *was* to blame. Prue was his wife, and he'd left her vulnerable to the machinations of his jealous, vindictive former mistress. She'd been hurt, because of *him*. If he wasn't to blame, then who was? "Of course, it's my fault, Grandfather."

"No, it isn't, lad. This is the doing of that she-devil, Lady Archer."

Jasper dropped back into his chair, the anger draining from him as quickly as it had surged. "But who's to blame for putting Prue in Selina's sights?"

"Why, Lady Archer is to blame for that as well, of course! You didn't do anything wrong. Don't lose sight of that, lad. This is a devil of a thing, and I don't pretend otherwise, but—"

"I *did* do wrong. I didn't betray Prue, no, but my past wrongs were bound to catch up to me sooner or later, and now they have."

And the worst of it was, they'd caught up to Prue, as well.

But his grandfather was shaking his head. "No, Jasper. That's not so. Do you remember that day at Basingstoke House, after the, er . . . shooting incident? I told you that day that Prudence Thorne would be the making of you, but I didn't—"

"And so, she has been. But what of Prue, Grandfather? Did you ever think of what marrying me would do to *her*? You didn't see her this morning. Her face . . ." As long as he lived, he'd never get over how devastated she'd looked, how her breath had caught when she'd begged him to let her go to Montford Park.

This, and they'd only been married for two weeks. What would he see in her face after a year? After ten?

"You didn't let me finish, lad. I told you marrying Prudence Thorne would be the making of you, but what I didn't say was that you'd also be the making of *her*."

Jasper let out a harsh laugh. "That's a lovely thought, Grandfather, but I think we can both agree the evidence doesn't bear out your optimism."

"Not yet, perhaps, but it will."

"How? My God, for the better part of my life, I've made one misstep after the next. Being sent down from Oxford for fighting? The wagering, the drinking, the mistresses? Don't say you've forgotten all that."

"None of that matters now. Listen to me, lad—"

"It does matter." Bitterness welled up inside him, the force of it pressing with such insistence on his chest, a stream of words he'd never intended to say spewed from his lips. "I . . . I never meant to . . . I tried to . . . I'm sorry I've been such a disappointment to you, Grandfather."

Silence fell between them, thick and fraught, until at last his grandfather broke it, his voice soft. "Don't ever say that, Jasper. Don't you *ever* say that again."

The words fell between them, fierce and throbbing with some emotion Jasper couldn't explain. He jerked his gaze up to meet his grandfather's. "I thought . . . I don't understand."

"No, you don't, and that's my fault."

His grandfather crossed the room and rested a gnarled hand on top of Jasper's, and it was . . . God, it was strange, the touch of that thin, papery skin, the bony fingers gripping his.

He couldn't remember the last time his grandfather had taken his hand.

Not since he was a child.

"You've never been a disappointment to me, Jasper. *Never*. I should have told you that more often. Every day, even. I never wanted you to think . . . I never should have allowed you to believe for one moment that I've ever been anything but proud of you."

Proud of him? Jasper stared. "But the wagering, and the mistresses, and the—"

"Yes, yes." His grandfather waved a hand. "I haven't forgotten it, and I don't deny there were times when I wanted you to take a different path than you did, but I've never once felt ashamed of you, Jasper. Whatever failings you may have, they mean nothing when weighed against your heart. You've got a good, honorable, loving heart, lad. You're a good boy." His grandfather's voice broke. "A good *man*."

A good man. Of all the things he'd always believed of himself—that he was a rake, a blackguard, a wastrel, and a scoundrel—never once, in all of his twenty-eight years, had he ever thought of himself as a good man.

Not once.

But Basingstoke thought so, didn't he? He'd said it on more than one occasion, and Grantham had as well, and the Duchess of Basingstoke, who'd always maintained he was one of her favorites.

Why hadn't he ever listened to them?

"You've always been guarded with your heart, Jasper." His grandfather swallowed. "And that's my fault. I—I blame myself for that."

"*Your* fault? How could it be—"

"Hush." His grandfather held up a hand to quiet him. "Let me speak, lad. When you came to me as a boy, after . . . after Eugenia and your father died, you were such a sad, lost little thing. You were small for your age, you know, Jasper, though one wouldn't know it to look at you now, and you had those big dark eyes, just like Eugenia's."

Jasper stilled, listening. In the twenty-two years since his parents' death, his grandfather had only ever said their names a handful of times, and he rarely spoke about Jasper's boyhood. He hadn't realized how much he'd longed for it, but to hear his grandfather now was like a cup of cool water raised to his parched lips.

"You used to sit and stare at their portraits. Do you remember, lad? You spent hours in that deserted portrait gallery, just staring up at them."

"I remember." So much about that first year after he'd come to live with his grandfather was lost to him now, like a dream he could only half remember, but he *did* remember that. "One day, the portraits were gone."

"Yes. I had them removed. Your preoccupation with them troubled me, at the time. I thought it couldn't be good for such a young boy to yearn for what he could never have again. I thought it was better if you forgot them, so I took the portraits away, and after that, I hardly ever spoke of your parents to you. It seemed the right thing to do then, but now I . . . I think you were trying to grieve for them, lad, and I—I stopped you."

Jasper tried to remember if, after the portraits had disappeared, he'd felt as if it were wrong to think about them, or as if he weren't permitted to speak of them. It was too long ago to know, the memories so far away they'd become flickering images only in his mind, hazy and indistinct, but there was one thing . . .

"I remember missing the scent of her perfume. She smelled of orange blossoms."

"She did." His grandfather's voice was hoarse, and tears were standing in his eyes, but he was smiling, too. "She was everything that's lovely, just like your Prue."

His Prue. Was she his? Had she ever been his?

"I've thought about this a good deal lately, Jasper, and now I wonder if there wasn't selfishness in the way I went about it. I think I told myself we needed to put the past behind us for your sake, when the truth was, it was easier for me to pretend as if we'd never lost them. I almost couldn't bear it when they died, and I think I told myself I was protecting you when really, I was protecting my own heart."

"Perhaps, but who could blame you? She was your daughter." He forgot that sometimes, didn't he? When he thought of his parents, he thought of them as *his*, but they'd been his grandfather's, too.

"Not a soul would blame me, Jasper, least of all *you*. You see how generous you are with me? I wish you could be as generous with yourself. You've kept your heart locked up tight all these years, afraid of getting hurt again, but your duchess, well, you're going to have to open it back up for her, otherwise you'll lose her, and I don't know . . ." His grandfather shook his head, his face twisting. "I don't know what will become of you if you lose the lady you love."

"I do love her." The ache in his chest whenever she was near, the way he thrilled to her laugh, the fierceness with which he wanted her. That was love.

His grandfather smiled. "Who could know her, and not love her?"

"It's as simple as that, isn't it?" Despite everything, Jasper's lips twitched. Because his grandfather was right. Who could know Prue, and not love her? And who but

Colonel Cornelius Kingston could have put it so plainly even Jasper couldn't fail to see the truth of it?

"If it's complicated, then it isn't love. Love is the purest, simplest thing there is, but you can't do it by halves. It's all, or nothing." His grandfather folded his hands on top of his walking stick and sat back, considering Jasper. "So, lad? What's it going to be? All, or nothing?"

"All." It would be all, because it was *Prue*. How could it be anything less?

"Ah. I thought so. Well, then, it just so happens I have a bit of information that may help you set things right with the duchess."

Jasper snorted, shaking his head. Of course, he did. "I've always said, Grandfather, that of all the busybodies in London, you're the busiest."

"Eh, well, I do pick up a tidbit here or there. A man can't know too many secrets, Jasper. They do prove useful on occasion, like now."

Jasper's heart began to pound. "How useful?"

"Very useful, indeed. You see, an acquaintance of mine happened to see Lord Quincy skulking about Basingstoke's ball. Quincy's a sly one, to be sure, but not quite sly enough, this time."

Jasper leaned forward, his fatigue dropping away in an instant. "Oh?"

"Yes. It seems Lord Quincy was wandering about inside Basingstoke's house where he had no business being. My acquaintance saw him and grew suspicious, so he followed him, and what do you think he saw? Lord Quincy, sneaking a lady into Basingstoke's house through one of the conservatory doors. My acquaintance didn't see the lady's face, but she was wearing a scarlet ball gown. Curious, isn't it? You didn't happen to see a lady in a scarlet ball gown at the ball, did you, lad?"

"Now you ask, I believe Lady Archer was wearing a scarlet ball gown."

"Was she, indeed? Well then, I can't help but wonder if Lord Quincy has any notion what Lady Archer may have said to your duchess. Perhaps we should find Lord Quincy and ask him."

CHAPTER 25

Lord Quincy wasn't at White's. He wasn't at Tattersalls or Manton's, nor was there any sign of him in St. James's Street or Pall Mall. He wasn't frittering away his fortune at the gaming hells in Covent Garden or squiring one of the celebrated courtesans through the streets of Piccadilly.

He was nowhere, it seemed.

"Every blade, rake, and dandy in London is wandering the streets today," Jasper muttered to his grandfather as the carriage made its way from Piccadilly to Regent's Street. "So, where the devil is Quincy?"

His grandfather grunted. "He's made himself scarce, that's what. You can be sure we're not the only ones who know about that trick he pulled at Basingstoke's ball. Every gossip in London will be whispering about it by now."

If that was the case, they'd never find him. Like most villains, Quincy had a keen sense of self-preservation. If the *ton* was already whispering, then he'd likely guessed Jasper would be looking for him, and he was taking care to keep out of sight. "He's probably run off to his mother's house in Sussex by now."

"Then we'll go to Sussex and drag him out from behind his mother's skirts," his grandfather said stoutly. "Not to worry, lad. We'll have him one way or another."

They would, yes. The question was, how long would it take before he could wring the man's neck until Lady Archer's secrets burbled like a fountain from his lips? There were any number of squalid corners in the city where a rat like Quincy could hide.

They were running about like dogs chasing their tails.

If Quincy really had fled London, it could be days before they caught up to him, and meanwhile Prue was alone at Montford Park, imagining . . . what? That he'd run right into Selina's arms as soon as she was gone from Berkeley Square? That he was in bed with Selina even now, laughing at her, and congratulating himself on finally being free of her?

He dropped his head into his hands. God, this was a nightmare.

"Now, none of that, lad." His grandfather laid a hand on Jasper's back. "Quincy will be brought to heel, I promise you. But it's nearly two o'clock. Shall we return to Berkeley Square and find out what Basingstoke and Grantham have discovered?"

"Yes, alright, but let's stop at Angelo's first."

Between Basingstoke, Grantham, and Jasper's grandfather, poor Keating had had a trying morning. His friends had appeared on his doorstep late this morning, grim faced and promising to force their way into Jasper's study if Keating didn't stand down at once.

It seemed that Prue had sent a note to Park Lane informing Franny that she was leaving for Montford Park at once. Basingstoke hadn't wasted any time fetching Grantham, and the next thing Jasper knew, two outraged dukes had appeared on his doorstep, demanding to know what must be done to bring his runaway duchess home.

What, indeed? If it hadn't been for his grandfather, Jasper, Basingstoke, and Grantham might still be in Jasper's study even now, blinking helplessly at each other, but the colonel, with great presence of mind, had sent Basingstoke and Grantham off to interrogate a few of Quincy's fellow scoundrels, in hopes of discovering the man's whereabouts.

They were meant to meet up again at Jasper's townhouse by four o'clock. It was nearly four now, but Jasper couldn't bear to waste a minute, and they were only a few blocks from Angelo's Fencing Academy.

He didn't have much hope he'd find Quincy there. If the villain was clever enough to avoid White's, then he wasn't likely to appear at Angelo's, but then Quincy fancied himself quite a Corinthian, and spent a good deal of time at Angelo's and Gentleman Jackson's.

"Something's afoot," his grandfather observed as Ruddick, his coachman, brought the carriage to a stop on Bond Street. "It's a crush."

"Yes, far more than usual for this time of year." The street was a tangle of carriages, and the clamor of gentlemen's voices and laughter could be heard on the other side of the closed door. "Though I suppose the *ton* was already in town for Basingstoke's ball."

But the moment he was over the threshold, he knew it was more than that. A dozen heads swung in his direction when he entered, and an odd hush fell over the gentlemen nearest the door, only to explode in whispers in his wake as he pushed his way through the crowd.

He soon discovered why.

Lord Quincy was lounging against the wall, with a crowd of admiring gentlemen surrounding him, the picture of fashionable elegance in a smart, olive-colored morning coat and brown striped waistcoat.

He had a practice foil in his hand, but he wasn't fencing.

He was laughing. *Laughing*, as if he hadn't a single care in the world.

Jasper must have made some noise—a hissed breath, or perhaps even a growl—because his grandfather caught his arm, his white eyebrows raised in alarm. "Now, don't act hastily, lad. You don't want to do anything you'll regret."

"I *won't* regret it, Grandfather. I assure you." Quincy had schemed against Prue, *insulted* her. This was no time for cool-headed calm. This was a time for bloody vengeance. "As you said yourself, it's all, or nothing."

His grandfather watched Quincy for a moment with pinched lips, then shrugged. "Go on, then, but don't kill him before he tells you what that she-devil said to your duchess."

"No, indeed. I'll kill him directly afterwards."

Half of the gentleman gathered inside Angelo's had seen Jasper by now, but Quincy hadn't. He was too busy holding court, no doubt regaling the nest of scoundrels surrounding him with his tale of how he and Lady Archer had humiliated the Duchess of Montford.

Well, let him laugh while he could, because he'd have precious little to laugh about once Jasper was through with him. "I beg your pardon, gentlemen." He began to push his way through the crowd toward Henry Angelo, and soon enough the gentlemen fell back, clearing a path for him.

"Your Grace." Angelo offered him a bow. "I did wonder if I might see you today."

"And here I am. A rapier if you would, Angelo."

Angelo's eyebrows rose. "You mean a practice foil, Your Grace?"

"No. I haven't come to *practice*. A rapier, if you please."

Henry Angelo was far too well acquainted with the particular habits and peccadillos of London's gentlemen of fashion to be easily shocked, but it wasn't every day a duke strolled into his establishment and publicly challenged an earl.

It was enough to render him momentarily speechless, but he recovered quickly. "You demand satisfaction from Lord Quincy."

It wasn't a question.

"I do, and I intend to have it. *Now*."

Angelo glanced past him. His patrons had caught on to what was passing by now, and they'd pressed closer, all of them holding their breath at once as they waited to see if Angelo would permit the bout to go on, or if he would disoblige the Duke of Montford by sending him out the way he'd come in.

In the end, Angelo did what any savvy businessman would do.

He selected a rapier from the rack of swords and handed it to Jasper. "I beg, Your Grace, that you do not kill Lord Quincy in my establishment. If you wish to murder him, you may do so in the usual way, after a proper challenge and appointment of seconds."

Jasper tested the point of the rapier with his finger. "Very well." It wasn't precisely what he'd hoped for. He would have relished the chance to reduce Quincy to a gory mound of shredded flesh, but Prue was waiting, and even as circumscribed a duel as this would be enough to humiliate Quincy as he deserved.

Quincy, who'd at last caught on, spoke up then. "You

say His Grace may not kill me, Angelo, but you haven't restricted me in the same manner. Am I to be permitted to kill His Grace, then?"

A ripple of laughter rose from the crowd.

"You may try, my lord, but I rather doubt it." Angelo gave Quincy a cool smile. "I've seen His Grace fence."

Quincy's face darkened at that, but he removed his coat, tossing it to a companion, and accepted the rapier Angelo offered him, slicing the blade through the air. "I await your pleasure, Your Grace."

"And a pleasure it will be, Quincy." Jasper strode toward Quincy, and the knot of gentlemen fell back to gather around them, clearing a circle in the center of the room.

"Two touches only, gentlemen," Angelo called. "Only those to the chest shall be deemed valid, but in deference to the insult paid to the Duchess of Montford, you may bloody yourselves as much as you please. *En garde*."

Jasper offered Quincy a shallow bow, which Quincy returned with a flourishing one of his own, then Jasper attacked, lunging forward with a straight thrust directly at the center of Quincy's chest.

It was a powerful stroke, quick and efficient, and for all Quincy's boasted skill as a swordsman, he only just managed to catch the tip of Jasper's rapier and deflect with a circle parry. It was badly done, and Quincy was forced to drop back, his blade whipping through the air in an attempt to slice Jasper's hand.

But he wasn't quick enough. The edge of his rapier found only air, and then Jasper was on him again, lunging forward. This time the tip of his blade found its mark, and a murmur went up among the spectators as a patch of dark red blossomed on Quincy's elegant striped waistcoat.

Quincy's blood wasn't as red as his face, however.

"Damn you, Montford." He lunged again, but he was flustered now, the patch of blood on his waistcoat spreading ever wider, and his attempt to beat Jasper's blade back failed.

Jasper could have ended the bout right there and then, but he wasn't in a merciful mood.

He feinted, then feinted again, forcing Quincy into parrying, but it was no use. Quincy was already tiring, and his reflexes were slow. Jasper renewed his attack, and the edge of his blade found Quincy's shoulder. It wasn't a deep wound, but he followed it with a swipe at Quincy's arm, and with one quick stroke, he ripped Quincy's shirt from his elbow to his wrist, leaving a long, thin slash mark that oozed blood.

Another gasp went up from the surrounding gentlemen. Quincy staggered, and nearly toppled backward onto his arse. If the man's crime had been anything less than a malicious attack on Prue, Jasper might have felt sorry for him.

As it was, he merely waited, his rapier balanced casually between his fingers, while Quincy regained his feet. "You're looking a trifle ill, Quincy. Shall we put an end to this? You may yet save the last shreds of your dignity, provided you agree to tell me what I want to know."

"Never," Quincy snarled, his voice shaking with mortification and rage.

Jasper shrugged. "Very well, then. *En garde.*"

Quincy attempted a riposte, but Jasper easily blocked his advance, and with a flick of the tip of his rapier he sliced open Quincy's cheekbone.

Quincy cried out and jerked his hand to his face, paling when it came back dripping with blood. "Damn you, Montford, you bloody savage."

After that, it was all but over. Quincy made a few

more shaky attempts to draw Jasper's blood, but he was bleeding badly by now, particularly after Jasper delivered another jab to Quincy's chest, opening a new wound and ending the bout.

Angelo called it then, declaring Jasper the victor.

"A word, Quincy." Jasper passed his bloodied rapier to his grandfather and strode toward Quincy, pushing aside one of Quincy's friends, who'd come forward to help Quincy to his carriage. The man paled, and backed away.

Quincy gave him a sulky look. "I don't have to tell you a cursed thing, Montford."

Jasper smiled. "Of course not, Quincy, but if you don't, then you may choose your second, because you'll be meeting me at dawn on Primrose Hill the day after tomorrow."

Quincy visibly blanched. "Yes, alright. What do you *want*, Montford?"

"Not here. The carriage." He grabbed Quincy by the collar of his shirt and dragged him past dozens of gawking gentlemen out the door of Angelo's, nodding to his grandfather as he passed.

"What did Lady Archer say to my wife at Basingstoke's ball?" he demanded, once they were seated in his grandfather's carriage with Ruddick standing guard in front of the closed door. "Every detail, if you please, and don't even think of lying to me."

"How should I know what she said? I don't deny I let Selina into the ball, but I wasn't there when she spoke to the duchess."

"Perhaps you didn't understand me, Quincy. *Every bloody word*, or else."

Quincy glanced at Jasper from the corner of his eye, and whatever he saw there made him gulp. "Selina, ah . . .

she said something to me about—now, don't take this the wrong way, Montford—but Selina insisted she knew beyond a doubt that the duchess wasn't innocent when she came to your bed."

Jasper stared at him in shock. Prue, not innocent?

He'd tortured himself imagining the dozens of different lies Selina might have told Prue, but *this*? Good God, but Selina had truly outdone herself. It was utterly absurd, of course, but the accusation had so overset Prue, she'd hidden herself in Basingstoke's study, as if she were ashamed.

There must be something to it, then. Not truth, no— he'd never for a moment doubted Prue's innocence, and he didn't now—but some question or doubt must be lingering in Prue's mind.

"And just how does Lady Archer presume to know anything at all about my wife, or the state of her innocence?" God, it was so ridiculous he'd be tempted to laugh, if it weren't for how badly Prue had been hurt.

"That lady's maid. I can't recall her name . . . was it Stitch, or Stritch? Your duchess dismissed the woman quickly enough, but she was there the morning after your wedding night, and she attended the duchess."

Mrs. Stritch? He'd forgotten all about her. "*And?* What does Mrs. Stritch have to do with anything? Get on with it, Quincy, before you succumb to a swoon."

Quincy shot him a look of pure loathing. "Mrs. Stritch works for Selina, Montford, or she did. You can imagine the rage Selina fell into when the duchess dismissed the woman, though by then, she had what she needed."

"Which was?" Had any man ever taken so much time to say so little as Quincy?

"Pristine sheets, Montford. Not a drop of blood to be found anywhere, or so Mrs. Stritch told Selina. I don't know many virgins who don't bleed on their wedding night, do you?"

Pristine sheets? *This* was Selina's proof that Prue hadn't been an innocent when she came to his bed? For God's sake, there were dozens of reasons why a lady might not bleed on her wedding night. A lack of blood didn't prove a damned thing, any more than the plentiful flow of it did.

One needn't look any further than the Covent Garden brothels for proof of *that*.

Of course, he'd noticed Prue hadn't bled on their wedding night. He'd never thought twice about it, but how *he* felt was neither here nor there. What mattered was what *Prue* felt, and she must have been confused by it, or else Selina's accusation wouldn't have done the damage it did.

Did Prue imagine their marriage hadn't been consummated? Or, dear God, did she think *he* doubted her innocence? He fell against the squabs, his head spinning, but no sooner did the question rise in his mind than he knew the answer.

Of course, she did.

Prue must believe *he'd* been the one who told Selina about the sheets. Either she didn't realize that Mrs. Stritch had noticed them, or else she'd forgotten about the woman as quickly as Jasper had.

Dear God, was it any wonder Prue believed he'd taken Selina as his mistress again? There was no way—leaving Mrs. Stritch out of it—that Selina could possibly know such a thing if Jasper hadn't told her.

"Well, Montford? Are we done? I don't know anything more, I swear it."

"We're done, if only because I can't stand another moment of your bleating. Get out." Jasper rapped on the window of the carriage to alert Ruddick, but he caught

Quincy by the back of the shirt before he could flee. "One last thing, Quincy. Tell Lady Archer she's earned herself a powerful enemy in me. If she ever dares to come near my wife again, she won't like the result."

He released Quincy so suddenly the man tumbled into the street, right at Jasper's grandfather's feet. The colonel looked down his nose at him, then stepped around him as if Quincy were a pile of horse droppings.

But he stopped short at the door of the carriage. "That scoundrel bled all over my carriage seats!"

"Yes, I beg your pardon, Grandfather. He's seeping everywhere. I'll see to it you have new seats, or a new carriage, whichever you prefer."

"Eh, no matter." His grandfather climbed in, skirting the bloody seat, and settled himself on the other side of the carriage. "So, did that scoundrel spill Lady Archer's secrets, or not?"

"He did. It seems Selina revealed something Prue believed was known only to her and myself, something of an . . . intimate nature."

His grandfather didn't ask for details, thankfully. The old man might poke his nose far deeper into Jasper's business than was comfortable, but he'd never ask Jasper to reveal any of Prue's secrets. He was a gentleman, after all.

"I need to leave for Montford Park at once, Grandfather."

"Today?" His grandfather glanced out the window. "It'll be a devil of a drive, with this rain."

Was it raining? He hadn't noticed. The only thing he could think about, the only thing that mattered, was getting to Prue as soon as possible. "Yes, today. I don't want to wait any longer, Grandfather."

His grandfather considered him for a long moment,

then nodded. "Berkeley Square, Ruddick, my good man," he said to his driver, then sat back in his seat, rubbing his hands together with glee. "I can hardly wait to tell Basingstoke and Grantham how you punished Quincy and made him cry out for his mother."

Jasper frowned. "I don't think he *did* cry out for his mother."

His grandfather gave him a mischievous wink. "Maybe not, but when I tell it, lad, he will have."

CHAPTER 26

"May I fetch you more tea, Your Grace?"

Prue glanced away from the window to the doorway of the drawing room where Montford Park's housekeeper, Mrs. Bingham, stood wringing her hands. She was a plump, grandmotherly lady with kind blue eyes, eager to please her new mistress, but she didn't seem to know quite what to make of Prue.

It seemed duchesses did not, in Mrs. Bingham's experience, spend long, silent hours alone in their grand drawing rooms without issuing a single command, or making a single demand. Without, in fact, saying a single word, but only staring out the window, as quiet as a mouse.

"That's kind of you, Mrs. Bingham." Prue had yet to touch the tea tray Mrs. Bingham had left an hour ago, but she nodded with a smile. "I'd welcome more tea, thank you."

Mrs. Bingham beamed. "Right away, Your Grace!" She bustled off, looking relieved to have something to do, at last.

Mrs. Bingham *was* kind. All the servants at Montford Park were as kind and accommodating as any servants possibly could be, from the housemaid who'd lit the fire in her bedchamber this morning, to Mr. Whitehurst, the groom who'd shown her around the stables, to Mrs. Bingham, who'd hovered just outside the drawing room door for most of the day, and offered Prue more tea than she could drink in a lifetime.

As for Montford Park itself, it was as lovely as Prue had imagined it would be. One couldn't stir a step without stumbling upon another of its beauties, whether it was the ornate wood paneling, the elegant plasterwork ceiling medallions, or the extensive walled gardens redolent with the scents of roses and lavender.

It was the castle in the clouds she'd always dreamed of, as much as any place ever could be, but from the moment she'd set foot inside the grand entryway, she found herself sinking under a misery more profound than any she'd ever endured, as if heavy weights were attached to her limbs, dragging her downward.

Despite the dozens of servants, the place felt wretchedly empty.

It shouldn't have, when everything she'd never even dared to dream of was *here*, right at her fingertips. Servants at her beck and call, a lovely home with sunlight streaming through the windows, a stable full of exquisite horses, and vast, open space in which to ride them.

Was none of this enough for her, now that she was a duchess?

It seemed not.

It didn't make sense, really. It wasn't as if her girlhood dreams had ever included a husband. How selfish she was, to be pining for a thing she'd never wanted! But since she'd arrived at Montford Park, a shadowy figure with lovely dark eyes, a headful of tousled hair, and a smile that was both wicked and teasing at once had followed her everywhere she went, as if she were dragging a silent ghost along in her wake with every step she took.

She couldn't escape him.

How was she ever going to survive a month here, if she couldn't even manage a single day without him? She'd go mad.

She leapt to her feet, unable to sit still a moment longer, and hurried to the window. The afternoon sun was still shining, filtered through a cocoon of white, puffy clouds, but darker, more foreboding clouds were massing in the distance.

It was going to rain, possibly for hours. Days, even. She'd be trapped indoors with nothing to occupy her mind, no way to escape the weight of Jasper's shadowy presence. No, she couldn't bear it. She must get outside now, at once, before she lost her chance.

She whirled around and raced for the drawing room door, but just as she reached it Mrs. Bingham appeared, carrying a tea tray in her hands. "Your Grace?" The housekeeper paused in the doorway, her eyebrows drawing together. "Do you require assistance?"

"No, Mrs. Bingham, I just . . . I was taken with a sudden urge for a walk, that's all. If you'd be so good as to leave the tea, I'll have it when I return."

Mrs. Bingham glanced at the window, where the steel-edged clouds seemed to be advancing with astonishing speed, swallowing the weak rays of sunshine as they came. "Oh, but I think it's going to rain, Your Grace. You wouldn't like to get caught in a downpour."

"You needn't worry, Mrs. Bingham. I won't be gone long." Prue edged past the housekeeper and into the hallway, resisting the urge to turn and flee. "I'll take care to dress warmly, as well."

"Very well, Your Grace." Mrs. Bingham nodded, but

Prue could feel the housekeeper's worried gaze on her back as she hurried down the hallway to the staircase. Sarah had given her a similarly anxious look this morning, when Prue had sent her tray back to the kitchens with her breakfast untouched.

It was becoming quite the thing, for people to follow her with worried gazes, wasn't it?

She took the stairs two at a time, desperate to be outdoors where she might draw in draughts of the fresh, cool air. "Sarah?" She burst through the door into her apartments, but Sarah wasn't there.

Prue glanced at the bell but decided against summoning Sarah. She couldn't bear to wait another instant, and all she needed was a warm cloak and a hat. She could fetch those for herself easily enough.

She strode through her bedchamber to her dressing closet—a rather grand room with green-figured silk wallpaper, a great many tufted settees, and fit for a far grander duchess than she, and began to rummage among the shelves.

Goodness, she'd acquired a great many new gowns, hadn't she? Too many to wear in a lifetime. There was more than one warm cloak among them, but they were all too fine for a damp romp in the countryside.

She pushed gowns, pelisses, capes, and shawls aside, hardly knowing what she was looking for until at last she came to the end of the row, and there, tucked behind her old navy riding habit, was the worn brown cloak she'd brought from Wiltshire when she first came to London a few weeks earlier.

A few weeks. It felt as if a lifetime had passed since then.

The cloak looked shabbier now than ever, next to its newer, more costly and fashionable sisters, but it was no less beloved for all that, not to mention much more practical, the rough wool rather like the embrace of an old friend. She seized the first hat she laid her hands on— a rather flimsy straw bonnet that would do little to protect her in a downpour—and then she was off down the stairs and out the entryway door.

The main drive that led from the public road to the entrance of Montford Park would do well for a walk. It was wide and smooth, with lovely, old growth English oak trees with broad, spreading crowns that would provide ample protection from the rain.

But it felt too public, too exposed. Anyone who happened to look out one of the front windows of the house would be able to see her, and soon enough she'd have Sarah out here following her about, or Mrs. Bingham with her tea tray.

Perhaps she'd come back that way.

For now, she skirted around the side of the house where she'd noticed a beautiful walled garden when she'd returned from her visit to the stables this morning.

She might wander there alone, without encountering a servant.

A low iron gate was set into the stone wall. She pushed it open, ducked inside, and spent some time wandering along the gravel pathways. The roses were just beginning to fade, but there were plenty of pretty blue asters, and dahlias in every shade of yellow, red, and orange.

Beyond the back of the walled garden, she could just make out what looked like an extensive fruit orchard. She couldn't tell from here whether it was pear or apple, but there was likely another gate set into the back wall.

Perhaps she'd wander out and see.

But she never made it as far as the orchard, because hidden in the back corner of the garden she found a charming little nook with a stone bench tucked inside it, shaded by the overhanging branches of an apple tree. It was a tiny, secluded little place, a secret garden hiding within the larger garden, the soothing sound of trickling water coming from a cistern built into the wall behind it.

It seemed to beckon to her, as if it had been put there for her exclusive use.

She settled herself on the bench, drawing her cloak tighter around her. The wind had picked up, and a few drops of rain from the dark clouds she'd seen earlier plopped onto the top of her straw bonnet, but she remained where she was, her mind drifting.

She hadn't intended to think about Jasper, but he was forever there in her mind, waiting for a silent moment to drift into her conscious thoughts. This time, she didn't try to stop him. She let her thoughts float about as they pleased, like a butterfly flitting from flower to flower.

If anyone had asked after Franny's ball, she would have said she didn't have any happy memories of the past few weeks, but as she sat there listening to the water flowing into the shallow cistern, she found it wasn't true.

There were happy memories waiting there, as surely as there were sad ones.

There'd been that wager, in the billiard room at Basing-stoke House. Of course, she'd lost that wager, and with it any claim she may have had to Thornewood, but there'd been more than one moment when she'd basked in Jasper's smile, when she'd felt warmed by it, all the way down to the very depths of her heart.

And their wedding night—oh, she'd never forget it,

how sweet he'd been, how tender, and even that wager over fencing at Angelo's . . . well, of course Jasper had behaved abominably over that—very high-handed, indeed—but then dukes did tend to be so, and he'd only been trying to protect her from the *ton*.

Rightly so, as it turned out.

But this business with Lady Archer . . . she raised her face to the sky, blinking against the raindrops falling into her eyes.

Now she was calmer, and could think rationally, it struck her that something wasn't quite right about it. Lady Archer's claim, when considered with a cooler head, didn't make much sense.

Jasper hadn't behaved at all like a man with a mistress in those ten days before Franny's ball. Why, he'd nearly reduced her bedchamber door to kindling just to get to her!

All this, during the same time Lady Archer claimed he'd been frolicking in her bed.

Surely, if he'd been languishing in Lady Archer's arms, she would have noticed prolonged, unexplained absences? But that hadn't been the case. Everywhere she'd turned, Jasper was there, watching her, his gaze hungry, the corners of his lips twitching in that wicked grin.

As for the accusation she'd made about Prue's innocence, while she couldn't imagine how the woman could know such intimate details about her marriage bed, wasn't it possible there was some other explanation for it other than Jasper having told her?

He'd sworn to her Lady Archer was lying. He'd begged her to listen to him, to believe him, and now, thinking back, she recognized that his words had had the ring of truth to them. Couldn't she simply choose to believe him, regardless of whether there was an explanation? Could it be as easy as simply choosing to trust her husband?

Oh, she didn't know!

It was raining in earnest now. The wind had grown colder and was whipping through the thin layer of her cloak. She rose to her feet, shoving her hands into her pockets to warm them, and began to trudge back through the garden toward the house.

But she hadn't even taken a step when she stopped. There was something in her pocket, tucked way down into the corner, half buried in the clumsily stitched seam. It felt like . . . a pebble?

Whatever it was, it was too tiny to grasp, so she tore off her gloves and delved into the pocket again with her bare fingers. Yes, it felt like two small, perfectly smooth, round pebbles. She pinched them between her thumb and forefinger and pulled them loose, cradling them in her palm.

But they weren't pebbles at all. On her palm sat a pair of tiny, perfect pearls.

She stared down at them, her heart suddenly roaring in her ears. These weren't just any pearls. They were the pearls that had dangled from the ends of Jasper's ruby earrings. She'd know them anywhere.

But how? How in the world could they have ended up in the pocket of her cloak? Where had they come from, unless—

Jasper.

The last time she'd worn the cloak had been that night she'd sneaked downstairs to meet Jasper in the billiards room. He'd kissed her that night, his lips sweet and gentle against hers.

She'd fled from him that night after he'd ordered her

to go, but she'd accidently left her cloak behind. Jasper had still been in the billiards room when she'd left, and he'd had the earrings. He must have . . . dear God, he must have pried the pearls loose from the setting and slipped them into her pocket!

They'd been there all this time, waiting for her to find them.

But why? Why would he give the pearls to her?

She'd *stolen* them from him. *Blackmailed* him.

Yet he'd given them to her anyway, right after the first time he'd kissed her.

She raised her hand to her lips, a soft sob catching in her throat. She'd been so certain that kiss had meant nothing to him, but maybe . . . maybe . . .

She gathered her skirts in her hands and began to run.

"Perhaps it wasn't a good idea for us to come to Montford Park after all, Loftus."

Jasper peered out into the dusk beyond his carriage window, misgivings tightening his chest. Prue had asked him for one thing only. To come to the country *alone*. Now here he was, jaunting merrily up the drive to the entrance of Montford Park in utter disregard of her wishes.

Good Lord. Even now she was likely looking down on him from one of the windows, cursing the day she became his duchess.

Loftus turned to Jasper with wide eyes. "Er, yes, Your Grace, but I'm afraid it's rather too late now."

"I suppose so." Jasper slumped back against his seat. It wasn't as if he could have done otherwise. Surely, a husband whose wife suspected him of the worst sort of betrayal—and with the worst sort of villainous female, no less—surely that husband must do everything in his power to clear his name, and set things back to rights with the lady he loved?

Not to mention his having nearly sliced Quincy to ribbons to get here.

Yes, these were all very good reasons why a husband might chase his wife into the country after she'd specifically asked him not to, yet doubts continued to niggle at him.

What if she sent him away again? Or worse, what if she *wept*? He couldn't think of anything worse than watching tears leak from those lovely hazel eyes. No, he couldn't bear it. "We must turn around at once, Loftus! This instant!"

Loftus jumped at Jasper's sudden shout, and his mouth dropped open. "Turn around? Now? But . . . I beg your pardon, Your Grace, but we've only just—"

"You don't understand! The duchess doesn't want me here, Loftus."

"I don't like to contradict you, as you know, Your Grace, but I think Her Grace is—"

"Her Grace specifically requested I not join her at Montford Park! We've made a terrible mistake, Loftus, and must go back to London at once."

"Of course, if Your Grace wishes it, but might I venture a word first?"

Jasper huffed out a breath. "Yes, if you must, but I warn you, there isn't a single thing you can say that could possibly change my mind."

"Of course not, Your Grace, but you see, I, ah . . . well, perhaps I should have told you this sooner, but I didn't like to betray Her Grace's secrets, and—"

"Secrets?" Loftus was in possession of Prue's secrets? Why hadn't he said so at once? "What secrets?"

"I don't like to tell tales, Your Grace, and . . . oh, dear." Loftus wrung his hands. "Perhaps it would be best if I didn't say."

Not say? *Not say?* Jasper clenched his fists to keep from shaking poor Loftus until all of Prue's secrets fell from the man's lips. "It's quite alright, Loftus. Whatever it is, you may tell *me*."

"Yes, Your Grace. This morning, before Her Grace left for Montford Park, I found her . . ." Loftus hesitated, biting his lip.

"Yes? Found her *what*, Loftus?"

"In your bedchamber, Your Grace. Alone."

"Prue was in my bedchamber?" And he'd missed it? God above, he was the unluckiest husband alive.

"Yes, Your Grace. I found her at your dressing table, and she was . . ."

"Yes, yes? What was she doing?"

"Your cologne, Your Grace. She had a handkerchief, and she was scenting it with your cologne."

Jasper fell back against his seat, stunned. Prue had stolen some drops of his cologne? But why would she . . . oh. *Oh.* "That would seem to imply, Loftus, that she was . . . that she thought she might . . ."

"Miss you, Your Grace?" Loftus smiled. "Yes, that was my impression, as well."

"Did she say so?"

"No. The duchess was a trifle embarrassed, I think, Your Grace."

"And what did you say to her, Loftus? What did you do?"

"I didn't say anything much at all, Your Grace. I simply helped her to a few droplets of your cologne, and she went on her way."

Jasper shook his head, a smile rising to his lips. "Good man, Loftus. Good man."

"Thank you, Your Grace. You do see why I'm persuaded that the duchess does wish for your presence at Montford Park, despite what she said, Your Grace?"

"I do, yes. I'm glad you told me, Loftus."

The carriage continued to make its way up to the drive, and God above, it seemed to take forever. Who had decided they must have such a long drive leading up to the house? Not him, that was certain. The shorter, the better—

"My goodness, isn't that . . ." Loftus frowned, his gaze on the window. "Isn't that her Grace, just there?"

"Where?" Jasper leaned past Loftus and pressed his nose to the rain-streaked window. It had grown dark quickly once the rain began to fall, but he could just make out a lone figure in a brown cloak running around the side of the house, her skirts caught in one hand and the other holding on to the droopy, sodden straw hat on her head.

By God, it *was* her. He slammed a fist on the roof of the carriage. "Stop at once, Farnham."

Farnham brought the horses to such an abrupt halt, both Jasper and Loftus nearly toppled from their seats to the floor of the carriage. "Second coachman," Jasper muttered, giving Loftus a hand back into his seat.

"I'll be pleased to see Norris again, Your Grace."

Jasper hardly heard him, nor did he wait for the carriage to come to a full stop before he wrenched open the door and leapt out, running to catch up to his wife. "Prue! Wait!"

She froze for an instant, then turned, her mouth dropping open when she saw him. "Jasper? My goodness, Jasper! What are you doing here?"

Jasper ran up to her and seized her hands. "I came to . . ."

To tell you the truth about Lady Archer. To reassure you that I didn't betray you. To fetch you home with me.

But none of the words made it past his lips. Instead, he blurted out the only words that truly mattered. "I came to tell you I love you, Prue."

CHAPTER 27

The eyes are the window to the soul.

A poet had said that once, hundreds of years ago, and lovers had been repeating it for centuries since. Prue had heard it dozens of times, but she'd never truly felt the truth of it until this moment, when she stood in the rain with cold water dripping down the back of her neck, gazing up into Jasper's eyes.

He'd been shouting something as he ran up to her. She'd heard him say her name, but the wind had snatched the rest of his words and sent them whirling into the twilight surrounding them.

But she didn't need to hear the words. Who needed words, when everything he felt for her was right there in his warm, dark eyes?

Oh, those eyes! They'd held her captive for weeks now. Even in her worst moments, when she'd been angry with him, unsure of him, she'd sought out his eyes every hour of every day they were together, and then dreamed of them at night.

How was it that she hadn't been able to see what his eyes had been telling her all along, until just now?

"Prue, please, you must listen to me." He was gripping her hands, rain dripping from the ends of his dark hair and trickling down his face, his thick eyelashes starry with raindrops. "I promised you I wouldn't come here, but I couldn't stay away. I never should have let you walk out the door yesterday. I won't be separated from you. Not ever again, Prue."

She gazed up at him, her throat working, thousands of words rushing to her lips, but it was too much to say all at once, so she said the only thing she *could* say. "Thank God, Jasper, thank God." Her voice caught on a sob. "Thank God you came."

He let out a long, slow breath, and then he gathered her into his arms. "I missed you so much."

She gripped the edges of his coat, holding on tight. "I—I made a mistake. I should never have—"

"No." He pressed her closer, his arms warm around her, crooning against her hair. "No, sweetheart. You didn't do anything wrong."

They might have stood there forever with the rain pounding down on their heads if Loftus hadn't alighted from the carriage just then. "Er, Your Grace? I do beg your pardon for interrupting you, but it *is* rather wet. Might I help you and Her Grace indoors?"

Jasper smiled, but his gaze never left her face. "Is it wet, Loftus?"

"Er, well, just a trifle so, Your Grace, but if you'd rather stay—"

Loftus didn't get any further, because the front door swung open then, revealing Mrs. Bingham. "Oh, there you are, Your Grace! I was just about to send a footman out in search of—" Her gaze fell on Jasper then, and her eyes went wide. "Oh, Your Grace! That is, Your Graces! I didn't realize. . . well, never mind. Please come in out of the wet, Your Graces!"

Jasper and Prue did as they were told, and patiently endured the usual chaos that ensued when the master of the house arrived unexpectedly, with Mrs. Bingham bustling about, sending servants scurrying to retrieve the baggage and see to the horses, all the while clucking like a mother hen.

Meanwhile, Jasper took her hand and led her upstairs to his apartments, where Loftus had already seen to it that the lamps were lit and a fire was roaring in the grate. "Alone, at last." Jasper closed the door behind them and leaned back against it, his gaze on her.

Prue stood in the middle of his bedchamber, plucking nervously at the folds of her skirts. They were damp still, and she should have been freezing, but the heat in his eyes was setting every inch of her skin on fire.

"Come here, Prue."

There was nothing in the world she wanted more, and she flew to him, straight into his arms. He caught her, tugging her tightly against him and sinking his hands into her hair, words tumbling from his lips. "I left Lady Archer's bed months ago, Prue, and I haven't returned to it since. I haven't even been tempted. I don't want her. I don't know any more how I *ever* wanted her. I only want you. I know you don't trust me, and that's my fault, because I've never given you any reason to, but—"

"Shhh." She pressed her fingers to his lips. "I do trust you, Jasper. I do."

He brushed her damp hair back from her face. "But

how? How can you trust me? What's happened since you left Berkeley Square to change your mind?"

What had changed? Nothing and everything, all at once. "I hardly know where to begin."

"Begin at the beginning, sweetheart."

There *was* no beginning, not really. Even now she couldn't say when or why everything had changed, but as she'd sat on the bench this afternoon with the branches of the apple tree sheltering her from the wind, she'd just *known*.

Or, perhaps it hadn't happened then.

Perhaps she'd known all along, and had only needed a quiet moment to herself to realize it.

Jasper had never betrayed her. Not with Lady Archer, and not in any other way. She knew it, in the same way she knew that raindrops were wet, and sunshine was warm, and that she'd never before loved the scent of orange blossom so much as she did now, after she'd smelled the scent on *him*. She knew it innately, instinctively, the truth of it tucked into the deepest depths of her heart.

But for his sake, she would try and explain it. "I know who Lady Archer is—what she is. You told me from the start. But when she found me that night, those things she said . . ."

"She knows how to lie."

"Yes. I never thought anyone could be so cruel, and I wasn't prepared." She'd been looking down at their joined hands, but now she looked up into his eyes, her own eyes damp. "Once I had a chance to think about it, I knew it was all lies."

"Clever lies, yes. It was Mrs. Stritch who told Selina the lie about our wedding night."

"Mrs. Stritch!" She stared up at him. "Of *course*! My God, I never even thought of her, but she was there that morning. She saw the bedsheets and must have drawn her own conclusions."

"Or Selina did. I daresay Mrs. Stritch merely told Selina what she'd seen, and Selina seized on it as a thin justification to spread an outrageous lie."

"Then you never believed, that is, you never thought . . ." She swallowed, her gaze dropping away from him. Oh God, she couldn't bear to say it.

"Look at me." He caught her chin and raised her face to his. "No, Prue. Not *ever*."

"Oh." She let out a breath, her shoulders sagging with relief. "It was silly of me to think—"

"No, sweetheart, it wasn't. The fault lies with me, not you. I should have realized you might have questions and talked to you about it. Did you think our marriage hadn't been consummated?"

"It, ah, it might have occurred to me, yes." Dear God, her cheeks were on fire.

He gazed down at her, his eyes bleak. "I'm sorry, Prue. If I'd done as I ought to, we might have avoided all this."

Perhaps there was truth to that, but what did it matter now? He was here. That was all she cared about. "How did you find out about Mrs. Stritch?"

"Lord Quincy. As it turned out, it was Quincy who let Selina into Basingstoke's house that night."

"Ah, I see. Did Lord Quincy simply volunteer this information about Mrs. Stritch, then?" She'd wager every last gown in her wardrobe that wasn't the case. Jasper could be formidable, indeed.

"Not exactly, no. He, ah . . . well, he became a good

deal more forthcoming once I had a blade pressed against his chest."

"Jasper! You didn't fight a duel with Lord Quincy?" Good God, he might have been killed!

"Just a little one. But I don't want to talk about Quincy anymore, or Mrs. Stritch, or that devil Selina. They don't matter." He cradled her face in his hands. "You're all that matters. I love you, Prue, so much I think I may have panicked at first. I've never loved anyone the way I love you."

Oh, my. Had she truly thought she didn't need to hear those words from his lips? Her heart melted into a puddle inside her chest. She drew in a shaky breath, lifted her arms, and twined them around his neck. "I love you, too, Jasper. More than anything."

He squeezed his eyes closed. "You love me, Prue?"

"Yes." She looked into his dear, handsome face, his features lost in shadows, that silky lock of tousled dark hair lying across his forehead. "Take me to bed, Your Grace."

Jasper's hands were shaking as they fell to her waist, his fingers curling against her as he backed her toward the bed, but he was gentle, always so gentle as he laid her down and eased himself on top of her. "Like this?"

"Yes. Just like that." She caught a handful of his thick hair and urged his head down. "Now kiss me."

He took her lips with a groan, his mouth sweet and demanding at once, his tongue slipping out to tease the seam of her lips until she opened to him with a gasp. "That's it, sweetheart," he whispered. "Give me everything, Prue."

She did—oh, she did, because it was *him*, and she couldn't do anything less, her body straining against his as he took her mouth again and again, her heart overflowing with love.

"Did you think of me when we were each in our separate bedchambers, Prue? Did you miss me?"

She grasped a handful of his shirt in her fist to bring him closer. "Yes, I—I thought about you, and about our wedding night."

He let out a desperate moan, trailing his lips down her neck. "Did you touch yourself when you thought of me? Did you caress that sweet little spot between your legs, and bring yourself pleasure?"

Dear God, he was wicked, his words inflaming her almost as much as his touch. She arched her neck, going mad from the warm drift of his breath against her damp skin. "Yes, yes."

He sucked in a breath, his hand cupping her breast, his thumb tracing her nipple. "I thought of you, too. You're all I can think about, Prue."

She squirmed in his arms, wanting more of his touch. "Jasper."

His gaze remained on her face as he traced his fingertip over one hardened nipple and then the other—once, then again and again until she was whimpering, his caresses both too much and not enough at once. "Jasper. I need you."

He gazed down at her, his eyes wild, his chest heaving with each breath, then he reached for the hem of his shirt and tore it off, tossing it to the floor. "Sit up for me."

She did as he bid her, holding onto his bare shoulders to steady herself as he made quick work of the buttons down the back of her dress, the cool air kissing her skin as he drew the sleeves down her arms, then eased the gown over her head.

Once he'd stripped her down to her shift, she settled back against the bed. He followed her down, and a soft moan escaped her at the flutter of his hot breath against her ear.

"Come here." She sank her hands into his hair and brought his face down to her breasts.

She whimpered as his tongue snaked out to lick her nipples, her head falling back against the pillow as he tugged and teased and nipped at her. Dear God, it was so good she thought she might climax with just his mouth on her breasts.

He suckled her, his lips and tongue hot and rough and perfect. "Jasper . . . oh, yes."

He growled against her damp flesh, his hand creeping under the flimsy linen of her shift and up her thigh, then he shifted to kneel between her knees, spreading her wider with a gentle nudge of his hips. "Want you, Prue."

"I want you, too, Jasper. So much." But first, she wanted something else, something she almost didn't dare to want, but he was her husband, and more than anything, she wanted to make him feel as good as he made her feel whenever he touched her.

She slid her hand down his taut stomach and trailed her fingers underneath the edge of his pantaloons. He gasped when she flicked open the buttons of his falls, and he reached for her wrist with shaking fingers. "Do you know what you're about there, Your Grace?"

"Not really." She gazed up at him, her lips twitching. "Not yet, that is." She let her fingers trail lower, spreading the fabric of his falls wider so she could stroke the crisp line of hair that led from just under his belly button to the still-mysterious organ between his legs. "Lie back. I want to see you."

He gave her a scandalized look that made her laugh, but he did as she asked and rolled onto his back, pausing only to drag his pantaloons over his lean hips and kick them off.

She sucked in a breath. Goodness, he was beautiful. She ran a hesitant hand over his muscled chest and shoulders and that long, lean torso, his smooth olive skin stretched tight over the grooves of his abdomen. Narrow hips, taut thighs layered with muscle, long legs dusted with dark hair, and . . . dear God, his legs seemed to go on forever.

"If you keep looking at me like that, this is going to be over before—" He broke off with a gasp when she leaned over and touched her lips to his belly. Then, in a moment of bravery, she wrapped her hand around the rigid length of him rising proudly against the hard plane of his torso.

"Prue." He hissed out a breath, his hips jerking.

"Oh." She hadn't expected his skin would be so soft here. She leaned closer, her lips hovering over his, her hand still moving steadily, stroking him. He met her clumsy strokes with desperate jerks of his hips, pushing his hard length through her fist, and dear God, she'd never seen anything more beautiful than Jasper lost in pleasure, writhing against the bed, deep, husky moans spilling from his lips with every stroke of her hand.

She tightened her grip a little, amazed at the way he pulsed and throbbed against her palm, stroking him more quickly, her tongue creeping out to touch her bottom lip. He grew more frenzied, and then, on impulse she leaned down and pressed a hesitant kiss to his damp, flushed tip.

"Ah!" He threw his head back with a sharp cry, and the next thing Prue knew she was flat on her back on the bed with him on top of her, his chest heaving and his dark hair hanging in a damp tangle over his fierce dark eyes.

"Jasper!" She squirmed underneath him, but he reached up and pinned her wrists to the bed. "I want to make you feel as good as you made me feel."

"Prue." His face softened and his grip around her wrists loosened. "You *did* make me feel good. No one's ever made me feel as good as you do. I love you, sweetheart. Everything you do makes me feel good. But I want to be inside you. I want to watch your face, and look into your eyes, and I want us to find our pleasure together."

"Oh, Jasper." She laid her palm on his cheek. "I want that, too."

He settled between her legs, panting with desire. "I want you so much, Prue," he murmured, his eyes dropping closed as he slid his palms down her thighs and eased her legs open a little wider. "That's it, sweetheart. Open your legs for me."

Prue gasped, and let her knees fall open, her lips parting on a soft moan as Jasper slid his hand between her thighs, his fingers finding the tiny, needy bud where her pleasure was centered.

"God, Prue." Jasper took his cock in his hand and pressed it against her, but he held back, stroking them both. The sensation of his hard length just breaching her body while his fingers played with her was almost more than she could take.

"You're so wet," he groaned against her ear. "You're going to make me come." He thrust his hips, rubbing the head of his cock against her. She watched, mouth open, as Jasper undulated above her, taking them both right to the edge of release before pulling back with a gasp, his teeth clenching as he stroked her slippery core with his fingers.

"Need you." She was pleading, her hips rising and falling into Jasper's every teasing caress. "I want you. Please."

"Soon, love." Yet still he held back, his jaw tight as he teased and stroked her, spreading the wetness there. He waited until she was panting, incoherent pleas falling from her lips, then he eased inside her and began to move.

"Oh, oh . . ." She dragged her nails across his back, straining against him. "More," she pleaded, punctuating the demand with a desperate thrust of her hips.

"You want more of me, love?"

"Yes, yes!" Her head thrashed against the bed.

He thrust inside her, once, twice, and again, his eyes sliding closed as he worked her core in time with his thrusts. Her body bowed, arching off the bed, her core drawing as tight as a fist and then finally, finally releasing with a rush of pleasure. "That's it, Prue. Come for me, sweetheart."

He urged her on as her body climbed higher, then higher still, until with a hoarse cry he followed her over the edge. "Ah, God, yes. So good, Prue."

She fell back against the bed when the pleasure released her at last, dazed, and he came down on top of her, crooning to her as he stroked her damp hair back from her face. "You're so beautiful, Prue." He gave her a crooked grin that made her heart lurch in her chest. "I already want you again."

She smiled and reached up to stroke his sweat-slick hair back from his face. "I'm not going anywhere."

"No, you're not, and neither am I. Never again." He gathered her against him, urged her head down to his chest and pulled the blankets up over them. "Sleep, sweetheart." He pressed a kiss to her temple. "Sleep."

Jasper watched Prue come awake slowly some hours later, her eyelids fluttering over those glorious hazel eyes.

The minute she saw him she smiled, and it was like the sun coming out. He dragged his thumb over her lower lip, still swollen with his kisses. "You never opened your gift, Your Grace." He nodded at the long, flat package on the table beside the bed. She'd left it behind when she'd gone to Montford Park, so he'd brought it with him from London.

She gave him a sleepy smile. "Another gift?"

"Another one?" He leaned down and kissed that smile, because he couldn't resist. "I don't believe I've ever given you a gift before, have I?"

"Yes, you did." She rolled over, retrieved her discarded cloak from the floor, and rifled through the pockets, then held her palm out to show him. "You gave me these."

He stared down at the pair of tiny pearls he'd slipped in the pocket of her cloak . . . well, it felt like ages ago. "I thought they'd gotten lost."

"No. Just hidden for a little while." Her gaze met his. "Why, Jasper? Why did you slip these into my pocket?"

"Because, I . . ." He cleared his throat. "I wanted you to have them."

She searched his face. "Is that all?"

He toyed with a lock of her hair that had fallen against his chest. "Not exactly." He glanced up at her, his cheeks heating. "You were meant to win the wager over billiards, so I could give your father his money back."

"Meant to win?" She frowned. "You mean to say you *tried* to lose that game?"

"Well, yes, but you sent all my schemes awry when you missed that shot!" He took her hand and pressed a kiss to her knuckles. "So, you see, it's all your fault, Your Grace."

"Why, that's the most manipulative, wonderful, sweetest thing I've ever heard! You mean to say you were trying to give Thornewood back to me, all those weeks ago?"

Without warning, she threw herself into his arms, and he caught her with a grunt.

"So, you gave me pearls instead?"

"I gave you the pearls because I wanted you to have them, because they're beautiful, and so are you, inside and out, Prue." He kissed her hand again. "If you'd let me, I'd give you a pearl every day for the rest of our lives."

"I don't need pearls, Jasper. I just need you." She reached out to trace his mouth, a small smile on her lips. "Is that what's in this box, then? A pearl?"

He grinned. "Not exactly."

"Jasper! That big box better not be filled with jewels."

"Open it, and find out." He reached for the package and set it on the bed between them, his heart pounding.

She bit her lip as she unsnapped the brass latches and raised the lid of the box. When she saw what lay inside the box, she slapped her hand over her mouth, her bright hazel eyes wide. "Oh," she breathed. "Oh, Jasper. It's . . . I can't believe it." She reached out a finger to stroke one of the pearls that studded the grip of the rapier nestled inside. "It's so beautiful."

"Deadly, too." He dragged his thumb lightly over the edge of the blade, taking care not to cut himself. "As pretty as it is, it's no toy, but a real rapier, for a real swordswoman."

She tested the tip with her finger. "My, it certainly is. Does this mean I may go to Angelo's without displeasing my high-handed husband?"

"You won our wager, so, of course you shall go, and your husband will be very pleased indeed, as long as his extraordinary wife is happy. But if you like, I'll also give you fencing lessons of my own." He caught her against him and nuzzled his face into her neck. "Very, er . . . particular fencing lessons. *Corps-à-corps*, you know."

"*Corps-à-corps*?"

"That, Your Grace, is when two fencers come into physical contact with each other." He caught her lower lip between his teeth, nipping gently. "The literal translation is 'body to body.' It's never appealed to me much, but suddenly I find it a great deal more intriguing."

"Body to body?" She gave him a saucy little grin. "But can't I learn that at Angelo's?"

He tumbled her onto her back on the bed and fell on top of her. "No, you may not. Only I will instruct the Duchess of Montford in *corps-à-corps*." He dropped a kiss on her nose. "It's safer for everyone that way."

"I love my gift. Thank you, Jasper." She reached up and dragged her fingers down his cheek, pausing to caress the corner of his mouth. "I'm quite madly in love with you, you know."

"How fortunate, as I'm quite madly in love with you, as well."

She gave him such a sweet smile his chest pulled tight. Later, he'd tell her again just how much he loved her. Or maybe he'd show her, and she'd smile like that, just for him.

"And there will be no more wagers between us," she murmured, stroking the hair on his chest. "Not now that we've broken the one rule of wagering."

"Oh?" He pressed a kiss to the tip of her nose. "What rule is that?"

"Never wager anything you can't afford to lose." Her hazel eyes were shining as she gazed up at him. "I have your heart now, Jasper, and I will never risk it. Not for anything."

"I lost it before I realized I'd risked it at all. I lost it to you." He caught her hand and pressed a kiss to her fingertips, his eyes finding hers. "I lost it to you."

EPILOGUE

Montford Park
Seven months later

"Keep your eyes closed." Jasper wrapped his arm more firmly around Prue's waist as they neared the carriage house, guiding her over the rough cobblestones. "My dear duchess, do you imagine I can't see you peeking?"

Prue laughed, her fingers tightening around the sleeve of his coat. "I'm only peeking a little!"

"Peeking is peeking. I won't hesitate to blindfold you, if necessary." He brushed his lips over the smooth skin of her cheek, inhaling the scent of honeysuckle. "In fact, this can wait until the afternoon, surely? Perhaps I'll take you back to our bedchamber right now, and—"

"Certainly not! You've been teasing me with this surprise for weeks."

"Patience is not your virtue, Your Grace. Very well, then. Here we are." He nodded to Whit, Montford Park's coachman, who was waiting for them beside the open door of the carriage house.

"Can I open my eyes?" Prue was hopping up and down. "I can't wait another moment."

To be fair, it had taken him a bit of time to decide on this particular purchase, as he'd wanted it to be just right, and he had been teasing her rather mercilessly in the meantime, but really, that was her own fault, because she made it so delightful to tease her.

"In a moment. Stand right here. No, just a little to the left—"

"Jasper!" She stamped her foot. "I'm opening my eyes."

He laughed. "Alright, no more teasing. You may look, Your Grace."

She opened her eyes, blinking for an instant at the elegant, high-perch phaeton standing in the carriage house courtyard, before she let out a gasp. "Oh! My goodness, Jasper!"

"Do you like it?" God, he hoped so, as he'd gone to a good deal of trouble to find just the right carriage for her, and driven both Franny and Basingstoke mad in the process.

"*Like* it? Of course I do, you silly man! How could I not? It's perfect!"

She gave him a smile that dispelled any last lingering doubts he had. "That's fortunate, because Basingstoke forbade me from saying another word about it, which is bound to prove awkward when they come to dine on Sunday, and you insist on showing him your new phaeton."

"I can hardly wait to take Franny driving! What a pretty color it is. I don't think I've ever seen a carriage this color before."

"No, this is the first of its kind." The wheels and top were a shiny, lacquered black, but he'd had the body done in a particular shade of green—somewhat darker than apple, but lighter than emerald—a shade that he fancied would particularly flatter his wife's lovely coloring.

Especially her hazel eyes.

It was the very equipage for a lady who had no experience driving, wished very much to learn, and would prefer to drive a lively mare, or in time, a matched pair rather than a pony.

"I can hardly believe it. Indeed, Jasper, I don't know what to say." She turned to him with glistening eyes. "I've always wanted to learn to drive, but I never imagined I'd ever have the chance, much less in a carriage as lovely as this."

"It wasn't meant to make you cry, Prue." He gathered her into his arms and dropped a kiss on the top of her head. "It's meant to make you happy."

"I *am* happy." She pressed her face against his chest and mumbled something he couldn't make out.

"What did you say, sweetheart?" He caught her chin in gentle fingers and tipped her face up to his. "Don't hide."

She gave him a shy smile, a blush staining her cheeks. "I said, *you* make me happy. So happy, Jasper."

"My love," he whispered, touching his forehead to hers. They stood thus for a few moments, a silent communication passing between, one that grew stronger with every day they spent together, a silence that said more than words ever could.

As it happened, Basingstoke had been right all along. Love *did* make all the difference.

He pressed a brief kiss to her lips, then drew back, grinning down at her. "Now, I suppose you want to drive it, don't you?"

"Yes, please!" She clapped her hands.

"Whit, will you be so kind as to hitch Dolly to the phaeton?"

"Dolly?" Prue's brows lowered. "But Athena is much faster than Dolly, and—"

"And that's precisely why we're taking Dolly. She's a sweet, gentle thing, and not liable to startle. She's just what we want for your first drive. Don't you think so, Whit?"

"Indeed, Your Grace. Dolly's a good girl and will do very well."

"Very well. Where shall we go? I daresay the main drive will do for us."

"I believe we'll save the main drive until your second week of lessons. There's a private road just past the stabl with a turnabout at the top. We'll start there."

"But surely, the main drive isn't dangerous? Why, i as wide as the Thames!"

"It's dangerous enough if you send us into that ditc He pointed toward the shallow channel that ran along eastern edge of the drive. "If we hit that at the wr angle, we could break a wheel, or worse, a horse's l

"That's not a ditch. It's barely a furrow, and I w never risk a horse's wellbeing with reckless driving dry, and that's a nice, smooth bit of road."

"That nice, smooth bit of road will still be there you're ready for it. I'll not trifle with your safety,

Her face softened. "Of course, you're right. deny going around in circles in a turnabout doesr like nearly as much fun as trotting up and down but perhaps it's best to start slowly."

They waited while Whit harnessed Dolly a her to the traces of the phaeton, then Jasper around to a small circular bit of road behin

well shaded by the spreading branches of a copse of elm trees.

He remained in the driver's seat for their first half dozen turns, showing Prue how to hold the reins properly, guide the horse to the right and left, and bring her to a stop. "Now, if you'll promise to take it slowly, and do as I say, you can take the reins."

"Yes indeed. I promise it."

"Very well, then." He brought Dolly to a stop with a twitch of the reins, and handed them over to her.

She kept her promise and kept Dolly at a slow, steady walk. Dolly, sensing a confident horsewoman at the other end of the ribbons, responded well to her commands and promenaded cheerfully enough, her ears flicking lazily at the insects buzzing about her.

"My father never let me drive. Did I ever tell you that, Jasper? He claimed it was because a lady's hands were too small, and their fingers too short and slender to skillfully manipulate the ribbons, but I always suspected he thought it wasn't proper ladylike behavior."

Jasper snorted. "*Your* father, who thought it was perfectly fine for his daughter to wear breeches and learn how to box, thought *driving* wasn't proper ladylike behavior?"

"Yes. According to my father, ladies don't drive. Period."

"Perhaps we won't tell him I've bought you a phaeton, then. He'll have my head."

The awkwardness between Jasper and his father-in-law had vanished when it became clear to Major Thorne how much Jasper loved his daughter, though it was in also thanks to his grandfather. He and Major Thorne

had become fast friends, and the colonel wouldn't hear a bad word said against his grandson.

Prue laughed. "No, he won't. He adores you. He always wanted a son, and now he has one."

And Jasper now had a father, in addition to his grandfather, and perhaps in time, a son or a daughter with golden-brown hair and hazel eyes.

A brief silence fell over them, the only sound the gentle clop of Dolly's hooves against the soft ground, but then Prue said quietly, "I suppose, deep down, my father must have thought I couldn't manage the ribbons, but you never do that, Jasper. You always believe I can do anything."

"Because you can." He reached out and gave a loose lock of her hair a gentle tug. "You're extraordinary, Prue. You can do anything you set your mind to."

She brought Dolly to an easy stop and scooted closer to him, so her thigh was pressed against his. She kept hold of the reins with one hand, took his hand with the other, and pressed a soft, sweet kiss to his knuckles. "Because I have you."

Visit our website at
KensingtonBooks.com
to sign up for our newsletters, read
more from your favorite authors, see
books by series, view reading group
guides, and more!

Become a Part of Our
Between the Chapters Book Club
Community and Join the Conversation